Ann Brashares

Ann Brashares grew up in Maryland, USA, with her three
brothers, and attended a Quaker school called Sidwell Friends.
She studied Philosophy at Columbia University in New York City.
Expecting to continue to graduate school, Ann took a year off after
college to work as an editor, hoping to save money for school.
Loving her job, she never went back, and instead, remained in
New York City and worked as an editor for many years.
Ann made the transition from editor to full-time writer
with her first novel, *The Sisterhood of the Travelling Pants*.

Ann lives in Brooklyn, New York, with her husband, Jacob Collins,
an artist, and their three children, Sam, Nathaniel and Susannah.

Carmen's the one who found the jeans, in a second-hand store.
They didn't look all that great: they were worn, dirty, and speckled
with bleach. But Tibby liked the look of them. And then Lena tried them,
and Bridget. And that's when the magic began ... because the pants fitted
each of the four girls perfectly. Not 'sort of okay', not 'just about right',
but PERFECTLY. Even Carmen (who never thought she looked good
in anything) admitted the jeans looked great on her too.
And over a few bags of snack food and some bad eighties music,
the Sisterhood of the Travelling Pants was born ...

www.sisterhoodcentral.com

Praise for *The Sisterhood of the Travelling Pants*:

'It's great to read a fantastically written, fresh novel every once in
a while that really makes you feel good.' Suzi, age 15

'A must-read for any person who has ever faced hardships
and felt they were alone.' Bec, age 18

Praise for *The Second Summer of the Sisterhood*:

'In one word, inspiring ... it makes you laugh and it makes
you cry but most importantly it makes you feel.
I give this book a 9 out of 10.' Carlie, Year 11

All quotes taken from the Young Australian Readers' Award website,
www.yara-online.org

ForeVer in BLUE

the
fourth
summer of the
sisterhood

Ann Brashares

RANDOM HOUSE AUSTRALIA

For my sweet Susannah
... when she's ready

Acknowledgments

With admiration I thank Jodi Anderson, first and always.

After four books and six years together, I thank my cohorts at Random House with ever-deepening warmth and appreciation: Wendy Loggia, Beverly Horowitz, Chip Gibson, Judith Haut, Kathy Dunn, Marci Senders, Daisy Kline, Joan DeMayo, and many others who have invested themselves wholeheartedly in this project. I thank Leslie Morgenstein and my friend and agent, Jennifer Rudolph Walsh. What a lovely time we've all had.

I thank my parents, Jane Easton Brashares and William Brashares, and my brothers, Beau, Justin, and Ben Brashares. You can't pick your family, they say, but I would pick them.

I lovingly acknowledge my husband, Jacob Collins, and our three children, Sam, Nate, and Susannah.

And see she flies

And she is everywhere

—Nick Drake

PROLOGUE

Once upon a time there were four girls. Young women, you might even say. And though their lives traveled in different directions, they loved each other very much.

Once upon a time before that, these same girls found a pair of pants, wise and magical, and named them the Traveling Pants.

The Pants had the magic of teaching these girls how to be apart. They taught them how to be four people instead of one person. How to be together no matter where they were. How to love themselves as much as they loved each other. And on a practical level, the Pants had the magic of fitting all four of them, which is hard to believe but true, especially considering only one of them (the blonde) was built like a supermodel.

Okay. Full disclosure. I am one of these girls. I wear these Pants. I have these friends. I know this magic.

I am in fact the blonde, though I was kidding about the supermodel part.

But anyway, as it happens with most kinds of magic, these Pants did their job a little too well. And the girls, being extraordinary girls (if you don't mind my saying so), learned their lesson a little too well.

And so when the girls' lives changed that final summer, the Pants, being wise, had to change too.

And that is how this tale of sisterhood began, but did not end.

The only true paradise is

paradise lost.

—Marcel Proust

Gilda's was the same. It always was. And what a relief too, Lena found herself thinking. Good thing you could count on human vanity and the onward march of fitness crazes requiring mats and mirrors.

Not much else was the same. Things were different, things were missing.

Carmen, for instance, was missing.

"I can't really see how we can do this without Carmen," Tibby said. As was the custom, she'd brought her video camera for posterity, but she hadn't turned it on. Nobody was quite sure about when posterity started, or if maybe it already had.

"So maybe we shouldn't try," Bee said. "Maybe we should wait until we can do it together."

Lena had brought the candles, but she hadn't lit them. Tibby had brought the ceremonial bad eighties aerobics music, but she hadn't put it on. Bee had gamely set out the bowls of Gummi Worms and Cheetos, but nobody was eating them.

"When's that going to be?" Tibby asked. "Seriously, I think we've been trying to get together since last September and I don't think it has happened once."

"What about Thanksgiving?" Lena asked.

"Remember I had to go to Cincinnati for Great-grandma Felicia's hundredth birthday?" Tibby said.

"Oh, yeah. And she had a stroke," Bee said.

"That was after the party."

"And Carmen went to Florida over Christmas," Lena said. "And you two were in New York over New Year's."

"All right, so how about two weekends from now? Carmen will be back by then, won't she?"

"Yeah, but my classes start on June twentieth." Lena clasped her hands around her knees, her large feet bare on the sticky pine floor. "I can't miss the first day of the pose or I'll end up stuck in a corner or staring at the model's kneecap for a month."

"Okay, so July fourth," Tibby said reasonably. "Nobody has school or anything that Friday. We could meet back here for a long weekend."

Bee untied her shoe. "I fly to Istanbul on June twenty-fourth."

"That soon? Can you go later?" Tibby asked.

Bridget's face dimmed with regret. "The program put us all on this charter flight. Otherwise it's an extra thousand bucks and you have to find your own way to the site."

"How could Carmen miss this?" Tibby asked.

7

Lena knew what she meant. It wasn't okay for any of them to miss this ritual, but especially not Carmen, to whom it had mattered so much.

Bee looked around. "Miss what, though?" she asked, not so much challenging as conciliating. "This isn't really the launch, right?" She gestured to the Pants, folded obediently in the middle of their triangle. "I mean, not officially. We've been wearing them all school year. It's not like the other summers, when this was the huge kickoff and everything."

Lena wasn't sure whether she felt comforted or antagonized by this statement.

"Maybe that's true," Tibby said. "Maybe we don't need a launch this summer."

"We should at least figure out the rotation tonight," Lena said. "Carmen will just have to live with it."

"Why don't we keep up the same rotation we've had going till now?" Bridget suggested, straightening her legs in front of her. "No reason to change it just because it's summer."

Lena bit the skin around her thumbnail and considered the practical truth of this.

Summer used to be different. It was the time they left home, split up, lived separate lives for ten long weeks, and counted on the Pants to hold them together until they were reunited. Now summer was more of the same. Being apart wasn't the exception, Lena recognized, it was the rule.

When will we all be home again? That was what she wanted to know.

But when she thought about it logically, she knew: It wasn't just the answer that had changed, it was the question. What was home anymore? What counted as the status quo? Home was a time and it had passed.

Nobody was eating the Gummi Worms. Lena felt like she should eat one or cry. "So we'll just keep up the rotation," she echoed wanly. "I think I get them next."

"I have it written down," Tibby said.

"Okay."

"Well."

Lena looked at her watch. "Should we just go?"

"I guess," Tibby said.

"Do you want to stop at the Tastee Diner on the way home?" Bridget asked.

"Yeah," Tibby said, gathering the effects of a ritual that hadn't happened. "Maybe we can see a late movie after. I can't handle my parents tonight."

"What time are you guys taking off tomorrow?" Bee asked.

"I think our train's at ten," Tibby said. Lena and Tibby were taking the train together: Tibby was getting off in New York to start film classes and her Movieworld job, and Lena was heading up to Providence to change dorm rooms for the summer. Bee was spending time at home before she left for Turkey.

Lena realized she didn't want to go home just yet either.

She picked up the Pants and cradled them briefly. She had a feeling she could not name exactly, but one she knew she had not had in relation to the Pants before. She had felt gratitude, admiration, trust. What she felt now still contained all that, but tonight it was mixed in with a faint taste of desperation.

If we didn't have them, I don't know what we would do, she found herself thinking as Bee pulled the door of Gilda's shut behind them and they walked slowly down the dark stairs.

One's real life is so often

the life that one does

not lead.

—Oscar Wilde

"Carmen, it is beautiful. I can't wait for you to see it."

Carmen nodded into the receiver. Her mother sounded so happy that Carmen had to be happy. How could she not be happy?

"When do you think you'll move in?" she asked, trying to keep her voice light.

"Well, we will need to do some work. Some plastering, painting, refinishing the floors. There's some plumbing and electrical to do. We want to get most of it out of the way before we move in. I hope it will be by the end of August."

"Wow. That soon."

"*Nena*, it has five bedrooms. Is that unbelievable? It has a beautiful backyard for Ryan to run around in."

Carmen thought of her tiny brother. He could barely

walk yet, let alone run. He was going to grow up with such a different life than the one Carmen had.

"So no more apartment, huh?"

"No. It was a good place for the two of us, but didn't we always want a house? Isn't that what you always said you wanted?"

She'd also wanted a sibling and for her mother not to be alone. It wasn't always easy getting what you wanted.

"I'll have to pack up my room," Carmen said.

"You'll have a bigger room in the new house," her mother rushed to say.

Yes, she would. But wasn't it a bit late for that? For having a house with a yard and a bigger room? It was too late to redo her childhood. She had the one she had, and it had taken place in her small room in their apartment. It was sad and strange to lose it and too late to replace it.

Where did that leave her? Without her old life and not quite coming up with a new one. In between, floating, nowhere. That seemed all too fitting, in a way.

"Lena dropped by yesterday to say hi and see Ryan. She brought him a Frisbee," her mother mentioned a little wistfully. "I wish you were home."

"Yeah. But I've got all this stuff going on here."

"I know, *nena*."

After she hung up with her mother, the phone rang again.

"Carmen, where are you?"

Julia Wyman sounded annoyed. Carmen glanced behind her at her clock.

"We're supposed to be doing a run-through on set in . . . now!"

"I'm coming," Carmen said, pulling on her socks as she held the phone with her shoulder. "I'll be right there."

She hustled out of her dorm and to the theater. She remembered along the way that her hair was dirty and she'd meant to change her pants, because the ones she was wearing made her feel particularly fat. But did it matter? Nobody was looking at her.

Julia was waiting for her backstage. "Can you help me with this?" For her role in the production, Julia wore a long tweed skirt, and the waist was too big for her.

Carmen bent down to work on the safety pin. "How's that?" she asked, pinning the waistband in the back.

"Better. Thanks. How does it look?"

Julia looked good in it. Julia looked good in most things, and she didn't need Carmen to tell her so. But Carmen did anyway. In a strange way, it was Julia's job to look good for both of them. It was Carmen's job to appreciate her for it.

"I think Roland is waiting for you onstage."

Carmen stepped onto the stage, but Roland didn't appear to be waiting for her. He didn't react in any way when he saw her. These days she felt her presence had the same effect as a ghost—nobody noticed her, but the air suddenly got cold. Carmen squinted and tried to make herself small. She did not like being onstage when the lights were on. "Did you need something?" she asked Roland.

"Oh, yeah." He was trying to remember. "Can you fix the curtain in the parlor? It's falling off."

"Sure," she said quickly, wondering if she should feel guilty. Was she the one who put it up last?

She positioned the ladder, climbed up three rungs, and aimed a staple gun at the plywood wall. Set building was strange in that it was always about the impression, made to be seen from particular angles and not made to last. It existed in space and time not as a thing, but as a trick.

She liked the *chunk* sound of the staple clawing into the wall. It was one of the things she'd learned at college: how to operate a staple gun. Her dad was paying a lot of money for that.

She'd learned other stuff too. How to gain seventeen pounds eating cafeteria food and chocolate at night when you felt lonely. How to be invisible to guys. How to not wake up for your nine o'clock psychology class. How to wear sweatshirts almost every day because you felt self-conscious about your body. How to elude the people you loved most in the world. How to be invisible to pretty much everyone, including yourself.

It was lucky she'd gotten to know Julia. Carmen was very fortunate, she knew. Because Julia was one of the most visible people on campus. They balanced each other out. Without Julia on the campus of Williams College, Carmen privately suspected she might disappear altogether.

We are having carmic disturbances around here.

I know you're in your hibernation and I, of all people,

get what that's about.

But Carma, it's June. Time to come out and be with

your friends who love you.

We tried to go to Gilda's, but without you we could not go on.

Could not.

The buzzing Bee

It was different being a girl with a boyfriend.

Bridget meditated upon this as she walked along Edge-mere Street on the way from Lena's house to her own. Her meditation had begun moments before, when a guy she knew vaguely from high school leaned out of his car and yelled "Hey, gorgeous!" and blew her a kiss.

In the past she might have shouted something at him. She might have blown him back a kiss. She might have given him the finger, depending on her mood. But some-how, it all seemed different now that she was a girl with a boyfriend.

She had spent almost a year getting used to it. It was particularly complex when you only saw that boyfriend for a day or two every month—when he went to school in New York City and you went to school in Providence, Rhode Island. Your status was more theoretical. For every guy who shouted from his car window, for every guy you passed on the way to Freshman Psychology who sort of checked you out, you thought, *What he doesn't realize is that I have a boyfriend.*

Each time she saw Eric's remarkable face, each time he appeared at the door of her dorm room or came to meet her at Port Authority in New York, it all came back. The way he kissed her. The way he wore his pants, the way he stayed up all night with her getting her ready for her Spanish midterm.

But it became theoretical again after Eric told her about Mexico. He'd gotten a job as assistant director at their old camp in Baja.

"I'm leaving the day after classes end," he'd told her on the phone in April.

There was no uncertainty in it, no question or lingering pause. There was nothing for her.

She clamped her hand harder around the phone, but she didn't want to betray the chaotic feelings. She wasn't good at being left. "When do you get back?" she asked.

"End of September. I'm going to stay for a month with my grandparents in Mulegé. My grandmother already started cooking." His laugh was light and sweet. He acted as though she would be as pleased for him as he was for himself. He didn't fathom her darkness.

Sometimes you hung up the phone and felt the bruising of your heart. It hurt now and it would hurt more later. The conversation was too unsatisfying to continue and yet you couldn't stand for it to end. Bridget wanted to throw the phone and also herself against the wall.

She had presumed her and Eric's summer plans would

unfold together in some way. She thought having a boyfriend meant you planned your future in harmony. Was it his certainty about her that made it so easy for him to leave, or was it indifference?

She went for a long run and talked herself down. It wasn't like they were married or anything. She shouldn't feel hurt by it. She knew it wasn't personal. The assistant director job was a windfall — it paid well and put him close to his faraway family.

She didn't feel hurt, exactly, but in the days after he told her, she got that fitful forward-moving energy. She didn't feel like hanging around missing him. If she hadn't been caught by surprise, caught in a painful presumption, she probably wouldn't have signed up for the dig in Turkey quite so fast.

Eric couldn't expect her to sit around waiting for him. That was not something she could do. How long could she coast on having a boyfriend when that boyfriend planned to be away from May to late September? How long could they coast as a couple? She wasn't a theoretical kind of person.

It was after the conversation about Mexico that she really started to wonder about these things. After that it seemed like for every guy she saw on her way to class, she had the feeling that her status as a girl with a boyfriend was something demanded of her rather than something she had very eagerly given.

❖   ❖   ❖

Tibby glanced at the time on her register. There were four minutes left in her shift and at least twelve people in line.

She scanned in a pile of six movies for a prepubescent girl wearing sparkly silver eye shadow and a too-tight-looking choker. Were the girl's eyes bulging or was Tibby imagining it?

"You're gonna watch all these?" Tibby asked absently. It was Friday. Late fees kicked in on Monday. The girl's gum smelled strongly and fakely of watermelon. As the girl swallowed, Tibby thought of fishermen's pelicans, with the rings around their necks so they couldn't gulp down their catch.

" 'Cause I'm having a sleepover. There'll be, like, seven of us. I mean, if Callie can come. And if she can't, I shouldn't be getting that one, because everybody else hates it."

Were we like that? Tibby wondered while the girl went on to describe each of her friends' specific movie requirements.

Now her shift was over by two minutes. Tibby cursed herself for having begun the conversation in the first place. She always forgot that annoying fact of question-asking: People tended to answer.

She had eleven customers still to serve before she could reasonably close down her register, and she was no longer getting paid. "This one's closing," she called to incipient number twelve before he could invest any time in her line.

The next person up was a goateed young man with a Windbreaker over his doorman coat. When it flapped open, Tibby could see that his name was Carl. She wanted to tell him that his movie was all right, but the ending stank and the sequel was an insult to your brain, but she made herself think the comment and not say it. That would be her rule going forward. She might as well admit to herself that she liked talking more than listening.

She closed out her register, said her good-byes, and walked along Broadway before turning onto Bleecker Street and then into the entrance to her dorm. The bad thing about her job was that it paid barely over minimum wage. The good thing about her job was that it was three blocks away.

The lobby of her dorm was cool and empty but for the security guard at his desk. It was all different now that it was summer. No students jabbering, no cell-phonic symphony of ring tones. A month ago, the big bulletin board had been laden with notices twenty thick. Now it was clear right down to the cork.

During the school year, the elevator ride was socially taxing. Too much time to stare and appraise and judge. In the normally crowded space she'd felt a need to be something for each of her fellow passengers, even the ones whose names she didn't know. Now, with it empty, she felt herself merging into the fake wood-grain wall.

Tonight the halls would be empty. The summer programs didn't start until after July fourth. And even then there would just be new, temporary people, not her friends, and not the kind you worried about in the elevator. They'd be gone by the middle of August.

It was a strange thing about college. You felt like you were supposed to be finding your life there. Each person you saw, you thought, *Will you mean something to me? Will we figure into each other's lives?* She'd made a few actual friends on her floor and in her film classes, but most people she saw she kind of knew off the bat wouldn't mean anything. Like the swim team girls who decorated their faces with purple paint to demonstrate school spirit, or the guy with the fuzzy facial hair who wore the Warhammer T-shirt.

But then again, chimed in the voice she'd recently come to think of as Meta-Tibby (her do-right self, never hurried or snappish), who would have guessed that first day in the 7-Eleven that Brian would become important?

In the four years since she'd first met Brian, many things had changed. Though Brian insisted he'd loved her from the first time he met her, she'd thought he was a doofus for the ages. She'd been wrong. She was often wrong. Now she got a deep abdominal tingle whenever she thought of being near him. It had been nine months since they'd . . . what? She hated the term *hooked up.* Nine months since they'd swum in their underwear after hours in the public pool and kissed fiercely and pressed themselves together until their hands and toes turned pruney and their lips blue.

They hadn't had sex yet. Not officially, in spite of Brian's pleas. But since that night in August, she felt as though her body belonged to Brian, and his body to her. Ever since that night in the pool, the way they loved each other had changed. Before it they each took up their own space. After it they took up space together. Before that night if he touched his ankle to hers under the dinner table, she blushed and obsessed and sweated through her shirt. After that night they always had some part touching. They read together on a twin bed with every part of their bodies overlapping, still concentrating on their books. Well, concentrating a little on their books.

Tonight this place would be quiet. On some level she missed Bernie, who practiced her opera singing from nine to ten, and Deirdre, who cooked actual food in the communal floor kitchen. But it was restful being alone. She would write e-mails to her friends and shave her armpits and legs before Brian came tomorrow. Maybe she would order pad thai from the place around the corner. She would pick it up so she wouldn't have to pay the tip for delivery. She hated to be cheap, but she couldn't afford to lay out another five dollars.

She fit her key into the loose lock. So imprecise was the lock she suspected it would turn for virtually any key in the dorm. Maybe any key in the world. It was a tarty little lock.

She swung open the door and felt once again the familiar appreciation for her single. Who cared if it was seven by nine feet? Who cared if it fit more like a suit of clothes than an actual room? It was hers. Unlike at home, her stuff stayed the way she left it.

Her gaze went first to the light pulsing under the power button on her computer. It went second to the steady green light of her camera's battery, fully charged. It went third to the glimmer of shine in the eyeball of a large, brown-haired nineteen-year-old boy sitting on her bed.

There was the lurch. Stomach, legs, ribs, brain. There was the pounding of the heart.

"Brian!"

"Hey," he said mutedly. She could tell he was trying not to scare her.

She dropped her bag and went to him, instantly folding up in his eager limbs.

"I thought you were coming tomorrow."

"I can't last five days," he said, his face pressed into her ear.

It was so good to feel him all around her. She loved this feeling. She would never get used to it. It was too good. Unfairly good. She couldn't dislodge her worldview that things balanced out. You paid for what you got. In happiness terms, this always felt like a spending spree.

Most guys said they'd call you tomorrow and they called you the next Saturday or not at all. Most guys said they'd be there at eight and showed up at nine-fifteen. They kept you comfortless, wanting and wishing, and annoyed at yourself for every moment you spent that way. That was not Brian. Brian promised to come on Saturday and he came on Friday instead.

"Now I'm happy," he said from her neck.

She looked down at the side of his face, at his manly forearm. He was so handsome, and yet he wore it lightly. The way he looked was not what made her love him, but was it wrong to notice?

He rolled her over onto the bed. She pried off her running shoes with her toes. He pulled up her shirt and laid his head on her bare stomach, his arms around her hips, his knees bent at the wall. If this room was small for her, it barely contained Brian when he stretched out. He couldn't help kicking the wall now and then. Tonight she was glad not to have to feel guilt toward the guy in 11-C.

It was something like a miracle, this was. Their own room. No hiding, no fibbing, no getting away with it. No parent to whom you must account for your time. No curfew to bump up against.

Time stretched on. They would eat what they felt like for dinner — or at least, what they could afford. She remembered the night they'd had two Snickers bars apiece for dinner and ice cream for dessert. They would fall asleep together, his hand on her breast or the valley of her waist, and wake up together in the sunshine from her east-facing window. It was so good. Too good. How could she ever afford this?

"I love you," he murmured, his hands reaching up under her shirt. He didn't hang around for that beat, that momentary vacuum where she was meant to respond in kind. His hands were already up under her shoulders, unbending himself over her for a real kiss. He didn't need her to say it back.

She used to have the idea — an untested belief, really — that you loved someone in a kind of mirror dance. You loved in exact response to how much they were willing to love you.

Brian wasn't like that. He did his loving openly and without call for reciprocation. It was something that awed

24

her, but that set him apart, as though he spoke Mandarin or could dunk a basketball.

She plunged her hand under his T-shirt, feeling his warm back, his angel bones. "I love you," she said. He didn't ask for the words, but she gave them.

... and down they forgot

as up they grew

—e. e. cummings

There were so many things you took for granted. So many things you hardly noticed until they were gone. In Carmen's case, one of those things was her identity.

She did have one once, she thought as she put the last of the props away in the darkened and empty theater.

She had once been the only child of a single mother. She had been one quarter of a famously inseparable foursome. She had been a standout math student, a fashionista, a good dancer, a control freak, a slob. A resident of apartment 4F. Now these things were gone, or—for the moment, at least— undetectable. She had come up with nothing to replace them. Except for maybe Julia. She was lucky to have Julia.

Ideally, you grew up in a house with a family and then you went to college. You left your home and family there, kind of waiting for you. You left a hole roughly the size and shape of you. You got to come home and fill it every once in a while.

Maybe this was only an illusion. Nothing stayed the same. You couldn't expect your family to sit there in suspended animation until you came back. That required a babyish narcissism that not even Carmen could muster. (Well, maybe she could muster it a little.) But so what if it was an illusion? Illusions could be really helpful sometimes.

The important thing was that home stayed where it was and you got to move. You could always plot your location in the world by your relationship to it. *I'm so far from home*, you could think, when in, say, China. *I'm so close to it*, you could think, when you turned the last corner and saw it again.

As Carmen's mother liked to point out, teenagers and toddlers were very much the same. They both liked to leave their mother, so long as their mother did not move.

Well, Carmen's mother did move. She was a moving target. Home was a time and no longer a place. Carmen couldn't return to it.

As far as Carmen was concerned, that made the leaving a lot harder. It also made the plotting of your location very tricky indeed.

For the first seven months of the school year, nothing felt familiar and nothing felt real. Except for maybe food. She felt as though she'd stepped out of the flow of time. She watched it go past, but she didn't take part. She just waited there, wondering when her life would start again.

She had lived big before. She really had. She was ambitious, she was pretty. She was a young woman of color.

Now she felt like a ghost. The pale, starchy cafeteria food made her pale and starchy. It blurred her lines.

She depended too much on her context to know herself. The faces of her friends and her mother were mirrors to her. Without them she couldn't see herself; she was lost. She'd first realized it that strange and lonely summer in South Carolina when she'd met her stepfamily.

She and Win Sawyer, the guy she'd met last summer, had gotten together a couple of times in the fall, but she had purposely let it trail off. She didn't know or like herself enough to be knowable or likable when she was with him. She had nothing to offer.

It turned out that she wasn't very good at making friends. That was one of the problems that came of having three pals, ready-made, practically waiting for you to be born so they could befriend you. She hadn't had to work that muscle you use to make friends. She doubted she even had that muscle.

Her first mistake was believing that she and her room-mate, Lissa Greco, would be instant friends, and that their relationship would be a stepping-stone to social conse-quence. Lissa set her straight pretty quickly. She'd arrived at Williams with her two best friends from boarding school. She was petulant and undermining to Carmen. She wasn't looking for another friend. She accused Carmen of stealing her clothes.

In the beginning Carmen was disoriented by her loneli-ness and wanted desperately to see Tibby, Bee, and Lena. But as time passed, she started to avoid them in subtle ways. She didn't want to admit to them or herself that she wasn't quite making the go of college that she'd hoped.

Once, she went to Providence and saw Bee in her glory: her soccer friends, her glorious roommate, her eating friends, her partying friends, her library friends. She saw Lena in her different kind of glory, quiet in the studio, surrounded by her beautiful sketches. The weekend she spent in New York with Tibby, it was three of them to the room, including Brian, and Tibby won a departmental prize for her first short film.

Carmen didn't want them coming to see her here, where she had no glory at all. She didn't want them to see her like this.

She first met Julia in the late winter in the theater department, where Carmen was signing up for a playwriting class. Julia mistook her for a theater type. "Have you worked on sets?" she'd asked Carmen.

Carmen couldn't figure out whom she was talking to. "Me?" she'd finally asked. She wasn't sure which was more surprising: that Julia took her for a set builder or that Julia was talking to her at all.

How low I have fallen, Carmen thought miserably. Nobody in high school would have mistaken her for a set builder. She'd been one of the cute girls, particularly by the end of high school. She showed off her belly button in tiny shirts. She flirted outrageously. She wore red lipstick to take her SATs.

Carmen tried to scrape together a little bit of dignity. "No, I'm not really a set person," she said.

"Oh, come on. Everybody's a set person. Jeremy Rhodes is directing a production of *The Miracle Worker* for senior week, and we're getting desperate," Julia explained.

Carmen recognized Julia from the cafeteria. She was one of the few freshmen that people knew about. She was beautiful and somewhat dramatic-looking, with her pale white skin and her long black hair. She wore vintage jackets and long bohemian skirts and made a certain amount of noise with her various pins and beads and bangles. She was small and thin but used the oversized gestures of a person who knew she was being looked at.

"Well, sorry," Carmen said.

"Let me know if you change your mind, okay?" Julia said. "It's a really cool group of people. Really tight."

Carmen nodded and fled, but she did think about it. She thought wistfully of having things to do and "really cool" people to do them with.

Julia approached her again in the cafeteria a few weeks later. "Hey, how's it going?"

Carmen felt self-conscious because she was eating alone. She was torn between being unhappy that Julia was seeing her this way and being happy that all the rest of the people there were seeing her with Julia. "All right," Carmen said.

"Did you get into the writing class?"

"Nope," said Carmen. "How's the play going?"

"Really good." Julia smiled a winning smile. "Still looking for people to join up."

"Oh, yeah?"

"Yeah. You should really think about it. Jeremy's very

cool. There are only three performances and they don't start until after exams. Why don't you come tonight? We have a rehearsal at seven. Just see what you think."

"Thanks," Carmen said, feeling almost absurdly grateful. Grateful that Julia had noticed her, remembered her, talked to her, invited her to something. Did Julia know how alone she was here? "Maybe I will," she said.

So grateful was she, she probably would have agreed if Julia had invited her to drink poisoned Kool-Aid.

And that was how, one week later, Carmen found herself standing on a ladder wearing a tool belt. If her friends saw her, they would not recognize her. No one in her high-school graduating class would recognize her. Or at least, she hoped they wouldn't. She didn't recognize herself. But really, who was herself? Who?

If she knew that, she probably wouldn't be standing on the ladder wearing the tool belt.

And now, six weeks after that, Carmen was doing the same thing, only it had lost its feeling of absurdity. She belonged there more than anywhere else. You could get used to almost anything.

And she did appreciate having something to do, someplace to go after dinner besides her dorm room. She appreciated that Julia was nice to her. Julia introduced her around. She made sure that if the cast and crew were going to get cappuccinos after rehearsal, Carmen came too. Carmen appreciated the hilariously mean impression of Lissa that Julia did to cheer her up when her roommate did something nasty.

In the theater group, which included many upperclass-men, Carmen felt like she was an add-on to Julia, a low-budget hanger-on friend. She had to remind people of her name too often. But still. It was better being out and about as a friend of Julia than eating candy in her room as a nobody.

Once in a while she felt sorry for herself. She felt like the prince in "The Prince and the Pauper," being mistaken for someone unimportant. *Do you even know who I am?* she thought. *Do you even know who my friends are?*

But really, if someone called her bluff, what would she say? Maybe she could answer the second question, but not even she knew the answer to the first.

What are you getting out of this? she silently asked Julia, these weeks later, as she pinned Julia's skirt for the third time and Julia gave her a squeeze of thanks. That was the part she couldn't figure out.

When Julia came to her in April with brochures from the Village Summer Theater Festival in Vermont, Carmen was startled and, of course, grateful.

"These are full-scale productions with a lot of really well-known actors," Julia said. "Do you want to do it? It's mid-June through the second week in August. It's hard to get in for acting, but they're always looking for crew. It could be a great experience."

Carmen was so pleased to be invited, she would have agreed for the sole reason that she'd been asked. Later she had to get her parents to agree to pay.

"Carmen, since when are you interested in theater?" her father had wanted to know when she called him to ask for

33

the check. She'd reached him on his car phone on his way home from the office.

"Since, I don't know . . . Since now."

"Well, I guess you've always been dramatic," he mused aloud.

"Thanks a lot, Dad." This was the kind of stuff you had to put up with when you asked for money.

"I mean that in the best sense, Bun. I really do."

"Right," she said tightly.

"And I remember you as the fierce carrot in the salad in your first-grade play."

"Tomato. Anyway, I'm not doing acting."

"Then what are you doing?"

"Behind-the-scenes stuff."

"*Behind-the-scenes* stuff?" He acted like she'd said she was going to eat her own ears.

"Yeah." She was starting to feel defensive.

"Carmen, sweetie, you've never done anything behind the scenes in your life."

He was in quite the chatty humor, wasn't he? she thought darkly.

"So maybe it's about time," she said.

She heard him turn off the car's ignition. It was quiet. "Bun, if this is really what you want, then I am willing to pay for it," he said.

It was easier when he was being annoying. When he was nice, she found she actually had to think.

Was it what she wanted? She thought of Julia. Or was Carmen just wanting to feel wanted?

She took stock of her options. Bee was going to Turkey, Tibby was taking classes in New York, and Lena would be in Providence. Her mother and David were ditching her apartment—her home—and fixing up a large suburban house on a street she had never even heard of.

"It's really what I want," she said.

Bridget stood in the bathroom looking for a toothbrush in the disorderly medicine cabinet, realizing just how long it had been since she'd spent a night at home.

It wasn't the product of any design. It was just one thing and then another. Over Thanksgiving, she'd stayed up so late talking at Lena's she'd just crashed on the couch. She'd been in New York over Christmas break, first with Eric uptown, then with Tibby downtown. She'd gone down to Alabama to visit Greta for spring break. She'd taken all-night buses the time she came home in February.

And now, on the eve of her trip to an excavation in a remote place halfway across the world, she was touching down at home.

She kept her eyes straight ahead in the hallway. She didn't want to see how badly the carpet needed to be vacuumed. She wasn't going to spend her short time here cleaning the stupid house.

In her room she sifted impatiently through her duffel bag again. She didn't feel like putting any of her stuff on the shelves. She had piles of laundry, but she wouldn't do it here. She kept her contact points minimal: her feet and whatever bit of floor space was required by the bottom of her bag. To sit or lie down extended that contact uncomfortably.

She remembered her seventh-grade camping trip, the ranger teaching them the principle of low-impact camping. "When you leave the wilderness, make it like you were never there." That was how she lived in her own house. Low-impact living. She ate more, drank more, laughed more, breathed more, slept more at any of her friends' houses than at her own.

She knocked on Perry's door. She knocked again. She knew he was in there. Finally she pushed the door open. He was staring at his computer screen. He had big earphones on, that was why he hadn't heard her.

What was it with her dad and her brother and their damned earphones? The house was as quiet as a crypt.

"Hey!" she said, about a foot from his ear. He looked up, disoriented. He took off his earphones. He wasn't used to being disturbed.

He was deep into one of those online war games he'd been playing since the beginning of high school. He did not want to chat. He wanted to get back to his game.

"Do you have a spare toothbrush somewhere? I thought I packed mine, but I can't find it." She always felt bullish and noisy in this house.

"Sorry?"

"An extra toothbrush. Do you have one?"

He shook his head without thinking about it. "Uh-uh. Sorry." He turned his eyes back to the screen.

Bridget stared at her brother. For some reason she

thought of Eric, and with that thought came the dawning of a certain set of objective facts. Yes, her family was alienated. On their best days they were eccentric. They were not happy; they were not close. But still. Here she was standing in front of Perry, her own brother—her twin, for God's sake—whom she had hardly seen this year.

She pushed a pile of techie magazines out of the way and hoisted herself onto his desk. She was going to talk with her brother. They hadn't had a single real conversation since Christmas. Out of guilt alone, she would torture him.

"How's school?"

He fumbled with something on the back of his monitor.

"What have you been taking this semester? Did you do the wildlife class?"

He continued to fumble. He looked at her once, wishfully.

"Hey, Perry?"

"Yeah. Oh, sorry," he said. He left the computer alone. "I've actually been taking time off this semester." He spoke to the arm of his chair.

"What?"

"Yeah. I haven't been taking classes this semester."

"Why not?"

His look was blank. He wasn't used to having to answer questions. He wasn't used to having to present his life or explain his decisions.

"What did Dad say?" she asked.

"Dad?"

"Yeah."

"We didn't really discuss it."

"You didn't really discuss it." She was talking a little too quickly, a little too loudly. Perry made a face like his ears hurt.

"Does he know?"

Perry's eyes would not engage. She felt as if she were speaking over a PA system rather than specifically to him.

She didn't care if he wouldn't look at her. She made herself look at him. She wanted to see him through objective eyes.

His hair had always been darker than hers, and now it had turned completely brown, probably accelerated by his staying inside all the time. He had untended fuzz on his upper lip, but otherwise he looked as though he had barely entered puberty. She glanced away, a churning feeling in her chest.

He was so slight and she so tall it was a wonder they were related, let alone twins. But then, maybe it wasn't a wonder at all. Maybe it was part of the harsh duality of being born together. What one got, the other didn't. And Bridget had always been strong. She couldn't help picturing them stowed together in her mother's stomach, taking what resources they could.

It was the zero-sum problem with twins. If one was smart, the other felt dumb. If one was bossy, the other was meek. The equation was too easy.

Bridget knew she'd always taken more than her fair share. But was it her job to stay small to encourage him to be big? If she withdrew, would he come forward? Was it her fault he had come out this way?

"I guess Dad knows," Perry finally answered.

She stood up. She felt frustrated. What was Perry doing if not going to school? He didn't have a job. Did he have any friends? Did he ever leave his room?

"I'll see you later," she said tightly.

"You could ask him," he said.

She turned around. "Ask who?"

"Dad."

"About what?"

"About the toothbrush."

Fill what is empty,

empty what is full, and

scratch where it itches.

—Tallulah Bankhead

Lena didn't feel lonely easily. Somehow, knowing she had friends was enough to keep her happy. She didn't actually have to talk with them or see them all the time. It was like other things: So long as she had an aspirin in the cabinet, she didn't really need to take one. So long as the toilet was readily available, she could wait until the last second to use it. As long as the basic resources existed for her, her needs were small.

She thought of this on the first day of her summer painting class. The instructor was new to her, the monitor was new. The students were unfamiliar. She was using a new kind of brush. She would probably like these things once she got used to them.

And in the meantime, Tibby and Carmen were on the other end of her cell phone. The Traveling Pants would come her way soon. Annik, her former teacher, was available for art-related crises, even the little ones. Her old kind of brush was sitting there at the ready, just in case. These were the things that made her bold.

But did it count as boldness when she kept herself so covered?

"Up there. There's a space," she heard the instructor, Robert, saying to a late arrival. Lena's main hope for the other students was not that they provide friendship or commiseration. It was that they not set up too close to her and obstruct her sight lines. She tensed up as the new person came closer and relaxed again when he/she passed behind her and kept on going to the far side of the studio. Potential threat averted. She didn't need to take her eyes from the model.

When the timer dinged and the model broke her pose, Lena finally looked up. She saw dark brown hair poking above the newly set-up canvas, curly and not very well trained. A tall person, most likely male. She quickly looked down. It was familiar dark brown hair. She tried to think. She kept her eyes down as she went into the hall.

Lena had developed the habit years before of avoiding eye contact. It was a sad capitulation, in a way, because she loved to look at people's faces. She wanted to be an artist, after all. She had good, informative eyes, and she liked to use them. The trouble was, whoever she looked at was usually looking back. And though she liked looking, she did not like being looked at. Brain-wise, she was perfectly designed for invisibility. Face-wise, she knew she was not. She'd always been striking. She'd always gotten attention for it.

That was one of the things she loved about drawing and painting models. It was the only time in her life she got to look and look and look and nobody looked at her.

She walked back to her easel after the five-minute break, gearing up for the next twenty-five minutes of concentrated work. The late person with the hair was still at work. It made her sort of curious. She saw a hand and a palette. It was a man's hand.

For the first minutes of the pose, she thought about the hair and the hand across the way and not about her drawing. That was strange of her. Well, maybe she did avoid eye contact, but she apparently fell for a mystery as hard as the next person.

At the break, she waited for the face to emerge from behind the canvas. She waited for him to find her face and look at her. Then the world would be normal. He would look at her for a few seconds too long and then she could not care about him anymore.

Did she know him? She felt like maybe she did.

Another break passed and he did not so much as peer around his canvas. How frustrating. She actually positioned herself to get a look at him. She had to laugh at herself in the process, craning her neck. The laugh brought in the smell of linseed oil and oil paint and she felt happy in a visceral, smell-induced way.

Desire was just the dumbest thing. You wanted what you wanted until it was yours. Then you didn't want it anymore. You took what you had for granted until it was no longer yours. This, it seemed to her, was one of the crueler paradoxes of human nature.

She remembered a pair of brown wedge boots. She'd seen them at Bloomingdale's and passed them up because they cost over two hundred dollars. They probably had lots of pairs in the back, she'd thought. Certainly they would have her gargantuan size in stock. She could always come back.

And yet when she did go back two days later, they were all gone. She asked the saleslady, who said, "Oh, those wedge boots sold out instantly. Very popular. No, we're not getting any more."

At which point, Lena became obsessed. It wasn't that other people wanted them. It was that she couldn't have them. No, that wasn't completely it either. Partly, at least, it was the fact that they were genuinely lovely boots. She scoured the Internet. She researched the manufacturer, she searched eBay. She would have bid three hundred dollars for those two-hundred-dollar boots, and yet she never found them. "The boots that got away," Carmen said jokingly once, when Lena rhapsodized about them.

So how did desire, hopelessly tricky as it was, relate to love? It wasn't the same. (She hoped it wasn't the same.) It wasn't entirely different. They were certainly related. By blood, though, or more like in-laws? she wondered.

What about Kostos? There was desire, no question. What else? Would she have continued to love him if he had continued to be available to her? Yes. The answer came before she finished thinking the question. Yes. There was a time when he loved her and she loved him and they both believed they could be together. Indeed, such a time it was, it had effectively wrecked all the rest of her times.

But could she have gotten over Kostos if he hadn't been taken from her so forcibly? If she'd just been allowed, over the course of months or years, to discover that he snored or that he was prone to zits on his back or that his toenails grew inward and made his feet stink?

She stopped. Wait a minute. Objection. She demanded that her mind rephrase its question. Would she have gotten over him *more easily* had he not been forced away? She was over him now. Yes, she still thought about him, but not nearly as much. No, she hadn't yet been with anyone else, but . . .

For the rest of class, Lena found herself looking again and again at the hand to the right of the canvas across the way and the shock of hair above it. He was a lefty, she realized. Kostos was a lefty.

He worked through the breaks. She couldn't get so much as a peek at him.

The last pose ended and Lena packed her things away slowly. She hung around, pretending to be thinking (well, she was actually thinking, wasn't she). At last she drifted into the hallway.

And because the truth must be told, Lena (who didn't care) loitered for fourteen minutes in the hallway until he finally came out of the classroom and she got her look at him.

She did know him. Okay, no, she didn't know him. But she knew of him. He wasn't her year. Maybe one or two years older. She had certainly seen him.

He wasn't the sort of person you would forget, appearance-wise. He was tall, with raucous hair, dark gold skin, and some very good-humored freckles.

His name was Leo, and she knew that because he had a reputation. Not for being a player, so far as she knew, but for being able to draw. And that, of all things, was a turn-on to one Lena Kaligaris, Greek virgin.

Her small circle of friends and acquaintances at RISD, art geeks that they were, whispered most fervently about the people who could or couldn't, did or didn't. Draw, that was. And this young man of the hair and hand stood among the few, almost legendary people who could.

She watched him with a surprising little thrill in her stomach and waited for him to notice her. How often did she want that? Not often. What she really wanted, she informed herself, was for him to look at her in a particular way. It wouldn't matter if he had a serious girlfriend or wasn't even into girls at all. She wanted him to give her the look, the slightly extended appraisal that would drain him of his mystery and transform him into a regular person. (She did want that, didn't she?) It was this familiar look that confirmed her peculiar power, easily possessed and rarely wanted.

These were the things that freed her. These were the things that made her bold.

But he didn't look at her like that. He didn't look at her

at all. He fixed his eyes ahead and he kept on walking, bringing to mind for the second time that afternoon the memory of the brown wedge boots.

"I got in."

Brian slipped the news in between the mu shu pork and the fortune cookies.

"You what?" Tibby demanded, unsure she had heard him properly.

"I got in."

"You did?"

He looked slightly sheepish. He cracked his fortune cookie in quarters and then eighths, and then it was a crumble.

"That's so great! I knew you would. How could you not?"

Ever since Brian had hatched the idea of transferring to NYU from the University of Maryland, his grades had been faultless.

"I just want to sleep beside you every night," he had told her back in December. "That's all I want."

She knew he would get in. She knew he would make it work. That was how he was.

"What does it say?" he asked, pointing to the fortune in her hand.

" 'Beware the prevalence of ideas,' " she read. She crunched on her cookie. "My lucky numbers are 4 and 237. How about yours?"

" 'You are sexy,' " he read.

"No way! It doesn't say that. Let me see it!"

He smiled suggestively and handed it over.

It actually did say that. How unfair. "So what about the money?" she asked, tossing her fortune into the remains of the plum sauce.

"Well."

"Not good?" She felt the sesame noodles climbing back up her esophagus.

"I got six thousand."

"Oh." She swallowed. "Dollars?"

"Dollars."

She tried to think. The waiter slapped the bill down on their table without stopping.

"Out of twenty-two thousand."

"Oh."

"Not including room and board."

"Oh." She flicked her chopsticks around. "How come not more?"

"My stepfather has more money than you'd think."

"But he doesn't give you any of it," Tibby burst out. In her world, parents paid for college, and if they couldn't cover it, they helped you get the loans to pay the difference.

Brian didn't look bitter in the least. He didn't even look irritated. What Tibby thought of as a right, Brian didn't hope for. "I know. Yeah. But that's how it works."

"It's not fair that they count his money against you. Can you explain that he's not going to pay *anything*?"

Brian shrugged. "I'm saving."

"How much have you got?"

"One hundred and seventy-nine." He picked up the bill. She grabbed it from him. "I've got this."

48

"No. I want to."

"You're saving."

"I know. But I can save and also buy you dinner."

"And take the bus up here almost every weekend and buy me CDs?" She didn't mean to sound mad at him.

He took out his wallet. She saw a corner of the condom he'd stashed there three or four months ago. "So we're ready, when we're ready," he'd told her when she'd first noticed it. He fished out a bill—a twenty, crumpled and weary, as though it were the last of its kind.

"Come on. Please let me." She got her wallet out too.

"Next time," he said, getting up, leaving her clutching her extraneous wallet.

He always said that. His arms were around her as soon as they made it to the sidewalk. It surprised her that they could walk in that degree of embrace.

On the way up in the elevator they took advantage of being alone. As soon as they were inside her room, Brian went to his duffel bag and unzipped it. "To celebrate," he said, pulling out a bottle of wine.

"Where did you get that?" she asked. Brian was not your fake-ID type.

He tried to look mysterious. "I found it someplace."

"Like in your house?"

He laughed. "It was sitting around. It's old."

She picked it up and looked at it. It was red wine from 1997. "Very funny."

"Hang on." He disappeared down the hall and came back with a corkscrew and two plastic cups from the communal kitchen. He didn't really know how to use the corkscrew and neither did she. At last, laughing, they poked the cork into the wine bottle. First he poured two cups and then he put on a Beethoven CD, the fifth concerto for piano, which he knew she loved.

"It's loud," she said.

"Nobody's here," he said.

"Oh, yeah."

They sat cross-legged, facing each other on the floor. When they touched cups, the soft plastic gave, making no sound.

"To us together," she said, knowing how happy it made him by the flush of his skin. She felt shy all of a sudden. She wanted to say something ironic, but nothing came. She took a long drink of wine.

"Is it good?" he asked, pulling her feet to get her to come closer.

"I don't know. Is it?"

He drank some more. "Tastes kind of old."

"I think I like it," she said. She liked all the things about that moment, and the wine went along with them.

"Here's more."

"You have some too."

She turned and lay back against him, wine in her blood and music in her ears. She guessed there were people who lived their whole lives without getting to be this happy. That thought was the single note of unhappiness in her happiness.

He whistled along with the violins for a few bars. "I

think this is the best night ever," he said in a quiet voice, thinking her thoughts, as he often did.

"Except maybe the night of the pool."

"Right." He considered. "But I didn't know you as much then. I thought I did, but now I know I didn't. And imagine how it will feel next year or the one after?"

Brian was unafraid to think of the future, believing she was in it. He talked about them when they were thirty as easily as when they were twenty. He talked about babies and who would get Tibby's extra-long second toe. He wanted all of it. He wasn't afraid of saying so.

He liked to tell her his dreams, and he always dreamed in *we*. "Who's *we*?" she asked the first time he recounted to her a long, complicated scenario.

He looked at her, perplexed, as though she was kidding around with him for no good reason. "You and me."

It couldn't keep getting better, Tibby decided. It just couldn't. There was a law of physics that prohibited it. Seriously, there was some kind of law. Conservation of joy. No joy could be added to the sum in the universe without some being taken away. They were taking more than their share as it was.

He poured more wine. She realized in an indistinct way that she was getting drunk. She realized it on one level and felt it on another.

The bottle and the plastic cups were somehow shoved out of the way and now they were kissing on the linoleum floor.

The second movement of the concerto began, too beautiful for anything. "How about the bed?" she suggested faintly.

Usually she was the one who kept guard in these situations. She'd made the decision that they weren't supposed to make love yet. They were both virgins. He was more than ready, but she still wasn't sure. And as much as he pleaded, he didn't push; he was a gentleman.

Now she pressed against him, her hips seeming to know what to do without even bothering with her brain. Her shirt was off, without her quite noticing. Some time ago, Brian had gotten the knack of her front-fastening bra.

She managed to free him of his shirt. There was nothing better than feeling his bare skin against hers, and those few fine hairs in the middle of his chest.

If he was doing this, she wondered vaguely, and she was doing that, then who exactly was minding the store?

They were hurtling forward now, doing the things they often did, but faster and more. Her body wasn't consulting her at all anymore. She wanted to be closer to him; she wanted him inside her.

She meant to stop. To say hang on, wait up. Just to think, at least. To get her whole self on board. But she couldn't say stop. She didn't want to. She wanted to feel him inside. He was so close now.

"Do we have . . . ?" she began faintly.

"Yes," he said almost before a word was out of her mouth. He fumbled for less than a second before locating the familiar condom and tearing it open.

"Do you want to . . . ?"

"I don't know. . . ."

She loved him. She knew she did.

And then in a moment, simple and pure, they were together in a way they hadn't been before.

oh, life is a glorious cycle of song, / A medley of extemporanea; / And love is a thing that can never go wrong; / And I am Marie of Roumania.

—Dorothy Parker

Opening night came and went. Carmen wore dark clothes and knocked herself out changing sets and managing props. She kept her focus tight; there was no room for error. Although she did good work, it was the kind of job where people only noticed you if you screwed up.

Of all the people Carmen clapped for, she clapped the loudest for Julia as Annie Sullivan. She made sure there was a bouquet of roses to be presented to her onstage. She was proud of her friend. With Julia, even pride took on the tint of gratitude.

Carmen had worked hard. She'd learned things. She'd answered her own questions without needing help. She was largely invisible, granted, but there was something to be said for plain competence.

Afterward she gave Julia a silver bracelet. Julia countered with a plate of brownies for Carmen, which she brought to her room late that evening.

"Hey, did you get your room assignment at Village Theater yet?" Julia asked. She had her paper in her hand.

"I think so," Carmen said, finding the letter on her desk that had arrived that morning from Vermont.

"Forte House, room 3H," Julia read. "Did they put us together?"

"3H. Yep."

"Oh, good."

Once again, Carmen felt fortunate and also relieved. How lucky she was that Julia wanted to room with her. She'd been half afraid when she got the assignment that Julia would prefer a stranger.

"My brother said he'd drive me up. He's visiting some girl at Dartmouth and it's not too far out of the way. Do you want to come? Do you have a ride yet?"

Julia's brother, Thomas, was a conspicuously handsome senior at Williams. Carmen was too overwhelmed in his presence to chirp out a single word. She was not only invisible but mute. "That'd be great. I hadn't planned a ride yet."

"Oh, good," Julia said again, looking genuinely pleased. "Do you want to go get coffee?" she asked.

"Sure," said Carmen, and as she wandered along next to an exuberant Julia, she felt herself in awe of Julia's Mexican skirt, of the particular dark red color of her tank top, of her thinness and her confidence to wear a tweed cap that would have fallen pretty flat on almost anyone else. Again Carmen felt the gladness to have someone to do things with. Not just any someone, but one of the most striking people in the school.

Carmen stood in line at the student union to get them both lattes and arrived back at the table to see Julia holding court among a bunch of sophomore boys. Carmen slipped in silently beside her. She laughed at Julia's witticisms and admired her ease.

For the hundredth time she wondered what Julia saw in her. This friendship was an incredible boon to Carmen, but what was Julia getting out of it? There were other girls around campus as glamorous as she was. As friends they would have suited Julia a lot better, and yet she hung around with dull, mute, invisible Carmen.

Carmen stared into her coffee cup while Julia told a funny story about the sound system going haywire in the second act of the play. Carmen felt bad for not being a worthier friend. She should think of things to say too, not sit there like a moron. She should have *something* to offer.

Julia did not belong with a loser in an oversized sweat-shirt. If for no other reason, Carmen determined she would pull herself together for Julia's sake.

Lying against Brian, her face sticking to his sticky chest, Tibby felt warm, thin tears dripping from the corners of her eyes, running over the bridge of her nose, tap-tapping onto his rib cage. They were some of the truest and most mysterious tears she had ever cried. When she put her hands up to his face, she realized his eyelashes were also wet.

She wanted to stay like this forever. She wanted to sink into his body and live there. She also realized she really had to pee.

Sometime or other she rolled onto her back and he sat up. She touched her flushed cheeks.

"What—" An odd sound occurred in his throat.

She sat up too, caught by it.

"What?" she said, dazed.

"I—there was—I'm not sure—"

"Brian?"

"The condom—I think it was— It's not—"

"Not what?" She didn't even want to look.

"Not . . . on."

"What do you mean?" Her voice was flat, but her muscles were coiling.

"God, Tib. I'm not sure. Maybe it broke. I think it broke."

"You do?"

He was investigating, his hair falling forward over his face. He reached a hand toward her, but she had already stood up, dragging the covers with her.

"Are you sure?" Her voice was rising. Worries were seeding and spreading, pushing up stems like in a time-lapsed movie.

"It'll be okay. We'll— I'll—"

"Are you sure it broke?" She was clutching the covers around her with two hands. She thought with hatred of the incompetent condom that had lived in his wallet all these months.

He sat like Rodin's *Thinker* on the bare bed. "Yes, I'm pretty sure. I don't know when it happened."

She could get pregnant. She could be getting pregnant

right now. What about STDs? Herpes? What about, God, AIDS?

No, he was a virgin. He said he was a virgin. He had to be. He was, wasn't he? "It happened when we were having sex," she said sharply.

He looked up at her, trying to understand the strange tone of her voice.

She could get pregnant! Easily! This was exactly how it happened! She needed to think. When was her period? These were the things that happened to tragic girls who weren't nearly as cautious or practical as Tibby.

What should she do? What did this mean? For all this time, being in all these strange places in her life, she had taken a certain refuge in the fact that at least she was still a virgin. At least that category of fears was not hers to fear. It was the single transom she had not crossed.

She wasn't a virgin anymore! Why had she let herself forget that it mattered?

She looked at Brian, almost as far away as he could be in a room so small. She should be having these worries aloud, with him, not just alone. But she couldn't help it.

She wished she could dress without his seeing. She turned away.

"Tibby, I am sorry. I'm so sorry this happened. I didn't even know—"

"It's not like you did anything. . . ." Her words were backed by minimal breath and floated to the wall.

"I just wish . . . ," he said.

❖　❖　❖

Bridget's stomach had been groaning since she'd woken up that morning, but when her father put a plate of eggs on the table for her, she fitfully roved around the kitchen instead of sitting down with them.

"Dad, why did you let Perry quit school?" she asked.

Her father was dressed in shapeless twill trousers and a tweed jacket, the same outfit he'd worn to work as long as she could remember. He was a history teacher and associate dean at a private high school, and he was clueless in the way she imagined only a longtime high school administrator could be. He'd made a career of tuning out teenagers. He was in good practice when it came to his own.

"He didn't quit. He took some time off."

"Is that what he said?"

Her father adopted his look of silent retreat. He didn't like to be demanded of. He resisted her in his passive way. "You should eat if you want me to drop you on my way to school," he said quietly. He was always eager to drop her places.

"Why is he taking time off? Did you ask him that? Three courses at Montgomery Community College is not exactly overwhelming."

He poured his coffee. "Not everyone belongs in the Ivy League, Bridget."

She glared at him. He was trying to force her to back off. He knew she was neither a scholar nor a snob, that she felt defensive about going to Brown. He probably calculated that this would shut her up, but it wasn't going to work. "So he's going back to school in the fall?" she said volubly.

Her dad put forks on the table. He sat down to eat. "That's what I expect."

She tried to grab hold of his gaze. "Is that really what you expect?"

He salted his eggs. He paused, waiting for her to sit down. She didn't want to sit down. When it came to him, she was a passive resister, too. It was one of the few things they had in common.

He'd made these eggs as a gesture. He'd done it for her. And yet the sight of them turned her stomach. Why couldn't she receive what few overtures he made?

He refused to give her what she wanted. She refused to take what he gave.

She sat down. She picked up her fork. He ate.

"I'm worried about him," she said.

He nodded vaguely. His eyes wandered to the newspaper on the table beside him. On most mornings the *Washington Post* was his breakfast companion, and she sensed he wasn't enjoying the break in routine.

"It seems like he's just . . . rotting away in his room."

Her father looked at her finally. "His interests are different than yours, but he does have them. Why don't you eat?"

She didn't want to eat. She didn't want to do what he said. She felt that if she ate, she'd be acceding to him, to this life in the underworld, and she wasn't willing to do it.

"Does he see anyone? Does he leave the house? Do his interests include anything other than staring at a computer day and night?"

"Don't be so dramatic, Bridget. He'll be fine."

All at once she was furious. She was standing and her fork was clattering around on the floor. "He'll be fine?" she shouted. "Just like Mom was fine?"

He stopped chewing. He put his fork down. He looked not at her but through her, past her. "Bridget," he said in a low rumble.

"Why don't you look around! He is not fine! Why won't you see it?"

"Bridget," he intoned again. The more times he said her name, the less she felt she was even in the room with him.

"This is no way to live! Can't you see that?" She felt the tears in her throat and behind her eyes, but she wouldn't cry. He wasn't safe enough for crying, and hadn't been in a long time. *It's too lonely this way.*

He shook his head. Of course he couldn't see it. Because it was how he lived too.

"Bridget. You live the way you choose. You let Perry do the same."

And me. You let me be, he might as well have added.

She wouldn't sit down. She wouldn't eat his eggs. But she would live the way she chose. She would do that for him.

She grabbed her duffel bag and her backpack and walked out of the kitchen and out of the house. That was what she chose.

"So when he called, I told him I couldn't talk," Julia explained, sitting cross-legged on Carmen's twin bed in their small dormitory room in Vermont. "I felt bad and everything. I don't know how to tell him that I'm not going to be into it this summer."

It was funny. The setting was new—the campus of a performing arts center that housed the theater festival—but the situation was the same—Julia sitting on a dorm-room bed at night telling Carmen the latest episode in her off-again relationship with Noah Markham, scholar and stud.

Carmen nodded. She had finished putting all her stuff away, so she started refolding things.

"I mean, what if I meet someone here, you know? Have you looked around? There are a lot of good-looking guys. Probably half of them are gay, but still."

Carmen nodded. She hadn't really looked around yet.

"A place like this, anything can happen. You know how costars are always falling in love on movie sets and ruining their relationships?"

Carmen read *Us Weekly* often enough to know the truth of this. She put a bottle of the shampoo they both liked on Julia's dresser. She saw the familiar black-and-white picture of Julia's mother in the silver frame. Julia kept it in her dorm room at school. It was a glamorous picture taken by some famous photographer whose name Carmen only pretended to know. Julia's mother had been a model, Julia told her. She was beautiful, certainly, but Carmen also registered that Julia's mother almost never called.

Carmen didn't put out any pictures of her family, but taped inside the cover of her binder she kept a small picture of Ryan on the remarkable day that he was born. She'd also taped a picture of the Septembers at Rehoboth Beach, the last time they'd all been together. Sometime during the winter she'd moved it from inside the front cover to inside the back cover, because though the sight of it made her happy, it made her happy in the saddest possible way.

Julia watched Carmen arranging the room. "Hey, did you pick up the Teramax conditioner?"

Carmen raised her eyebrows. "I don't think so. Was it on the list?"

Julia nodded. "I'm pretty sure I wrote it on there."

Carmen scoured the pharmacy bags but couldn't find conditioner of any sort. "I must have missed that somehow." She felt guilty, though she didn't even use it.

"Don't worry about it," Julia said.

"I'll pick some up when we go into town," Carmen said apologetically.

"Seriously, it's fine," Julia assured her.

Julia fell asleep at some point, but Carmen lay in her bed. She had to remind herself where she was.

After a while she got up and checked the list that she and Julia had made for her to take to the pharmacy. Teramax conditioner was not on it.

She went out to the hall to call Lena. Lena didn't answer, so she left a message. Tibby didn't answer either, and Bridget had already left for Turkey.

Even though it was late, she called her mom.

"*Nena*, hi. Is everything okay?" her mom asked in a groggy voice.

"Fine. We're just settling in here."

"How does it seem?"

"Good," Carmen said without really thinking about it. "How's Ryan?"

Her mom laughed. "He threw his shoes out the window."

"Oh, no. His new walking ones?"

"Yes."

Carmen pictured Ryan and his tiny sneakers and she pictured her mom racing around trying to locate them.

"Street or courtyard?"

"Street, of course."

Carmen laughed. "So what else is going on?" she asked, somewhat wistfully.

"We met with the painters today." Her mother said it as though she'd met with the president.

"Oh, yeah?"

"We're having them skim coat every wall. We're starting to choose colors."

Carmen yawned. She didn't have much to say about skim coating.

"Okay, Mama, well, sleep tight."

"You too, *nena*. I love you."

Carmen tiptoed back into the room and crawled into bed, careful not to wake Julia, who was a light sleeper.

Carmen knew her mother loved her. That used to provide a certain sufficiency. That alone had been enough to make her feel like somebody.

It used to feel like she and her mother were almost one person, living one life. Now their lives were separate. Her mother's identity wasn't one she could tag along with anymore.

It didn't mean her mother didn't love her. She'd given Carmen life, but she couldn't be expected to keep giving it. And yet Carmen wasn't sure how to live by herself.

She tucked her hands under her pillow, and even though she could hear Julia's breathing a few feet away, she felt terribly lonely.

When Lena got to her room that night, she called Carmen back, hoping it wasn't too late. "I have to ask you something and don't jump all over me," she said, after giving Carmen a chance to relocate to the hallway.

"As if I would," Carmen said, too curious to pretend to be hurt for long.

"Am I over Kostos, do you think?"

"Did you meet someone else?" Carmen asked.

Lena gazed at the ceiling. "No."

"Did you *look at* someone else?"

Lena felt herself blushing and was glad Carmen couldn't see. Carmen had always combined an extravagant capacity for near psychic brilliance and total obtuseness, but she rarely used them both at the same time. "Why do you ask?"

"Because I think you will be officially over Kostos when you talk about—even really look at—somebody else."

"Isn't that a little simplistic?"

"No," said Carmen.

Lena laughed.

"One of these days you are going to fall in love and forget about him. Sooner or later it has to happen. I'd hoped it would be sooner."

Lena crossed her feet under her on the bed. Could she forget Kostos? Was that what she was supposed to be striving for? She'd so far aimed at "getting over" him, whatever that meant, and she often prided herself on making strides toward that goal. But it was hard to imagine forgetting. She wasn't really the forgetting type.

"I don't know if that's possible."

"I think it is. I think it will happen. And you know what else I think about Kostos?"

Lena sighed. She had reached her limit of saying the name Kostos out loud and far exceeded her limit of hearing it said by others. "No, smarty. What?"

"I have this weird premonition that as soon as you forget about Kostos, you are going to see him again."

Lena felt activity in her stomach. It had both the heavy quality of sickness and the fizz of excitement. She was glad the bathroom was right there.

"Oh, you do, do you." Lena tried to calibrate her voice for lighthearted sarcasm, but it sounded dark as mud.

"I really do," Carmen answered solemnly.

Lena hung up the phone with the suspicion, perhaps even the hope, that Carmen had veered into the obtuse.

Pain is inevitable;

suffering is optional.

—Greta Randolph

She'd had her period on the drive from school home to Bethesda, hadn't she? Tibby tried to remember the usual accompaniments — the stained underwear, the forgetting to buy tampons or pack them, the needing to stop at a gas station to take care of urgent matters.

"Tibby Rollins?"

She and Bee had driven down together. Bee had borrowed her roommate's car in Providence and picked her up in New York on the way. Tibby remembered at least two gas station stops. One was for actual gas, the other for more of a personal emergency. But was the emergency bleeding through her pants or was it needing a box of Krispy Kremes? She couldn't remember. She was a virgin then, and virgins were entitled to blessed ignorance about when their periods came and went.

"Tibby Rollins?"

She turned with irritation toward the sound of her manager's voice. Charlie always called her by first and last names, as though there were three other Tibbys on the premises.

"Charlie Spondini?" she said back.

He frowned at her. "The return box is so jammed up nothing will fit in the slot. Do you mind?"

"I do mind. That is inconsiderate of our customers and our financial dependence on late fees." Sometimes she could make him laugh, but today she knew she was just being rude. She almost wished he would fire her.

"Tibby Rollins . . ." He looked more tired than angry.

"Okay, fine," she said. She moved to the giant cardboard return box under the counter and began unloading.

She and Bee had driven down on June fourth. If she did have her period then, that meant . . . What did it mean? Was she supposed to know when she ovulated? She hated that stuff. She'd been through her mom's fertility treatments, the thermometers and kits. She didn't want to live in the same world as that.

"Excuse me?"

Tibby looked up. It was a customer. He had tinted glasses and a gray comb-over. "Do you know if you have *Striptease*?"

"What?" She glared at him with distaste.

"*Striptease*?"

Ick. "It's in Drama if we have it."

"Thanks," he said, and turned to the aisles.

"It's a total piece of crap," she informed his back.

At home her message light was blinking. Usually she found sustenance in Brian's sweetly romantic messages. Tonight she had to force herself to listen.

"Tib, I found out about the pills you can take." His voice sounded strained and worried. "I don't think it's too late. I'll come up tonight if you want me to go with you. I have the address of the Planned Parenthood. It's not far—just on Bleecker Street. I can—"

She jabbed the Erase button and her room was quiet. She didn't want to know the address of Planned Parenthood. She didn't want to have that kind of life. She didn't want to get examined by a gynecologist and fill a prescription. She wanted her sexual experience to be strictly over the counter.

Why had she done it? Why had she let Brian talk her into it? *He didn't really talk you into it*, said the voice of Meta-Tibby. There hadn't been much talking going on at all.

But he was the one who wanted to so badly. He was the one who'd wanted it and pleaded all these months. He was the one who'd carried the shoddy condom around in his wallet. He was the one who'd been so sure that doing it would bring them closer.

Every black thought she had stuck itself to that stupid condom and to Brian for carrying it so eagerly and so long.

Tibby flipped on her tiny TV. The local news was on channel seven. Tibby kept it on this station, because there was an anchorwoman she liked. She was older, probably almost sixty, and her name was Maria Blanquette. She had brown skin and intelligent and imperfect features, and unlike most news talkers, who wore thick masks of makeup, Maria looked like an actual person. She did this "Manhattan Moments" segment where she was supposed to showcase all the celebrity doings in New York City. But instead of adulating the celebrities, as most entertainment spots did, Maria laughed, and she had a laugh unlike anything else on TV. It was loose and raucous and totally unpolished. Tibby sat through hours of news for those moments.

Tibby watched hopefully, but Maria didn't laugh today. Tibby suspected her producers had probably warned her to can it.

Usually Bridget liked airplane food. She was one of the very few people who did.

If you scarfed it all down while it was steaming hot, it tasted pretty good. It you thought about it too much and let it get cold, she now realized, it wasn't so appealing. That was true of many things in life.

Tonight it sat on her tray table. Eric was in Baja. She imagined he was diving into the Sea of Cortez. It was almost dinnertime there, and he always used to swim before dinner. And here she was, thirty-five thousand feet over the Atlantic. Both of them suspended over water, neither of them with their feet on the ground.

"Eric acts like I don't need anything," she'd said to Tibby on the phone a few days before.

"Maybe you act like you don't need anything," Tibby had said. She'd said it gently, but still it cut its way into the center of Bee's brain.

She felt a tingle of anxiety, being so far from the ground and hurtling so quickly in the opposite direction of Eric and home and the things she needed.

It was dark in the cabin, dark outside her window. She wasn't completely alone. Interspersed throughout the cabin were lots of people from her program. She'd be spending her summer with them. They were strangers now, but friends theoretically. It was too bad Bridget wasn't a more theoretical person.

She liked short flights better, where you stayed in the same day. She felt faint discomfort at flying directly away from the sun.

She put her cold hands on the Pants, feeling the comfort of uneven stitches of yarn and the puffiness of the fabric paint Carmen used.

What did she need, really? She needed her friends, but she had the Traveling Pants. It was like having her friends with her. The Pants allowed her to hold on to her friends no matter what.

Greta was in her house in Burgess, where she always was. If Bridget calculated the time there, she could figure out exactly what Greta was doing. Tuesday at seven was bingo. Wednesday morning was shopping. No matter how fast or far Bridget went, Greta stayed still.

And there was Eric. One time in her life she had needed

Eric and he had been there. He had known exactly what to do. She never forgot that.

And home. Technically speaking, that meant a dingy clapboard house containing her brother and her father. She swallowed hard. She gave her uneaten tray of food to a passing flight attendant. Did they need her? Did she need them?

These weren't the right questions. They were N/A. She remembered getting three N/As on her first-grade report card and worrying that she'd failed those subjects. When she told her father, he'd laughed and fiddled with her hair. "That means Not Applicable, Beezy. It doesn't mean you failed anything." He'd been able to comfort her back then. Back then she'd tried harder, too.

Now it wasn't a home where needs were had or met. If Perry or her dad needed her, it didn't matter, because they wouldn't accept her help anyway. If she needed them . . . well, she didn't. They had nothing to give that she wanted.

She couldn't help them. She didn't need them. That was the truth. Not everybody got a close family. Not everybody needed one.

She was flying away from the sun, but it would be there to meet her when she landed. They were just taking different routes to the same place.

She felt herself relaxing into her seat, unsticking her mind from the continent behind, looking to the one ahead. She couldn't help her dad or Perry. She couldn't. Her job was to look forward, to make as good a life as she could. She didn't need to look back anymore.

She pulled off her sneakers and tucked her feet under her. She crossed her arms and held her hands in her armpits to keep them warm. When she woke up, she'd be in Turkey. On another continent, in another hemisphere, on another sea.

She felt the tingle starting. But this was the tingle of excitement instead of fear. The one that made you hungry rather than sick. The one that came from looking ahead and not behind.

In a way it was the same tingle. It just felt a lot better.

Carmen doodled on the handouts while aspiring theater types—known here as apprentices—from all over the country sat listening to the presentations in the main theater building. Julia painted her toenails, which seemed like kind of a ditzy thing to do. But she painted them black, which seemed to Carmen like an actressy thing to do.

Carmen looked around at the number of decked-out kids. Julia wasn't the only one in layers of vintage clothes and inky black eyeliner. It almost made Carmen laugh to think that though Julia stood apart from all the schlumpy kids at school, Carmen stood apart from the glamour queens here.

The director of the big and coveted Main Stage production, Andrew Kerr, made his presentation first.

"This year we're putting on *The Winter's Tale*. As I'm sure you know, for every decade anniversary of the theater we do an all-Shakespeare summer, and this year is number thirty. We've got some wonderful professional actors involved.

Here's the thing." He cleared his throat to get attention. "This Main Stage mounts a professional, Equity production. But by tradition we open only one role to an apprentice. One role, and it's typically not a lead. That's the way it is every year. You are welcome to try out, but callbacks will be minimal. Don't waste too much energy on it. There are many great roles for you in the Second Stage and community productions. All of you will have some part in one of them."

Most of the kids knew this already. But it was hard not to be hopeful. Carmen suspected a lot of them were going to waste a lot of energy on it, regardless of what Andrew Kerr said. She was beginning to realize that actors, as a general category, were hopeful, and they also had strong self-esteem.

"All the auditions begin together. Then we'll follow up with separate callback lists for each of the three productions."

Was anyone else here going straight to crew? Carmen wondered. Was she the only predefeated theater apprentice in America?

"Auditions begin not tomorrow, but the day after. Sign-up sheets are in the lobby. Good luck to all of you."

Carmen wondered whether she'd get the chance to work on sets for the big production. She guessed not. There were actual known set designers and builders arriving here. Well, she'd be happy working on one of the other shows.

After the meeting, Julia was inspired. "Let's go back to the room and get to work."

"I don't think I have anything to work on yet," Carmen said, falling a little bit behind Julia's energized stride.

"I was hoping you would run lines with me," Julia said.

Some bodies like change better than others. The rest of Bee's group was sacked out over the three rows of the old Suburban, one of several large and battered vehicles owned by the Consortium for Classical Archaeology. Bee sat straight as a palm, studying the countryside between Izmir and Priene. Now they were close enough to the coast that you could see the Aegean out the right-hand windows.

"Ephesus is a few kilometers to the left," said Bob Something, a graduate student, who was driving the car. "We'll spend at least a day there this summer."

Bridget squinted eastward, remembering the pictures of Ephesus from her archaeology class. The sun had indeed arrived along with her.

"Also Aphrodisias, Miletus, and Halicarnassus. These are some of the best ruins you'll ever see."

She was glad she was awake, because otherwise Bob would have had no one to tell this to and she wouldn't have heard it.

"What about Troy?" she asked, beginning to feel a little breathless. Here she was in this incredible place, farther from home than she'd ever been. There was as much history here in this soil as anywhere on earth.

"Troy is north, up near the Dardanelles. It's fascinating to read about, but there isn't as much to look at. Nobody from our group is making that trip, as far as I know." He had a faded orange alligator shirt and a round face. She thought he must have recently shaved a beard, because his chin and lower cheeks were pale and the rest of his face was pink.

"I read the *Iliad* in school last semester," Bridget said. "Most of it." In addition to her ancient archaeology class, she'd taken Greek literature in translation. She hadn't realized it at the time, but looking back, she considered it by far her most engrossing academic experience. You couldn't always know what would matter to you.

When they pulled into the site, Bridget was surprised at how small and basic it was. Two very large tents, several smaller ones, and beyond them, the dusty, roped-off shapes of the excavation. It sat on a high hill overlooking a river plain and, just beyond that, the Aegean.

She left her bags in one of the tents, which had canvas walls over a wooden platform. It held only four cots and some open shelving, but it seemed quite romantic to her. She was nothing if not a veteran of rustic summer venues.

The new arrivals groggily gathered for a welcome meeting, and Bridget exercised the bad habit of looking around and deciding who was the best-looking guy in the room. It was a habit that predated her being a girl with a boyfriend, and she hadn't entirely managed to eradicate it.

In this case, the room was actually a large, open-sided tent, which would serve as their meeting room, lecture room, and cafeteria. The best view was of the Aegean, but there were a few good faces, too.

"This is a comparatively remote site, folks. The plumbing is rudimentary. We have four latrines and two showers.

That's all. Make friends with your sweat this summer," said Alison Somebody, associate director, in her not very welcoming welcome. She had a kind of boot-camp mentality, Bridget decided. She was excited about privation.

Well, Bridget could get excited about privation too.

"We've got a generator to serve the field laboratory, but the sleeping areas are not wired. I hope nobody brought a hair dryer."

Bridget laughed, but a couple of women looked uneasy.

It was a small and fairly new dig, Bridget gathered. About thirty people altogether, a mix of university and scientist types and a few civilian volunteers. It was hard to tell, amid all the T-shirts and cargo pants and work shirts and Birkenstocks, the professors from the graduate students, from the college students, from the regular citizens. Most of them were American or Canadian; a few were Turkish.

"There are three parts to this site, and all of us spend some time in each of them. If you are a student and you want credit, you must attend lectures Tuesdays from three to five. We'll take a total of four trips to other sites. The schedule's on the board. All trips are mandatory for credit. That's the school part. That's it. Otherwise, this is a job and we work as a team. Questions so far?"

Why were organizational types so joyless? Bridget wondered. Who wouldn't want to see the Temple of Artemis at Ephesus?

It was lucky, in a way, that Brown University was situated in a relatively urban setting and not in a tent, because it was difficult to concentrate with the sea winking at you like that. She began to tune Alison out in favor of her habit. There was one good-looking guy who she guessed was also a college student. He had black curly hair and very dark eyes. He was Middle Eastern, she thought. Maybe Turkish, but she heard him speaking English.

Another one was sort of good-looking. He looked old enough to be a graduate student. He had reddish hair and so much sunscreen on his face it cast a blue tint. That was maybe not so sexy.

"You're Bridget, right?" Alison asked, startling her from her habit.

"Yes."

"You're in mortuary."

"Okay."

"What does mortuary mean?" Bridget asked a tall girl named Karina Itabashi on their way to the field lab.

"It means dead people."

"Oh."

After lunch Bridget settled in for her first lecture and discovered an interesting thing: The best-looking guy was neither the possible Turk nor the sunscreen-slathered redhead. The best-looking guy was the one standing in front of her, lecturing about artifacts.

"Okay, folks." The best-looking guy had been holding an object behind his back, and now he presented it to them. "Is this object in my hand a technofact, a sociofact, or an ideofact?" The best-looking guy was looking directly at her, wanting her to answer his question.

"It's a tomato," she said.

To his credit he laughed rather than throwing the tomato at her. "You have a point, uh . . . ?"

"Bridget."

"Bridget. Any other ideas?" Various hands went up.

She'd thought he was a graduate student when she'd first seen him eating a sandwich under an olive tree earlier that day. He didn't look like he could be thirty. But he'd introduced himself as Professor Peter Haven, so unless he lied, he was one. He taught at Indiana University. She tried to picture Indiana on the map.

At sunset that night after dinner in the big tent, a bunch of people gathered on an embankment on the hilltop to watch the sun go down. Several six-packs of beer were on the ground. Bridget sat next to Karina, who had a beer in her hand.

"Do you want one?" she asked Bridget, gesturing to the supply.

Bridget hesitated, and Karina seemed to read her expression. "There's no drinking age here, as far as I know."

Bridget leaned over and took one. She'd been to enough parties over the last year that she'd formed a solid acquaintanceship with beer, if not an actual friendship.

On Karina's other side, Bridget recognized one of the directors, and she was struck here, as she had been at dinner, by the mixing of the team. The group wasn't hierarchical, the way school was. Age-wise, it wasn't nearly as homogeneous. If anything, people assembled more according to the area of the site where they worked than according to age or professional status. She realized how accustomed she was to looking out for authority figures, but here she wasn't finding any.

"Where are you digging?" she asked a woman who sat down next to her. She recognized her as Maxine from her cabin.

"I'm not. I'm a conservator. I'm working on pottery in the lab. What about you?"

"Mortuary. For starters, at least."

"Ooh. How's your stomach?"

"Good, I think."

She saw Peter Haven at the other end of the group. He was also drinking and laughing over something. He had a nice way about him.

The sun was down. The moon was up. Maxine lifted her beer bottle and Bridget tapped it with hers. "To mortuary," Maxine said.

"To pottery," Bridget added, never having drunk beer with a conservator before. It was good to be an adult. Even the beer tasted better here.

It's innocence when it

charms us, ignorance

when it doesn't.

—Mignon McLaughlin

If Leo had looked at her as planned, Lena wouldn't have had to think about him several times that night, or tried to figure out his last name so she could Google him.

She certainly wouldn't have felt the need to go to the empty studio on a Saturday morning when all self-respecting art students were still in bed. She went there to sneak a look at his painting, secretly hoping that maybe his artistic skills were not all that his reputation promised.

She checked first on her own painting. It was a standing figure of a thick-thighed woman named Nora. Lena could convince herself of Nora's beauty only as long as Nora was standing still. As soon as she changed her expression or opened her mouth, the concept crashed to the floor and Lena had to build it again at the start of each pose.

But those thighs of Nora's did have their strange grace and, more importantly, presented Lena with an unsubtle view of mass, so hard to re-create in two dimensions. Lena liked how that part of her painting was coming.

Now, embarrassed even though she was alone, she edged across the scuffed linoleum. She considered the empty model stand, the unmanned easels, the high, creaky casement windows, the fern that nobody watered, the leftover smells. An empty studio reminded Lena of the world at night. It was hard to reconcile that the night world was the same place as the day.

Lena remembered a summer lightning storm when she was in middle school. She was wide awake at midnight and bravely made her way down the stairs in her nightgown to sit on the front porch and watch. A burst of lightning flashed, midnight became noon, and Lena was jarred to see that all the things in the mysterious night world were exactly the same as they were in the cheery, prosaic day.

After that she spent a lot of time convincing herself that what you saw, even what you felt, had an unreliable relationship to what was actually there. What was actually there was reality, regardless of whether you saw it or how you felt about it.

But after that she'd started drawing and painting and had to unravel all the convincing she'd done. There was no way to access a visual reality beyond what you saw. Reality was what you saw. "We are trapped in our senses," her old teacher, Annik, told her once. "They are all we have of the world."

And so they are the world, Lena remembered thinking then, and many times since.

You couldn't paint a thigh based on how you knew it was, in darkness or in light. You had to paint a thigh based exactly on how the light particles entered your eyes and how you perceived it from that angle, in that room, at that moment.

Why did she spend so much of her life unlearning? It was so much harder than learning, she mused as she timidly made her way around Leo's canvas.

She was almost scared to look—scared of its being worse than it was supposed to be but more scared of its being better.

She waited until she was fully in front of his painting to take it on.

After three days in the studio, his painting was really only begun. More suggestion than execution. And yet it was so far beyond hers she felt like crying. Not just because hers looked so amateurish in comparison, but also because his had a gesture and a quality, even at this young stage, that was unaccountably sad and lovely.

She was devoting her life to art school, and she knew she could learn a lot of things here, but in a flash of recognition, she also knew that this couldn't be taught. She couldn't say why this painting struck her so, what was the particular insight into the pathos of Nora, but she felt it. And she felt her own set of standards and ambitions swirling down the toilet. She could practically hear the flush.

She put her fingers to her eyes, unnerved to feel actual wetness. She had hoped these would be conceptual tears, not wet ones.

She thought of Leo. His hair and his hand. She tried to reconcile the look of him with this painting.

And in a rush she felt ashamed of her fatuous games as she realized she was going to be thinking about him whether or when or how he ever looked at her.

LennyK162: Hellooooo, Tibby. Are you in there? You are not answering calls and your friends are concerned. Bee is writing up the missing person report and I am designated to call Alice. Please advise.
Tibberon: I am here, O hilarious one.

"Please call me back before five if you can, Tib," Brian said.

Tibby lay on her bed as she listened to the end of his message. She didn't want to call him back. If she actually spoke to him, rather than leaving him messages when she knew he was at work, she probably wouldn't be able to be angry at him.

"It'll be okay, Tib," he said in closing.

Why was he always saying that? What power did he have to make it so? Maybe it wouldn't be okay. Maybe she really was pregnant.

Anyway, okay for whom? Maybe it was her body and not his.

And what if she was pregnant? What would he say then? What if he wanted her to keep the baby? He had talked about babies before. What if he secretly wanted something like this to happen?

Meta-Tibby had something to say about this, but regular Tibby shut her up fast.

Brian probably romanticized the notion of having a baby. He probably thought it would be this beautiful thing between them. Well, Tibby had seen the whole process up close and personal, and it wasn't pretty. She had seen her mother's gigantic belly, pregnant with Nicky, with all the scary red stretch marks across it. She knew how little you slept and how much babies cried. And in one of the most surreal experiences of her life, she had weathered the whole bloody, bloody thing as Christina's unwilling labor partner. She knew the power of birth, both for beauty and terror. She was the last girl in the world who could write it off as cute and sexy.

She couldn't be. What if she was?

If her last period had ended on the fifth, say . . . or maybe it was the sixth? And then you counted twenty-eight days. No, it was twenty-one days, right? From the last day? From the first day?

Tibby had puzzled over this question at least one hundred times, and still she got confused in all the same places.

Brian worked as a busboy at a Mexican restaurant in Rockville on Wednesday evenings. She waited until she knew his shift had started to call him back.

"I don't think you should come this weekend. I think I'm going up to Providence to hang out with Lena. Okay? Sorry about that."

She hung up quickly. She felt her face twisted in an unpleasant shape. She was too preoccupied to feel her own shame at lying or even to do it convincingly.

If it had been the fifth, then her period — if it was going to come — was going to come by the twenty-sixth. But what if it hadn't been the fifth? It could easily have been the sixth or seventh. Then she would have to wait until Sunday. How could she wait that long?

And what if it didn't come on Sunday? What if it didn't come at all?

No. She couldn't think that thought. She couldn't bring herself to think it, and yet she couldn't fully think any other.

She wasn't really going to Providence. She didn't want to see her friends now. Not until she got her period. If she went, she would have to tell them what was going on. They knew her too well to accept her evasions or her lies. She didn't want to say the feared word out loud to her friends, because that would make it feel true.

She hated not telling them that she had finally done it. She needed to tell them such an important piece of information. But the aftermath of having done it was too painful to share, and the two things were inextricable.

She couldn't see Brian right now. She didn't want to talk about what had happened. What if he wanted to have sex again? He would, wouldn't he? What would she do?

Brian shouldn't have been so insistent on it, she found herself thinking. *We should have just stayed how we were.*

She didn't feel like eating, she didn't feel like sleeping. There was nothing to look forward to, nothing to feel happy about, and nothing she could bring herself to do.

And yet she had very specific plans for the weekend. She would wait and hope for the one thing she really wanted. She would wait and hope that it would come.

"Oh, my God. It's a piece of a skull. Somebody get Bridget."

Bridget laughed and turned around.

Darius, the good-looking Middle Easterner, turned out not to be Turkish, but Iranian by way of San Diego. He was also in mortuary, and at this moment he was pointing to a wall of dirt.

She moved in. She put down her usual pointy trowel in favor of finer instruments. In a little over a week she had already earned a reputation for fearlessness. In the face of moldering bones, snakes, worms, rodents, spiders, and bugs, no matter how big, she was unperturbed. Not even the stench of the latrines got to her. Though in truth she almost never peed inside.

At five-thirty in the evening, her dirty, sweaty colleagues were wandering toward camp, but she was still working on the piece of bone. It was actually quite a large piece. It was painstaking work. You couldn't just dig it out. Every bit of soil had to be cleared and screened with care. Every bit of bone, every fragment of clay or stone had to be sent to the lab. Everything had to be recorded in context by means of a large three-dimensional grid. She had to photograph each thing with a digital camera and number it by basket and lot.

"The difference between looting and archaeology is preserving context," Peter had told her. "The object itself, whatever its worth, represents a small fraction of its value to us."

By six-thirty, only Peter was still there with her. "You can go," she said. "I'm almost done."

"I don't feel right, leaving you alone in a grave," he said.

She liked him there, with the sun behind him. She'd let him stay.

"I've named him Hector," she said, coaxing the skull from the dirt.

"Who?"

"Him." She pointed to the hole that would have been his nose.

"That's a heroic name. Why do you think it's a he?"

She wasn't sure if he was asking her or quizzing her. "By the size. We found a part of a female skull yesterday."

He nodded. "And what did you name her?"

"Clytemnestra."

"I like it."

"Thanks. I'm keeping an eye out for the last few bits of her. Her skeleton is almost complete."

"Oh, so that's Clytemnestra. I heard about her in the lab."

Bridget nodded. "The biology guys are excited about her."

Once almost all the dirt was processed, she gingerly lifted Hector's skull. She began to brush out the grooves as she'd been taught.

"It doesn't get to you, does it?"

She shrugged. "Not really."

"Something will eventually. It seems so far back, I know, but something always gets through."

"But there isn't much tragedy in a death that took place three thousand years ago, is there?" Bridget mused aloud. "Old Hector would be long dead no matter what great or awful things happened in his lifetime."

Peter smiled at her. "It puts mortality in perspective, doesn't it?"

"Yeah. Why do we worry so much about everything when we're just going to end up here?" she asked. She felt quite cheery considering she was standing in a burial site holding a large section of a human skull.

He laughed at her, but he seemed appreciative. He sat down at the edge of the trench to consider. She had the odd perception that he had fine ears. He seemed to hear the full extent of what she said and meant, no matter how loudly or quietly she spoke. When you shared a context, it made hearing easier.

"No question a recent death feels more tragic," he reasoned. "I guess because we're still experiencing the world that the dead person is missing. We are still around to miss them."

Did he have such a tragedy in his life? she wondered. Could he tell that she did?

She pushed her hair back. She realized she'd drawn a streak of dirt across her forehead. "Our moral connection to people expires after a certain amount of time. Don't you think? Otherwise how could we dig up their graves?"

"You are exactly right, Bridget. I couldn't agree more. But how long a time? Two hundred years? Two thousand? How do you calculate the moment when a person's death becomes scientific rather than emotional?"

She knew he was asking the question rhetorically, but she actually wanted to answer it. "I'd say you calculate it by the death of the last person whose life overlapped with theirs. The point when they lose the power to help or hurt a living soul."

He smiled at her certainty. "That's your hypothesis?"

"That's my hypothesis."

"But don't you think the power to help or hurt can extend far beyond a person's natural life?" he asked.

"I don't," she proclaimed, almost reflexively. Sometimes she felt the magnet of certainty more than truth.

"Then you, my friend, have a thing or two to learn from the Greeks."

Lenny,

I enclose the Pants with a little bit of ancient dirt and a picture of me with my new boyfriend, Hector. He's not so lively, you may say. But he's got the wisdom of the ages.

A whole lot of love from yer pal Bee
(and a toothy kiss from yer pal-in-law, Hector)

Carmen did run lines with Julia. She ran them for hours on end for two straight days. Julia wanted to try a range of parts before she settled on her audition strategy.

Carmen was relieved when Julia went to the office to photocopy more pages so Carmen could at least have a break and check her e-mail. She had a list of unread messages from Bee and Lena and her mom and her stepbrother, Paul.

When Julia got back, she immediately noticed a picture Carmen had printed out and left on her desk.

"Hey, who's this?" Julia asked. She picked up the paper and studied it.

It was a picture of Bee in Turkey holding a human skull and pretending to kiss it. Bee had sent it over the Internet, and it had made Carmen laugh so much she'd printed it out.

"That's my friend Bridget," Carmen said.

"Really?"

"Yeah."

Carmen knew it was strange of her that she didn't talk about her friends more to Julia. She mentioned them in passing once in a while, but she never expressed what they really meant to her. She wasn't sure why. It was as though she had put them and Julia into two different compartments. They didn't mix. She didn't want them to mix.

"She's your friend?" Julia looked vaguely doubtful, like perhaps Carmen had clipped the picture from a magazine and was just pretending.

Maybe that was why, Carmen thought.

"She's amazing-looking. Check out those legs," Julia said.

"She's a jock."

"She's pretty. Where does she go to school?"

It was funny. Carmen didn't think of Bee as pretty, exactly. Bee didn't have the patience for it. "Brown," she said.

"I thought about going there. Williams is a lot more intellectual, though."

This from a girl who read not only *Us Weekly* each week, but *Star* and *OK!* as well. Carmen shrugged.

"Her hair looks kind of fake. She should use a darker shade."

"What?"

"Does she color it herself?"

"Bridget? She doesn't color her hair at all. That's her hair."

"That's her real hair?"

"Yes."

"Are you sure?"

"Yes."

"That's what she tells you, anyway," Julia said, half jokingly, but Carmen didn't find it funny.

She looked at Julia, wondering what was up. Was she honestly competing with a girl she'd never met?

"Hey, let's go pick up something quick for dinner and bring it back here," Julia suggested later, after another hour of lines. "I want to keep studying."

"You can stay here," Carmen offered. "I'll go get it." She

was frankly glad to get away from lines, glad to be outside. The grounds of the place were beautiful, especially in the evening light. There were miniature weeping trees along the paths and huge annual gardens around the main buildings.

In her appreciation of the flowers, she lost track of the cafeteria, known by the apprentices as the canteen. She walked until she got to a pretty hillside overlooking the valley. It was lush and so sweet in this light.

Carmen stood there looking at it for a long time. She was already lost—she couldn't really get more lost, could she? When you belonged nowhere, you sort of belonged everywhere, she mused.

She wondered how long it had been since she'd used her senses to perceive beauty. It was like she had been frozen for all these months and was only now beginning to thaw.

She realized that another person from the campus was nearby, appreciating the same view. It was a woman she had not yet seen or met.

"It's beautiful, isn't it?" the woman said.

Carmen sighed. "It really is."

They fell into step together along the path. "Are you part of the theater program?" the woman asked. She was wide hipped and somewhat graceless. She wasn't an actress, Carmen decided, and felt a sense of camaraderie.

Carmen nodded.

"What are you trying out for?"

Carmen pushed a stray hair behind her ear. "Nothing. I'm doing sets, hopefully."

"You're not going to try out for anything?"

"No."

"Why not?"

"Because I'm not an actress."

"How do you know? Have you tried?"

"I guess not. No." *Though my father claims I'm dramatic,* she added silently.

"You should try it. It's really the strength of this program."

"You think so?"

"Absolutely."

"Huh." Carmen spent two seconds pretending to consider this so she wouldn't seem rude. "Hey, would you point me in the direction of the canteen? I got off track and I have no idea where I'm going."

"Sure," the woman said. She pointed to the left when the path split.

"Thank you," Carmen said, looking over her shoulder.

"What's your name?" the woman asked.

"Carmen."

"I'm Judy. Good to meet you, Carmen. You try out, okay?"

Carmen couldn't say okay if she didn't mean it. "How 'bout I'll think about it?"

"That's all I can ask," the woman said.

Later, when Carmen was trying to fall asleep and all the lines and lines and lines were scrabbling around in her head, she did think about it. She mainly thought of why she would not do it.

Right now I'm having

amnesia and déjà vu at

the same time.

I think I've forgotten

this before.

—Steven Wright

Lena walked around with that overstimulated feeling. She didn't like it very much. She forgot to eat and she wore eye makeup to painting class. She forced herself to look at Leo only once every pose and to keep to herself during breaks. She hoped, she silently begged for him to notice her. She racked her brain to find ways to hedge these hopes, to keep them safe.

She looked at her painting in a new way. At first she was so disgusted by it, she could barely look at all. But then she settled down. She tried to relax and see better and deeper than she had before. She felt like a track runner who was pushing herself to break a five-minute mile only to have somebody tell her it could be done in four. If it could be done, then she had to reframe her sense of possibilities. She had to at least try.

She thought about Leo. She asked around a little, casually, she hoped, and learned that he was in his third year, that he didn't live on campus and was rarely seen at campus events. His mystique only grew.

The next Saturday the Traveling Pants arrived from Bee. Lena wore them for courage and struck out from the safety of her dorm room. Not for the courage to talk to Leo; the courage to visit his painting again.

She was so intent on her agenda, so eager and yet so furtive, she almost felt like she had gone into the empty studio to steal something. She walked straight past her painting in favor of his. She stood in front of it, as she had been secretly longing to do all week. For every session he worked on it, she found herself wishing she could watch, to see exactly what he did. How could she now retrace a whole week's worth of work?

She needed to think about her own painting with as much vigor, she knew, but for now she was living in the world of possibilities.

If she could have crawled inside the paint, she would have, so desperate was she to understand what he did, how he did it.

"You learn a lot in art school by looking around," Annik had said to her on the phone a few nights ago.

How true this was. She found herself only wanting to hear what Robert the instructor said when he was talking to Leo.

The beauty of Leo's work waned as she took it apart, dissected it. And then she'd lose her focus for one second and it snuck up on her again. Finally she stopped trying so hard and let her eyes fuzz a bit as she just admired it.

It wasn't that she hadn't seen transcendent paintings before; she had. She'd stared at paintings that were far more accomplished than this. She'd been to the National Gallery hundreds of times. She'd been to the Met and other great museums, big and small.

But Leo was painting exactly the same subject she was — in the same studio, at the same angle (though in mirror image), by the same light. He was an art student, not a master. This was apples to apples: They were handling the same forms and dimples and hairs and shadows. It made her able to appreciate what he was doing in a thrilling though humbling way.

She just looked at it. The lines of the shoulders. The elbows. For some reason she thought of her grandfather. Emotions Lena usually stowed down deep came to hover at the surface. She felt a flush in her cheeks and the wateriest of tears flood her eyes. She thought of Kostos next, and she thought of the fact that she hadn't really thought of him in a few days.

Was Carmen right? Was she really capable of forgetting him? Was that what she should be striving for?

She wasn't sure she wanted to be striving for that. How disorienting it felt. She wasn't sure she wanted to be the forgetting type, even if she could be. If she forgot Kostos, she feared she'd forget most of herself along with him. Who was she without him?

"What do you think?"

Lena was so deep down in her brain she felt she had to travel miles to get back to the sound and the light. In quick succession she realized that Leo was standing a few feet away from her, that he was talking to her, that she was standing in front of his painting for no reason she was prepared to explain, and that she had tears running down her face.

Instantly her hands went to her face and she wiped them off. She pressed wet fingers to her thighs and remembered she was wearing the Traveling Pants. Well. These weren't the first tears to dry on the Traveling Pants.

He looked at her and she scrambled to think of what was supposed to happen. He was looking at her Pants. Should she try to explain them? But he had said something, hadn't he? He had asked a question. Did that mean she was supposed to answer it? So manic was the fluttering of her thoughts she feared it was audible.

"It's okay if you don't like it," he said, wanting to help her out.

"No! I do like it!" she nearly shouted at him.

"I'm having problems with the head." He reached out with his thumb, and to Lena's horror, actually smudged a patch of wet paint that composed Nora's jawbone.

"No!" she burst out. Why was she shouting at him? She made herself be quiet. She realized she didn't want him to look at her quite this hard.

"Sorry," she hurried to say. "I just—I like that part. I don't think you should smudge it." She wondered if she was more connected to his painting than he was.

"Oh. Okay." He thought she was crazy. She wished he would go back to not looking at her at all.

She tried to calm down. She wasn't going to be cool, so

she could at least be honest. "I really love your painting. I think it's beautiful," she said at a normal volume.

He looked at her in a different way now, trying to gauge her tone, surprised by her sincerity. "Well, thank you."

"The thing is, though . . . looking at it makes me realize I have no idea what I'm doing." Who could have known that Lena would actually talk to Leo? And that when she did, she would be so disarmed she'd be truthful?

He laughed. "Looking at it makes me realize I have no idea what *I'm* doing."

She laughed too, but miserably. "Shut up," she said.

Had she just told him to shut up?

"It's true, though," he said. "I look at it in a certain way and I only see what's wrong with it. Isn't that what we all do?"

"Yeah, but most of us are right," she said ruefully.

Was she actually having a conversation with Leo right now?

He laughed again. He had a nice laugh.

"I'm Leo," he said. "Where are you set up?"

She pointed to the easel directly across the room from his, trying not to feel too crushed by the fact that he really hadn't noticed her at all. "Lena," she said in a slightly defeated voice.

"Are you a year-rounder or here for the summer?"

"All year," she said crampily. "I only finished my first, though."

He nodded.

The fact of this conversation settled upon her at last.

Here was Leo. In an otherwise empty studio. Did he have a girlfriend? Did he have a boyfriend? Did he make time in his life for such frivolity?

She realized he wanted to work on his painting. She suddenly felt so self-conscious she couldn't carry on. She made an excuse and fled.

When she got home, she twisted and turned in her un-made bed for a while, and then she called Carmen.

"Guess what?"

"What?"

"I think I have a crush."

Carma,

Here are the Pants and a little sketch I made of Leo. From memory, not from life. (And no, I'm _not_ thinking of him day and night. _God_.)

Funny hair, huh?

He did not realize I was in his class. I think I'm making a big impression around here.

Love you,
Len

At seven-thirty the light waned and Peter still sat with Bridget at the edge of the trench. She knew he felt he had to stay because he was supervising, and also to show her he appreciated her work ethic. She only hoped he was enjoying it as much as she was.

"Hey, Bridget?" he said at last.

"Yeah?"

"Can we go get some dinner?"

"Oh, fine, fine." She pretended impatience. "Let me finish recording."

"We'll drop the stuff by the lab on the way."

They fell into step companionably. She tried wiping her face and made it even dirtier.

"Would you call me Bee?"

"Bee?"

"Yeah, as in bumble."

"Okay."

"That's what my friends call me. You can call me Bridget if you want, but I may think you are slightly mad at me."

He smiled at her. "Bee, then."

They washed up hurriedly by the outdoor pump, but dinner had been cleared from the big tent by the time they got there.

"It's my fault," she said.

"It is," he agreed in his agreeable way.

The Turkish ladies who provided most of the food service kindly found some leftover bread and hummus and salad for them. One of the ladies brought over an unlabeled bottle full of strong red wine. It was a tricky business drinking wine after working in the sun all day. Bee mixed hers with water.

Was this awkward? she wondered.

It wasn't awkward exactly. It was good, slanty fun. He was handsome and he was nice and she was drawn to him for these and probably other reasons.

Would it be less awkward if he weren't so handsome and nice? Would it be less fun?

What about the fact that she was a girl with a boyfriend? That he was . . . who knew what?

Was having a boyfriend honestly supposed to make you not feel attracted to people? Was it supposed to make you not attractive?

And now she wondered, how did he see her? Was it all in her mind, this tension she felt in the way they reached for things and shared the space?

Oh. She felt like smacking herself. She was incorrigible. Why was she feeling this way?

Hmm. Was she feeling this way?

What way was it, exactly?

The sun was long past set, but they walked along the hillside toward the embankment. She felt the dizziness, the giddiness of the wine. Was his tread a little happier, a little less directed too? They intended to join what was left of the party like they did most nights, but it had mostly scattered. There was some awkwardness about whether to sit down. At least in her mind. He did sit down and she joined him. Was it strange that they should be spending time together like this?

No. If she weren't incorrigible, it wouldn't be.

Incorrigibly, she pulled the elastic out of her hair. It was coming out anyway, she told herself, though she didn't quite buy it. Her hair was unusually long from not having Carmen around to trim it since they'd gone to college. It was down to her elbows, almost, halfway down her back. It had the particular feature of absorbing moonlight. She knew he had to notice it. He was probably wishing he hadn't sat down with her.

Why was she behaving this way? She was older now. She'd learned her lessons. What was she trying to prove?

Her limbs had that forward tingle. She couldn't help herself.

Was it all in her mind?

It was, wasn't it? Maybe that was for the best.

She looked at his eyes to try to gauge the mood of the moment faithfully, but he unexpectedly met her gaze. They stayed there for a moment too long before they both looked away.

Shit.

He fidgeted. He clapped his hands together as if he were summarizing an argument. "So, Bridget," he said. "Tell me about your family."

She felt her body bending away from him without actually moving. She had nothing to say about her family at present. "So, Peter," she said, a little too fierce. "Tell me about yours."

How much the air had cooled. In a dry place like this the sun left and took all the heat. There was nothing in the air to hold it. "Let's see. My kids are four and two. Sophie and Miles."

His kids were four and two. Sophie and Miles. It had seemed to her that this might come at the end of the questioning rather than first thing out. She had somehow thought he'd tell her about his parents or his siblings. Her brain fitfully worked backward. He was a father, which presumably meant he was a husband.

"And your wife?"

"Amanda. She's thirty-four."

"Are you thirty-four too?"

"Almost thirty."

"Older woman."

"Right."

She had misread him. She had let her thoughts get away from her. It was time to get them all back.

Do not spoil what you

have by desiring what

you have not.

—Epicurus

The Traveling Pants called to Carmen from under her bed. The other times Carmen had gotten them in the last several months, she had carried them from place to place, but she had not actually worn them.

The Pants were outstanding, and Carmen hadn't been in the mood to stand out very much. She hadn't been in the mood to answer questions Julia would certainly ask about them. It was again the issue of the compartments. She couldn't figure a way to introduce that Carmen to this one. Also, she was scared she was too fat.

She pulled her suitcase from under her bed and felt for where she'd stashed them earlier that morning when they'd arrived by FedEx from Lena. There they were, carefully folded into her suitcase like a false bottom.

For some reason, on this day, she had the urge to put them on. Maybe because it was beautiful outside or because she'd had a lot of coffee. Maybe it was because Lena had a crush on a guy named Leo, and that made Carmen happy and also made her think that the world was opening up.

It was a slightly scary urge, because she was worried about what she would discover. Though she had opted not to try on the Pants, they had never opted not to fit her. She didn't want to force them.

But she also knew that since she'd started working on *The Miracle Worker* in the spring, she'd almost completely stopped her late-night affair with candy. During the past two months she'd been careful about what she ate, mostly in her efforts to be a more worthy friend for Julia.

Holding her breath, sucking in her stomach, wishing she could suck in her backside, she pulled them up, up, up, and over. They went. Who could doubt their magic now? God, they fit. How good they felt. How happy they made her.

She went to the mirror and really looked at her reflection for the first time in months. She pulled on a pink T-shirt and struck out for the wide world. For the first time in ages she didn't feel ashamed of herself.

It was certainly because of the Traveling Pants that she wandered into the lobby of the theater where the auditions were taking place.

"You're in the next group," a woman with a clipboard told her. "Go ahead in."

The woman was mistaken, Carmen knew, but she went in anyway because she was curious. Had Julia gone yet?

A guy was up there reading from *Richard III*. Carmen sat in a seat toward the back and listened. She grew sleepy, enjoying the language if not necessarily absorbing the meaning.

"Carmen?"

She heard her name and she looked around. Had she actually fallen asleep?

She squinted.

"Carmen, is that you?"

She leaned forward. A woman was standing up in the second row. She realized it was Judy, who had pointed her on the path to the canteen the night before.

Carmen waved, feeling self-conscious.

"We're going to break for the afternoon in a few minutes," she said, "but we'll take you now if you're ready."

Meaning they would take her now to audition? Judy must have thought she'd come to try out. It certainly looked that way. Otherwise, why was she here?

Carmen meandered toward the stage. She paused at Judy's aisle, where Judy was sitting with Andrew Kerr and a couple of other people Carmen didn't know.

"I didn't really . . . I didn't really prepare anything," Carmen whispered, hoping her voice would reach Judy but not the others. "Do you want me to come back another time?" *Like never*, she thought.

"Just go ahead," Judy said. She must have been one of the assistant directors, Carmen thought.

Carmen walked up onto the stage, wondering what in the world she was doing. She did not feel comfortable standing under these lights. She had nothing to say, nothing to read. "I'm more interested in sets," she said lamely to the assembled group. She thought she heard someone laugh in the back.

The other people in Judy's row looked annoyed, but Judy was patient. She came up to the stage and handed Carmen some pages. "Just read Perdita. It's fine. I'll read Florizel's lines."

"Are you sure?" Carmen asked. She felt stupid. Everyone else had memorized parts and prepared them and performed them with a clear sense of intent. Here she was reading from pages she had not even provided.

She did know some of these lines, though. They were from *The Winter's Tale*. She'd practiced them with Julia. That spurred her on, because the words, though strange, were familiar and pleasing to her.

Judy started the scene as Florizel, and then gave way to Carmen with an obvious lead-in.

Carmen cleared her throat.

> "Sir, my gracious lord,
> To chide at your extremes, it not becomes me—
> O, pardon, that I name them!—your high self,
> The gracious mark o' the land, you have obscur'd
> With a swain's wearing; and me, poor lowly maid,
> Most goddess-like prank'd up."

She stopped and looked up.

"Keep going," Judy said.

So Carmen kept going. She was getting to the part she most liked, and she read it with a certain joy. At the end of the last page she stopped. She looked around. She felt stupid again.

"Okay. Thanks," she called to them generally, squinting to see Judy in spite of the lights blasting her retinas. "Sorry about that."

She trundled offstage and let herself out the back door into the sunshine.

She actually laughed aloud when she got outside, because the whole thing was so bad and ridiculous.

Oh, well. Another adventure for the Pants, she thought affectionately.

There were so many odd reversals on the way to growing up.

Tibby was fourteen before she got her period for the first time. She was the last of her friends. She wished for it. She imagined how it would be. She bought a box of maxi pads and kept them under her bathroom sink just in case. It stayed there unopened for months. She worried she would never get it. She worried there was something wrong with her. She wished and wished for that first spot of blood to bring her into union with her friends.

And then it came. The happiness at getting what you want is not usually commensurate with the worry leading up to it. Relief is a short-lived emotion, passive and thin. The agony of doubt disappears, leaving little memory of how it really felt. Life aligns behind the new truth. Her period was always going to come.

Three months later she had fallen into the convention of

hating her period and dreading it just the way everybody else did. She suffered the cramps badly. She lay curled up in her bed for hours. She took Midol. The pads, once prized, became a nuisance. Why had she ever wanted them? She stained all her clothes and washed them herself, because she was embarrassed to have Loretta see.

And now, almost five years later, she was back to pining for her period. She kept a constant monitor on her abdomen, at work, at home. She watched TV with part of her brain and thought about her uterus with the other. Was that a cramp she felt, that little twinge? Was it? Oh, please?

She thought about her uterus straight through work Friday and Saturday morning. She thought about it as she walked to Fourteenth Street to buy food and a magazine. She thought about it as she walked past the places that had become meaningful to her over the last year—the place where she'd gotten a terrible haircut with her friend Angela; the Mexican place favored by film students where they served cheap margaritas and almost never carded. She thought about her uterus through the long afternoon and night while she ignored her ringing phone and listened to messages left by people who loved her.

I'll just get through this, she thought. *Then I'll call everybody back.*

She worked Sunday. She wore a pad, just in case. She thought she felt a cramp.

"Tibby Rollins, where are you going?"

Tibby froze on her way through the Comedy aisle. She cleared her throat. "Uh. Nowhere?"

She couldn't say she was going to the bathroom again. She'd already been six times and it wasn't even noon. Every time, she checked her underwear hopefully. Every time, she returned to the floor in an agony of worry.

"Do you mind taking register three?"

"Okay. Fine."

If it didn't come today, was it officially late? Did that mean . . . ? A wave of panic mounted and broke. But maybe her last period hadn't really ended on the sixth. Maybe it had been the seventh.

This was her pattern. She talked herself up. She panicked. She talked herself down.

A customer was waving his hand in her face.

"Sorry?" she said, blinking.

"Have you seen this?" he asked. He was in his twenties, she guessed. Yeesh. So strong was his cologne she could practically taste it.

"Yes," she said, trying not to breathe in.

"Is it a good date movie?"

Tibby didn't mean to roll her eyes. It just happened.

He murmured something unfriendly and walked away.

She watched him go, considering her uterus. Was that a cramp she felt? Or was she just hungry? She made sure Charlie wasn't looking when she snuck off to the bathroom again.

❊   ❊   ❊

Julia was a nervous wreck for callbacks the next day.

"It'll be good," Carmen assured her. "I'm sure you were great."

"Let's hope Judy thought so," Julia said nervously, chomping on her pinky nail.

"Judy?"

"She's the casting director."

"Really?"

"Yeah. Why? Do you know her or something?"

"Not exactly, no."

Most of the kids were eating lunch when word went out that the lists were posted. Carmen was waiting in line to get coffee for her and Julia, and she feared she might get trampled like a hapless British soccer fan.

She watched the stampede. She drank her coffee by herself, enjoying the relative quiet.

Later, after the hoopla had died down, Carmen did wander by the lobby to check the lists. Why not? She checked the community theater list first, thinking it the least absurd possibility, and then the Second Stage. Her heart did pick up a little speed as her eyes passed from *I to J* to *K to L*. To *M*. Her name was not there.

Not exactly a surprise, she said to herself as she walked outside, taking the long way back to her room. She was mildly embarrassed that she'd even looked.

Was she disappointed? She wanted to read her heart honestly.

No. She felt pretty happy. She was wearing the Traveling

Pants and they still fit her, and even on an empty path she felt herself among friends.

O Tibbeth,
  Wherefore art thou ignoring thy friends?
  I sendeth thou a phone card. Please calleth me backeth.
  And I encloseth the Pants.

Loveth,
Thy loving and
most theatrical wench,
Carmen. Eth.

When Bridget reported for duty the next workday, Peter was not in the grave. She casually waited until around noon to casually ask cabinmate Carolyn why not. "I think he moved over to the house excavation."

"Oh," she said casually.

He was not the Tuesday lecturer, and she didn't see him at dinner the following night.

"A bunch of people went into town for dinner," Maxine mentioned.

Town was about thirty-five minutes away and Bridget had not yet been there, but suddenly she felt herself growing curious about it.

The next day, Alison announced to the team in mortuary that they'd made a big advance in the house dig, and asked for a couple of volunteers to shift. Bridget's hand shot up.

"We found a new part of the foundation and a new floor," Peter explained animatedly to the newly expanded group after lunch.

Was he surprised to see her there? Did it matter?

"We've cleared the floor in one small area, and we want to keep going. It's a tamped-earth floor, made of . . . well, earth. It can be hard to distinguish from the rest of the earth, if you know what I mean."

Bridget found herself on her hands and knees with her trowel. They were deep in, the shadows were long. Other members of the crew were carefully lifting off layers of the ground in front of her. Where she knelt there was less than a foot of loose dirt where they'd left off with the coarser tools.

She felt around with her hands, cupping mounds of it into the nearest bin. Peter had told her what to look for, but she sensed she would do better with her hands. She most urgently did not want to dig through and wreck the integrity of the floor.

She kept two palms on the edge of the flat and moved them along, feeling with her hands. It was all earth, yes, but some of it had been constructed and maintained purposefully and the rest had poured haphazardly into the negative space. Even after two and a half millennia, she could begin to feel the difference.

That was the thing with digging, she was starting to understand. You went into it with the instincts of a looter: Dig around, find something valuable and cool, and bring it to a museum. She'd fancied herself a wannabe Indiana

Jones. But the real thing was finding the effects of the human will. The planning, the wanting, the attempting of these ancient people was what connected you to them. Their effort was the difference between the random, all-over, everywhere-including-your-scalp dirt and this precious floor.

That was what they could learn from the gravesite, Peter had explained to her. You could learn a lot more about a people from how they buried, cared for, and commemorated their dead than from an ancient body randomly struck down by the side of a road.

"We do not like random," she'd teased Peter after one of his pep talks.

"No, we don't, do we?" he said, laughing, as he was quick to do.

This floor was not random. She closed her eyes and concentrated all of her self into her palms, almost in a trance as she felt along. She knew she probably looked ridiculous, but she didn't care. She remembered her grandfather describing how Michelangelo sculpted bodies out of blocks of marble. Her grandpa had been reading a book about the artist during a long-ago summer she'd spent in Alabama with him and Greta. She remembered him saying how Michelangelo looked for the body inside the block. He saw it and sensed it in there, and with his chisel he freed it.

Well, Bridget thought, a floor was a more prosaic thing, granted, but she was going to free it.

Her fingers were so sensitized she almost shouted when they ran into something hard and quite purposeful, but not the floor. Carefully she shook it off and held it in the patch of sunlight.

"Look at this," she called.

Peter hopped down into the room, followed by Carolyn and another guy. "Wow. That's great. That's most of a lamp. Look, you can see some of the painting on it."

She felt the moist terra-cotta against her fingers and followed the smooth, molded shape.

"That's where they would pour the oil. Probably olive oil." Peter pointed to a little well at the top. "They'd float the wick right there." He nodded at her approvingly. "I bet you can't find the missing piece."

She was such a sucker for a dare. He could obviously tell that.

"I found it," she said less than a minute later.

He hopped back down again, mirth spread over his features. She was glad to provide so much entertainment.

"Well done, Bee." He raised a hand to whack her on the shoulder, but put it down again without making contact. "Do your recording and bring it to Maxine. She'll be happy to have a whole one."

Always carry a flagon of

whiskey in case of

snakebite, and

furthermore, always carry

a small snake.

—W. C. Fields

"*Love's Labour's Lost* is such a great play," Carmen declared. "You were awesome reading the speech of Lady What's-Her-Name."

"Rosaline," Julia said flatly.

Carmen was trying to cheer Julia up about the fact that she'd gotten called back for the community production, the least desirable in her mind, and not the other two. But Julia wasn't having it.

"Rosaline. Right. You have to admit the play's a whole lot funnier than *Richard the Third*."

Richard III was the production on the Second Stage. Carmen could already perceive a hierarchy developing between the kids who'd gotten called back for Second Stage and the larger number who'd gotten called back for the Community Stage.

"Yeah. But they don't even sell tickets. It's, like, free. It's outdoors. It's not even real."

"How can you say that? Of course it's real. Andrew said it's the best attended of all of them, by far."

"That's because it's free," Julia said. "Anyone can go."

"That's a *good* thing. Anyway, at least you got called back," Carmen said. She wasn't even sure why she said this. She had made up her mind not to tell Julia about her ludicrous tryout, but here she was eager to debase herself to make Julia feel better.

"Everyone got called back," Julia said.

"That's not true."

"What are you talking about? Melanie Peer said that everyone who tried out got called back for something."

"No, they didn't."

"How do you know?" Julia was sitting up straighter now.

"I didn't get called back," Carmen said, with a perverse note of triumph.

Julia looked at her in outright astonishment. "You tried out?"

"Yeah."

"You're kidding."

"It *was* kind of a joke, but no. I really tried out."

"Really? Why?"

"I have no idea. It was kind of a mistake, actually."

"Who did you read?"

"Perdita."

"No."

"Yeah."

Julia looked like she might laugh, but she made a wince of sympathy. "You didn't get called back."

"No way."

"Oh, well. It was brave of you to try."

"That and stupid."

Julia patted Carmen on the arm and laughed. It looked like this method of cheering her up really was working.

Lena wasn't sure how much of it was attributable to Leo, but she knew that every hour she wasn't in her painting class she wished she were.

"Hi, Lena," he said to her on Thursday as she was leaving painting class, girding herself for three long, bleak days of not painting and not getting to see Leo.

"Hi," she said, taking almost absurd pride in the fact that he still knew her name.

"How's it going?" he said.

"Pretty good," she said blandly. She smiled blandly. "How are you?" she asked blandly.

"Just fine."

Please be interesting, she begged of herself.

She was wearing her hair down and had put on mascara for the fourth day in a row. She was boring as crap, but at least she looked good.

"I don't know if I can make it to Monday," Leo said. He distractedly pushed his hand around in his hair and made it stand up more.

"What do you mean?"

"I mean no painting. I'm right in the middle of this thing I'm trying to figure out. It'll be gone by Monday. It's too long to go, you know?"

She nodded. Oh, how she knew. She wasn't sure her reasons were quite as pure as his, but she was taken aback to think they felt exactly the same way.

"I'm thinking of seeing if Nora would work extra hours over the weekend. I'd have to ask Robert, I guess." He pushed his hair around again despondently. "Would you want to go in on it with me?"

She was nearly frozen by the thought. She cherished his phrasing. "Uh."

She tried to figure. She'd have to come up with around eight or nine dollars an hour. How could she do that? She had no money. She ate Cup O' Noodles almost every night from the twenty-four pack she'd bought at Costco with her parents' membership. That was as close as her father got to financial aid. Her mother had slipped her eighty dollars at the beginning of the summer, and she'd made it last for almost three weeks.

But how could she say no? She couldn't. She'd pawn her watch. She'd steal her mother's diamonds. She'd borrow money from Effie, for God's sake.

She swallowed. "I'd love to go in with you," she chirruped.

"Are you Carmen Lowell?"

Carmen looked up from the table at the canteen to see a guy she didn't know staring at her with odd intensity.

She was so surprised she didn't answer. A year ago she might have imagined he was staring at her like that because he thought she was cute, but now she was so conditioned to invisibility she found his gaze disturbing. Suddenly she worried she'd set off all the sprinklers in her dorm or something.

"Yes, she's Carmen Lowell," Julia said, looking mildly impatient with both of them.

"Well, dude. Congratulations. Sophia over there thought it was you, but I said I didn't think you were trying out."

Carmen could not have been more mystified. She would have liked to say something, but she just gaped like a hooked fish.

"Congratulations for what?" Julia asked.

"The callback," he said.

Julia put her fork down. She cast a protective look at Carmen. "She didn't get called back."

Carmen nodded.

"I'm pretty sure you did." Why did this guy proceed to talk as if to Carmen and not to Julia, who was the one conversing with him? This added another unsettling layer. "Didn't you check the list?"

"She did check it," Julia said, almost combatively.

"Then maybe you should check it again," the guy said to Carmen.

"He has no idea what he's talking about," Julia muttered once he'd left, resuming her dinner of salad and Diet Coke.

Carmen stood up. She had an odd idea blossoming in her mind and she needed to choke it off before it really started to get to her.

"You said you checked, right?" Julia asked.

"Yeah. I might go check again, though." Carmen picked up her tray with the remnants of her dinner on it.

Julia stood too. "I'll come with you. I'm done."

As they walked toward the Main Stage, Julia talked and Carmen fretted.

"That guy probably looked at one of the tech lists and got confused," Julia said.

"Yeah, probably."

But the thing Carmen was thinking when she pushed open the doors to the lobby was that she had checked the lists, but only two of them. She hadn't thought to check the third, because it was somewhere else, she didn't know where, and it just seemed too preposterous to go around looking for it.

Wordlessly, both she and Julia walked to the lists and ran their eyes along the columns. Indeed, Carmen's name was not there.

"One thing," Carmen murmured on the way out. She bent her steps to the other side of the entrance, where she now saw a much smaller list posted.

"That's the Main Stage list," Julia said.

Even so, Carmen walked up to it and looked. There were seven names on the list, and hers was one of them.

Carma,

I have a new love. Don't tell Hector.

I have fallen in love with a dirt floor. I am obsessed. I am devoted.

I am its humble servant.

I am going to marry it. I am going to have dirty, flat children with it.

But fear not, Carma. I'll still love you guys even though you're rounded and clean. Just, you know, not in that way.

Love,

Mrs. Bee Vreeland Dirtfloor

After the initial shock wore off, Julia wanted to talk about it.

"It's unbelievable, Carmen, it really is," she said.

She wanted to know every detail of Carmen's happening into the theater, her discussion with Judy. She wanted Carmen to reenact every word of her muddled tryout.

And then, all of a sudden, Julia didn't want to talk about it anymore. She said she was tired and fell asleep in under five seconds.

So Carmen lay there twisting in her sheets, wondering if Judy was playing some subtle trick on her. What could it mean?

And now she was supposed to prepare for a real audition for the following evening? How was she supposed to do that? She had no idea how you did that.

Anyway, what was the point? She was not an actress. She did not like the lights. She would not get the part.

Her audition had proven to her that she had no business on the stage, even if it had failed to prove so to Judy.

The next morning she got up early. She walked around until nine o'clock, when she could find out the location of Judy's office and, subsequently, Judy.

"I think you might have made a mistake," she said, hovering nervously in front of Judy's desk.

Judy took off her reading glasses. "What mistake?"

"You put me on the callback list for *The Winter's Tale*."

Judy looked at her a little strangely. "That wasn't a mistake."

"I think it might have been."

"Carmen, are you the casting director or am I?" Judy didn't look mean, exactly, but her straight-across eyebrows were intimidating.

"I know. I know. It's just that I don't think I'd be right for it."

"You don't even know which part we're going to cast!"

"Well, that's true, but I don't think I'd be right for any of them."

"Can you please leave that to me?" Judy was getting annoyed now.

"Judy. Seriously. I don't know how to prepare for an audition. I'm bad at memorizing. I would not do a good job. I think there are so many people who would do a good job. My friend Julia Wyman, for instance, would do a great job. I heard her read Perdita, and she did it so much better. She memorized the whole thing." Carmen realized how juvenile she probably sounded.

"Carmen, no offense to your friend Julia, but I see that girl twenty times a day."

Carmen was puzzling over how this could be, until she realized Judy was speaking figuratively.

"She's polished, she's poised and ambitious, but that's not what I'm looking for right now. When she reads Perdita I hear a shepherdess who thinks she's a princess. I want a shepherdess who thinks she's a shepherdess."

Carmen did not completely follow, but she didn't want to argue.

"I'm looking for somebody who is a little more porous, you know? Someone who is fragile, who is less sure of everything."

Carmen nodded, imagining for the first time that Judy wasn't completely out of her mind.

When she got home, she called her mother.

"Carmen, congratulations! That's exciting!"

"Mama, it's not exciting. It's scary. I don't think I want to do it. I don't know how." Her voice never sounded whinier than when she spoke to her mother. "You know I'm not an actress!"

Her mother was silent while she mulled this over. "Well, *nena*, you have always been dramatic."

"Mama!"

Why did everyone keep saying that?

Never had a weekend passed more slowly. Lena remembered the old adage about knowing whether you'd chosen the right career by how you felt on Sunday night. Well, what light did it shed on your personal life when you abhorred Friday night?

She lived for Monday painting class. She lived twice when Leo came up to her easel at the first break.

"Robert says we can't do it," he said unhappily.

"Why not?" she asked.

"We can't use the studio. Some bullshit about insurance and you need a security person in the building. I don't know. He says we can't hire Nora off the books either."

"Really?"

He shook his head.

"That sucks," she said, though a little too happily. She was elated that he was seeming so much like her friend.

"Yeah."

Well. It was good not to have to steal her mother's diamonds. But how could she get through another weekend?

The timer dinged and they both went back to painting. At the end of class she took a long time putting away her stuff and was thrilled when he wandered back over to her easel.

"It's not that I have to paint Nora," he said as they walked together down the hall and out into the sunshine. "I mean, that would be great. But I just want to keep painting. We should be working every day. I feel like I start over every Monday."

"I know what you mean," she said boringly.

He walked pretty fast, she realized. She practically jogged to keep up with him.

"I could work on a still life or something," he said. "But I'm doing the figure this summer. That's what I want to think about. It's not the same to stare at a couple of pears."

"Yeah."

He stopped. "Do you want to get a cup of coffee?"

"Sure," she said.

He led her around the corner. "This place has good iced coffee," he said.

"Great," said she. His freckles were nice.

He ordered two. "Do you have time to sit down for a minute?"

How 'bout an hour? she felt like saying. *How about seven?* She couldn't help laughing at herself a little.

"I do" was what she said.

They sat.

"I have a lot of minutes," she added overhonestly.

"Yeah?"

"Yeah. I guess I am kind of underscheduled this summer." Why was it that when her mouth obeyed her she was chokingly boring, and when it didn't she was mortifying? Where was the in-between?

He looked at her. Did he feel sorry for her? It wasn't exactly sexy to admit you had nothing to do.

"I mean, I have painting," she hurried to say. "I have work-study in the library eight hours a week. But none of my friends stuck around this summer, so . . ."

"Right."

"Yeah."

He shook the ice around in his iced coffee. He looked regretful. "I have to be at work soon. But what are you doing tomorrow night?"

She turned pink. She felt stupid. Charity and romance did not go together. "Well. That's really nice of you, but—"

"But what? Come over for dinner. You can't go acting like you have other plans."

She laughed. "I can't, can I?"

"Anyway, it will be good. Here." He fished around in his bag for a piece of paper and a pen. He wrote down his address. "About seven?"

"Okay," she said weakly.

When he left the coffee shop, the air slowly leaked out of her. Leo had asked her to dinner. She had a date with Leo.

Some part of her was pleased. Other parts knew there was nothing like the artifice of a date to ruin a relationship. Especially a date born out of pity.

It is a characteristic

of wisdom not to do

desperate things.

—Henry David Thoreau

The Traveling Pants came on Monday. Tibby's period did not. A watched period, she worried, does not come.

She decided to change her strategy. She would tempt fate. She wore a pair of slight, lacy underpants and pulled the Traveling Pants on over them. She went to register for her summer classes.

With a small part of her brain, she filled out forms in the lobby of the main film building and consulted the catalog. With the remainder of her brain, she thought about not thinking about her uterus anymore.

Since the first time she'd ever worn the Traveling Pants, she'd had this secret worry that she would get her period while wearing the Pants. You couldn't wash the Pants, of course. It was the first and most infamous rule. Tibby had often imagined the shame of bleeding on the Traveling Pants and then needing to send them on. She imagined secretly washing them and hoping no one would ever find out.

It was this fear that led her, from the first summer onward, to wear her hardiest underwear whenever she wore the Pants, and also to wear a liner of some kind. She happened to know she was not the only member of the Sisterhood to do so. It was kind of a basic courtesy at this point.

But not today. Today she took the ultimate risk. Whatever it took she would do, she both thought and did not think as she strode into her dorm room late that afternoon.

"Tibby?"

She reared back against the door. Her blood whisked around her veins in a hectic way. In all the times Brian had appeared in her room, he had never truly startled her before.

"Sorry," he said, recognizing her distress. Usually he sat on her bed, but today he was standing. When he tried to put his arms around her, she shrugged away.

"Today isn't a good day," she said.

"You didn't answer the phone. I wanted to make sure you were okay."

"Okay."

"Are you?" He wanted so much to talk to her. She could see that. But she was holding herself too carefully. She couldn't open up a little or at all.

"Don't you work tonight?" she asked.

"I traded shifts."

"What about tomorrow morning?"

"I'll be back for that," he said.

"You're going back tonight?"

He nodded. "I just wanted to see you."

This was her first moment of relief. He wasn't staying.

"Okay. Well."

His hair was lank. When did he last take a shower?

"I know you're worried. I'm worried. I just wish I could—"

"You can't," she said quickly. She looked at the ground. "This is where you are happy that you're the boy and I'm the girl."

He wore his hurt openly. "I'm not happy."

She saw how miserable he was, how miserable she was making him. She thought of the Pants and her single-minded wish. What wouldn't she ruin? What wouldn't she sacrifice for a dot of blood?

"I know you're not happy," she said regretfully.

"I wish I could do something."

She wanted him to leave. That was what he could do. She wanted to be alone with her uterus. "If I think of something, I'll tell you," she said, opening the door and stepping aside for him to go through it.

"Will you?"

"Yeah."

"You promise?"

"Yeah."

"Tibby?"

"Yeah?"

He looked like he might cry. He wanted to be able to talk.

We shouldn't have done it, she wanted to say. *We opened ourselves up to all this. Why did you want to so much? Why did you make me believe it would be all right?*

She knew she should be having this talk with Brian. Instead, she had it, once again, with herself.

"What?" she pressed, knowing full well what he wanted.

He looked at her for another moment and turned to go.

She felt mean. She was mean. She hated herself more than she hated him.

He walked to the elevator. He had come all this way, and now he was going all the way back. Only Brian would do a thing like that.

Usually these gestures moved her. She appreciated the way he was, the way he trusted himself and her, regardless of how the rest of the world worked. Usually she understood the particular ways he felt and the things he did.

Tonight she felt differently. After she closed the door she wondered what half-sane person would travel twelve hours to see a girl for ten minutes.

Julia worked on the Princess of France while Carmen, self-consciously, worked on Perdita.

"Perdita means lost child, did you know that?" Carmen asked, looking up from her book the night before the callback. The room had been silent for so long, she wanted the comfort of a little conversation.

"Yes. I know that," Julia said flatly.

Carmen tried not to feel hurt. "Do you want me to read Berowne or the king for you?" she asked.

"No, thanks."

Later, it seemed to her that Julia felt bad. "Do you want me to read with you?" Julia offered.

"Um, sure. That's really nice. Do you want to be Polixenes?"

"Fine."

"Okay, so I'll start where she goes." Carmen squinted at the page, knowing she should try it from memory. "Uh, 'Sir, welcome . . .' "

"Go ahead."

" 'Sir, welcome! / It is my father's will I should take on me / The hostess of—' "

"No," Julia interrupted. "It's 'hostess-ship,' not 'hostess.' And you don't say 'of.' It's a contraction. You say 'o.' You say 'hostess-ship o' the day.' "

"Right," Carmen said. She tried it again.

Julia stopped her after another three lines. "Carmen, have you read Shakespeare before?"

"Not that much. Not out loud. Why?"

"Because your meter is all wrong. Rhythmically it just sounds wrong."

"Oh." They were close enough friends that Carmen had trouble believing Julia meant to sound as mean as she sounded.

"And it's not like I have time to teach it all to you either," Julia said. "I have a lot of work to do for my own callback."

"Fine," Carmen said. She felt like she was going to cry.

Julia shut her book, seemingly blind to what Carmen was feeling.

Carmen kept her eyes on her script.

"Listen, Carmen, no offense, but are you sure you should bother with this? It doesn't seem like your kind of thing, you know? It's going to take a lot of work, and the chances of it working out are pretty small. Maybe you should just blow it off. That's probably what I would do if I were you."

Carmen did not want to cry. "I already tried to get out of it," she said almost inaudibly. "I told Judy she'd made a mistake."

"You did?" Julia's voice was loud and quick. "And what did she say?"

"She said she didn't."

Julia's normally pretty face did not look pretty at this moment. It looked pinched and suspicious. Carmen tried to use her imagination to restore its prettiness, to remember why they were friends.

"Didn't what?"

"Think she'd made a mistake."

"Well, yeah. But you know yourself better than she does."

Carmen nodded wordlessly. She lay on her bed and turned her face to the wall. What was wrong with her? Julia was being a witch to her and all she felt like doing was crying. Where was the famous Carmen temper? She was a master at standing up for herself.

But that Carmen felt like someone she only knew about from a long time ago. That Carmen wasn't this Carmen.

This was a faded Carmen. She'd lost her mojo for that kind of thing.

Maybe you needed to feel strong to stand up for yourself. You needed to feel loved. She'd always been better at acting up with people she trusted to love her.

She wished she could just fall asleep and sleep straight through her callback audition and forget about the whole thing. Maybe Julia wasn't simply being mean. Maybe she was being honest and it was the honesty that was tough to swallow. Carmen didn't know how to read Shakespeare. Her meter was undoubtedly wrong.

She wished she could sleep, but she couldn't. Even long after Julia turned off the light, Carmen lay there feeling wretched about herself. She felt despair, and apart from the Pants, she couldn't think of a way to feel better.

And then she thought of one small way. Quietly she picked up her script from the bottom of her bed. Quietly she walked out of the room and into the hallway.

She sat down outside her door in a spot where the light was good. Feeling an odd sense of rebellion, she stayed in that spot and studied the lines.

She read them all. Not just Perdita's, but the whole play. She read it again, and then, through the remaining hours before morning, she read Perdita's part, each time with more care. She didn't try to memorize it or figure out what Julia meant by the meter. She just tried to understand the play.

Carmen didn't know how to act like an actress. But it

dawned on her that she wasn't supposed to. She was supposed to act like Perdita. She was supposed to act like the lost daughter of estranged parents — a flawed but repentant father, a beleaguered but upright mother who gets carried off to sea. Maybe that was something she could try to do.

A single day is enough to

make us a little larger.

—Paul Klee

As Lena dressed for her alleged date, she realized she hadn't thought of Kostos in two days. Compared with how she used to be, two days was forever. Was she forgetting yet? Did that constitute forgetting? Maybe the fact that she was still asking meant no, not yet.

Lena wanted to look pretty, but not date pretty. She didn't want to try too hard, but she did want him to notice that she was attractive. Or was thought to be so. That struck her as funny. *You may not have noticed it, Leo, but I am thought to be attractive.*

She liked and admired Leo for not seeming to notice, but she did also want him to. Here she had this supposedly striking quality, and it mostly caused her strain and annoyance — vapid attention and endless comments and people assuming she was a princess or a snob. She might as well take advantage of it once in a while.

Without meaning to, she was suffused with the memory

of the last time she'd wanted to take advantage of it. It was at her bapi's funeral, when she knew she'd see Kostos.

Lena lost track of her preparations. She dropped the eye pencil on her dresser. She sat on her bed, her hands tucked under her. That was the hardest day to remember.

She stared at her feet for a while and then out the window at the building across the way. This did not count toward forgetting, she realized.

When she finally got up, she dispensed with the makeup and the hair fiddling. She changed back into her comfortable shoes that made her feet look like the boats they were. She hedged; she left herself how she was.

She walked along with the address flapping in her hand. Where did he live? Did he have a roommate? Was this going to go along a standard date format? Or was this simply the gesture of a charitable friend? She wasn't sure which she wanted less.

She turned onto his street. She knew the street, but not this part of it. It was deserted and a little bit dodgy, she recognized, and yet the old industrial loft buildings were staunchly romantic.

She stopped in front of 2020. She buzzed 7B. 7B buzzed back. She pushed into the building and made sure the door was shut behind her.

Of all the hundreds of possibilities she had considered, one of the few she hadn't met her at the door.

"Hi, I'm Jaclyn. You're Lena?"

Lena gaped for a moment too long and then stuck out her hand. "I am. Hi."

Jaclyn was a tall African American woman who appeared to be in her early forties. She was wearing a paint-spattered denim work shirt over olive green cargo pants and elegant brown slides. She had three sparkly clips in her long braided hair. She was beautiful.

Lena's brain was rushing around as she looked past the woman into the apartment. It was a gigantic loft. The ceiling must have been twenty feet high in the main room, and around it was a balcony suggesting a second floor. The railings were hung with huge tapestries and a few ancient-looking carpets.

The effect of the woman and the place were quite dazzling to all of Lena's senses, but her brain was wondering how she, Lena, could possibly fit into it. Leo was less conventional than she'd even guessed. And apparently he liked older women.

Leo appeared behind Jaclyn. "Hey. Welcome. Come in."

She followed them through the big room to an open kitchen under the balcony. The table was set, and pots were steaming on the stove. The air was spicy and garlicky.

"I hope you like, uh, flavorful food," Jaclyn said. "Leo uses a head of garlic every time he makes dinner."

Another sense dazzled. Another surprise about Leo. Lena nodded. "I'm Greek," she said.

Jaclyn smiled. "Excellent," she said.

Leo was manning all four gas burners with an admirably cool head. Lena had grown up in a family of cooks, but she couldn't manage even one burner.

"Mom, could you get me the butter?" Leo called.

All the bits and pieces swirling in Lena's head came apart and recombined. Jaclyn was his mom?

Jaclyn got the butter. More evidence that she was indeed his mother. There wasn't anyone else around who could be his mother.

Lena looked from Jaclyn to Leo and back. Huh. She considered Leo's dark gold skin. It made sense now. Lena saw, now that she really looked, how much of his mother's beauty Leo had.

Lena realized that as a dinner guest it was not desirable to be completely mute. "Can I help with anything?" she asked politely.

"I think we're set," Jaclyn said, looking for something in the cupboard. "Leo, how's it going?"

"A couple minutes," he said. "Hey, Lena, will you bring me the plates and I'll fill them up here?"

She was glad to have a job. She gathered and carefully stacked the yellow plates. "These are beautiful," she murmured.

"They're my mom's," Leo said.

It took her a second to realize that he didn't just mean that his mom owned them.

"You mean like . . ."

"She made them. She's a ceramicist. Mostly."

"You made these?" she said stupidly to Jaclyn, who was setting glasses on the table.

"Yep. Water with dinner? Juice? Wine?"

"Water, please," Lena said. She couldn't help looking at Jaclyn with bald admiration. She was beautiful. She was young. She made exquisite yellow dinner plates. Lena suddenly wondered about Leo's dad. Was there a dad? There were only three plates.

Lena thought of her own mother with her tailored beige clothes and her shiny briefcase.

Lena's taste buds were her only sense yet undazzled, and a few bites of dinner did the trick. It was a spicy curry with lamb and vegetables over some eventful and delicious kind of rice. "This is so good," she said to Leo, her awe undisguised. "I can't believe you made this."

He laughed and she realized it hadn't come out all compliment, as she had intended. "I mean, not because you don't seem like you could cook," she added lamely. "Because I'm so bad at it."

Why was she always putting herself down in front of him? What charm, exactly, did that hold?

"You probably haven't practiced that much," Leo said.

"That's true. Everybody else cooks in my family, so I haven't needed to yet." She thought of all her ramen noodles with silent shame. "My grandparents owned a restaurant in Greece."

The conversation rolled on from there. Jaclyn wanted to hear all about her family and how her parents ended up in America. Lena talked for a while, and when she remembered she was shy and lost, Jaclyn rescued her with a funny story about the time she went to Greece with an old boyfriend, lost him in a market near the Acropolis, and never saw him again.

After that Lena discovered that Leo's dad was a

businessman from Ohio who was no longer in the picture and that Jaclyn had brought up Leo mostly on her own.

"She supported us selling her ceramics and her tapestries," Leo explained with obvious pride.

Lena admired the tapestries and then all the other lovely things lining the walls and shelves. The whole place was filled with things the two of them had made. Drawings, pots, sculptures, paintings. It was almost overwhelming to Lena.

She thought of the empty beige walls of her house and of the hard, minimal surfaces of metal and polished stone. Her parents, hailing from a romantic, disheveled homeland, had grown up in ancient, disheveled houses. Now they wanted only American sleekness.

You grow up, Lena thought, about herself and them. *You leave home. You see other ways of living.*

Lena looked around, intoxicated by her sense of longing. She wanted this.

It was late and Bee still had two hands and two knees against the floor. She had cleared several more feet and could not leave it. She'd work through dinner. She'd do it by moonlight if she had to. She could do it in the dark. She'd dreamed about it the past three nights. She simply loved the feeling of finding the floor, inch by inch, under her hands. By now she really trusted herself to know where it was.

The difference tonight was that Peter was kneeling two feet away, clearing next to her. He had not yet learned the floor as she had, but she was slightly proud to note that he had put aside his trowel and adopted her technique. She was faster, smoother, and surer every hour she worked.

"You can go," she said. "Seriously. I'm fine. I'm a crazy nutjob, I know. I can't help it. But I swear I won't ruin anything."

"I know you won't," he said almost defensively. "I'm not staying for you."

She laughed. "Good to know."

He had the slightly abstracted look she also wore when she had her hands on the floor. "I mean." He raised his dirty hands. "It's addictive."

"Don't I know."

"Worse than pistachios."

"So much."

He disappeared briefly to find a spotlight and hook it up to the generator. He hopped back down.

"Hey, look," she said. She held up a large piece of pottery. "Another one." They had piles of them. They had left off with the proper labeling as it got later and later in the night.

"From the kalyx krater," he said.

"I think."

"Dude. We might find the whole thing." He was excited. He did what he did for good reasons. She could understand wanting to spend your life like this.

"Dude, we might," she teased him back.

He left again later to find a few pieces of pita bread and

a large chocolate bar and a half-empty bottle of red wine. He gallantly shared them with her.

After the eating were long periods of silent work. Occasionally she heard laughter from over the hill, where the nightly party was rolling on.

"Another sherd," he said. "It's from a lamp."

"Arrrrg!" she erupted. "Say *shard*! Don't say *sherd*." The word *potsherd* was the single thing about archaeology she really did not like.

He passed her a challenging look. "Sherd."

"Stop it!"

"Sherd."

"I hate that."

"Sherd."

"Peter! Shut up!"

"Sherd."

She reached over and shoved him hard. He was not only startled, he was poorly balanced. He fell over into the dirt.

Even though she felt bad, she was laughing too hard to stop. She walked over to him on her knees. She wanted to say sorry, but she couldn't get it out.

He reached up and shoved her in retaliation. She fell onto her back, laughing so hard she was practically suffocating. They both lay in the dirt, punch-drunk and wine-drunk.

Once he'd gotten his breath and sat up, he reached out his hand. "Truce?" he said, hauling her up.

She was back on her knees. He was still holding her dirty hand in his. He pulled it toward his chest.

"Truce," she meant to say, but she started laughing again midway through.

"Sherd," he said.

"How'd it go?" Julia asked when Carmen joined her for a late dinner after her audition. By Julia's expression, it looked to Carmen as though she had a specific idea in mind about how Carmen should answer.

It was a disaster, Carmen was supposed to say. *I made a total fool of myself.*

She could tell that that was what Julia wanted to hear, and that if she said it they could both laugh over it and be close again.

Carmen put her tray down and sat. But if Julia was actually her friend, why did she want to hear that? And if Carmen was so good at standing up for herself, why did she feel the need to say it? Why did Julia require that she be a failure, and why did Carmen go along with it?

"I'm not sure," Carmen said slowly, honestly. "I couldn't really tell."

"Did Judy say anything?" Julia looked impatient, unsatisfied.

"She said 'Thanks, Carmen.' "

"That was it?"

"That was it."

So cool was the air between them, Carmen figured they'd spend the rest of the meal in punishing silence. But a few minutes later two girls from their hall came up. "Hey,

Carmen, I heard you had a great audition," Alexandra said.

Carmen didn't try to hide her surprise. "Really?"

"That's what Benjamin Bolter said. He said that your energy was very fresh."

Carmen wasn't sure exactly what that meant. "Thanks. I was nervous."

"Nervous can be good," the other girl, Rachel, said.

"Anyway, I really hope you get it. How cool would that be?"

Carmen watched them go, suddenly wishing she were eating dinner with Alexandra and Rachel and not with Julia.

When they were leaving the canteen, Carmen realized that a bunch of kids at the front table were watching her. One of the ones she'd met, Jack something or other, waved at her. "All right, Carmen!" he called out.

She felt herself blushing as she went out the door. She wished she were wearing earrings and some makeup. She felt the drumming of excitement in her chest. It was kind of a responsibility, being visible.

To: Tibberon@sbgnetworks.com

From: Carmabelle@hsp.xx.com

Subject: call me call me call me

Hey, you girl of urban mystery. Will you call me? I have something cool to tell you and I'm not writing it here. You have to call me. Ha.

And don't do that thing you do of leaving a message when you know I won't be there.

❉   ❉   ❉

By eleven o'clock that night, Lena was relaxed and happy. Her stomach was full. She knew she was in love. If not with Leo, then certainly with his mother.

"So I asked Nora about posing, even though we're not supposed to hire her," Leo said as they picked at the last of the raspberries and the shortbread cookies.

"What did she say?" Lena asked, her elbows on the table.

"She said she'd think about it. I'm not too optimistic."

"The truth," Lena said, "is I really want to do it, but I probably can't afford to. Unless I steal my mom's jewelry. Which I have considered."

Leo laughed. "It's only eight bucks an hour if we split it."

Lena put her hand to her temple. "I know. But I have *no* money. I'm kind of on my own with school, and it's . . ."

"Ludicrously expensive," Jaclyn filled in. "Did you try for financial aid?"

"I didn't qualify," Lena explained. "My parents have the money, but my dad doesn't really . . . support the idea of my being an artist." Lena usually kept this to herself, feeling ashamed of them. But tonight she said it with a note of pride.

"You should apply for a scholarship," Leo said. "That's what I did."

"Did you get full tuition?" she asked.

"Tuition, stipends, everything. It helps being black," he said. "I qualify for almost every scholarship they've got."

It helps being the best painter in the school, she thought. "I have a partial one," she explained. "I'm applying for the big one for next year. I'll find out in August."

"I'm sure you'll get it," Leo said. "But I'll help you with your portfolio if you want."

Lena flushed with pleasure. "Thanks," she said. She wasn't sure she could let him see all those drawings she used to think were good. "I just need a few finished paintings, you know?"

Jaclyn got up to clear the teacups. "You should do what we used to do when I was in art school."

"What's that?" Leo asked, his feet, in faded blue socks, propped on the corner of the table.

"We used to trade poses with each other. We'd do portraits, figures, whatever. It's free, it's fair. Most of my drawings and paintings from my art school years are of my friends."

"I don't really know that many people in the summer program," Lena admitted.

Jaclyn gestured to Leo. "You know each other. You two can do it."

While Leo was getting on board, Lena was realizing what this meant. She stopped being quite as relaxed. "You mean, like, I pose for Leo and he poses for me?" The way they looked at her, she felt both childish and dumb.

Leo was starting to look eager. "We could split it up however we want. Maybe I could pose for you on Saturday and you could pose for me on Sunday. We could work like that for the next bunch of weekends."

Lena knew she was gaping. She tried to cover a little more of her wide eyes with her eyelids.

"It's good for an artist to pose, too. I've heard that," Leo was saying, though his voice sounded distant to her. "It's good to see the process from the other side. It makes you better at working with models."

Lena felt her head nodding.

"And you know we could each have a finished figure painting by the end of the summer."

Lena was alone, trapped in her head with her loud, slow-moving thoughts. He was going to pose for her for a figure painting? The dryness of the shortbread was caked and rough in her throat. She was going to pose for him? "Or a portrait," she choked out nervously.

"You can do a portrait," he said, not seeming to register what this meant. "If you want."

Lena simply could not swallow the cookie. It sat there, choking her. She knew that prudishness had no place in the training and career of a figure painter, but still.

She tried once again to swallow. Maybe her father was right after all.

In the depth of winter,

I finally learned that

within me there lay

an invincible summer.

—Albert Camus

The next morning Carmen unearthed a pair of red flared pants she hadn't worn since the end of last summer. She'd worn them to Target, where she'd gone shopping for college supplies with Win. She'd also worn a bandana, do-rag style, and he'd kissed her massively in the parking lot.

God, that felt far away.

She put on a sexy black tank top and big silver hoops. She wore a shade of red lipstick that she knew looked good on her. She let her long, unruly hair out of its ordinary clip. She felt like a completely different person as she walked out of the dorm and into the sun. But like a familiar person.

She wanted to make her way slowly to the theater lobby. She wanted to keep the motor running low, to keep her expectations in check. The chances of seeing her name on the cast list were small, she knew. One out of seven under the best of circumstances, and she knew she wasn't as prepared or as capable as the other six.

Two days ago, she was in Judy's office trying to get out of it. Now . . . what?

Now she wanted it. She had stayed up all night working and thinking and studying, and it had culminated in her wanting it.

As she walked into the theater, she felt the mad walloping of her heart in her chest, so strong it seemed to shake her entire body. In some ways it had been easier not wanting it.

But the wanting felt good. Even if she didn't get it. Wanting was what made you a person, and she was glad to feel like a person again.

The scene in the theater lobby was dreamlike. It seemed that all seventy-five of the apprentices were standing in there. But instead of noise and chaos, Carmen had the strange impression that they were waiting for her.

So strange it was, she thought her imagination must be firing in step with her perceptions, but this was how it seemed to her: It seemed like the crowd parted for her and made a path to the spot on the board where the cast list was posted. And it seemed like they were all urging her forward to look at it. And when she stood in front of it, it seemed that one character and one name were bigger and bolder than all the rest.

Perdita, it read. And next to that it said *Carmen Lowell*.

❄   ❄   ❄

She hadn't said yes, Lena said to herself as she got out of the shower the morning after her dinner at Leo's loft. Maybe she had indicated assent, but she hadn't said the word *yes*.

He would be so disappointed if she backed out.

She looked at her naked self in the steamy mirror. The mirror was too small to see all of herself, which was just as well.

She was a prude. She had to admit it. She was modest. Overly modest. She was Greek. Her parents were traditional. She couldn't even look at herself without feeling embarrassed.

She tried to imagine Leo seeing her like this. Just the thought flooded and fizzled her circuits. How could she actually do it?

She was uptight. She wished she weren't so uptight. What was the problem, anyway? Her body was fine. She wasn't overweight or awkwardly built. There were no major patches of cellulite, as far as she knew. She didn't have hair in unexpected places. Her nipples went in the right direction. What was the big problem?

She wished she were more like Bee. Bee showered in the staff locker room at soccer camp next to guys she barely even knew. When Lena gawped and stuttered in disbelief at this revelation, Bee just ignored her. "It's not that big a deal," she said.

She thought back to Kostos and the swimming episode in Greece the summer they'd met. For a girl who liked to keep covered, fate had played a couple of pretty mean jokes on Lena.

To: Carmabelle@hsp.xx.com
From: Beezy3@gomail.net
Subject: YAAAAA!!!

Carma! I screamed so loud when I read your message my co-digger almost called an ambulance.

I am so proud of you!

Set builder turned star. You can't keep your darn light hidden, can you?

If it didn't come on Tuesday, Tibby would buy a pregnancy test.

If it didn't come on Wednesday she would buy a pregnancy test.

If it didn't come on Thursday.

If not by Friday.

Tibby stood in Duane Reade on Saturday morning. She studied the box as though it were a cobra. Aptly, it was kept behind the counter, behind Plexiglas. You couldn't just snatch it from the shelf and toss it facedown on the counter. They made you ask for it. How could she ask? She tried the question in her mind. *Can I have the bllllllll? One of the rrrrrr, please? The box with the mmmmm?*

If she couldn't think it, what were the chances she could say it?

The nearest salesperson was a man with extravagant sideburns. She couldn't ask him. She'd come back.

She touched her belly. Her fingers related to it differently than at other times.

She walked outside. She looked up. The sun carried on its serene business of exploding, unmuffled by a single cloud. She had a free day, a blue sky, but she felt a throttling sense of claustrophobia. There was nowhere to go where the worry wouldn't go. Not even sleeping gave her respite.

Her legs went along and she found herself in Washington Square Park. Clumps of friends hung by the central fountain. A man and a woman kissed on a bench. Tibby wondered if part of what she felt was loneliness.

She thought of her friends. She felt a melting sensation in her muscles begetting a looser kind of sadness.

Oh, you guys. I had sex! I'm not a virgin! Can you believe that? I did it. We did it!

But then there was the other part of the story, inseparable from the first. Tibby was a natural believer in the other shoe dropping, and this time it had really clobbered her. It had turned happiness into agony, love into umbrage.

Wasn't that just how the world worked? You had sex for the first time with a person you really loved and the condom broke, leaving you most likely *prrrrr.*

Cynicism was a great hedge, of course. When the bad thing came true, at least you had the pleasure of being right. But that pleasure felt cold today. She didn't want to be right. For the first time in her life, she longed to be wrong.

"Do you know what time it is?" a young man in a corduroy cap asked her.

"I have no idea," she replied. She could have looked at her cell phone, but she didn't.

She couldn't make herself sit down anyplace. She walked past Duane Reade again.

Did she really have to buy the test? She couldn't. Did she have to find out? Maybe she could just play dumb for the next nine months. How far could she take the denial? She could be one of those girls who gave birth in the bathroom between classes.

She walked downtown. She crossed Houston Street and headed into deepest SoHo, packed as it was with shoppers. Tourists flocked here for the supposed urban grit, but all they found was each other.

She walked all the way to Canal Street, dipped briefly into Chinatown. She passed the stairwell to a second-floor restaurant where she'd once eaten gelatinous, scary, and delicious things with Brian and two of the girls from her hall. They'd sat at a table by the big picture window and watched the snow fall that night. Now it was ninety-five degrees. That night she'd been happy and now she felt miserable. Tibby turned north again. Her legs led her, without asking, back to Duane Reade. She paced in front of the store. She couldn't go in and buy the thing, but she couldn't do anything else. Denial could be very absorbing.

She walked past a homeless woman for the third time. She reached into her bag and found a five-dollar bill. As the puffy-faced woman graciously accepted the money, Tibby wondered what had happened to this woman. Why had she ended up like this?

Tibby put her head down and walked on. Probably all started with a teenage pregnancy.

Peter was as crazy about the dirt floor as she was. Usually Bridget was attracted to people who were more solid than she, but in this case it was the feeling of finding a soul mate that really got to her.

It was Sunday. Everyone else had gone to the beach. Bridget and Peter were left at the site, working on their floor.

"You two are crazy," Alison had commented before she left. They had both nodded acceptingly.

They were more than two-thirds done. They had cleared and exposed a generous square room, a source of excitement to everyone at the site, finding two perfectly beautiful and intact late-sixth-century Attic pots and the pieces to comprise at least five more. It had turned out to be a bigger find, a more prosperous house, than even the director had imagined. Other members of the team had worked on the walls, exposing patches of plaster and the suggestion of a fresco.

"I don't know what I'll do with my life after we finish this thing," Bridget said musingly, her hands alive in the dirt.

"I know what you mean," Peter said.

"I love it. I'll miss it. I think my life's meaning will be gone."

He nodded. He didn't act like this was so strange. He was as consumed, moment by moment, as she was.

"This is a satisfying way to dig, you know?" he said. His voice was a bit lazy under the hot sun. "It's not always like this."

"I'm spoiled."

"You've had a lucky start," he agreed.

"I am lucky," she heard herself say.

"Are you?"

"Yes. In all but the important ways."

He stopped and sat back. "What does that mean?" For days he'd been disinclined to look right at her, but now he did.

She put both hands flat on her dirt floor. "My mom died when I was pretty young." It was always clarifying to get that out there. She always knew she was somewhere once she'd said it out loud. It was like her version of scent marking.

"I'm sorry."

"Yeah. Thanks." The fact of her mother's death seemed to connect to her dirt floor, but she wasn't sure how.

"That's why you don't like to talk about your family."

I don't have a family to talk about, she was going to say, but she realized that it wasn't true. She did have a family. They were all under twenty and none of them related to her by blood, but they made her who she was. They represented the best of her. "I have an unconventional family," she told him.

He left her alone with the digging for a while. She appreciated that.

"These people lived big, I think," he said, after the sun had begun to dip. "They painted their pots, they painted their walls, they made their sanctuaries and told their stories on every surface they had."

"They did, didn't they?" she said wistfully. She was starting to feel tired.

"That's why I picked this specialty, instead of something closer to home, as I probably should have done. These people left so much of themselves for us to find."

She nodded and yawned. She sat back against the wall to rest in the shade. In these long days outside, the sun had turned her skin brown and her hair a whiter yellow.

She thought of her own house, where she lived as small as possible. What could an archaeologist ever find of her? Of her mother? They told their stories nowhere. What about the old photographs, their old things? Where were they now? Had her father thrown them all away?

She crawled back on her hands and knees to where she'd left her love, the floor. She'd go slower. She'd make it last.

"Hey, what are these?" she asked. She rubbed off the dirt and passed the heavy pieces of metal into Peter's hands.

He studied them carefully. "You know what they are?"

She shook her head, even though it was a biding-time kind of question.

"I think they're loom weights. I've seen pictures, but I've never found any before." He seemed excited about them. "Make sure you record the location."

She nodded. She wiped her hands on her shorts and took the digital camera out of her pocket. She took out her Sharpie to make the label.

"You know what this makes me think?"

"No," she said.

"It gives me an idea of this room, what it was. The orientation of it, away from where we think the road was. The kind of pots we've found. Now these."

She waited patiently. She let him think and talk.

"I'm guessing it was the gynaikonitis. We'll talk to David when he gets back. He'll be thrilled with this."

"What do you call it?"

"It means the women's quarter. Big houses had them. Men didn't like to let women be seen in public or even in their own homes. Women usually stayed in a remote part of the house where they wouldn't be seen."

"Why?" Bridget asked.

"Why? Because —" He paused to think. "Because men are jealous, I guess. What else is there?" He looked at her with a certain frankness. Maybe too much frankness. "We are jealous, fallible creatures. We look in our hearts and that's what we see."

"Hello?"

There was one reason Tibby picked up the phone Sunday evening and one reason only: She was waiting for a soup delivery and she thought the security guard was calling her room to tell her to come down to get it.

"Hello? Tibby? Are you there?"

She never would have picked up if she'd known it was Lena.

"Tibby? It's me. Please talk to me. Are you there?"

At the sound of Lena's voice, Tibby felt the long-suspended tears take position. Up came the worry, the misery. Up, up, and over. Tibby tried to keep her noises to herself. She held the phone away. A tear made a dot on the thigh of the Traveling Pants. One dot and then another. Her body was shaking. A sob made it out.

"Tibby. I'm here. I'm not in a hurry. Just say something so I know you're there."

Lena's softness opened Tibby up in a way that sharpness never could. She tried to suck in enough air to make a word. Her nose was full of snot and tears. Her hand was wet from wiping it. The thing that came out was more of a gurgle than a word.

"Okay, Tib. That's good. I hear you. You don't have to say anything if you don't want."

Tibby nodded and cried. Discordantly she remembered how she once yelled at her little sister, Katherine, for nodding into the phone rather than saying yes.

"I'll just hang out here for a while," Lena said.

"Okay," Tibby gurgled.

Tibby thought of the times in middle school, before IM'ing really caught on, when they would hang around for hours on the phone playing songs for each other, watching TV shows together.

She thought of the nights she would stay on the phone with Carmen when Carmen's mom had to work late and Carmen thought she heard noises in the apartment. More than once Tibby had fallen asleep with the phone beside her on the pillow.

Tibby struggled to make some words, if only not to be

spooky. "I'm scared—I could be—I might be—" The critical word drowned in salt water. She couldn't get it out.

Lena hummed in sympathy. Most people when they sensed a crisis got despotically curious, needing to stake out the far boundary of trouble. Tibby appreciated that Lena wasn't doing that.

Lena was patient while she cried. It took a long time.

"Lenny. I'm a mess," Tibby said finally. She laughed and accidentally blew her nose at the same time. She was a mess, but even so, she felt a tiny bit closer to sane for admitting it.

"I'm coming, okay?"

"You don't need to."

"I want to. It's easy to."

"Are you sure?"

"Yeah."

Tibby sighed.

"Is there anything I can bring?" Lena asked.

Tibby thought. "Actually, there is."

"What?"

Tibby tried to clear her throat. "Do you think you could bring a pregnancy test?"

"I thought I was going to be working on sets, actually," Carmen said to the loosely assembled group drinking iced coffee together on the steps of the theater Sunday evening.

"I heard you didn't even try out for the other two plays," said Michael Skelley, a guy from the floor below her.

A certain myth was developing around Carmen's ascent,

she recognized, and she was trying to both cultivate it and set the record straight at the same time. "Only because I didn't think I was going to try out for any of them. I was watching auditions and Judy told me to read Perdita. That's kind of how it started."

Many heads nodded.

"So what's Ian O'Bannon like?" Rachel asked.

He was the well-known Irish stage actor playing Leontes.

Carmen laughed. "I'm still getting up my nerve to say something to him. At the first read-through you would have thought he'd been playing Leontes for the last twenty years."

It was strange having all these people look at her, after having almost no one look at her for months. They didn't know she was adrift in the world, standing outside the current and watching it go by. They didn't know it, maybe, because she didn't feel that way right now.

These people were excited for her. They had all made a point of congratulating her. They didn't know that she was lost and undeserving.

There was really only one person who hadn't congratulated her and did not appear to be happy for her. That one person did know she was lost and undeserving, and unfortunately, that one person happened to be her friend.

Julia had been cast in the Community Stage production. A choral bit called "Winter" at the very end of the play, wherein she was supposed to dress up like an owl.

Carmen wondered if Judy harbored a certain vitriol for girls she had seen too many times a day.

One must have a good

memory to keep the

promises one has made.

—Friedrich Nietzsche

Tibby cried into her soup when it finally came. "I'm scared I'm pregnant," she told it. The carrots and peas made no reply, but she felt better for having told them.

She fell asleep in her clothes. In the morning she changed into her pajamas. She waited for Lena in her pajamas. And then she got too impatient for the sight of Lena's face, so she waited in her pajamas in the lobby instead.

Her underwear felt damp. She registered this almost absently, but she was now too fixed on Lena's coming to go up and check.

Tibby was standing at the glass door when Lena turned the corner. Tibby went out to the sidewalk and nearly mowed her down. She wasn't sure if Lena looked more surprised by her clobbering hug or the sight of her pajamas on the bright New York City sidewalk.

Lena held her hand as they went up in the elevator.

"Can you hang on a minute?" Tibby asked when they arrived on her floor.

"Sure."

Tibby went into the bathroom and came out again less than five seconds later.

"Guess what?" She felt as though her whole body had come undone.

"What?"

"Something got here right before you." She wanted to keep from smiling, but she couldn't help it.

"Really?"

"Yeah."

"I guess we don't need this, then," Lena said happily, holding up the plastic drugstore bag.

Tibby took the box out and studied it. It had struck such terrible fear in her in the store. Now it wasn't scary. "Man, these are expensive."

"Do you think it will stay good for a decade or two?" Lena asked.

"You keep it," Tibby said. "I don't think I could." She suddenly felt so tired, as though she hadn't a bone in her body. She fell onto her bed.

"So," said Lena. She couldn't be expected to hold off forever. "Are you ready to tell the tale?"

Tibby was. She lay on her bed while Lena sat in the chair by the window. Tibby talked and Lena took out her sketchbook and drew Tibby's bare feet while she listened. Tibby rode every cramp with the pleasure of a surfer after a hurricane.

What relief. *I will remember this feeling,* she promised herself, *I really will. I won't take anything for granted again.*

On Thursday Nora began a new four-week pose. They drew numbers to pick their spots and Lena got third. She tucked herself up close. She worried through the rest of the picks about another student encroaching on her space. She felt like a bullfrog, swelling up to look as big and dangerous as possible every time a classmate came near.

Leo had the fourteenth and last pick. He set up, to Lena's astonishment, on a low stool right at Lena's knees. She thought he was kidding at first. She would have been furious had it been anyone else, but when the pose began he started broadly blocking out the figure, and she was electrified.

Lena could see the model without any obstruction. She could also see the whole of Leo's back and hands and canvas. She could watch him work. Had he any idea how much she wanted this? How much she knew she could learn from him?

She watched him breathlessly at first. And when she began to paint, she drew such intensity from his work, she felt as though she had connected her mind to his by a broadband cable and she was conducting a download.

Yes, she was impatient with her old work and her old standards. She was full of self-criticism. But she wasn't pessimistic. She hadn't known the possibilities then. Now she was seeing them right in front of her.

They worked straight through the breaks, both she and

Leo. By four o'clock Lena's arm was aching and her legs were asleep, but she didn't care. The rhythm of her painting life was marked by breakthroughs, and she'd had more today than in the course of the entire school year.

She and Leo packed up silently and walked out together. It was hard to come down. She was speechless with stimulation and gratitude and excitement. She was like a closet packed too full. If you pulled one thing out, the rest would tumble after.

He seemed to know how she was feeling. He put a hand on her arm by way of good-bye. "I'll see you Saturday," he said.

That night as Lena lay in her bed, her body and her head were achingly full. She wasn't sure under what categories to store these different feelings.

There was desire. Maybe love. Or lust. There was the excitement of the breakthrough. The visitation of the art spirit. How these things fit together she didn't know.

In rare nights of swollen-hearted yearning (as painful as they were sweet), she allowed herself to fall asleep to amorous thoughts of Kostos: the things they had done, the things she fantasized they had done, the things she imagined they would do if they ever had the chance to be together again, impossible though that was.

Tonight she let the amorous images roll. But tonight she thought of Leo.

Bridget sat in the field laboratory doing some cursory recording and paperwork. She stamped and mailed a letter to Greta and waited to use the computer. She hadn't checked her e-mail in four days. Eric was probably wondering what happened to her.

She let big parts of days, whole days, go by without thinking of him. How could she let herself do that? Well, she was occupied with her floor, of course. But more worryingly, whenever she was around Peter, she let herself forget about Eric. That was wrong.

Almost since the day Eric had left for Mexico, she had been unable to picture his face. It was puzzling. She could sort of see the outline of his head, the general shape of his hair, but the middle was a blur. Why was that? She could picture people she didn't care about. She could easily picture the fat-faced bursar at school. She could picture her roommate Aisha's older sister, who had visited once. Why couldn't she picture her own boyfriend? Why couldn't she hold Eric in her mind when he was not with her? She knew intellectually that she loved him, but she couldn't find a way to *feel* it just now.

And why not? Why couldn't she reconstruct feelings that were so powerful when she was in his presence?

Because he wasn't in her presence.

Was there something wrong with her heart? Was it failing to function? Did nothing get to her?

She thought of Peter and felt her heart kick up. No, it was working. It was working all too well.

But it was a limited heart, she realized, a literal heart that seemed to beat only in the present tense. Like desert air, it couldn't hold on to heat once the sun was gone. Like a sluice, it seemed to work in one direction—forward, not back.

What would she write to Eric? What would she say? Would he detect that her tone was forced or evasive? Was he jealous? Was he fallible?

A guy named Martin came out of the office as she stood up to go in. "Don't bother," he said. "The satellite system is down."

"No e-mail at all?" she asked.

He shook his head.

Guiltily, she felt happy to have the excuse rather than sad to have the problem. She passed Peter on her way out. "Is the hookup still down?" he asked her.

She nodded. "I hadn't realized."

"Since this morning," he said. "We're cut off, I'm afraid."

On her way through the lab she checked the mortuary section. "How's my girl Clytemnestra?" she asked the main biologist, Anton.

He seemed to enjoy the fly-by visits from Bridget. "We've got all of her. We're doing some good work."

"Like what?" she asked breezily.

"How old she was, what she ate, how she died."

"Really. How did she die?"

"In childbirth."

Bridget felt her face changing. "You can tell that?"

"Not with certainty. But it's likely."

She nodded. "How old was she?"

"Probably around nineteen or twenty."

Bridget's step was heavier as she left the lab than when she'd entered. She found herself wondering whether Clytemnestra's baby had lived. What if they found a tiny skeleton as well? Would they call the fearless Bridget over for that?

Bridget bowed her head low passing the gravesite. Clytemnestra was thousands of years old, but it occurred to Bridget that she would always be nineteen or twenty.

Oh, Lordy, Bee.

I've got a lot of stuff to tell you. I think your e-mails might not be getting through. I can't write it in this letter, but call me soon, okay?

Have fun with these here Pants and don't do anything I wouldn't do. Which should severely limit your options. But, ahem, may include one thing you might not THINK you could do but which I might in fact be capable of doing or even have done. Hint, hint.

Did I just write that sentence?

Love you,
Tibby

* * *

180

"Maybe not this weekend," Tibby found herself saying to Brian over the phone.

"I could come just for Sunday."

"I have to work on Sunday. And also, I have to get my stuff ready for classes starting on Monday."

"Oh. Right."

She could hear Brian walking around his room. She knew the tread of his shoes, the creaky sound of the floor, and the particular ratio of carpet to wood.

"I could just come for the night on Wednesday," he suggested.

Why couldn't Brian see that he should let it go for a while? Why was he so obtuse?

"Midweek isn't good," she pronounced. If he was going to be obtuse, she wasn't going to bother with intricate excuses.

"Next weekend, then."

"Maybe."

She heard him pacing. "Tibby?"

"Yeah?"

"The thing we were really worried about . . ."

He wanted her to interrupt him, to put words in the blank, but she did not oblige.

"You said before . . . you're not . . . worried anymore?"

"No. I told you. I think it's okay."

She'd been so joyful at this news on Sunday. Why couldn't she let him be a part of it? She was stingy with the bad news and even stingier with the good.

She hung up the phone and sat on her floor, wondering. Why was she annoyed at him? Her period was full force; she was no longer afraid of pregnancy. No foul, no fault. (Or how did that go?) Why couldn't she go back to feeling happy? She'd thought the single red spot on her underwear would put everything back to right, but it hadn't. Why not?

It was as though something inside Tibby had gotten turned in the wrong direction.

The uncertainty in his voice, the number of times he called, his desperate desire for reassurance. Why did this bother her so much?

But strangely, this question she meant to ask was undermined by a deeper question she didn't mean to ask: Why hadn't it bothered her before?

Leo appeared, as a good model should, at exactly the designated hour of nine o'clock.

Lena opened the door to her tiny dorm room and let him in. She'd been sitting on her bed in her quiet room for the preceding twenty minutes, hands sweating, mind blank.

She could not hide her nervousness. There was no point.

"You ready?" he asked. Was his voice pitched slightly higher than usual?

"I think so," she squeaked. She gestured toward her French easel, upon which was perched her freshly gessoed eighteen-by-twenty-four-inch canvas. Her palette was ready. Her paints were assembled.

With him inside it, her room was almost comically small.

How, exactly, was this going to work? How could she get far enough away to see more than three inches of his rib cage? She hadn't thought this through very well. (She couldn't even manage to think about it.)

"Should I be . . . on the bed?" he asked. He was uncertain too. His uncertainty made her both more terrified and slightly more in control. Somebody had to steer the ship.

"I thought . . . yes. Only—"

"Yeah, you can't exactly—"

"Yeah, it's pretty close."

"What if I . . ."

He tried lying across the bed a few different ways, clothes blessedly on. Each time she found herself staring directly, and at close range, into his crotch.

Somewhere deep inside, Lena knew this was funny, but so panicked was she, she could no more access a laugh than if she were in the middle of a plane crash.

He seemed to recognize this. He sat up. "What about a seated pose?" he said.

He tried a few of those.

Lena backed up as far as she could. With his help she moved her dresser and sat with her back pressed against the wall. She shook her head. "I think this only works if we cut a hole in the wall and I paint you from Dana Trower's room."

He shrugged. "Dana might not go for it."

Was it too soon to give up? They'd given it the old summer-school try. Maybe they could just go have another iced coffee.

"I think I know the answer," he said.

Iced coffee? She cleared her throat. "What's that?"

"Foreshortening."

"Yeah?"

He dragged her bed to the end of the room. "I'll show you."

He positioned her easel in the corner. Then he lay on the bed, his head closest to her, his feet farthest away.

She stood at her easel and looked at him lying there. It was a strange angle. She would have to paint his shoulder and his head very big and his feet very small. His shoulder was like giant Greenland in one of those projected world maps, and his feet were way down there, little, like the Cape of Good Hope. But then again, his private areas would be somewhat less apparent in this pose. Like maybe Ecuador.

This was about as good as could be hoped for.

"I think this will work," she said.

"Okay. Good."

"Okay."

"Okay, so I'll just . . ."

"Okay." She looked down at her paints, her cheeks flaming. She was such a baby. What would Bee say?

He sat up and pulled his T-shirt over his head. She kept her head down. "I've never done this before. It's kind of strange."

She couldn't even make a noise come out.

"It seems so ordinary for the models in the studio, you know?"

She nodded, still staring at her cadmium red.

"I mean, it's just a pose. It's for a painting." He talked himself through the unbuttoning and removal of his jeans.

"Yeah," she attempted to say, but it came up more phlegm than word.

Was he really going to take off his underwear? Arg. She was such a baby.

"Hey. It's not like there's something else going on here. . . ." His voice faded uncertainly. He tripped out of his underwear and was lying on the bed in under one second.

How could she look? How could she concentrate on painting?

He didn't think there was anything going on here? She thought there was something going on here!

Her face was sweating. Her hands were sweating and also shaking. She tried to hold the brush. If she lifted the brush, he would see how badly her hand was shaking.

He said there wasn't anything else going on here. Hey. What was that supposed to mean?

"All set," he said. "Can you time the pose?"

No. She couldn't. She couldn't do anything. She couldn't even make her eyeballs move in their sockets.

"Are you okay?" he asked. She registered that his voice was actually quite sweet.

She tried to shift her weight. "I'm Greek," she said finally. Her catchall. For garlic, for shame.

"Oh." There was some understanding in the way he said it. "Can you try to think of me as a regular model in class?"

She made her eyes shift upward slowly. His shoulder,

his face. His face was flushed, like hers, though not sweating as profusely. Their eyes met for a moment, which was not what she intended.

He didn't think there was anything else going on here?

This was not how she felt when Nora posed. This was not how she felt when Marvin posed. Not even a twenty-millionth of this.

Her indignation kept her eyes up, though her pupils did not focus. She clamped her fingers around her brush and aimed it at the canvas. It was not a good technique. She made some clumsy strokes.

Too flustered to look at her canvas, she looked at him. Frying pan to fire. She looked down his body, down all the golden skin. Oh, my. She saw what was there. How could she not? It wasn't Ecuador. It was more Brazil.

She looked away quickly. There was too something else going on here.

She let her brush rest on the palette.

"Let's take a break," he said.

And if the blind lead the blind, both shall fall into the ditch.

—Matthew 15:14

"You'd be so lean, that blasts of January
Would blow you through and through.—Now, my fair'st
    friend,
I would I had some flowers o' the spring, that might
Become your time of day—"

Carmen looked up, caught her breath.
    In spite of the fact that Polixenes was played by an actor Carmen had seen in at least four movies, he bore an almost uncanny resemblance to her uncle Hal. As she stood across from him, she tried to pretend he was Uncle Hal, because otherwise she felt too nervous. He nodded at her to keep going.

"That wear upon your virgin branches yet
Your maidenheads growing:—O Proserpina,

For the flowers now, that, frighted, thou lett'st fall
From Dis's waggon!"

She was addressing herself now to Florizel, her supposed love interest. He was at least ten years older than she, wore cakey makeup, and seemed frankly more interested in Polixenes.

She was relieved when they finally got to take a break. They were now in rehearsals almost ten hours a day and costume fittings at other times.

She saw Leontes where he'd been watching from the side of the stage and nervously attempted to swing wide around him. He was so magnificent that she had not yet drawn up the courage to say a word to him that wasn't one of Perdita's.

The swing did not work. He was looking directly at her.

"Carmen, that was absolutely lovely," he said to her as she scuttled along like a baby turtle racing for the sea.

"Thank you," she squeaked in response, perspiring from every one of her pores.

But outside, she couldn't keep down her joy. "Lovely," he had said. "Absolutely lovely."

"Absolutely lovely." That was what he said. She laughed to nobody. The armpits of her T-shirt were soaked through in a way that was not absolutely lovely.

It was astounding to her. It really was. She had never in her life felt like she was naturally gifted at anything. In the past she had felt like she'd worked, willed, begged, bossed, or stolen everything she'd ever gotten.

She was good at math because she spent twice as many

hours on it as the people who weren't. She scored well on her SATs because she studied vocabulary lists and took practice tests every week for two years. She got an A in physics because she sat to the right of Brian Jervis, an overachieving lefty who never covered his test paper.

And now here she was, managing with little discernable effort to be absolutely lovely.

The joy of it. The loveliness.

Prince Mamillius came out the side door. When he saw her he sat down next to her. She couldn't remember his actual name. Though he was technically her brother in the play, he died before she was born, so they didn't share the stage.

"How's it going?" he asked.

When he was the prince, he spoke in pristine Shakespearean English, but when he wasn't, she was amused to hear, his accent was more like central New Jersey.

"Good," she said. He had a tattoo of a badger on his ankle. He was actually very cute.

"Nice flowers," he said.

Carmen lifted her hand to her ear. Andrew Kerr had asked her to wear flowers in her hair during the romancing scene to prepare for her elaborate costume as Flora. "Oh." She felt stupid, and then she decided she didn't.

He leaned over, very close to her, and smelled them. "Yum," he said. She could feel his breath on her hair.

"Can I get you a lemonade?" he asked, standing up again. He was a jumpy sort of person.

She thought of saying no, but then she said yes. "I'd love that," she said.

He raised his eyebrows at her before he turned to walk away. She realized in slow motion that Prince Mamillius, her own brother, had most likely just flirted with her.

Three hours later, Lena had squished several dollars' worth of paint around on a perfectly well-made canvas. She had wasted both, as well as Leo's time. Her painting wasn't even a painting. Her sister, Effie, would have made a better painting.

For the third hour, Lena's cheeks smoldered deep purple. There was no way she could let him look at her so-called painting.

"Let's call it quits for the day," she said defeatedly.

"Are you sure?" He didn't sound opposed.

"Yeah."

He was undeniably awkward too. "Sorry I'm not a better model."

"No. No, you're fine. It's just."

She washed her brushes in the bathroom while he got dressed. When she came back they sat side by side on her bed.

"That didn't go quite as well as I'd hoped," he said.

She breathed out in relief. That he was dressed. That she wasn't trying to hold a paintbrush.

"It's my fault," she said.

"No, it's not."

They were quiet for a while.

"Are you a virgin?" he asked.

She looked at him in surprise.

"Sorry. That's getting kind of personal, I know. Don't answer if you don't want."

She didn't want to answer at first. But his face was nice. He looked at her intently. He wore his own version of disarray, and his was beautiful.

"That's okay. God. Is it so obvious?"

"No. And anyway, it's nothing to be sorry for."

He put his hand over her hand. Not holding hers, quite, just lying there.

After he left, Lena fell into her bed in a heap of exhaustion and didn't move for an hour. Somewhere in the back of her mind pressed the knowledge that in the pose-trading bargain, today was the easy part.

Bridget had spent all day Saturday touring Halicarnassus, now a city called Bodrum. In the van she'd nearly made herself sick to her stomach reading books that Peter had lent her, gobbling up information spanning the time from the first settlements of the Greeks in Asia Minor all the way to the Persian invasion that nearly destroyed them.

Once inside the ruins of the city, she'd darted around to every column, every path, every step of the ancient stadium. She'd loved it, but she was happy to get back to the site, where a package from Tibby that contained the Traveling Pants was waiting for her, as was her floor.

Now she was sitting on the floor in her Pants, glad to think that they would forever harbor a few particles of this old dirt. She savored her time with both of them. And with

Peter, too. The fact that it was just her and Peter, and the satellite was still down, made her feel that much more insulated from the regular world.

There were only a few feet left to clear. They were both going slowly now.

"What time is it?" he asked. The sun had set hours before, and they'd spent a long, meditative stretch of quiet digging and sorting.

"I don't know. Do you want me to find out?"

He nodded. "Would you?"

She stood up.

"Hey, I like your pants," he said. It was like him to notice.

She went closer to him and stood in the light so he could see. "These belong to the unconventional family I mentioned."

He nodded, studying some of the pictures and inscriptions on the front. Then he grabbed her by a belt loop and slowly rotated her to look at the rest.

You are looking at my Pants, she told him silently, but she also suspected that he was looking at the shape of her underneath.

Self-consciously she climbed out of the room by the makeshift wooden stairs and went to the embankment party, which was just winding down. "Does anybody have the time?"

Darius had a watch. "Twelve-forty," he told her.

She went back down into the room to tell Peter.

"Guess what?" he said.

"What?"

"I'm thirty."

"Right now?"

"Forty minutes ago."

"No way! Happy birthday! That's a big one."

"Thanks." He sat back against the wall. He dusted off his hands. Suddenly he looked suspicious. "If you tell anyone I'll kill you."

"That would be kind of an overreaction."

He laughed. "You're right. But don't anyway, okay?"

"Okay." It seemed perhaps too natural that he should be sharing his secrets with her. She studied his face. Thirty didn't seem very old on him now that she knew him.

"You've got to have a cake or something, don't you?"

"I think I'll manage without it. I have a childhood fear of being sung to by strangers."

"Interesting."

"Yeah. Anyway, I'm happy to become thirty with just the floor." He stopped and looked at her. "And you."

She tried to shrug it off, but her face burned. "Thanks. I'm honored." She felt his mood wavering between heavy and light. She wasn't sure how to read him.

"Me too," he said. They didn't need to pretend they hadn't become close these weeks. That was undeniable.

She had an idea. "Okay, then. Hold on a minute."

The kitchen area of the big tent was empty, but she found a flashlight and, with the help of that, a half tray of baklava, a votive candle, and a bottle of wine. She found matches and two plastic cups and took the stash back to Peter.

Sitting across from him on their smooth floor, she poured two cups of wine. She lit the candle and set it next to the baklava. "I don't think you want me to sing," she said. "But happy birthday, my friend." She said it seriously and she meant it. It was a big deal, a big day. She glanced down at the floor as he blew out his candle and made his wish.

Because he was her friend and she felt solely responsible for bringing him into a new decade of his life, she lifted her cup to tap his and at the same time she leaned in. She wasn't sure what she meant by it. Maybe she thought she'd hug him or kiss his cheek, the way she did with lots of people.

But he misinterpreted her closeness, or maybe she did. Her cheek pressed against his cheek and then her mouth pressed against his cheek. And then he turned, whether to get closer or farther away she couldn't be sure. But the effect of it, accidentally or on purpose, was that her mouth touched his mouth.

The first touch was bumbling and awkward. The second touch was almost certainly on purpose. She felt herself pulled into the heat and smell of him. She touched his face, which you don't do with lots of people. She kissed him purposefully and she felt his purposeful hand on the back of her neck.

"That was a happy birthday kiss," she said, forcing herself to pull away. She was dizzy. She was not quite in her mind. She needed to keep alive the possibility of turning back. Did he need that too?

He stood up quickly and she followed. "Do you want to walk?" he asked her.

They both needed that. A walk, a breeze.

They walked toward the sea, up to the top of the hill and over it to a nice perch of soft brown summer grass laid out under a trillion stars.

She had the urge to run all the way down to the water and jump into it and swim for another shore. She had the urge to kiss Peter again, to throw herself against him and bury her face in his neck.

She was still wearing a filthy white tank top from the morning. She might have been cold but she couldn't feel it.

Peter took her hand in his and put them together on his thigh. "Bee."

"Yes."

"I have to confess to a very monstrous addiction to you." He said it slowly and with some deliberation. "I was hoping it wouldn't get to this, but I'm also hoping it might help to say it out loud."

She rested her cheek on her hand, looking across at him. "I have that kind of addiction too," she said.

"To the floor."

"To the floor. To you."

"To me?"

"To you." It did feel good to say it. *But will it really help?*

"I shouldn't be happy about that," he said, appearing to defy his words as he said them.

"No. And I shouldn't either."

She felt her hair fluttering in the light wind, tickling his arm, working its magic. She wasn't sure she wanted more magic right now.

"It's very tricky . . . ," he began slowly, his speech punctuated by consideration and a few uneasy breaths, "not to feel like I'm falling in love with you now. It's such a strong feeling and a good feeling having you right here like this. Looking at you, it's hard to keep in my mind the reasons why I can't."

"Do you want to talk about them?"

He looked genuinely unhappy for a moment. "No."

She looked at him with the hint of a challenge in her eyes. "Then what do you want?"

The reckless happiness was creeping back. He couldn't help himself. He was like her. He couldn't keep it down. "Do you really want to know?"

She nodded, knowing she shouldn't. She shouldn't have asked. She shouldn't want to know.

"Here's what I want to do. I want to pull you on top of me and roll you down this hill. Then I want to take off your clothes and kiss every part of you. And then I want to make passionate love to you on the grass right there." He pointed to a place near the bottom of the hill. "And then I want to fall asleep holding you. And then I want to wake up when the sun is rising and do it all again."

She kept her eyes closed for a minute. These were dangerous places they were passing through. How could she not picture it and feel it and want it the way he said it?

"And what will you do?" she asked, her voice hardly above a whisper.

She could practically see the opposing forces duking it out in his head. She wasn't sure which side was winning or even which side she was rooting for.

A weariness came into his eyes, giving her a clue. "We'll kiss, because it's my thirtieth birthday and it's what I've been wishing for. And then I'll walk you to your cabin and say goodnight."

"Okay," she said, happy and sad.

He did kiss her. He rolled her over onto the grass and kissed her passionately. His hands reached under her shirt to press against her naked back. She felt the strength of his longing and it made her woozy.

She sat up before they could be sucked into the next phase of what he wanted.

They held hands on the way back to camp. He kissed her on the cheek at the entrance to her cabin.

"You better get out of here before this thing goes the other way," he whispered in her ear. "You know, the rolling-down-the-hill way."

She nodded against his cheek. "Happy birthday, mister," she said out of the side of her mouth as if she were Mae West.

And so she lay on her crappy metal cot in a cloud of desire. But even in her cloud she perceived a buffeting sensation, a brooding feeling of discomfort beneath her.

They had withstood this night for the most part, but what about the next one and the one after that?

She had the taste of him now. She had the feel of his

body. They had said things you couldn't forget and couldn't take back. All the ordinary boundaries between them lay in ruins. What was going to keep them apart now? She feared they had both seen the place where they could have turned back and, knowingly, they had passed it by.

Experience is a hard
teacher because she gives
the test first.
the lesson afterward.
−Vernon Law

Leo looked surprised to see Lena at the door of his loft on Sunday morning. She was surprised to be there.

"I wasn't sure you'd come," he said.

"I wasn't either."

"I'm glad you did," he added. He did look happy, and also uncertain. He was looking at her in a different way.

"I'm nervous," she said honestly. "But fair is fair."

His eyes on her were different. She couldn't say why. "You are fair," he said. "But you don't have to do it."

She smiled nervously. "Thanks."

"Do you want a cup of coffee?"

"Sure." She considered the state of her nervous system. "Maybe tea," she mumbled, following him into the kitchen.

He put the kettle on and sat down. Northern light—artists' light—fell all around them from the high windows.

"Where's your mom?" Lena asked.

"She volunteers all day at our church," Leo said. "I thought the privacy might make it easier."

She nodded.

"But I understand if you don't want to."

"Okay."

She sat and thought.

He looked at her, his elbow resting on the table, his chin in his hand. When she saw him looking, he smiled. She smiled back.

She thought of drinking her tea and going back home. She thought of staying here and taking off her clothes and letting Leo paint her. The second alternative didn't seem possible, but in a strange way, neither did the first. She had the odd sense of pushing off the edge into unknown territory. She had already let her mind travel. There were possibilities now. It wasn't enough to go back and forget. She wasn't the forgetting type.

"I think we should try it," she said.

"You do?"

"Do you?"

"I do."

"So let's."

"If you're uncomfortable, we'll stop."

She shrugged with a laugh. "I will be uncomfortable. We'd have to stop before we start." She breathed deep. "But I think we should try it anyway."

Leo's bedroom was spacious and skylit. He had dragged a

small ruby-colored couch into the center and draped a pale yellow sheet over it. His easel was folded in the corner.

"I was thinking of here," he said a bit sheepishly. She could tell he'd made the effort to set it up more like a painting class, not just put her in his bed. "We could do it somewhere else, though."

The colors glowed. The light dusted over the drapery in a beautiful way. She could almost see the painting. "No. This is good."

He disappeared for a moment and came back with a robe, probably his mother's. He handed it to her with a question on his face. *Do you really want to do this?* "I really won't be upset with you if you don't," he said.

"I think I might be upset with me," she said.

He nodded. "It's just a painting."

It wasn't just a painting for her. She needed to do it anyway.

"I'll give you some privacy," he said.

"Not for long," she joked nervously. It was like when the doctor left the room as you undressed and dressed again. As if the nakedness weren't embarrassing if you could transition into it alone.

She took off her clothes quickly, before she could think about it and stop. Tank top and loose yoga pants and flip-flops in a pile on the floor. She was too nervous to fold them. She had dressed herself like she'd observed the models did—loose clothes for easy on and easy off. No weird red marks from a tight waistband or pinching bra strap.

She'd thought to shave her stubbly parts so she was smooth and unremarkable.

She hurriedly propelled herself into the robe. To what end? she wondered. She just had to get right back out of it. But models always had the robe. Maybe it could be like Superman's telephone booth. She'd go into the robe a terrified and prudish virgin and come out of it a seasoned artist's model.

She took the robe off. She sat on the couch. She lay on the couch. She rearranged herself on the couch. Leo knocked on the door. "You ready?"

Every one of her muscles contracted. She felt her shoulders, neck, and head fuse into one ungraceful mass. Apparently she had come out of the robe the same way she had gone in.

"Ready," she whimpered.

"Lena?"

"Ready," she said a little louder. This had the quality of a bedroom farce. She wished she could find it funny.

He was nervous too. He didn't want to affront or embarrass her by looking too quickly or too much. He occupied himself with his easel as though there weren't a naked girl in the room. She said some things about how it was hot out, also pretending there wasn't a naked girl in the room.

"Okay, my friend," he said. His paintbrush was poised in his hand. He was ready to work. He looked at her through his painter's eyes.

"Okay," she breathed. This "my friend" business might

be doing it for him, she thought sourly, but it wasn't doing it for her.

He moved the easel to the left. He pushed it a couple of feet closer to her. He came out from behind it. "Head up a little," he said, coming closer.

She did.

"Perfect." He came closer still. He was looking now. "Okay, hand more like this." He did it with his own hand rather than touch hers.

She obliged. She wished she could make her muscles soften a little.

"Beautiful," he said. He kept studying her. "Legs a little . . . looser."

She let out a nervous laugh. "Yeah, right."

He laughed too, but vaguely. She could tell he was starting to really think about painting now. Why hadn't she been able to do that when it had been her turn to paint?

"Okay. Wow." He went back to his canvas. He raised his eyebrows. She could tell he was excited. He was excited about his painting.

Bridget was crouched over her cereal bowl the next morning groggily spooning in the Frosted Flakes when she noticed the unfamiliar car pulling into the makeshift parking area. She didn't make anything of it at first. Her mind was too full and unkempt as it was.

She dimly registered the slams of a few car doors and some stir at the other end of the tent. Slowly it made its way to her.

"Have you seen Peter?" Karina asked her.

She blinked and swallowed her mouthful of cereal. "Not this morning," she said. Something about the question started the slow tick of alarm. At the far end of the tent an unfamiliar woman was talking to Alison. Then into Bridget's view bounced a very small person, a little girl with a messy ponytail that had migrated to the side of her head. It was unusual to see a child here.

None of the pieces stuck together until she saw Alison marching toward her looking agitated, which doubled for excited in the case of Alison. "Do you know where Peter is? His wife and kids are here to surprise him."

His wife and kids. They were here to surprise him. The ticking accelerated into a wild knocking. His wife and kids had popped out of their theoretical ether and appeared here. To surprise him.

For his birthday, Bridget realized, her thoughts bumping and scraping along. His secret birthday, which she had somehow believed belonged to her. It did not belong to her, she acknowledged with a messy ache in her chest. It belonged to them.

Peter's wife and kids were far enough away and backed by flooding sunlight, so she couldn't really see them.

"No. I don't know where he is," she said robotically. Suddenly she felt the shame of Eve. Why did everybody keep asking her? What did they know? What did they suspect? She wished she hadn't stayed up late all these nights. She found herself wanting to be sure that her cabinmates knew she'd woken up among them every morning.

How would his wife feel with everyone seeking information about her husband's whereabouts from the tired blond girl with the kissed lips and the starry expression? She felt the urge to defend herself, but to whom?

She was stuck there in her chair, midchew, unable to swallow her cereal or spit it out, when she heard Peter's voice somewhere behind her. She realized she needed to get out of there before this reunion took place. For her sake, but even more for Peter's. She didn't want him to see her there. She crouched lower. She momentarily considered crawling under the table and hiding.

He had a wife. A *wife*. Theoretical and now real, with dark brown hair and a canvas bag over her shoulder. A wife like you had in a real family. Kids like you had in a real family. Kids who jumped around and needed things.

In her mind she switched from identifying with the wife to identifying with the daughter. A daughter like she was a daughter. A person with wishes and disappointments of her own.

These were dangerous places indeed.

Tibby finally let Brian come that Sunday, but not for the reasons he hoped.

She intercepted him in the lobby. It would be worse if he came up to her room.

"It's pretty nice out. You feel like taking a walk?" he asked her gamely, innocently.

She used to adore his innocence. Now she wondered about him. Was he a bit stupid? No, not stupid, really. She didn't mean that. He had a high IQ and all. But was he kind of like an idiot savant?

"Yes," she said dishonestly.

Maybe, Meta-Tibby suggested, she liked his innocence better when her own heart wasn't so black.

They didn't walk far. She turned on him in the middle of Astor Place.

"Brian, I think we should take a break," she said. That was the phrase she had decided upon.

He looked at her, his head cocked like a Labrador retriever's. "What do you mean?"

"I mean, I think we shouldn't see each other for a while."

"You are saying that . . ."

The sadness and surprise was beginning to wear through his trusting expression, but she couldn't feel anything for him. She saw it, but it didn't go past her eyes. There were times in her life when she felt his pain more acutely than he did. Why not now?

"But why?" he asked.

"Because. Because . . ." This was such an obvious question and she hadn't thought up an answer for it. "I just think . . . because of the long distance and everything . . ."

"I don't mind coming up here," he said quickly.

She glared at him. *Just protect yourself and go away, would you?* She felt like shouting at him. *Get mad at me. Call me a bitch. Walk away from me.*

"I don't want you to," she said flatly. "I want to be by myself for a while. I can't even explain it very well."

He was processing. His T-shirt blew against his body. He looked thin.

Brian didn't confine himself to the mirror dance. He did what he did, he chose what he chose in the bravest possible way. She used to love this about him. But now the best thing had turned into the worst thing. She thought he rejected the dance as small-minded and fearful, but now she wondered if he even knew it. Was it rejection or total ignorance? Why, for once, couldn't he just follow her lead?

There is no such thing as too much love. That was what a doe-eyed and slightly creepy friend of her mother's had once said to Tibby, seemingly out of the blue. *Well, yeah, there is*, Tibby thought now.

"Is it because of—" he began tentatively.

"I don't even know what it's because of," she snapped. "I just know that I don't want to keep going like this."

He looked up and then he looked down. He watched people cross Lafayette Street. He considered the banner snapping over the entrance to the Public Theater. Tibby was worried he would cry, but he didn't.

"You don't want me to come up and see you anymore," he said.

"Not really. No."

"You don't want me to call you?"

"No."

Had Brian ever taken a hint? Had he always required a total clubbing over the head to make him comprehend even the most obvious point?

Suddenly she felt an insidious suspicion. She saw this

version of Brian in the eyes of the world, and she saw herself, too. Did people think he was basically a moron? Did they laugh at her for being with him?

Tibby hated herself for this cruelly disloyal thought. But who in the world has a brain she can force to think only the acceptable things?

Do I hate him? she wondered about herself. *Did I ever really love him?*

On that fateful night they'd had sex, it seemed to her that she'd fallen asleep one person and woken up another. She couldn't remember the hows and whys of who she used to be. It was bewildering. Like hypnosis or a magic spell or a dream that had broken on her waking.

"Then we should say good-bye," he said.

Her head shot up. She could see by his face he understood now. She could see it in his eyes. They were no less hurt, but they had stopped questioning her.

"Y-yes. I—I guess," she stammered. If anything, he had gotten ahead of her.

She hadn't pictured him storming away, though she might have wanted that. But neither had she figured on his sticking around for a proper eye-to-eye good-bye.

"Good-bye, Tibby." He wasn't angry. He wasn't hopeful. What was he?

"Bye." Stiffly she leaned in to kiss his cheek. It felt wrong, and midway through she wished she hadn't done it.

He turned and he walked toward the subway, carrying his worn red duffel bag over his shoulder. She watched him, but he didn't turn back to look.

He walked in a way that struck her as resolute, and she recognized that she was the one left standing alone and confused.

She realized all at once the deeper thing that bothered her, the thing that made him not just irritating but intolerable: how he kept loving her blindly when she deserved it so little.

oh, darling, let your body in,

let it tie you in,

in comfort.

—Anne Sexton

Lena realized a strange and comforting fact of life: You could get used to almost anything. You could even get used to lying naked on a ruby-colored couch under the gaze of a young man you hardly knew while he painted you. You could do that even if you happened to be a Greek virgin from a conservative family whose father would die if he knew.

For the first hour, Lena agonized.

Sometime in the second hour, her muscles began to unkink, one at a time.

In the third hour, something else happened. Lena began to watch Leo. She watched him paint. She watched him watch her. She saw how he looked at her different parts. She kept track of which part he was working on, feeling a thrill in her hip when he painted that and along her thigh when he got there.

As much as she ordinarily dreaded being looked at, this

felt different. It was a different way of looking. He looked at her and through her at the same time. He only held any one image long enough to get it onto his canvas. It was like water through a sieve.

His intensity built and she began to relax. His relationship, she realized, was with his painting. He was relating to his version of her more than to the actual her. It freed her mind to wander all around the apartment. Were all relationships this way, to some extent? Whether or not they involved any artistic representation?

She liked the way the diffuse sun felt on her skin. She began to like the way his eyes felt on her skin as she became free to wander.

He put on music. It was Bach, he said. The only instrument was a cello.

In the fourth hour, he looked at her face at a moment when she was looking back. They were both surprised at first and looked away. Then, at the same moment, they both looked back. He stopped painting. He lost his way. He looked confused and then found his way back.

In the fifth hour, she stopped taking breaks. She was under a spell. She was languorous. Leo was also under a spell. They were under different spells.

In the sixth hour, she thought about him touching her. The blood that came to her cheeks was a different blood. It came for a different reason.

He put on more Bach. It was music for solo violin this time. It sounded raggedly romantic to her.

He was painting her face. "Eyes up," he said. She looked up. "I mean at me," he clarified.

Was that really what he meant? She looked at him.

And for the next hour, he looked at her and she looked back. And like in a staring contest, the stakes seemed to rise and rise until it was almost unbearable. But neither of them looked away.

When he finally put down his brush, his cheeks were as flushed as hers. He was as breathless as she. They were under the same spell.

He came over to her, still not breaking eye contact. He put his hand lightly on her rib cage and leaned down and kissed her.

In the past when Bee was overwhelmed or depressed she took to her bed. But this was too awful even for her bed. This was a more active misery, a hunt-you-down-and-find-you kind of pain. In her bed she'd be a sitting, lying duck.

Barefoot, she walked from the dining tent. Once in the clear, she spit her mush of Frosted Flakes into the grass. She was afraid she might throw up what was in her stomach as well.

She was so grateful she had left the Pants on her cot. She didn't want them to see her like this.

She walked from the camp and kept going toward the sun. She would just keep going. If you set out for the east, you could walk practically forever. To India, China.

She walked and walked and her feet grew sore. How sore they would be when they got to China.

Sometime later the sun passed over her head and she realized she was walking away from it now. She didn't want to walk away from it, but if she walked with it, she would have to turn back around, and she couldn't turn around. She shivered. Was it cold in China?

She felt like a reptile, relying on the sun to warm her blood. She didn't feel the capacity to generate her own warmth.

She had known almost from the beginning that Peter was married and had children. There had been nothing new divulged this morning. That wife and those children were no more real now than they'd ever been. But now she'd seen them. That was what destroyed her peace.

Out of sight, out of mind. How could she allow that of herself? That was for people with amnesia and brain damage. That was for newts and frogs. What was wrong with her? Why couldn't she hold things in her mind? There was no comfort to be taken from her inability, no excuse.

This was a different game she was playing. Not a playground challenge or a warm-up or a scrimmage. It was real and it counted. Peter was an adult. She was an adult. They had real lives to make or lose.

She could flit around and show off in front of the married man. She could kiss that married man and pretend it was all big, mischievous fun. But it wasn't.

As she walked she shuddered. It was time to grow up. She looked ahead of her and saw the crest of a hill. That crest stood for growing up, she decided as she willfully crossed it.

She stood up her straightest, to her full woman's height of five feet and ten and a half inches. If she didn't take her life seriously, who would? She was becoming the person she'd be for her whole life. Each thing she chose contributed to that person. She didn't want to be like this.

Carmen liked being in the theater. Even the longest, crankiest late-night rehearsal was preferable to being in her dorm room. Andrew Kerr could take her down with a look, but even at his scariest he was friendlier than her roommate.

Carmen had transformed from invisible to visible in the eyes of everyone on campus except for one person. For two long weeks, even though they shared a small room and slept within five feet of each other, Julia had acted like Carmen wasn't there.

Which was why it surprised Carmen in the third week of rehearsals when Julia turned to her and said, "How's the play going?"

Carmen was pulling off her socks at the moment it happened, exhausted but also excited at having tried on her costume for the first time.

"It's going pretty well. At least, I hope so."

"How is it working with Ian O'Bannon?" Julia asked.

She asked this like they'd been having friendly chats night and day. Carmen was scared to believe it was actually happening.

"He's . . . I don't even know what he is. Every day I think I can't be more amazed and then I am."

"Wow. Lucky you, you get to work with him."

Carmen sifted through these words, girding herself for jeering or sarcasm, but she didn't hear it.

"It is really lucky," Carmen said warily.

"It's like . . . the experience of a lifetime," Julia said.

Again Carmen weighed these words, studied Julia's face. Julia's face, which had seemed so beautiful and commanding at one time and now seemed furtive. The qualities Carmen had most admired in her seemed extreme now. She was too thin, too poised, too careful.

"I think it is," Carmen said.

Carmen fell asleep that night wondering what had brought about the thaw, scared to trust it, but more than anything, grateful that it had happened.

So that when she woke up the next morning, she was still doubtful, though still hopeful.

"You should wear those green pants. They look really good on you," Julia said when Carmen was rummaging through her drawer.

Carmen turned. "You think so?"

"Yeah."

"Thanks." Carmen put on the green pants even though she didn't think they looked so good.

"What are you rehearsing today?" Julia asked.

Carmen counseled herself to take the friendliness at face value and just be glad for it. "I think it'll be Leontes going bonkers for the first part. Perdita doesn't even come in until act four, scene four, but Andrew wants me to watch. 'Watch and absorb,' he always says, and he shakes his fingers over my head. He thinks that's entertaining for some reason."

"He's kind of an oddball, isn't he?" Julia said.

"He is," Carmen said, though she suddenly felt protective of his oddness. "I have no experience or anything, but I think he's a good director."

Julia could easily have said something cutting then, but she didn't. "He's got a huge reputation," she said.

"Does he?"

"Oh, yeah."

"Huh." This was enough pleasant conversation to last Carmen for the week, but Julia kept going.

"I can read with you if you ever want some extra practice," she said.

Carmen looked at her carefully. "That's nice. Thanks. I'll let you know."

"Seriously, any time," Julia said. "My part in *Love's Labour's* is not exactly consuming, you know?"

Carmen didn't want to be caught agreeing. "You have the last word, though. That's a big deal."

"As an owl."

"Well."

Julia's expression was openly rueful. "R.K., our director, asked me if I'd give a thought to helping with sets during my downtime."

Carmen tried to keep her expression neutral. "What did you say?"

"I said that sets really aren't my thing."

Carmabelle: Wow, Leo's black?

LennyK162: Yeah. Half, anyway.

Carmabelle: You really are trying to kill your father.

LennyK162: Pretty much any color boyfriend would do it.

Carmabelle: Does Leo identify more with his black side or his white side?

LennyK162: What?

Carmabelle: I'm a woman of color. I'm allowed to ask these things.

LennyK162: I still don't know what you're talking about.

Carmabelle: Okay, does he listen to U2?

Bridget ended up that evening not in China, but on her dirt floor with a bad sunburn stinging her shoulders.

She was glad to have her floor again. She had worried that the joy of her floor somehow depended on Peter, but she now realized it didn't. It was her own separate joy and could not be taken away.

She was glad to hear that Peter had gone with his family into town for dinner. She wanted to skip dinner, but she didn't want to skip it on his account.

She continued this busy overthinking, feeling it an annoying by-product of adulthood. Were people in her work team treating her too carefully?

At least her hands still knew how to seek out the floor. She was down to the final couple of feet left over from last night. She couldn't draw it out much longer.

She dug and sifted and sorted. At the final edge, her finger touched something hard. She was used to that by now. She assumed it was a piece of terra-cotta, like so many of the other bits were. She shook if off and held it up, but the sunlight was too faded to help. She felt it between her fingers. It was tiny. It wasn't porous like clay. It wasn't heavy like metal.

She recorded its provenience and hopped up the stairs to find a flashlight. Holding the little thing under the light, she felt her heart begin to thump.

She took it to the lab, glad that Anton was working late.

"What've you got?" he asked her.

She handed it to him. "I think it's a tooth." She was shaken by it. She felt a shaky chill in her abdomen.

He looked at it. He held it under magnification. "You're right."

"A baby tooth."

"It certainly is."

"Can you tell who it belonged to? I mean a boy or a girl?"

He shook his head. "You can't discern gender from any of a child's bones. Before puberty, boy skeletons and girl skeletons are exactly the same."

Why was Anton looking so jovial about this when she felt sickened by it?

"I found it in the house," she said. "In the new room." Her breathing was moist and a little bit ragged. "I expect to find this kind of stuff in mortuary, but not in the house." She really did not want to cry.

Anton looked at her carefully. "Bridget, it wasn't in mortuary because the kid didn't die."

"It didn't?"

"Or I should say, its death was not related to this tooth."

"It wasn't?"

"No." Anton smiled, apparently wanting to cajole her out of her somber face. "The tooth fell out, Bridget. It got lost on the floor. Maybe the kid's mother saved it."

Bridget was still nodding as she walked back to her floor, almost wanting to cry with relief. This person, whoever he or she was, had long, long since died. But the person hadn't died with a baby tooth. The little tooth did not represent death. It represented growing up.

I have drunk, and seen the spider.

—William Shakespeare

"Do you miss him?" Carmen asked.

"I don't think so. I'm not sure," Tibby said, holding the phone with her shoulder and picking her big toenail. Some of the summer students were crowded around a portable video game in the hall. It was too noisy for a serious conversation.

"You're not sure?"

"No. I don't know. I was pretty sure of needing to break up with him. I don't want to see him, but I do sometimes think about whether he's going to call or something."

"Uh-huh."

"I kind of think he will, but also that he won't. Does that make any sense?"

"Uh." Carmen's voice was high in her throat. "I think so."

Tibby could tell it didn't make sense to Carmen at all, and that furthermore, nothing Tibby had said about any part of the relationship since the summer began had made one bit of sense, but that Carmen was hanging in there nonetheless.

"Do you want to talk to him about anything in particular?" Carmen asked. Carmen's patient voice was among her least convincing. Tibby found it surprising to think that she was having so much success as an actress this summer.

"No, not really," Tibby said wanly, purposeless. There was an explosion of hooting out in the hall.

Most conversations, particularly with the Carmen of old, had some storyline, some momentum. Going toward intimacy or coming away from it. Achieving agreement on some subject or unearthing a probable conflict. Giving succor or getting it. This conversation had nothing. Tibby knew that was her fault, but she didn't feel motivated to take the steps to fix it. She felt tired. She was supposed to work on her script. She needed to take a shower. What was she going to eat for dinner?

"It's really noisy here. I'll talk to you later, okay?" she said to Carmen.

"Okay," said Carmen.

There was no satisfaction in being on the phone or in hanging up.

Tibby sat at her desk and pulled up the document on her computer that supposedly contained the script for her intensive screenwriting class. The document was eagerly titled "Script," but it didn't actually contain any scriptlike writing. She'd been in the class for almost three weeks and all she had was a page of notes, randomly spaced and or-dered. Not one of them seemed to have anything to do with another. She couldn't even remember writing half of them.

She let her computer fall back to sleep. She flicked on the TV. She could live a full life just going from one screen to another. Everything she needed was inside an electronic box.

She waited for her favorite newslady, Maria Blanquette, with the big nose and the laugh. An authentic island in a sea of fake. But Tibby was too late. The newscast had al-ready moved on to the weather.

She wondered again about Brian calling. He would prob-ably call her as he made his plans for the fall. He would call her with a good excuse—advice about housing or require-ments, or meal plans or whatever. He was almost certainly expecting that once he got to NYU in September, they would go back to being friends, at least.

And what would she do? And what would she say? Should she help him? Should she encourage him, or was that a mistake? Would that just make it harder for him to get over it?

Bridget still felt weepy when she called Tibby from the empty office late that night, deeply grateful that the satel-lite service was back up and running. She knew the call would cost a bundle, but she didn't care. She hadn't told any of them the truth about Peter, but now she needed to.

"I feel so stupid," she said. She let herself weep. She was a walking wound and she needed to get the fluid out.

"Oh, Bee," Tibby said soothingly.

"I knew he was married. I knew he had kids and I let it happen anyway."

"I know."

"I saw them this morning and I felt so disgusted with myself. But why weren't they important before?"

"Mmm," said Tibby to indicate she was listening and not judging.

"He's part of a family, you know? They depend on him. They belong to him. I'll never belong to him."

With that said, Bridget took a long break to cry. And as she did, she realized she had been more honest with Tibby than she'd intended.

"Beezy, it's okay. You belong to other people," Tibby said, her heart in her voice.

Bridget thought of her father and felt an overwhelming sense of despair. She thought of Eric and felt no right to his love. She thought of her mother and ached for the things she hadn't left behind. "I belong to you and Lena and Carmen, Tibby," she said through her tears. "I don't think I belong to anyone else."

On Monday morning, Lena got to the studio first. Leo got there second. He came over to her immediately. She was shy again.

"I've been too excited to sleep," he told her.

He did in fact look both very excited and very tired. Was it the painting? Was it her?

"I brought it," he said. He lifted the thin box. "Can I show it to you?"

"Not right here," she said. Already other students were wandering in.

"I know. But later. We'll go somewhere private."

"Okay," she said. She was nervous to see it.

She tried to concentrate on her painting. She tried to get into the trance of watching and working. It took a while.

He packed up fast after class. She had to hurry to catch up to him. He found an empty studio on the second floor and closed the door behind them.

He leaned the painting in its box against the wall. He drew her to him and kissed her. He pressed his face into her cheek.

"Nora's a great model," he said. "But now I just want to paint you."

He kissed her more until she was out of breath, furry headed, and furry limbed. "I never kissed a model before," he said. "I never painted a girl I kissed."

"You could try kissing Nora."

He made a face.

"Or Marvin."

He made a worse face.

"Okay. I'll show you," he said. He took the painting out of the box. He did it gingerly because it wasn't entirely dry.

It was hard to make herself look. She took it in one bit at a time, trying to think of it as just another student painting of a female figure. This building was loaded with such paintings.

But no. This was her. It was hard to set her appreciation

for Leo's work apart from her own self-conscious judgment. It was hard to look at it without distortion.

But when she could relax a little, she could see that it was beautiful in some objective way. And it wasn't a school painting either. There was something different about it. It was more intimate. It was a painting set in his room in the house where he had grown up. And it was of her, and she had belonged to him alone for those hours when he painted it.

She realized something else. Most school paintings were purposefully desexualized. This one was not.

"It's sexy, isn't it?"

His smile was inward and outward, too. "Yeah."

"Boy, I hope my parents never see this."

"They won't."

They were still awkward together. At a few different places in the relationship at the same time—seen each other naked, didn't know each other's friends.

When the pose had ended the day before, what if she hadn't put her robe on? What if she had let his kiss develop? She could tell it was what he wanted. She'd had all those thoughts too. But the sheer heft of the sexual energy between them had been too much for her.

"You did a lot better than I did in this trade," she said.

Leo looked genuinely regretful of that. "You were a better model."

"You were a better painter."

"Less inhibited, maybe," he said.

She could still feel the place on her ribs where his fingers had lain on her skin. "That's fair," she said.

"Maybe we could try it again."

"I don't know."

"Please?" He had a slightly desperate look. "Because if you don't paint me, I can't ask you, can I? And I *really* want you to pose for me again."

Was it just a painting he wanted from her? What would happen if she agreed? "You can ask me," she said.

"Will you? Please? I'll beg if you want me to."

"You don't have to."

"Sunday?"

It wasn't so bad being wanted. "I'll think about it."

"Say yes."

"Okay."

"Do you want to have dinner tomorrow?" He was happy. He packed up the painting. She knew he had to get to work.

"At your house?" she asked.

"We'll go out," he said as he led her down the hall. "I don't think I can kiss you in front of my mother."

Julia was waiting at the back entrance of the Main Stage when the cast broke for lunch. Carmen was taken aback, but pleased that Julia was looking friendly and ostensibly waiting for her.

Prince Mamillius, who was also called Jonathan, was walking next to Carmen, so Carmen introduced him to Julia.

"Are you coming to the Bistro?" Jonathan asked Carmen when they reached the split in the path. The Bistro was what they called the smaller, nicer dining room, which was reserved for the professional actors. Bistro people never went to the canteen and vice versa, Carmen understood, although Ian and Andrew and especially Jonathan tried to persuade Carmen to eat with them.

"No," she said.

"Oh, come on."

She was tired of having this argument. "I'm not supposed to."

"Shut up, miss. You know you are."

"Jonathan."

"You can bring your friend."

Carmen turned to Julia, who looked unmistakably excited by this idea. "Do you want to?" Julia asked Carmen.

Carmen didn't, actually.

"I just think it would be fun to see it," Julia said.

Carmen gave Jonathan a look. "It's supposed to be reserved for Equity actors," she said. "But if the prince here is so eager to eat with us, he can get takeout and bring it to the lawn."

Jonathan shook his head. "I am overmatched," he said. "Fine, Carmen, I'll meet you on the lawn."

"Give those apprentice girls a thrill," Carmen said wryly.

To Julia's delight, Jonathan did meet them on the lawn, the grassy area beyond the canteen where all the apprentices hung out. He brought three turkey sandwiches that tasted to Carmen exactly the same as the ones you got at the canteen.

His presence there did cause a stir. It seemed most of these people were more up to date with his filmography than Carmen. Julia chatted happily with him, discussing each thing he'd acted in.

Watching Julia, Carmen felt a certain mystery being solved, and she was relieved by it. Julia had become friendly again, Carmen realized, because she believed Carmen could connect her to real actors.

Carmen could have been annoyed by it, but for some reason she wasn't. So Julia was using her. So what. It was much better than the silent treatment.

Only in the last couple of days had Carmen acknowledged to herself just how painful it was to live with someone who wouldn't speak to you. She thought with earnest regret of the times she'd doled out that particular punishment to her mother.

Carmen had been unhappy with the fraught silence, but she'd also been uneasy about Julia's recent turnaround. Now that she understood it, she felt much better.

Later she saw Jonathan backstage and she thanked him. "The sandwiches stank, but I think my friend really appreciated your eating with us."

He laughed. He'd taken to touching bits of Carmen when he could, and he did it now, pulling on the end of a curl of her hair. "No problem, sister."

"Only now she wants to know what you're doing for dinner tonight."

Jonathan laughed again. "Yeah, well. Your friend is what we call a striver. You see a lot of that type in L.A."

❖ ❖ ❖

Well, Bridget had dug down to the bottommost thing. The most crushing thing. It was good to know where the bottom was, she thought, lying in her cot that night. She was a lying duck, lying at the bottom and letting the agony come for her. She was accepting it.

Peter had said she could learn a thing or two from the Greeks, and he was right. The Greeks knew about cycles of misery. They knew about family curses passed down through long generations. Even seemingly forgivable infractions started wars, infidelities, the sacrifice of children. They also ended in wars, infidelities, the sacrifice of children.

No—in fact, they didn't end that way. They didn't end at all. In the stories, the destruction kept on going, propagated by the blind bungling of human failure.

And that was the course she was setting for herself. Her family was unhappy. No family was allowed to be happy. On some level she didn't want Peter—or anyone—to have what she didn't have. She didn't even want his children to have it.

Now she wondered. Did the fact that Peter had a family dampen her interest in him? Or did it inflame it? How chilling that her most destructive impulses should mask themselves as romance.

Those blind, bungling Greeks always seemed to make the same mistake. They failed to learn from the past. They swaggered onward. They refused to look back. That was what she did too.

A child of five would

understand this.

Send someone to fetch a

child of five.

—Groucho Marx

Tibby cut back her work hours. Or Charlie recommended she cut back her hours, more accurately. He thought if she worked less, she might be more patient with the customers. He hired a girl who wore scented lip gloss and tiny pants and didn't care about which movies were good or bad. Charlie was too nice to fire Tibby outright.

Tibby didn't mind that much. She didn't have anyone to go out to dinner or to the movies with these days, so she didn't need the money as much. It gave her more time to work on her script. Or at least to open the file named "Script."

In late July she went home for a long weekend. Katherine and Nicky were doing a variety show at their day camp, and she thought she'd surprise them.

Would she see Brian? That was what she wondered as her train chugged southward and still wondered later as she waited for her mom to pick her up at the Metro station in Bethesda.

She would see him. She felt sure she would. How could she not? Brian loved her family. In fact, he appreciated them much more than she, an actual member of it, did and was appreciated much more in return. How was she going to feel about that now?

Indeed, on Friday morning, Brian appeared in the kitchen when Tibby was eating her Lucky Charms.

"Hi! Hi!" Katherine danced around him excitedly. "Are you taking us today?"

Was Brian surprised to see Tibby? She wasn't sure. At first she'd assumed he'd shown up with the idea of seeing her, but now, judging by the look on his face, she wasn't sure he'd known she'd be there.

"Hey, Tibby," he said.

"Hey." She kept her eyes on the little marshmallows. She wanted to be friendly, but she didn't want to lead him on.

"Brian takes us on Friday sometimes instead of Mom," Katherine explained happily. She had completely abandoned her own cereal in favor of Brian.

Tibby heard her mother upstairs yelling at Nicky to stop playing on the computer and get dressed. "Well, that's really nice," Tibby said stiffly. "You should eat your breakfast, Katherine," she added. She couldn't imagine volunteering to take her brother and sister to camp, and she was the one who supposedly shared their DNA.

But then, Brian didn't have any brothers or sisters. Desire came from deficit, and Tibby had a surplus.

"How come you're not hugging anymore?" Katherine asked, looking from Brian to Tibby and back.

Moments passed. Brian let Katherine stomp around on his shoes but did not answer the question. Tibby kept her pink face turned to her cereal bowl.

"Are you in a fight?" Katherine persisted. Now she appeared at Tibby's leg, both hands on one of Tibby's knees, leaning into her.

Tibby clutched her teaspoon and stirred. The combination of the pink hearts, yellow moons, blue diamonds, and so on turned the milk a sickly gray hue. "Not in a fight," she said. "Just . . . doing different things this summer."

Katherine did not immediately accept this answer.

"Do you want to come?" Brian asked Tibby politely.

"To . . . ?"

"To take us to camp!" Katherine got right on board. "Yes. Can you come?"

"Well. I guess I could—"

Minutes later, Tibby found herself in the passenger seat of her mother's car with her ex-boyfriend, who was driving her brother and sister to camp. But the true awkwardness began once the two noisy passengers had gotten out of the car.

"How's it going?" Brian asked into the silence.

He seemed more comfortable than she felt. But he wasn't the guilty one, was he?

"Pretty good. How about you?"

"Doing a little better, I guess. I'm trying to." He was

237

willing to be honest and she wasn't. That was why she didn't want to have a conversation with him.

She couldn't think of anything to say. They were stopped at the longest red light on record. She had always hated this light on Arlington Boulevard. Why had Brian gone this way?

"How's it going with school and everything?" she asked finally.

"What do you mean?" he asked. At last they were moving again.

"With financial aid and that stuff."

"I probably won't need it."

"Really? But I thought —" She was inside the conversation now.

"At Maryland, it's —"

"No, at NYU, I mean," she said.

He didn't say anything for a while.

She wished she could take back her words, remove herself once again from the interaction at hand.

"I'm not planning to go to NYU anymore," he said slowly, just as they were turning onto her block. "I withdrew my acceptance a couple weeks ago."

She was opening the car door before it had fully stopped. "Right. Sure." She forgot for a moment it was her mom's car and Brian would be parking it in her driveway. "That makes total sense. Of course," she said. She was flustered, spasmodically waving to him from the sidewalk on her way into her house.

He was looking at her, but she wasn't sure of his expression, because she wasn't really looking at him.

"I hafta run. So I'll see you later!" she declared as she disappeared into her house.

She walked up to her room and sat stiffly on her bed. She looked out the window but saw nothing.

Of course Brian wasn't going to NYU! He was only going because of her, and she'd broken up with him!

Brian, it seemed, had accepted the reality of their breakup. That much was suddenly clear.

But had she?

When Carmen got home after rehearsal ended that night, she was struck to see that Julia had left a stack of books for her on her bed.

"That one is about the Elizabethan stage in general," Julia said eagerly, pointing to the first one Carmen picked up. "The big one under it, that's about language and pronunciation. That will be really helpful. Then there's that one, which is just an analysis of *Winter's Tale.*"

Carmen nodded, studying them. "Wow, thank you. These are great."

"I think they might be useful," Julia said.

"Right. Definitely," Carmen said. The books struck a certain chord in Carmen. She wondered why she hadn't thought of going to the library. She, a girl who trusted herself to beg, borrow, study, and steal more than she trusted herself to be naturally good at something.

She was exhausted, but instead of going straight to sleep, she left the light on for a while and confused herself about the different kinds of verse.

The following night Julia coached her about looking through the text and beyond the text. And then Carmen read the passage Julia recommended about Leontes as self and antiself while Julia feverishly wrote something at her desk. Around midnight, when Carmen was getting ready to turn off the light, Julia presented it to her.

"Here, I marked this up for you."

It was a half inch of photocopied pages from the script, marked up with a dizzying number of symbols and annotations.

"I wrote the meter out for you," Julia explained. "I tried to put the beats in the way you're supposed to."

"Really."

"Yeah. It seemed like you could use some help with that."

"Okay. Yeah."

Julia pointed to the first line and started reading it, exaggerating the rhythm.

"I get it."

"Do you?"

"I think so."

"Do you want to try it?"

Carmen didn't want to try it. She didn't really get it at all and she felt stupid and she wanted to go to sleep.

"Just try a line or two," Julia prodded.

Carmen tried.

"No, it's like this," Julia said, demonstrating.

And so it went until Carmen was doubly exhausted and also had a headache.

On Sunday of that weekend, Tibby went to see Mrs. Graffman, mother of her old friend Bailey. Tibby was going back to New York by train that night, and she wanted to make some effort to see her before she left.

"Do you want to meet for coffee or something?" Tibby asked when she called.

"That's fine. Let's meet at the place around the corner on Highland."

"Perfect," Tibby said, relieved. She preferred not to go to the Graffmans' house if she could avoid it.

Tibby had tried to visit Mrs. Graffman, or at least call, the few times she'd been home in the last year. Usually she wanted to, but today it felt more like an obligation.

Tibby gave Mrs. Graffman a brief hug at the entrance where she was waiting. They got their coffee at the counter and sat down at a tiny table by the front window.

"How're things?" Mrs. Graffman asked. She looked relaxed in her yoga pants and slightly muddy gardening sneakers. She was more robust-looking than she'd been six months and a year ago.

Tibby considered neither the question nor her answer. "Pretty good, I guess. How about you?"

"Well, you know."

Tibby nodded. The "you know" meant that she missed Bailey and that life was only good or remarkable in a very limited context when you'd lost your only child.

"But work is fine. I switched firms, did I tell you that?"

"I think you had just switched last time," Tibby said.

"I redid the downstairs bathroom. Mr. Graffman is training for the Marine Corps Marathon."

"Wow, that's great," Tibby said.

"We try to keep our sense of purpose, you know?"

"Yes," said Tibby. Mrs. Graffman looked sad, but to Tibby's relief, she didn't look urgently sad in a way that needed tending.

"What about you, my dear?"

"Well, I'm taking this intensive screenwriting course. We're supposed to have a full-length script done by mid-August."

"That's exciting."

Suddenly Tibby realized that Mrs. Graffman was going to want to know what it was about.

"What's it about?" she asked cheerfully, right on schedule.

Tibby sipped her coffee too fast and burned her tongue. "I'm kind of working with a bunch of different themes, still. I'm kind of gathering images, you know?" She had heard someone say that once, and she thought it sounded cool. But in the air between her and Mrs. Graffman it sounded like the fakest thing ever.

"Interesting."

Which is another way of saying I haven't started, Tibby should have said, but didn't.

"And how about our friend Brian?" Mrs. Graffman asked with a smile. She was another one of Brian's many ardent parent-aged fans.

"He's . . . well. He's good, I guess. I haven't been seeing him as much."

Mrs. Graffman had a question in her eyes, so Tibby kept talking so she wouldn't get to ask it. "It's just been so crazy, because I have a job and school and he has two jobs and we're in different cities, and so . . . you know."

"I can imagine," Mrs. Graffman said. "But next year you'll be together?"

"Well." Tibby wished she could leave it at that. She wanted to go back to her tiny dorm room, hours from home, and watch TV. "I don't know. It's kind of tricky."

You see, I broke up with him. And now, oddly enough, it seems that as a consequence, we are not together anymore and our future is no longer shared. How mysterious. Who would have thought?

Mrs. Graffman was too sensitive to push into places Tibby didn't want to go. Which left them almost nothing to talk about.

"You're coming to my parents' party in August, right?" Tibby asked, gathering her things.

"Yes. We just got the invitation in the mail. Twenty years. Wow."

Tibby nodded blandly. She never wanted to do the math

243

as far as her parents' wedding was concerned. Here was yet another blocked conversation.

Tibby realized why she found comfort in simpler, more one-sided interactions, like with, say, the TV.

Lena had forgotten about forgetting about Kostos. That was how she knew. When you remembered to forget, you were remembering. It was when you forgot to forget that you forgot.

The thing that reminded Lena about Kostos came not from any movement in her brain (which would have constituted a failure to forget) but from a knock on her door on a hot Thursday afternoon at the very end of July.

It was simple. When she saw Kostos, she remembered him.

Why, what could she have

done, being what she is?

Was there another Troy

for her to burn?

—William Butler Yeats

It was after class that it happened. Lena had kicked off her flip-flops and fallen asleep on her bed in her shorts and T-shirt, her hair falling out of its ponytail. The knock came in the first deep part of sleep. She was groggy and disoriented and sweaty before she even opened the door.

When she saw the dark-haired man standing there, she only half believed that he could be Kostos. Even though he had Kostos's face and Kostos's feet and Kostos's voice, she persisted in thinking that maybe he was somebody else.

Why was this man, who looked so strangely like Kostos, standing in the doorway of her dorm room? Disjointedly she thought of calling Carmen and telling her that there happened to be a guy in Rhode Island who was almost identical to Kostos.

Then she remembered what Carmen had said about when Kostos would come, and she remembered about the forgetting.

She felt suddenly jolted and afraid. Like she'd woken up in the middle of her SATs. Did that mean it could be him?

But it was impossible, because Kostos lived on a Greek island thousands of miles away. He lived in the past. He lived unreachably inside the walls of a marriage. He lived in her memory and her imagination. That was where he spent literally all of his time. He existed there, not here.

He could not be here. Here was the leftover turkey sandwich from a hurried lunch in the studio and the ratty drawstring sweatpants she'd cut into shorts, and the mosquito bite on her ankle she'd ruthlessly picked, and the charcoal drawing she'd Scotch-taped to her wall two Mondays ago. Kostos did not live here or now. She'd question her eyes and ears faster than she'd question that.

She almost told him so.

"It's me," he said, sensing her confusion, faltering in his certainty that she would recognize him.

Well, she did recognize him. That wasn't the point, was it? She was hardly convinced. So what if he was me? Everyone was me. She was me. Who else was he going to be?

Just because he was Kostos and appeared at her door and said "It's me" didn't mean he was occupying space and time in her actual life. She thought of telling him so.

She had that frustrating dreamlike confusion of racking her brain for the answer and then forgetting what the question was. There was a question, wasn't there? She thought of asking him.

"I should have called first," he murmured.

She recognized that her heart was beating either many

more times or many fewer times than it was meant to. She considered. Maybe it would stop altogether. Then what was she supposed to do?

For some reason she pictured her chest opening like a cupboard door and her heart sproinging out at the end of a coil.

Was she awake? She could have asked him, but he was the last person who would know, having no place in reality himself.

"I think I might sit down," she said faintly. She was like a corseted girl in an old movie, taking the big things sitting down.

He stood in her doorway with the question on his face of whether he should come in. He looked worn out and rumpled. Maybe he really had come all the way here.

"Maybe you could come back later," she said.

He wore the look of being tortured. He didn't know what to make of her. "Can I come back this evening? Maybe around eight?"

She found herself wondering, did he mean eight her time or his time? She only confused herself. "That would be fine," she said politely. Could they really be in the same time?

If he came back at eight, she decided, listening to the door close, tipping over onto her pillow, that would strengthen the case for his being here.

On that same scorching Thursday at the end of July, the security guard called up to Tibby's room and told her she had a visitor.

Immediately she thought of Brian, even though she hadn't seen him or spoken to him since she'd returned from Bethesda. She felt her heart quicken. "Who is it?" she asked.

"Hold on." Tibby heard muffled conversation. "It's Effie."

"*Who?*"

"Effie. Effie? She says she's your friend."

Tibby's heart changed its stride. "I'll be there in a minute," she said.

She wet her hair down and pulled on a tank top and a ragged pair of shorts. Suddenly she was worried something might be wrong with Lena. She flew down the hall to the elevator.

Effie was practically in her face when the elevator door opened in the lobby. She backed up quickly, stumbling as Tibby burst out of it.

"Is everything okay?" Tibby asked.

Effie raised her eyebrows. "Yes. I mean, I think so."

"Where's Lena?"

"She's in Providence." Effie acquired that subtly damaged look she got when confronted with the reality that Lena's friends were not equally her friends.

"Oh. Right." Tibby realized it might sound mean to say *So what are you doing here?* Rather, she waited patiently for Effie to explain what she was doing there.

"Are you busy right now?" Effie asked.

"No. Not really."

"You're not like, rushing off anywhere or anything."

"No." Tibby was imploding with curiosity, with the sense that something was afoot. She'd been alone a lot.

"Do you want to go get a cup of coffee? Is there a place around here?"

Effie looked a bit nervous, Tibby decided. She was jumpy. Of her total of four hands and feet, not one was staying still. She was wearing a short strawberry pink wrap dress, which revealed an impressive amount of cleavage.

"There are a million places around here." Tibby counseled herself not to be impatient or mean. It was actually really sweet that Effie had come all the way here to see her. Did she want advice on something? Was she suddenly interested in film as a potentially glamorous career? Did she hear there was a disproportionate number of cute boys at NYU maybe? Not that there were. "We can get iced coffee at a place on Waverly."

"That sounds great," Effie said. She wiped a coat of sweat off her upper lip.

"Are you in New York for a while?" Tibby asked as they walked along, fishing for clues.

"Just the day," Effie said.

At last, equipped with a two-dollar iced coffee for Tibby and a five-dollar raspberry white mocha frappuccino for Effie, they sat at a dim, cool table in the back of the café. An opera in Italian was playing over the speaker to the left of Effie's head.

Effie's drink was so thick she had to really suck to get any of it. Tibby watched and waited.

"So you and Brian broke up," Effie said finally.

"Right."

"I couldn't believe it when I first heard it."

Tibby shrugged. Was this the preamble? Where was it going?

"Do you think you'll get back together?" Effie asked. Her expression was not demanding. In fact, she mostly fiddled with the paper from her straw.

"I don't think so."

"Really?"

Tibby tried not to be irritated. Was Effie just trying to make pleasant conversation? Because it wasn't all that pleasant.

"Really."

"Huh. Do you think you are over him?"

Tibby looked at her carefully. "Do I think I am over him?"

Effie opened her hands as though to show there wasn't anything in them. "Yeah."

"I'm not sure I would even know."

Effie shrugged lightly. She sucked on her drink. "I mean, like, would you be upset if you found out he was going out with someone else?"

As Tibby replayed those words, she felt her brain turning inside out like a salted slug. Her vision grew distorted and she blinked to get it back into focus. She tried to keep her face on, to remain calm.

What did Effie know? Had she seen Brian with another girl? Was Brian fooling around with some girl all over Bethesda? What had Effie seen? What was going on?

Tibby drank her coffee. She breathed the air. She listened to a tenor hollering just over Effie's head. She could not lose it in front of Effie. Effie, no matter what her cup size, was still a little sister.

She desperately wanted to ask Effie what she knew, but how could she without seeming like it bothered her? Like she was upset and disturbed and blindsided by the thought of it? She couldn't.

"You would be upset," Effie concluded.

Tibby had her pride, if nothing else. "No," she said finally. "I would be a little surprised, maybe. But look. I was the one who broke up with him, right? It wasn't like I didn't know what I was doing. I totally did. I didn't have any doubt that it was time for us to break up and that, for me, it was the right thing to do." Suddenly Tibby realized that talking felt better than thinking.

"Really?"

"Sure. I mean, it was really over. For me, it was over. Brian should do whatever he wants to do. He's totally free to go out with anybody he wants. Really, he probably oughta go out with somebody else if that's what he wants to do." Tibby felt like her head was teetering slightly on her neck. Like one of those dumb bobble-head figures people put in their car.

Effie nodded and sucked on her so-called coffee, her eyes wide, listening intently. "Would it matter if it was someone you knew?"

Never had Tibby imagined pure torture in the guise of Effie Kaligaris in a wrap dress sucking a pink drink. Someone Tibby knew? Who was it? Who was Brian with? Someone she knew? Brian was hooking up with someone she *knew*? Who was it? How could he do that to her? Tibby racked her brain to think of who it could be.

How could she ask and not betray her abject misery? How could she not ask and continue to suffer like this?

"It would," Effie proposed solemnly.

Once again, Tibby gathered herself. She could fall apart later. She could call Lena and get the truth. She could even call her mother if it came to that.

"Why should it?" Tibby said, tapping her fingers in a poor facsimile of nonchalance. "Why should it really matter if I knew the person?"

Suddenly every damn singer in the opera seemed to be screaming at the top of their lungs. "The point is that Brian is no longer my boyfriend and I am not his girlfriend." Tibby was almost shouting. "Who he goes out with is totally his business. Who I go out with is totally mine."

Effie nodded slowly. "That makes sense."

Tibby was actually quite proud of her answer. It sounded like exactly the right thing, even if it bore no relation to how she felt. She tried to catch her breath. She wished the opera singers would take it down a notch.

"That makes a lot of sense." Effie sucked more on her drink.

"So then . . ." Effie put her drink down and readjusted herself in her chair. Her eyes were now locked on Tibby. "You wouldn't mind if . . ."

Effie uncrossed her legs under the table. Tibby realized

she too felt the need to put both feet on the floor. For mysterious reasons, Tibby held her breath.

"You wouldn't mind if I went out with Brian?"

Things like this should not happen to Lena, Lena decided, looking at the bricks outside her window and then the gaps between them where the mortar had mostly worn away. They should happen to other people, like Effie. Effie, who, for instance, was more skilled at being a person.

The light got old and the bricks turned dark. The only concessions Lena made to the possibility of eight o'clock were putting on deodorant and brushing her hair.

In the latter movement was a memory, because she had also brushed her hair for him on the day of her bapi's funeral. That was two years ago.

The feelings of loss from that time were multiple: Bapi's death, her grandmother's agony, her father's harsh rigidity. And finding out about Kostos, of course. All of them had crashed together like malevolent winds. They had created a storm strong enough to suck in all the incidental qualities of that moment, however innocent: the particular pattern of clouds and the buzz of a certain kind of airplane, the smell of dry dirt and the feeling of having brushed your hair especially for a person you loved.

The storm had even sucked time into it—hours and days and weeks that didn't rightfully belong to it, so that the time before it struck was freighted with the knowing sorrow of inexorability, and the time after it bore the bleakness of wanting things she could never have.

Within the memory of brushing her hair for him hovered the foreknowledge that Kostos would abandon her.

She remembered certain things he'd said. They kept at her all this time, like a talk radio station turned very low at the bottom of her consciousness.

"Don't ever be sad because you think I don't love you," he'd said. "Never think you did anything wrong." "If I've broken your heart, I've broken my own a thousand times worse." "I love you, Lena. I couldn't stop if I tried."

The most haunting thing was not that he didn't love her anymore. She could have accepted that eventually. The most haunting thing was that he did. He loved her from afar. (Sometimes that was the way she loved herself.) He loved her in a way that was preserved in time, that couldn't be sullied. And she tended it in her careful, curatorial way.

She was lovable. She clung to that. She was worthy of being loved. That was what mattered, wasn't it? Even if he had married someone else? Even if he had wrecked her hopes?

She was lovable. It was what she had. In her dreams, she heard him say he still loved her, that he didn't forget her any hour of any day. She was unforgettable. That was the most important thing. Better, even, than being happy.

And where did that leave her? Alone on her Greek urn. Lovable but never loved.

She was free of risk. Bold within her limits.

It was the same old hedge.

❀   ❀   ❀

It reminded Tibby a little bit of the child-catcher's scene in *Chitty Chitty Bang Bang* where his candy truck is suddenly revealed to be a cage.

Sitting there across from Effie, her cup of melted ice sweating on the table, Tibby watched the four solid walls turn into the bars of a cage. She was trapped. She had walked right into it, pleased with her own cool, lying head.

What could she do? What could she say? Effie had played it masterfully. Suddenly Tibby understood everything Effie had intended, every question she had asked. Effie did not hail from the land of Socrates for nothing.

Tibby couldn't think anymore. She couldn't hope to combat Effie. Her head bobbled.

"You would mind," Effie concluded quietly, but Tibby could practically see the smugness peeking through. Effie looked ready to fly, to take her victory and run with it.

"No. That's fine," Tibby mumbled. What else could she say?

Up stood Effie. That was good enough for her. "Oh, my God. I am so relieved, Tibby," she gushed. "You don't know how worried I was. I couldn't do anything until I knew you'd be okay."

They were already on the sidewalk, Tibby following numbly.

Brian and Effie? Effie and Brian? Effie with her Brian? Was that what he wanted? He wanted to be with Effie? She thought of Effie's cleavage.

"I'm just so glad it's okay. Because Brian and I are like

the only two people left at home this summer, you know? And I've— Well, anyway. But I wouldn't even think of doing anything without making sure you would be fine."

"I'll be fine," Tibby managed to say, just to finish the charade properly. Then she went home and fell apart.

You shall know the truth,

and the truth shall make

you mad.

—Aldous Huxley

The alleged Kostos did come at eight.

Lena hazarded a touch to his wrist before she submitted to the belief that he was three-dimensional. He was too warm to be a ghost, figment, or hologram. He had eyes and lips and arms that moved. He was in her time, in her doorway. She had to accept him.

And so she stepped back, considering him silently and without regard to her own presence. She was a pair of eyes, not a person to be interacted with. If he insisted upon being present, maybe she could disappear.

So he was Kostos. She thought her memory of his face should certainly have diminished the reality of his face, but it hadn't. His face still had its power, she recognized, but as though from a distance.

He put out his hand and held hers, earnestly but without expectations. She stayed too far away to be read as wanting to embrace.

So he was Kostos and she was Lena, and after all this time and misery they were facing each other in a doorway of a student dorm in Providence, Rhode Island. She was watching it more than experiencing it. She was keeping track so she could tell herself about it later and brood appropriately.

There were people who lived in the moment, Lena knew, while she lived at a delay of hours or even years. And with that knowledge came the familiar frustration of wanting to club herself over the head with a combat boot if only to be sure of experiencing and feeling something in unison for once.

"I won't stay if you don't want me to, Lena." Tentatively he took one step into the small room. "But there are a few things I want to say to you in person."

She nodded, her mouth clamped and pointy like a bird's beak. The sound of her name in his voice was jarring.

They should walk, Lena decided. Walking was easier because they didn't have to look at each other. "We should walk," she said.

In single file they walked down the hallway and three flights of stairs. She led him out of the building and toward the river. The air had grown kind, warm but not steamy.

She had the vague thought that they would walk along the place in the river where fires burned in the middle of the water on summer nights. It was one of the few tourist attractions of Providence, but she was too disoriented to remember what time they were lit or even quite where they would be.

"I didn't know how you would feel," he said, walking beside her.

She didn't know how she would feel either. She had absolutely no idea. She waited to know as though someone might tell her.

She took him the wrong way. They wound up walking past a gas station and a 7-Eleven and picking their way along a busy road in the dark. She hadn't the gifts of a tour guide.

She thought of Santorini and how it was beautiful and how Kostos knew the way. The thought struck her heavily, almost like a boot, making her eyes sting.

"I'm not married anymore," Kostos told her between speeding cars. He looked at her and she nodded to show that she had at least heard him.

"I became officially divorced in June."

She was not freshly startled by this. Once she'd accepted his presence in her doorway, a part of her brain seemed to know he was no longer married.

With his solemn face he stood as they waited for a line of cars to pass. He was patient about it. They were both patient, perhaps overly so. They had that in common.

She steered them back in the direction of campus to a quiet bench in a green and dimly lit patch of garden between two administrative buildings. It was no olive grove, but they could talk.

"There's not a baby," he said gingerly. He seemed to have considered his phrasing in advance.

"What happened to it?" She felt bold to ask, but reasonable, too.

He looked at her openly. He hadn't the anger or guard-edness she'd seen two years ago. It was easier to talk about a baby that he didn't have.

"Well." His sigh indicated complexity. "Mariana said she miscarried. But the timing of it was hard to explain. Her sister told me privately that she hadn't been pregnant, but had wanted to marry and figured a baby would come in due course."

"But it didn't," Lena said.

She could tell by his gaze that he was measuring how much was the right amount to say. "I was angry in the be-ginning. I wanted to find out the truth. I refused to live . . . as a husband with her."

Lena wondered at the meaning of all of this. What American man would talk this way?

"We lived separately after the first half year, but stayed married. I thought I couldn't dishonor my grandparents by divorcing. It's not accepted among the old families. It's something that the newcomers and the tourists do."

Lena recognized how deep in Kostos's character was the need to please. The desire not to disappoint. It was an-other thing they had in common. He was the darling of all the families in Oia. He wanted to be lovable too, even if it meant setting happiness aside. His happiness and hers, it seemed.

What was this compulsive need to be lovable? They both had it, were driven by it, bound by it. They would even sacrifice each other for the sake of it.

But she sensed they were afflicted differently. He wanted

262

to preserve his worthiness in the eyes of other people. It was because of losing his parents; it had to be. Parents were the only ones obligated to love you; from the rest of the world you had to earn it.

And what about her? Whose love did she so compulsively doubt?

She knew without thinking. From her earliest memory she had perceived the chasm between how she looked and how she felt. She knew whose love she doubted. It wasn't her parents' and it wasn't her friends'. It was her own.

"And so what happened?" she asked dully.

"It was really my grandparents who mattered the most to me. You know they are old and very traditional. I held off doing what I had to do. I dreaded telling them."

He had thought about this part too, she knew. He had planned this speech. She nodded.

"When I finally told my grandmother, I thought she'd fall apart."

"She didn't," Lena guessed.

Kostos shook his head. "She told me she prayed every night I would have the courage to do it."

She pictured their two grandmothers, Valia and Rena, two old ladies full of surprises. How much did Valia know?

"Valia didn't say anything," she said.

"I asked her not to. I wanted to tell you myself."

Lena studied his calm face and suddenly felt affronted by it.

"I would be furious if I were you," she said.

"But who does that help now?" he asked.

She felt furious even though she wasn't him. She felt furious *at* him for having granted himself the right to dispense with her grievances too. "I would want to know what really happened," she said hotly.

Kostos looked pained, but he shrugged. "I had to let it go. What did it matter? What would it help to give out blame?"

What did it matter? Kostos could decide that it didn't. It was, technically speaking, no business of hers. And yet, in another bootlike strike, she felt quite sure, looking back on the past two years of her life, that it did matter.

That was the stupidity of loving someone from a different planet, wasn't it? You didn't just give yourself away to him. You put yourself in the path of crazy girls who made up babies, and strangling customs you didn't even care about.

That wasn't what she wanted for her life, was it? She had enough to stifle her without that. She thought bitterly of her father. She had enough of those old customs as it was.

And then, abruptly, she thought of Leo. Of his loft. Of his ruby red couch and the feeling of lying on it.

She lost her breath for a moment. It was almost intolerable to think of Leo in the same brain where she thought of Kostos. She felt unnerved, disassociated, as if she were living in two universes, being two people at the same time.

She had forgotten about Leo. The possibility of Leo. It came back to her like another kick.

Was she really so bad at forgetting? Maybe she was better than she thought.

There was the boot yet again, and it hurt. But wasn't that what she wanted?

No. It wasn't. *Leave me alone*, she felt like screaming. She didn't want the boot. She didn't need another crack over the head. She didn't want Kostos. She didn't want any of it.

"Carmen, what the hell are you doing?"

Carmen tried to be impervious to the devil glare coming from Andrew.

"I'm saying my line," Carmen said.

"What's the matter with you? You sound like a robot. You sound worse than a robot. I *wish* I could listen to a robot instead of you."

Carmen made herself stand firm. This wasn't Andrew's first tirade, though it was perhaps the first aimed so directly at her.

"Try it again," he ordered.

Carmen tried it again.

"Bleep. Bleep," harangued Andrew. "Robot."

She took a deep breath. She would not cry. He was tired. She was tired. It had been a very long day. "I think maybe I'll take a break," she said tightly.

"You do that," he said.

You are horrible and I hate you, she said to Andrew in her mind, although she knew he wasn't and she didn't.

She staggered to the back door and pushed it open. The air was hot and sticky and it offered no relief.

She sat down and rested her head in her arms. Andrew was being hateful, but he wasn't wrong. The lines had grown stilted in her mouth. She was thinking about them too much. Or more, she was thinking about the technicalities of saying them too much.

Some number of minutes later, Carmen looked up and saw Julia.

"Carmen, is that you?"

"Hey," Carmen said, sitting up straighter.

"What's the matter? Are you okay?"

"I'm having a bad rehearsal."

"Oh, no. What's wrong?"

"I think all the working on meter is just confusing me," Carmen said truthfully.

"Really?" Julia looked genuinely worried. She sat on the step next to Carmen. "That's no good."

Carmen closed her eyes. "I can't believe I have to go back in there."

"You know what the problem is?"

"What?"

"This always happens. The first time you learn the structural stuff it confuses you. Totally standard. The thing you've got to do is just keep going with it and then you get it. It becomes natural as soon as you get a handle on it."

"You think so?"

"I'm almost sure of it."

After Carmen was released from her rehearsal of pain, she went back to the room, where Julia was waiting.

"Here, I tried marking it in a new way," Julia said. "I think this will make it easier."

Carmen looked at Perdita's familiar words and they looked distant to her. Now that she was considering them in a different context, she couldn't access them in the old way anymore. She couldn't re-create the simplicity. She couldn't seem to go backward. So maybe Julia was right. Maybe she had to go forward.

She appreciated Julia's patience in staying up with her almost until dawn to make sure she worked through it.

Lena was angry. She couldn't sleep.

She'd been accepting, she'd been numb, she'd been sad, now she was angry. She was cycling through the stages of grief, but on fast-forward and in jumbled order.

In the middle of a night long ago, she'd gone to Kostos full of ardor, wearing her vulnerability in the form of a fluttery white nightgown. Tonight she knocked on his door at the Braveside Motor Lodge battened down in a slick black jacket held tightly closed against wind and rain.

He'd put on pants by the time he opened the door. She looked past him to a familiar bunch of suitcases, a familiar mess of clothes, familiar shoes. It all carried a familiar smell that hurt her. Why had he brought so much stuff?

"You shouldn't have come here," she said, noting as she did that she was the one knocking on his door at two in the morning.

Surprise, pain, defensiveness took turns on his sleepy

face. The creases of his pillowcase were still pressed into his cheek.

"Anyway, what are you trying to do? What did you think would happen?"

"I—" He stopped. He rubbed his eyes. He looked as though his own dog had bitten him.

"I just want to understand!" she exclaimed.

That was a lie. She didn't just want to understand. She wanted to catch him and punish him.

Maybe he didn't do that kind of thing. Maybe he was too good for it. Maybe blame didn't matter and people who ruined your life didn't matter to him. But maybe she couldn't get past it.

"I wanted to tell you what happened. I thought you had a right to know."

"Why? What business is it of mine?" she snapped. "You were married. Now you're not married. That was years ago. Why should it mean anything to me?"

Another lie. Far worse than the first. Even as she said it, she didn't know if she wanted him to believe her.

From the look on his face, he did believe her. "I—" He stopped himself again. He looked down. He looked at the night sky past her head. He looked at the few cars parked in the motor court. He did what he could to contain himself.

She clutched her jacket so tight around her middle she thought she might break a rib.

"I'm sorry." He did look sorry. He looked sorry in numerous ways. She wanted him to continue, but he didn't.

She felt like shaking him, screaming at him. *What are you sorry for?*

For coming here?

For thinking I'd care?

For caring yourself?

For breaking my heart?

For choosing other people instead of me?

For knowing how badly I want to hurt you right now?

For knowing I do care and that I hate you for it?

For having to see that I'm not who you thought I was?

She gritted her teeth so hard her ears ached. "Was I supposed to rush into your arms?" she asked derisively.

He looked taken aback. He was still believing she would be lovable. "No. Lena. I didn't expect that. I just . . ."

"Anyway, I have a boyfriend," she said conclusively, meanly, dishonestly. "Your timing is pretty terrible. Not that it matters."

There was something horrendously liberating about lying. It was an experience she'd never known before this.

He pressed his lips together. His body began to close in. It took a lot to make him distrust her.

A part of her wanted him to get mad, to prove himself as nasty and as unworthy as she was. Could he even do it?

She wanted an inferno. She'd preserved their love so carefully in her mind these years, but now she wanted to burn the thing down. She wanted every part of it broken and burned and wronged and done.

No, he couldn't do it. His stance was no longer open.

His face was shutting down. He was silent as she smoldered.

"I'm sorry for everything," he said at last.

She wanted to punch him, but instead she strode away. She turned the corner and listened silently for the click of his door.

On the way back to her dorm her walk turned into a run. She let go of her coat, let it flap heavily around her. She ran as fast as she could until she was out of breath and her heart was shuddering.

She realized later, shaking under the sheet in her underwear, that she'd never really gotten mad at anyone before.

Illusions are art, for the feeling person, and it is by art that you live, if you do.

—Elizabeth Bowen

When Lena awoke early the next morning, she was no longer angry. She was astounded. What had she done? How could she have done it?

A fearful, reckless energy prompted her out of bed and into clothes. She walked back to the motel, the scene of the crime, as if to prove to herself that she had actually done what she thought she had done. That it had really happened.

Had it really happened? What could she say to Kostos? Was she apologetic? She checked her heart.

She didn't find an apology there exactly. She couldn't quite define what was there: a strange brew of stridency and terror. What should she do?

As she walked along the open corridor, she was scared to see the remnants of the mess she had made.

She prepared herself to knock, but she saw when she got close that the door was already open. She thought of how much stuff there had been in the room, the number of suitcases and the piles of clothes. Now she looked past the housekeeping cart into a room clean and empty.

Tibberon: Oh, Len. Carmen told me what happened. Are you okay?

LennyK162: I'm okay. A little dazed maybe.

Tibberon: Do you want company?

LennyK162: I love your company, Tib, but I don't need you right now. I'm not really even sad. I'm relieved it's over. It's been over for a long time.

Love was an idea. Nothing more or less.

If you lost the idea, if you somehow forgot it, the person you loved became a stranger. Tibby thought of all those movies about amnesiacs where they don't even know their own spouse. Love lives in the memory. It can be forgotten.

But it can also be remembered.

Early in the summer, Tibby lost the idea of loving Brian. Because of the sex, because of the condom breaking, because of her worst fears seeming real. She couldn't know exactly why. But she knew the darkest parts of growing up had become linked to him that night. Those dark parts had attached to him and somehow overwhelmed the fragile idea of love.

Tibby distinctly remembered the strange sense that night that her idea of love had vanished. It was a spell broken, a dream ended, and reality took over. She had come to her senses and realized that she didn't love Brian, that his best qualities were actually his worst ones, and that furthermore, the fact that Brian inexplicably loved her was stupid and intolerable. She had awoken from a dream of love.

And yet.

Now it was all different again. Her dream had come back, and she didn't know if she was waking or sleeping, what was real and what was illusory.

She called Lena even though Lena had her own things to worry about.

"Do you have any idea what's going on?" Tibby raved. She was done with playing proud.

"With what?" Lena asked.

"With Effie and Brian!"

Lena was silent. Not for more than a second, but long enough for Tibby to know she knew something.

"Well." Lena sighed.

"What do you know?" Tibby practically exploded.

"I don't know anything for sure." Lena's voice was slow and steady. "I mean, I know Effie's had a crush on Brian. But that's been going on a long time. Everybody knows that."

Tibby felt she might swallow her tongue. "They do?"

"Oh, Tib. Just a crush. You know, a juvenile kind of crush. Brian is very good-looking, obviously."

"He is?" Tibby wasn't breathing at all anymore.

"Tibby! Come on. You know what I mean. I'm not trying to torture you. I'm just stating the facts of the case."

Tibby sat on her hand. "Okay," she squeaked.

"Do you want to talk about this?"

Did she? No! But there was nothing else in the world to think of or talk about. "I have to know," she said.

"I don't think there's much to know," Lena said, and her voice was pitched for comfort. "Effie has a crush on Brian, Brian is miserable over you. I think they've talked on the phone a few times."

"They have?" Tibby's hand was asleep. Her ear was hot from the phone.

"Tibby, I don't want to be in the middle of this. But I do want to be honest with you."

"They haven't . . . gone out together or anything."

"I don't think so."

"You don't *think* so?"

Lena sighed again. "It's the kind of thing Effie would mention. Trust me."

"Do you think Brian likes her?"

"I have no reason to think so. But I do think he's had a pretty lonely time."

"Because of thinking I broke up with him?" Tibby asked vacantly.

"Because you did break up with him."

"Oh."

"Hey, Tib?"

"Yeah?"

"I don't mean to bug you, but you really should have told Effie the truth."

"Gee. Thanks."

After she hung up with Lena, she sat at her desk and tried to unscramble her brain.

Effie wanted Brian. Brian was a dreamboat. Duh. Everyone knew that. Everyone wanted him. In fact, it so happened that he was way way way too good for Tibby.

It was base and painful how these things mattered.

Yes, Tibby had once forgotten how to love Brian, but her memory was now effectively jogged. Oh, how painfully she remembered.

Of course Brian was gorgeous! It wasn't like Tibby didn't know that! That wasn't even what mattered!

But all the other stuff did matter — that he was confident and good and that he was an optimist and could whistle Beethoven and didn't care what other people thought. That he loved Tibby! He knew how to love better than anyone. Or at least, he had.

Now the idea of loving Brian was back. Now she couldn't remember the idea of not loving him. When she thought of Effie and Brian, she wished she could remember the idea of not loving him.

A spell broke again, a dream ended, but this time in reverse. Now not loving him was the spell. Not loving was the dream she woke up from. That was how it seemed to her. But how confusing it was! How could you even know what was real? Or what would be real tomorrow? She was so scrambled she couldn't keep track.

Who was she that she could change her mind, her very reality, so completely? Could she ever trust herself again?

Over the next few days she wished she were working more at Movieworld. With her hours so much reduced, she had endless time to stare at her "Script" and wonder about these things. The more she wondered, the less she knew.

She tried to write her script. She had the idea it would be a love story. But she couldn't hold on to any thread. All she could think about was love's intermittency, and that made for no story at all.

Peter came to see Bridget in the lab a few days before she was set to leave for home. She had labels in her pockets, stuck all over her clothes. She had three different-colored Sharpies in her left hand and one in her right.

She'd avoided her lab responsibilities for almost the whole program. She knew she had won the notice of David, the director, for her work in the house, so she could get away with it. She liked being outside in the sun. She liked having her hands in the dirt. She did not like this part. So she'd saved her dues-paying until the end of the trip. She thought of Socrates before the hemlock. You had to pay up eventually.

She saw Peter and she removed the label she was holding in her mouth to say hello.

"How's it going?" he said. They were much changed since the kiss on the hill, both of them chastened.

She shrugged. "Okay."

He looked around to make sure they had privacy. "I didn't want you to go without saying good-bye."

She nodded.

"I feel bad about what happened."

"Probably not as bad as me," she said. She cringed inwardly. What a weird thing to be competitive about.

"Hard to imagine feeling worse," he said.

God, they were alike. Going overboard even at this stage.

"It makes me realize what a mistake it is for me to be away from my family for this long. I lose sight of what they mean to me, you know?"

She did know. She knew exactly. He was canny and he was hungry in all sorts of ways. He lived in the present just as she did.

"You're probably right about that," she said, also knowing that he was missing the deeper solution.

He grinned at her. "It could have been worse."

She raised an eyebrow. "You think so?"

"We could have rolled down the hill."

At that point, it would have just been gravity, but she didn't say so.

"I think back on that night. I feel like we dodged a bullet," he said.

She looked at him without saying anything. No, they hadn't. They hadn't dodged a bullet. The bullet had dodged them.

She thought of Eric, and for the first time in a long time she could actually begin to picture him. The set of his mouth when he concentrated on something. The crumple of his forehead when he was worried. The slightly jaunty overlap of his front teeth when he smiled. He came to her in little bursts, and she could feel, achingly, what it was to miss him.

She had gone to some lengths not to feel this, she realized. In spite of the sweetness and reliability of his e-mails, she had guarded against her feelings for him. She had long ago instituted a personal policy against missing people, based on the fear that you would spend your life missing people if you really got going on it.

The time had come to rethink that policy. You blocked the pain and you blocked everything.

Eric loved her. She trusted him more than she trusted herself. She appreciated the wisdom of loving someone built so differently than she was. She was stupid to let him go, even in her mind, even for a day. It was her loss.

As she said good-bye to Peter, she suddenly felt sad for him. He would do this same thing again. At some other place with some other misguided girl. He was already looking forward, shaking off the past—a past that now included her.

She made a vow to herself not to do that.

Tibby called her mother. Sad but true.

"Have you heard anything?" she asked. She had no pride. None. This would be unthinkable if she had any.

"Honey, no."

"Have you seen them together?"

"No."

"You know something. I can tell."

"Tibby."

"Mom. If you know something you have to tell me."

Her mother sighed in exactly the way that everybody

Tibby had talked to had sighed. "Your father saw them at Starbucks."

"He *did*?"

"Yes."

"Together?"

"Seemed like that."

"Brian doesn't like Starbucks!"

"Well, maybe Effie does."

That was the worst possible thing to say. Tibby felt the need to pout for a while.

"Tibby, sweetie. You sound like you are really upset about this. Why don't you tell Effie to lay off? Why don't you tell Brian how you are feeling?"

Typical her mom. These were the worst and least practical suggestions Tibby had ever heard in her life.

"I have to go," she said sullenly.

"Tib. Please."

"I'll talk to you later."

"You know what your dad said?"

"No. What?"

"He said that Brian did not look happy."

Tibby breathed out. That was the first and only good thing her mother said the whole time.

She cannot fade, though

thou hast not thy bliss,

For ever wilt thou love,

and she be fair!

—John Keats

"Hey, Carmen?"

"Yes, Andrew."

"What's going on?"

It was just the two of them in the empty lobby of the theater. Andrew Kerr seemed to have recognized that public humiliation didn't work, so he was trying to reach Carmen privately.

"I don't *know*." She put her face in her hands.

"Carmen, darling. Just relax. Just tell me what."

"I don't know what."

"You were doing so beautifully with this role. Even Ian said it. 'She's a miracle,' he said, and do you know what I said?"

Carmen shook her head.

"I said, 'Let's not jinx it.' "

"Thanks a lot, Andrew."

"Carmen, I know what you are capable of. I believe in you. I just want to know why you are not doing it."

"I think I'm thinking too much," she said.

Andrew nodded sagely. "Ah. Very bad. Don't think too much. Don't think at all."

"I'll try not to."

"Good girl."

Ten minutes later she was back onstage with flowers in her hair, trying to say the line about hostess-ship.

"Carmen!" Andrew thundered. "I hope you are not thinking again!"

"Are we on for Sunday?" Leo left the message on her answering machine.

"Are you there? Are you okay? Do you want to have dinner? What's up?" was his message on Saturday.

"Please, please call me, Lena," he said on Sunday morning.

So she did. When he asked her how she was, she couldn't quite figure out what to say.

"Can you pose today?" he asked hopefully.

Could she? An echo of the old terror sounded at the thought, but it was far away, more like a representation than the real feeling. "Okay," she said. She didn't have the stamina to think why not. "I'll be over in half an hour," she said.

She took a shower. Her skin felt cool and clean, a strange coating for her strange soul. She didn't try to organize her impressions or her anxieties. She just walked to his building and rang 7B.

Upstairs at the door he pulled her into the loft and hugged her and kissed her as though he'd been starved of love for his entire lifetime. Failure to return calls was a depressingly effective aphrodisiac, she thought fleetingly, even among decent guys.

She felt her body curve into him, her lips respond instinctively. Maybe she was starving too.

Leo was a little bit self-conscious when he drew her into his room. He closed the door behind him, which he had not done the week before. She sensed he didn't want the common rooms bearing witness.

The robe was ready. His bed was carefully draped. The little red couch was pushed against the wall.

"I was thinking . . ." His feet shuffled in a winning way. "You could be on the couch again if you want. Or . . ."

"Or?"

"Well, I was thinking maybe . . ."

She pointed to the bed. She could tell it was what he wanted.

"Right. Because. Well, I've sort of been envisioning this painting." He could not stand still. He was practically bouncing.

She could see how much he wanted it. Whether for her or for art she didn't know.

"Do you mind? If you are uncomfortable I totally understand." As he said it, his eyes pleaded with her to get on his bed.

"I don't mind," she said. For some reason, she didn't. The way he'd set it up was lovely. She could see how he wanted the painting to be. She was happy for him.

He politely disappeared and she shed her clothes, not bothering with the robe. She lay on her side on the bed. She laid her head on her arm. She loosened her hair over her shoulder and back and let it fan out behind her on the sheet.

Leo knocked timidly. He came in with the close-held expression of a man who didn't expect his desires to work out. But his face changed when he saw her.

"That's exactly, exactly what I imagined," he said, awestruck. The energy in his long limbs made him seem young to her. "How did you know?"

"This is how I would want to paint it," she said honestly. She wondered where all her millions of layers of self-consciousness had gone. It was strange. Where were the coiled muscles, the purple cheeks, the inability to follow a single thought?

Maybe it was depression. Maybe after the horrible incident with Kostos, she'd lost her will. Maybe she'd held the old hopes so tight that once they were gone, nothing much mattered anymore.

But she didn't feel sad, exactly. She would probably know if she were truly sad. She'd certainly known in the past.

She felt old, she realized. She felt tired. She felt like she'd lived a long time and could see her coquettish self of last week from a very far distance. She felt she hadn't the same things to hide. Or maybe she just lacked the energy to try.

Maybe she cared less. She looked at Leo gazing at her, poised with his brush. Maybe she cared differently.

Maybe it was just a relief to know that the epoch of Kostos was finally, finally over.

"Beautiful," he murmured.

She wasn't sure if he meant her or the painting. Maybe it didn't matter. In a strange way she felt as though she was off the hook.

She watched him paint. She listened to the music he'd put on. More Bach, he said, but this time orchestral and choral. She almost felt like she might fall asleep. Her mind unwound into drowsy thoughts about the sea and the sky as it looked outside her grandmother's kitchen window in Oia.

She might have fallen asleep, because when she opened her eyes the light was different. Leo had put down his brush and was studying her.

"I'm sorry. Did I fall asleep?" she said.

"I think so," he said. His eyes were intense, but in a way particular to painting. He was gathering his impressions, transferring them to his canvas without holding on to them.

"How's it going?" she asked.

"It's— I don't know. I'm afraid to say."

That meant it was going well, she understood. "I think I should take a break for a couple minutes," she said. Her arm was prickly all the way down to her fingers. She sat up and moved to the edge of the bed before he could put down his brush and his palette.

He paused halfway to the door. "Do you want me to go?" he asked.

"You don't have to," she said.

Leo watched her stretch and yawn on the edge of his bed. He was as unfamiliar with her behavior as she was. He drifted back to his canvas in some disbelief.

"What time is it?" she asked, shaking out her sleeping arm.

There was a clock on his desk. "Almost four."

Her eyes opened wide. "God. I really did fall asleep."

He nodded. "You sleep very still," he said.

Silence had fallen over Tibby's life. Lena claimed to know nothing. Tibby's mother claimed to know nothing. Carmen claimed to know nothing. Bee claimed to know nothing, but Bee was in Turkey. Bee was the only one Tibby believed.

In a low moment Tibby found herself on the phone with Katherine. She couldn't help herself.

"So have you seen Brian lately?" Tibby asked casually, hating every word as it came out of her mouth. And also hating her mouth and the weak body to which it was attached.

"Yes," said Katherine. Tibby suspected she was watching cartoons.

"Did he take you to camp on Friday?"

"Uh-huh." Now Katherine was chewing on something.

"Did you see Effie?" Oh, the shame.

"Huh?"

"Did you ever see Effie with Brian?"

"Effie?"

"Yes, Effie."

"No."

Tibby felt the relief flood through her body. Maybe Lena and everybody else were telling her the truth after all. Maybe there really wasn't anything going on.

"But she picked up Brian in her car," Katherine mentioned over the opening song of *Blue's Clues.*

"She did?"

"Two times."

What? What? "Are you sure?"

"Yeah. You know what I think?"

"What?" So intense was Tibby she had practically shoved the phone into her ear cavity.

"She has big boobies."

In the last hour of his light, Leo grew agitated.

"When's your mom coming home?" Lena asked, moving her mouth but not her head.

"Not till tomorrow. She went to the Cape with friends this weekend."

"Oh," Lena said. She began to consider a different explanation.

When the music ended, Leo put down his brush and stowed his palette. He walked over to her, and the fading light showed only half of his face.

"Are we done?" she asked.

He didn't answer, but he touched her calf lightly with his fingers. He put the palm of his hand against her hip. He waited to see if she would protest or move away, if she would feel around for the robe as she had done before.

She considered doing all of these things, but she didn't. She liked the feel of his hand on her skin. She wanted to know what came next.

He sat on the bed and leaned over her, kissing her. She drew in her breath as she felt his hand find her breast. She resumed the kiss as his hands explored her body, finding out a few things his eyes couldn't tell him.

He lay next to her and she unbuttoned his shirt. She recognized her own clumsiness, but it didn't register as shame.

She wondered at the intimacy of the sounds in his throat, the smell of his neck and his chest. She pushed her body against his wide, muscled expanse of skin. It was intimate, but not like what she'd had before. Her mind was peaceful. Her body was stirred and it was curious. She wanted to know how it would go.

This wasn't like it was with Kostos: the fierce want bordering on anguish, the longing intermingled with ache. It was something else. It was a simpler pleasure. Maybe you didn't have to go around feeling that much.

Two years ago, she'd stopped when she'd wanted desperately to go. Why not let it unfold? What was she waiting for?

She'd had enough dreams, enough fantasies. She'd read and she'd heard and she'd imagined. She knew what this was about.

"I have something," he murmured. She realized that he meant he had a condom and that he was asking her if she was ready, if this was what she wanted.

She paused, but only for a moment. "Okay," she whispered back.

I'm flying back to D.C. I'll be there Saturday.

Maybe even in time for the Rollinses' bash. I want to see you so much.

Leo wanted her to sleep over, but Lena realized she wanted to wake up in her own bed. He was sorry to walk her home, she knew. He walked her upstairs and to her door, and kissed her until she playfully shut the door in his face.

"We'll have lunch before class tomorrow," he said to her before he left. "I'll bring the sandwiches."

She sat on her bed for a long time without turning on the light. She considered the different parts of her body and how each of them felt. People said that the first time often hurt or felt bad. It didn't for her. She'd been lying naked in his bed for many hours, drowsy and stirred among his sheets and his pheromonal boy smells. She was ready when it happened. Her pleasure was tentative and new, but she was also able to take joy from Leo's more complete rapture.

She was his muse, he told her. The combination of the erotic and artistic had been a revelation to him. She was happy with that. Especially as she thought of her own painting and knew that he was a muse for her too.

Does he even know there is more?

Lena checked herself. She stopped her thinking and went back over the question, unsure of what she'd meant by it. More what? More sadness? More tragedy? More ragged exposure, like you had turned yourself inside out? Was that more?

What if Leo didn't know? What if he never knew? Maybe that would be a piece of good luck.

With Leo she didn't feel turned inside out. She was happy about that. She put on an old pair of pajamas, feeling very much outside in.

But when she woke up sometime in the early morning, she was crying. Her face and hair were soaked, her pillow was damp. How long had she been crying?

The crying kept going as she sat up and wondered about it, not seeming to will it. But she knew what the trouble was. She knew her dream self was permitting a sadness her waking self hadn't allowed.

All this time she'd been waiting for Kostos. She'd always thought her first time would be with him.

Remember to let her into

your heart.

—John Lennon and

Paul McCartney

Tibby tortured herself for the days leading up to her parents' anniversary party. But there was a strange comfort in the fact that at least she deserved it.

Brian and Effie were acting like a couple. No one was even denying it anymore.

"They are the only ones left at home," Bee said.

"Maybe they're just friends," Carmen said.

"Brian's lonely. He misses you," Lena said.

Tibby didn't believe any of it.

If Effie had used even half of the tactical brilliance on Brian that she'd used on Tibby, there was no hope. Effie would probably be wearing an engagement ring the next time Tibby saw her. It wouldn't even matter whether Brian liked her or not.

Silly old Effie, clueless little sister who couldn't tell time without a digital clock. Ha. In Tibby's mind, Effie had transformed into the devil herself.

Tibby's subconscious produced a new anxiety dream just

for the occasion. Tibby dreamed it night after night, all night long: Effie doing various bold things while wearing the Traveling Pants. Only once in all those dreams did Tibby get to wear them herself. And when her big chance came, Tibby somehow ended up with her whole body stuffed into one leg.

"Do you want me to disinvite Brian to the party?" her mother asked the week before Tibby was set to take the train home.

"Let me think about it."

Tibby called her mother back an hour later. "No, he should come. It would be wrong to tell him not to. Anyway, I'm going to have to see him sometime."

They were quiet for a minute.

"I can't exclude Effie," her mom said, naming the very thing Tibby was hoping for.

"You can't?"

"Honey, they're all coming. They are like our extended family. I couldn't think of not having Ari and George. And Lena? That's not a question. I can't exactly say everybody come but leave Effie home."

"Why not?" Tibby said sourly.

"Tibby."

"So would you mind disinviting me?"

More and more, Tibby spent her time watching TV. She'd given up on the computer and her "Script." She watched all the murder shows. All the makeover shows. All the soap operas. All the cooking shows. Even the bug shows and the history shows. She blew most of her savings buying a TiVo on eBay. With the rest she bought a used PlayStation. Everything she needed was right there in that little TV. She watched for Maria Blanquette, but she never came on anymore.

There were quiet moments, though, maybe in the middle of the night or the very early morning, when the countless hours of TV sanded her brain down so that she could see life's bigger patterns. And then Tibby had the sad thought that while she was staring at the screen, Brian, former Dragon Master, was being with a girl and living a life.

To: Tibberon@sbgnetworks.com; Carmabelle@hsp.xx.com; Beezy3@gomail.net
From: LennyK162@gomail.net
Subject: It

I truly cannot believe I'm writing a shotgun e-mail to tell you this, but I couldn't tell one of you without telling the others.

I did it. It it. Or we did it, I should say. Me and Leo.

Bee, I think it was you (was it not) who bet a dozen crullers it wouldn't happen before I was twenty-five. Ahem.

It's not that I was in a hurry or anything. I really wasn't. I would have forked over the donuts. I think I just realized that I was waiting for something that wasn't even real.

I'll have to give you the details in person when we are together. (Carmen??) I'm suddenly picturing my dad seizing my computer and reading everything I write.

Love, love, love, love, love,

Your Loving Lena

(Lover of Leo)

❖ ❖ ❖

Originally, Bee's return trip took her from Izmir to Istanbul to New York and ended with a short flight to Boston. Her plan at the time was to end up in Providence with a week and a half to get in shape for preseason soccer training camp.

But at the airport in Istanbul she switched the flight to Boston to a flight to Washington, D.C., instead.

And what made her happy, after a disorienting number of hours in transit, was seeing Tibby and Lena at the very front of the baggage area waiting for her. She ran at them, almost flattening them in her joy.

"I'm so glad you are here!" she shouted at them.

"We missed you," Lena said as Bee hugged and hugged them.

"I missed you," Bee avowed.

There was too much to say, so they didn't bother quite yet. They drove to Angie's downtown and stuffed their faces with pancakes and bacon even though it wasn't breakfast time, and felt happy to be together. Bee realized they were good at trusting that the moment would come when all would be shared and all would be known. They would wait until Carmen was with them for the true unburdening.

Bridget was lucky, she really was. In the ways that counted.

"I've got to take care of some things at home," Bee said as Tibby pulled her mom's car up to Bee's house. "But I'll come by your parents' party later, okay?"

"Good. It'll be you, me, Len . . . Brian and Effie," Tibby said darkly.

"Oh, no," said Bee. "Really?"

"Yes."

Bee looked at Lena, who shrugged. "Has Effie ever done what I wanted?"

"I'll bring my riot gear," Bee said.

Bee realized after she'd waved good-bye and watched them go that she did not have the key to her house. She didn't feel like knocking. She left her bags in front of the door and went to the back of the house. She still knew the tricks of the kitchen door. She jimmied it patiently and it opened for her. She walked purposefully inside.

Her dad was still at work, she guessed, and Perry would be in his room. She got her bags from the front of her house. She marched them upstairs. Without stopping to think too much she unzipped her duffel bag and began putting her things in her old, emptied drawers.

She opened a window in her room. When she was done unpacking, she walked down to the kitchen and opened a window there, too. She made a quick circuit around the small and overgrown backyard, stopping briefly to pull a few hydrangea balls from the neighbors' bush. She put the blue flowers in a glass in the middle of the kitchen table.

She looked in the refrigerator. There wasn't much there. A bottle of ginger ale. A half-full carton of milk. Some take-out boxes. A wilting bunch of celery in the bottom drawer.

In the cabinet were various cans, who knew how old.

Then she remembered the cereal. She opened the pantry door and saw the impressive lineup of boxes. Both her father and her brother were big on cereal.

She found a bowl and a teaspoon. She poured herself a short layer of cornflakes and added some milk, pleased that it had not yet expired. She sat herself down at the little kitchen table. She wasn't hungry and it didn't taste particularly good, but she ate it.

She left her bowl and spoon in the sink. She left her purse dangling on the chair.

For better and worse, this was her home, and she would remember how to live in it.

The magic had worn off. The loveliness had vanished absolutely. She was back to sweatshirt Carmen, though it was too hot to actually wear one.

She stayed in her bed, trying to sleep through rehearsal. She felt the old Destructo-Carmen impulse, and she tried to work it.

Julia was sympathetic. She brought her cookies and tea from the canteen. She brought her bags of salty Fritos and let her borrow her iPod. She promised they would never talk about meter again if Carmen felt like it was making it worse.

"Thanks," Carmen said tearfully.

She would have stayed in bed all day, but opening night was now four days away, and Carmen knew if she missed the afternoon part, Andrew would maim, mangle, dismember, and also kill her.

She dragged herself miserably to the theater. She was

slowly turning invisible again. Jonathan wasn't even bothering to flirt with her anymore.

She was unfortunately still visible to Judy, who was
waiting stage left to pounce on her.

"Carmen, c'mere," she said, walking briskly out back.

Carmen felt herself suffocating, even apart from the
ninety-five-degree heat and one-hundred-percent humidity.

"I don't like to think I have made a mistake."

"Me either," Carmen said dolefully.

"I'm trying to figure out what's wrong with you."

"Where to start," Carmen said.

Judy looked at her sharply. "You're wallowing."

"I know."

"It's too late to get someone else to do this."

Carmen felt the thud of her pulse in her head.

"And yes, I have thought about it."

Carmen was done with being smart. She had nothing
to say.

"You know, Carmen, the great majority of people achieve
real quality in acting by work and study. There are a few
people who have very strong natural instincts, and for
them it sometimes makes sense to just get out of the way
and let it happen. Do you know what I'm saying?"

Carmen nodded, though she didn't fully know what
Judy was saying.

"So you go home and figure out what the trouble is and
come back tomorrow for dress rehearsal and do your job."

Carmen gazed at Judy without confidence.

"One last thing."

"Yes."

"Trust yourself. Don't listen to anybody else."

Carmen tried not to roll her eyes, but it seemed to her a laughable command at this point.

Judy shrugged. "That's all I'm going to say."

"So look what I bought," Bee said to her father when he got home from work.

He was surprised to see her, first off, let alone the array of vegetables, fresh fruit, and pasta she'd bought at the new Whole Foods and left on the counter. "I'm only home for a couple of nights, so I thought we could make dinner together."

Once upon a time her father had enjoyed cooking. He used to listen to Beatles songs in the kitchen, and he played them loud, so the words made their way onto Bridget's sheets of homework.

She pushed him gently and amicably on the shoulder. "What do you think? You know how to make pesto, don't you?"

He nodded. He looked strained, shell-shocked, slightly frightened.

"Good. I'll get Perry. He can make the fruit salad."

This was an absurd notion, but Bee was ambitious tonight.

She dragged Perry downstairs, blinking like a mole pulled from the dirt. "You can go back to your game after dinner," she told him. She set him up at the counter next to her with a paring knife, a pile of fruit, and a blue bowl. "Cut off the peels and cut everything more or less into squares," she explained.

He was so startled he just did what she said.

She started chopping garlic for the pesto. "Like this?" she asked her dad. He looked up from washing basil.

"A little smaller," he said.

She plugged in the long-unused kitchen radio, an artifact of sorts, and tuned it to an oldies station. She bounced around a little as she grated the cheese.

"Penne or linguine?" she asked Perry, making the boxes dance in front of him. "You get to choose."

"Uh." Perry looked from one to the other. He seemed to take his job seriously. "Penne?"

"Perfect," she declared.

They worked in silence but for a dumb Carpenters song on the radio.

"Did you get pine nuts?" her father asked her.

She was so pleased that she had. "Here," she said, plucking them from behind a loaf of bread.

"Some people use walnuts," her father told them, "but I prefer pine nuts."

"Me too," said Bridget earnestly.

Perry nodded.

After she'd set the little kitchen table and lit a candle and helped Perry transfer his burgeoning salad to a bigger bowl, she heard "Hey Jude" come on the radio. She felt a sad and strange sort of exultation. She turned her face away from them for a moment and closed her eyes, caught in the grip of remembering how it used to be in this house, in this kitchen.

To her right, over the sound of water running in the sink, she heard her father sing along to two words of the song. Just the two, and yet it brought her a joy she could hardly contain.

Bouncing is for balls.

—Tibby Rollins

Tibby's parents' twentieth-anniversary party was for her, in a way, like a traffic accident taking place in slow motion over a long period of time. Sometimes she was in the accident and sometimes she was watching it.

It also had the feature, for Tibby, of having been foretold. And as with an accident, Tibby didn't dare look, but she couldn't not look either. Her better angels told her to look away. And she told those better angels to take a hike.

Lena brought her the Traveling Pants to wear. Lena and Bee hovered so close to her she felt like she'd grown two more heads. She finally told them they had to go away.

Tibby talked to various family friends. She acted like she was writing a real script, being a real film student, and not just playing one while watching TV.

The first time she saw Brian he was eating hummus. The next time he was eating shrimp dumplings. The third time he was eating stuffed grape leaves. How could he eat so much?

The fourth time, he was with Effie. It had to happen eventually. Tibby watched while Effie, in a fit of lurid effrontery, touched Brian on the back. In front of everybody. Tibby felt sick. Both Lena and Bee magically reappeared, each at one of Tibby's elbows.

Effie looked beautiful. She really did. Her cheeks were pink and her legs were tan and her breasts looked like they were ready to take over the room. To be fair, Effie wasn't overdressed. She wasn't overly made up. Effie was happy. That was the thing.

And by that standard of beauty, Tibby was a pure fright. A Boo Radley spooking around her parents' happy party.

Tibby spent some of the time in her room. At one point she went into the backyard and found Bee teaching soccer moves to Nicky and Katherine. Tibby tried to be zany and get up a game of spitting watermelon seeds, but who was she kidding?

"Can this just be over?" she asked Bee before the cake was even presented.

At last, in a blur of warm tidings and well wishes and drunken neighbors, it really was over. She ended up saying good-bye to Effie and Brian in order. She could tell it wasn't what they'd intended. Everyone looked embarrassed at the way it had fallen out.

Tibby kept her face on. And yes, there was Effie, close enough to smell. Tibby moved her mouth and formed words in the generally appropriate category. "Thanks. Great. Yeah. Blah, blah blah." Effie moved on.

Now it was Brian's turn. Tibby said the same robotic

and stupid things, but Brian didn't say anything stupid or robotic back. He just looked at her. Tibby's spirits were fried, but even so, her brain carried on. It continued to perceive things and have thoughts.

Yes, Effie was glowing. Effie was a goddess. But when Tibby looked with honest eyes she could see that Brian, all handsomeness notwithstanding, didn't look so happy. He was a second Boo Radley, but with a fuller stomach.

Tibby stopped whatever stupid thing she was saying in the middle of a sentence. Enough already. Brian held her hand. He held it and he looked at her straight on, eye to eye. She didn't look away. It was the first brave thing she'd done in three months.

There was the natural rhythm of things you knew without knowing. The natural rhythm dictated that Brian let her hand go now, but he didn't. He kept on and so did she. Before he got shoved along by a paralegal in her father's firm, Brian squeezed her hand. But so quickly and subtly she wasn't completely sure it was on purpose or actually that it had even happened.

She watched him go with a sad, slow feeling, as though she saw close things from miles away. She went up to her room without saying good-bye to anyone else.

She climbed into her bed and looked at the place by the window where Mimi's cage used to sit, where Mimi had lived her soft, simple guinea-pig days among her wood shavings and her pellets. Tibby wished she could go back to when Mimi was still alive. To when Bailey was still alive.

She thought about the first time she met Brian. It was Bailey, of course, who thought of it, who put them together. Bailey was uncanny in that way. Before Bailey died, she basically set Tibby up with everything and everyone she would need for a happy life. And Tibby mostly lost or forgot them.

It was so hard to live the right kind of life, even if you knew what it was.

Tibby wished she could at least go back to the night in June when she'd lost the idea of love. She didn't wish she could take back the sex. She used to wish that, but not anymore. She and Brian loved each other. They were old enough to know what they were doing. She wanted to be with him in every way, and that was one of them.

As she thought about it, she realized she wouldn't even change the condom breaking or her fears about pregnancy. If she really got a wish, she wouldn't want to be greedy or impractical. You couldn't turn back time or bring the dead to life. If she got a wish, she would hope to be more modest with it.

She remembered when she was around four or five asking Carmen if she believed the wish Tibby had made over her birthday candles would come true. "Yeah, if you wish for something that could actually happen," Carmen had said philosophically.

Tibby's wish would be to hold on to the idea of love even in the face of darkest doubt. Because that was the way in which she failed. Not once, but again and again.

❖   ❖   ❖

That night, Carmen tried to figure out what the trouble was. She walked around the campus. She sat on the hillside where she'd first met Judy. She called Tibby, and then she remembered about the Rollinses' anniversary party and she cried because she wasn't there with them.

Why are we always apart? she wondered. A voice on the phone wasn't enough sometimes. *Why have I kept away all this time?*

Because we have the Pants, she thought quickly. *The Pants make it okay to do that.*

She went back to her dorm room, and without bothering to take off her clothes or brush her teeth or turn out the lights, she crawled into bed.

She was lying there, eyes open, a while later when Julia came in.

"Look what I have for you," Julia announced gaily. She was in her Florence Nightingale persona.

"What?" said Carmen weakly.

"Those buttermilk scones you love. They make them at night. Did you know that? I have three in the bag and they are ho-o-ot!" She drew out the *O*, trilling it in song.

Carmen sat up. Scones were, in fact, the most comforting food in the solar system.

But as she looked up at Julia's face, something occurred to her. Julia looked happy. Not just cheering-up-a-friend happy, but genuinely happy. Carmen, on the other hand, felt—and undoubtedly looked—genuinely sad.

In the next moment another thing occurred to Carmen. She remembered the time, just a few weeks ago, when

Julia was the one who looked unhappy. And it happened to be at the same time that Carmen was feeling, and undoubtedly looking, happy.

Was this a coincidence? She thought not.

Julia was happy when Carmen was unhappy. In fact, Carmen's unhappiness was the very thing that seemed to make Julia happy. And, alternately, Carmen's happiness caused Julia displeasure.

There was a notable misalignment there. A serious one. What kind of friend thrived on your unhappiness?

She knew the answer. No kind of friend.

She lay back down, her mind whirring.

She thought of her pathetic resolution to be a more worthy friend to Julia, deciding that if she lost weight and pulled herself together, Julia would like her better. How wrong she had been! Julia liked her precisely for her unworthiness. All the ways Carmen failed made Julia feel better about herself. What few ways Carmen succeeded made Julia despise her. Even sabotage her.

Julia seemed to sense the change in mood, but she didn't want to let go. "Butter or jam? Butter *and* jam!"

Even now, even amid deepest doubt, confusion and misery, Carmen didn't want to let Julia down. Too ingrained was her idea of how friendship was. "No. Thanks," she said. "I'm just really tired."

"Are you sure? They are hot. They won't be hot in the morning."

Julia made it hard not to take what she offered. "No, thanks," Carmen said again.

Julia's face got a pinched look. "No problem," she said. "I'll just leave them on your desk."

"Thanks," said Carmen, dully. She picked herself out of bed, brushed her teeth, put on a sleeping shirt, and crawled back into bed. "Do you mind if I turn off the light?"

Julia grabbed a book from the floor. "I'm going to read for a while," she said.

Carmen tried to sleep, but she couldn't. Her despair was so big that she couldn't think of a way to feel better.

And then she remembered a way.

Under Julia's suspicious frown, Carmen took her script from the end of her bed and crept out into the hallway. She sat under the good light and tried to reacquaint herself with the lost girl.

When Tibby woke up, she lay in her old bed for a while and let the waking world come back to her slowly. And she realized her breath had an echo. That was kind of funny, to be breathing in twos.

Then she realized that the second breathing was not hers. She opened her eyes and saw Lena's face where she lay across the end of Tibby's bed. Lena's small, patient face, made with more precision, more fineness than ordinary faces. Most people would tap you and wake you up, but Lena was happy to just wait while Tibby slept.

"Hey," said Tibby. She wondered at how she could love one Kaligaris sister so much and really hate the other one.

Lena smiled. She seemed pretty satisfied with lying there in the sunshine.

"When do you go back?" Tibby asked, crooking her elbow and propping her head on her hand.

"I'm going to stay here for a few days. What about you?"

"I think Bee and I are going to take a train tomorrow night."

They were quiet for a while, but companionably so.

"I think you should get back together with Brian," Lena said finally.

Tibby felt as if she could see the words floating down like feathers freed from her comforter. "I can't, though."

"Why not?"

"It wouldn't be fair," Tibby said, earnestly hoping that Lena would not agree with her.

"It wouldn't be fair to whom?"

"Well, to Effie, I guess."

Lena studied Tibby's face thoughtfully. She seemed to want to project her thoughts from her eyes as much as her mouth. "I don't think you should worry so much about Effie."

"How can I not? She asked my permission and I gave it."

Lena looked sad. "Yes. I know. And Effie's my sister. And I don't want to side with you over her. It's not like I haven't thought about all this."

"I know, Lenny," Tibby said apologetically.

"I've waited to say anything, because I don't want to hurt Effie."

Tibby nodded. She'd worn her anger at Effie like a skin, protective and irritable. Now Tibby felt herself molting, slipping out of it not in bits, but as a piece. And like a molted skin, once disembodied, it sat dry and weightless beside her. It had captured her completely, and yet it didn't belong to her.

"Effie is strong, you know? She bounces."

I don't bounce, Tibby acknowledged to herself.

"She loves Brian. But she loves him in the Effie way. It's like she's going in circles a hundred miles an hour and he's practically standing still. She only sees him when she laps him, but still she thinks they're together."

Tibby laughed in spite of herself.

"Brian wants to cooperate, but it's not right for him."

Tibby marveled at Lena's perfect recapitulation.

Lena resettled her body so she was sitting cross-legged directly across from Tibby and holding her close with her eyes.

"Here's one thing I know," Lena said.

Tibby sat up too. Lena picked the important things carefully.

"There are some people who fall in love over and over."

Tibby nodded, understanding the particular melancholy as it revealed itself on Lena's face.

"And there are others who can only seem to do it once."

Tibby felt tears in her eyes just like she saw in Lena's. She knew Lena was talking about her and Brian. And she was also talking about herself.

And maybe . . .

you are a little

fat bear cub

with no wings and

no feathers.

—Else Holmelund Minarik

Bridget coaxed Perry into going on a bike ride with her. She'd gone to some lengths to borrow Carmen's stepdad's bicycle and helmet, but she'd tried to pass it off to Perry as the lightest of impulses.

"What do you say? We'll just go down to Rock Creek Park and back."

He looked doubtful.

"Please?"

She got on her old bike, not giving him too much chance to think. She was happy when he reluctantly followed. Perry had never been athletic, but he used to love riding his bike.

It was a beautiful late-summer day, not nearly as hot as it could have been. The traffic was blessedly light, as though the cars had purposely stayed away, knowing it was a fragile situation.

By the time they'd made it to the park, Perry was riding right up next to her, coasting along.

She stopped inside the entrance as promised. "Do you want to turn around?" she asked.

He shrugged. "We can keep going," he said, making her feel happy.

They biked for an hour more before they stopped at a cart and bought ice cream bars. Perry had money and wanted to pay. They sat on the grass by the creek and ate them.

There was so much she wanted to say to him. She wanted to get him to talk about their mother and about things he remembered. But she knew she had to go slow. It would be too easy to scare him away.

Before they got back on their bikes, she put her arm around him and squeezed his shoulders. How long had it been since anyone had touched him? He was a little stiff, a little uncomfortable. It probably wasn't what he wanted, but she felt in her heart it was something he needed.

On the way home they stopped at the pet store on Wisconsin Avenue. Perry had always loved animals, but he'd never been allowed to have anything but newts, because their mother was allergic to animals with fur.

They held hamsters first, and then an obese guinea pig. Perry held a baby white mouse with utmost care. Next they each picked up a rabbit. Perry's tried to climb down the front of his shirt and it made him laugh.

Soon after they got home from the pet store, Bridget's

cell phone started ringing. With a galloping heart she recognized Eric's cell number. He didn't have service in Mexico, did he?

"Hello?"

"Bee?"

"Eric?"

"It's me," he said sweetly. "Where are you?"

It had been so long since she'd heard his voice she thought she might cry.

"I'm in D.C. Where are you?"

"I'm in New York."

"You are in New York?" she screamed joyfully. She couldn't help herself. New York wasn't right here, but it was a lot closer than Baja. "Is everything okay?"

"Everything is fine. I really want to see you." He said it tenderly.

"I *really* want to see you." Whatever had happened this summer, the way she felt now, she could not doubt that she loved him.

"What time is it?" he asked.

She walked in view of the kitchen clock. "Almost noon."

"I'll be there in time for dinner."

"Here?"

"There. You better give me your address again."

"You're coming here?" She was screaming again.

"How else am I going to see you?"

"I don't know!" she shouted giddily.

"I can't wait until tomorrow," he said.

❋   ❋   ❋

316

Carmen dressed that morning under the watchful eye of Julia. She forced herself to wear lipstick, even though she didn't feel up to it. Sometimes you could trick yourself.

She didn't collect any of the books she'd taken to carrying around. She didn't even take her script. She could no longer see the words for all the markings.

She did, however, pick up the bag of scones from her desk and take them with her as she walked out the door. Julia looked pleased with that, at least.

Carmen carried the scones as far as the big front doors, where she dumped them in the garbage can.

At rehearsal she kept to herself. Andrew had an eye out for her, but he left her alone. Judy left her alone. Carmen didn't feel invisible to them. She felt they were trusting her to find her way. Either that or they had given up on her, but she didn't really believe that.

She sat in the back row, in the dark, and listened to Leontes rage about nothingness. She thought of the idea she'd had on the hillside the night she'd met Judy. Where there is nothing, there is the possibility of everything. When you live nowhere, you live everywhere.

She wished she had the Pants right now, but she didn't. She had to rely on herself. You have to be like a turtle, she thought; you have to figure out how to bring your home along with you.

She saw Hermione, Perdita's lost mother, bustle down the aisle in full statue costume and makeup. That was a fantasy, wasn't it? Your mother turns into a statue. William Shakespeare knew a thing or two about wish fulfillment.

The statue-mother stays exactly where you left her. You always know where to find her. She doesn't move, doesn't change, doesn't even age.

Carmen thought of her mother. She was hardly a statue. She didn't stay still for two minutes. And yet, even with her new husband and her new baby and her new house—with her *happiness*—Carmen always knew where to find her.

She thought of what it was to begrudge someone their happiness, and this brought to her a stinging set of feelings. She didn't want to think about Julia. She was afraid she would begin to seethe, she'd be sucked into the maelstrom of her old temper and it wouldn't help her. She didn't have the stomach for it. She didn't have the power. She didn't have the wherewithal right now to stake that kind of claim.

Instead, she thought of Ryan's walking shoes. She touched the Pants charm dangling from a chain around her neck. For some odd reason, she thought of Tibby's old guinea pig, Mimi.

Julia was waiting for her outside the theater when they broke for lunch. Carmen saw her there waiting with a smile and two big sweating iced teas, sandwiches, and bags of chips. She beckoned to Carmen and Carmen felt the familiar reactions, outmoded and dislodged though they were. She felt the old pull of gratitude. She felt needy and uncertain. She still clung to the notion of a friend, even a crappy one.

But Carmen didn't move. "No, thanks. Not today," she said finally, and she walked right by.

❋　❋　❋

Bridget fretted out loud in Lena's bedroom. Once the euphoria of getting to see Eric had quieted a little, she'd realized she had problems.

"I told Perry we'd all have dinner together again. He actually seemed like he wanted to. I can't blow it off."

"So you can eat together," Lena said.

"Together?"

"Yeah. Why not?"

There were many reasons why not. But were any good enough to prevent her from doing it?

"Okay, so what do I do with Eric?"

"What *do* you do with Eric?" Lena smiled craftily. "Only you can answer that."

Bridget pretended to punch her. "Come on. I mean where do I put him?"

"In your house."

"In my house?"

Lena shrugged. "That's my only idea."

Bee never brought anyone to her house. Not since middle school. Not even her friends. She hardly brought herself there. Certainly not a boyfriend. It was almost too strange to imagine. Did she need to ask her father? What would he make of it?

And more terrible, what would Eric think of them? How would he feel about her if he saw her house? If he met her father and brother? She had wanted to protect him from the truth.

"Lenny, you know how my house is."

"I think Eric can handle it."

"Do you honestly think that?"

"If he's good enough for you, Bee, I honestly do."

On the walk from Lena's, Bee's adrenaline started pumping. At home, she couldn't be still if she tried. She started with vacuuming, then dusting. She sprayed Fantastik on the walls, trying to make them look a little less gray. She opened all the windows. She brought a fan down from the attic. She mopped. She found boxes in the garage and started putting the ugliest stuff in them — plates, pictures, papers, odd bits of furniture. She stuffed them all out of sight in the basement. She shook out the rugs. She tried to rearrange them to cover the vomitously ugly wall-to-wall carpets. She cleaned the bathroom tile on her hands and knees. She stole more flowers from the neighbors' yard.

When her father arrived home, he looked as though he'd found himself in the wrong place.

"Hey, Dad," she said. "My friend . . . actually my boyfriend is coming to stay for a night. Is that all right?"

Her father's confusion was almost impenetrable. She had to explain it four times before he showed any light of understanding.

"Where will he stay?" he finally asked, with his faraway look.

"In the den. On the couch."

"In my den?"

"Yes. Unless you want him in your room." She meant that as a joke, but it didn't go over like one.

"I don't think so," her father said solemnly.

"In the den, then? Is that okay?"

He nodded and she went back to her cleaning, getting crazier as the hours passed. At five o'clock she corralled the two of them in the kitchen.

"No headphones outside of your rooms," she commanded.

They both nodded fearfully.

"Try to circulate a little. If Eric talks to you, it's a plus if you answer."

They both nodded again. They didn't even look offended.

"We'll have dinner at seven-thirty, okay? Dad, we'll have the leftover pesto and I'll make a salad."

More nodding.

"That's it. Just . . . be yourselves," she finished, which was the least helpful thing she could possibly have said.

By seven o'clock she ran out of steam. She floated along the hallway feeling sorry and hopeless and sad. She wished Eric weren't coming to this house. She wished she hadn't bullied her father and brother into hostile resistance. She wished she lived any life other than this one. Sometimes the past and the future could not be forced together.

But when she walked past Perry's room she saw him cleaning up his desk. When she went downstairs she saw her father carefully folding sheets and a blanket onto the couch in his den.

She'd thought they had nothing to offer her, but they did. She'd thought her efforts were lost on them, but maybe they weren't. She'd thought they had no power to hurt her or make her happy, but at this moment she knew that wasn't true.

They had meager offerings, all three of them. But if they could align what little they had, maybe they could start to make it better.

Tibby called Brian late on Sunday afternoon. "Will you meet me at the picnic table?" she asked him. It was their significant place, site of their first kiss. It stood under a giant copper beech tree in a tiny triangular park equidistant from their houses.

"Okay," he said.

"Now?"

She got there first. She pointed her face in the direction of his house and watched for him. At last he came, the sun drooping faintly behind him. She felt joy spilling over in her chest. Something about his face made her stand up and greet him with her arms. She put them around him courageously. He let her.

She took a step to the side so he could sit at the end of the picnic table. She was grateful that he obliged.

The perfect thing about this table was that when he sat on the end of it and she stood between his legs, they were at the exact right height for seeing each other eye to eye and also for kissing. They had done it many times in the past. She didn't try kissing him this time. But she put her face against his so her mouth was near his ear. "I am so sorry," she said.

He pulled away and looked at her carefully.

"I got scared. I panicked. I forgot everything that was important."

Sometimes it seemed to her that he could extract everything from her mind with his eyes. Sometimes it seemed like her words just got in the way of it.

"I knew that, Tibby. I understood. Why wouldn't you talk to me?"

A blink of her eyes released unexpected tears. "Because I can't lie to you as well as I lie to myself."

He nodded, seeming to understand even that.

"I promise I won't do that again," she said. His eyes tested her words, but she wasn't scared. She knew they were true.

Softly she held his two hands in her two hands. Brutally she shoved aside her chronic instincts of pride and fear. She had no business with them now. "I missed you," she said. "I wish we could go back."

He shrugged. "We can't."

"We can't?" Her agony stretched her words out over the abyss. Had she been wrong in believing that he would forgive her?

"We can go forward, though."

"Together?" She did nothing to temper the abject hope in her face.

"I hope so."

"Really?"

He nodded. "I won't be going to NYU, though."

She winced. "Because of me. Because I ruined everything." She was prepared to eat the blame like ice cream if he'd take her back.

"It's all right. Maybe it's not such a bad thing."

"I'll make it up. I really will. I'll take the bus back every weekend."

"You don't have to do that, Tibby."

"But I want to. I will."

"Let's see how it goes."

"Okay," she said, unnerved by his reserve, his reason-ableness.

She realized he was right when he said that they couldn't go back. For better or worse, it would be different now. In-nocence was not one of the things you could get back.

"Maybe we can trade off," he said.

Life's a voyage that's

homeward bound.

—Herman Melville

Eric had probably hoped for a dinner alone in a restaurant where they could laugh and kiss and play romantic under-the-table foot games to their hearts' content. Instead, he got underheated pesto, a distractedly made salad, and a lot of awkward silence from Bridget's two poorly socialized family members.

He might have thought he'd get to sleep in a bed in a nice suburban house, but he got a scratchy couch in a falling-down house occupied mostly by ghosts.

He tolerated all of it bravely, and his reward did come when she tiptoed downstairs and led him by the hand into her room and shut the door quietly behind her. She knew her brother and father were happily ensconced in their headphones, and this one time it made her glad.

She sat him down on her bed and he groaned with delight as she hitched up her nightgown and sat on his lap, wrapping her tan legs around him. She kissed him long and deep, tangling him up in her web of limbs and fingers and soft hair.

"Why did you come back early?"

"For this," he whispered.

"No, really."

"Really."

"Really?"

"I missed you."

"Did you?"

"A lot."

She hugged him harder.

"I thought of you everywhere all the time. On the beach. On the soccer field. In the water. Lying in bed I *really* thought of you."

His expression was so shameless she laughed. "I mean it, Bee. Every girl I saw I wished was you."

She looked at him with wonder. He was so much better at this than she was! She felt suddenly sad for herself and happy for him. Or rather, the opposite: She felt happy for herself, getting someone as wonderful as him, and sad for him, getting someone as wretched as her.

"Did you miss me?" he asked.

She looked at him thoughtfully. She didn't want to lie. She had some complicated things to tell him and she wasn't yet sure how. "When you told me you were going to Mexico, I wasn't sure what it meant," she said slowly. "I wasn't sure if it meant you wanted to . . . go our own ways for a while."

Each one of his features seemed to grow solemn in turn. "Did you really think that?"

"I wasn't sure what to think."

"Do you think that now?"

"No." She knew her answer right away.

He put his hands on either side of her face. "I never thought of going separate ways. I never wanted that. The way I looked at it was, when you're meant to be, what's a summer?"

She felt the ache in her throat. He didn't question his love. Why had she?

"So does that mean you didn't miss me?" he asked.

"I didn't realize how much until the end," she said.

"And the beginning and the middle?"

She rubbed her cheek thoughtfully. "I think I was missing the idea of missing," she said. "But I think I might have figured it out now."

He let her pull his T-shirt over his head. He let her kiss him. He obliged when she pulled at the waist of his boxers, and he seemed eager to get her out of her nightgown. He was going to trust her and she was going to be worthy of it.

It was maybe strange to want to make love to your boyfriend in your old bedroom after such a summer. But it was undoubtedly what she wanted.

Maybe it was her need to connect old and new. Maybe it was her desire to put a happy memory, an act of love, into this house that had seen so few of them.

❋ ❋ ❋

Carmen wore Perdita's flowers in her hair and she kept quiet. She spoke when she was onstage and otherwise she floated around in the state of a dream. For three days, she didn't look at her script.

The hardest part was the few hours in the middle of the night spent in her room. It was hard to be impervious to Julia's overtures. It was perhaps harder to be impervious to Julia's silent rage.

You don't want me to be happy, she said to herself to ward off Julia's poisonous spirit.

She wore her costume. She mused on the warmth of her skin and the sensation of new textures against it. She listened to Leontes. She listened to Polixenes and Autolycus and Paulina. She bathed her brain in luxurious language and mostly forgot about thinking.

She said her lines, but she did not look at Andrew and he said nothing to her. *We're trusting me to figure this out*, she knew.

In the morning Eric had to leave, he said. Maybe he just wanted to leave. But he promised Bridget he'd meet her in Providence in a few days. That was a relief. She wanted to practice being better at missing him, but not quite yet.

Before she left home she had a number of things to take care of. The last was retrieving the boxes of stuff she had shoved into the basement in her apoplexy of cleaning the day before.

She sensed that her dad and Perry were happy with some of her alterations, but she didn't want to go overboard. If

Perry needed to keep his Lord of the Rings calendar from 2003, then so be it.

She walked down to the basement and hauled up the boxes one at a time. Going down for the last load, she finally thought to turn on the light to make sure she wasn't forgetting anything.

Her eyes caught on a shelf holding a series of neatly placed boxes. She didn't remember them—neither the shelves nor the boxes. How long had it been since she'd looked around down here? She walked over to study them more carefully.

Each of the boxes was labeled with a name and a year or, in a few cases, a span of years. The writing was all capitals, but she recognized it as her father's.

In a state of breathlessness she took down *Bridget* from 1993. Was it kindergarten? Maybe first grade? Inside, carefully stacked and piled, were artworks, clay pieces, efforts at writing and tracing. There were pictures, some with notes on the back in her mother's handwriting. There was a card from Greta. A necklace she remembered beading. There was a photograph of her with Tibby and Lena and Carmen. There was a crayon drawing she'd made of Perry with a tiny head, holding a newt.

She took down the box that said *Marly, 1985–1990*. There were pictures from her parents' wedding, her mother's journals, pictures her mother had drawn, the beginning of a baby book for her twins. Bridget never knew that her mother had drawn pictures.

She took down another of her boxes, *Bridget 1994*. Here were many more photographs of the Septembers. Here was the first of her soccer trophies. Bridget picked up a tiny cardboard box, the kind you got when you bought a piece of jewelry. She shook it, and she knew without looking what it was. She remembered the celebration of little teeth tucked under her pillow, expecting money and usually getting it.

She put it back without opening it. She put the boxes back in place on their shelves and sat down on the dusty floor.

She thought about the vast amount of work her father had put into saving these things, the care with which he had preserved every single object. Out of sight, but still here. Her mother was here too. They didn't live big, maybe. But they lived.

She put her arms around her knees and hugged herself and let herself cry.

Lena extended her time in Bethesda by a few days because she sensed she might be needed there. Effie was leaving for a ten-day trip to Europe the following week, but until then, Lena sensed her sister might need some girly distraction. Lena was mentally preparing herself for round-the-clock manicures, pedicures, and home facials. One nice thing about Effie: There were few reversals in her life that a manicure couldn't fix.

Lena had the idea of calling Leo and telling him where she was and why. But when she actually got him on the phone she decided not to. He was happy to hear from her and eager to tell her about a new painting he had started, but he didn't need to know where she was or when she'd see him. That wasn't the way it would go between them. She knew that and she wasn't sorry.

Was she? Honesty required that she ask that question of herself a second time. No, she wasn't, she decided, trailing her hand over her bedspread, still looking at the phone. She would be happy to see him again. She admired him, she was attracted to him. But she wasn't sorry to let it go. The interlude in Leo's bed had been exciting and it had been clarifying for her, but even as it had unfolded she had sensed it was more like the end of the story than the beginning.

Lena went by Tibby's and Bee's houses that afternoon to say good-bye. Not long after she returned, she heard a knock at the door and Brian's voice downstairs and understood that he and Effie had gone for a walk.

She closed her door and sat on her bed and waited patiently for the noise to start. Within forty-five minutes it did. First Lena heard the front door slam. Then she heard the pounding on the steps and the slam of Effie's bedroom door.

She knew better than to relax. Minutes after Effie's door slammed the first time it slammed again, and then Lena's own door flew open.

"I cannot believe her!" Effie's face was red and her eyes were smeared with black. It had to have been an ambush of sorts, because Effie had an almost unerring instinct for when to wear waterproof mascara.

Lena deliberated with herself as to how much knowledge

to convey. She decided to be quiet. When it came to Effie, quiet usually worked best.

"Why did she tell me it was over? I gave her the chance! Why did she lie?" Effie's gestures were big with indignation.

Lena tucked her hands under her.

"Brian is an idiot! Why would he go back to her? After what she did? She doesn't care about him! She doesn't *love* him!"

Lena opened her mouth even though she shouldn't have. "How do you know that, Ef?" Instantly she regretted the mistake.

"What?" Effie came in closer, bearing down. "Are you saying she does?"

Lena kept her voice low and uncommitted. "Don't you think it's possible?"

"No! It's not! Do you know how she treated him?" She shook her hands emphatically. "You don't treat someone like that if you love them!"

Lena felt her own face warming. *Oh, but sometimes you do.*

"Lena? Lena!"

Lena looked up.

"You are siding with her, aren't you? I knew this would happen! You are taking Tibby's side, even after what she did!"

"Effie, no—"

"You are! Just admit it. Tibby lied to me, she treated Brian like *crap*, she betrayed me even after I went to New

York to get her *permission*, and you are still siding with her against your own *sister*!"

"No, Effie—" This had taken a wrong turn. The path to manicures had been forsaken.

"It's true!" Effie was really crying now, and Lena's heart felt frail. These were not histrionic tears, but sad, uncontrollable ones.

And Lena knew they had gotten to a deeper, harder thing, even harder than losing the boy you thought you loved.

"You always do that! You do! You always have. You know that?"

Lena felt the dull ache in her throat. "Effie—"

"You do. You do, Lena. I am your only sister, but you always choose them over me."

"Effie." Lena stood up to try to comfort her or touch her or even block her way, but it was too late. Sobbing, Effie fled.

Lena wished for a hearty door slam, but that wasn't what she got. Her door swayed quietly so that she could still hear her sister's tears. She minded them more than all the shouts and slams put together.

She tried to go to Effie's room a while later, but Effie wouldn't answer. The next day, Effie wouldn't open her door at all.

Lena left for a few hours in the late afternoon, and when she came back, Effie's door was still shut. She still would not answer.

Lena spent most of the evening hours quietly in her room, wondering whether she'd done the wrong thing. Had she really chosen Tibby over Effie? It didn't feel that simple. In a way that was almost more troubling, she felt like she'd chosen one way of being over another. She'd chosen Tibby's agony over Effie's joy. In a weird way, she'd chosen herself.

Before Bridget left home she went to the pet store and came home with a rabbit and a hutch.

"It's for you," she said to Perry, presenting it to him in the backyard.

He was startled and he didn't want to accept it at first, but as he held the little creature she could see his mind changing.

He began to get excited as they set up the hutch under the dogwood tree. He held the rabbit in his arms and fed it a stalk of wilted celery.

"I'll have to get a water bottle," he noted to himself and to her. "And carrots and lettuce and stuff."

"You can borrow my bike if you want," she said.

He nodded. How nice he looked with a little sun on his face.

She would come back home again in the next few weeks. She promised herself she would. And in the meantime Perry would have the company of this warm-blooded and furry thing. A reason to get out of his room and out of the house. Something to take care of, something that needed him. Something to nuzzle his neck and crawl down his shirt, to get him back into the practice of loving another soul.

She suspected that what he really needed were antidepressants, but until she could rally herself for that effort, a baby bunny rabbit was the next best thing.

He named it Barnacle. She had no idea why.

"She's got to come out eventually, right?" Lena said to her mother the next morning in the kitchen.

"Effie?" her mom said.

"Yeah. Have you seen her?"

"She left early this morning. Daddy drove her to the airport."

"What? You are kidding me! Where did she go?"

"She went to Greece."

Lena was stunned. "She went already?"

"She called Grandma last night and asked if she could stay in Oia for the week. Grandma was delighted. She wants Effie to help her paint her house. Your father changed the ticket on the computer."

How had she missed all of this? "She left this morning?"

"Yes."

Lena scratched violently at a bug bite on her wrist. She needed to think for a minute. "Did she seem okay?"

Her mother gave the first sign of knowledge. "Depends on what you mean by okay."

"Will she talk to me if I call her?"

"Maybe you should give her a few days."

Lena felt stricken. "That bad, huh?" She kept her eyes down.

"Lena, honey, she feels betrayed," her mother said, perching on a tall kitchen stool. Ari rarely gave in to a true sit.

Lena put her arms on the counter. "Brian didn't love her, Mom. She was going to have to notice that eventually."

"I think you're right. And I think Brian basically told her that as gently as he could," Ari said.

"You do?"

"I do. But I don't think it's Brian's love she's missing."

Carmabelle,
    Break a leg tonight. Break two!
We love you so,
Tibby + Bee + Lenny
P.S. Bee chose the blue carnations. Blame her.

Lena had thought she'd be needed here at home. Now she wasn't. She couldn't reach Effie on the phone to make anything right, and she was too guilty and fitful to hang around sidestepping conversations with her father about her plans for the future.

So she came up with an even crazier idea.

She fooled with the phone in her father's office until she managed to get Tibby and Bee on at the same time. Within two minutes she'd presented her crazy idea and they'd both agreed to it.

Once she secured the borrowing of her mother's car, she went upstairs to pack her bag.

"Hey, Mom?"

"Yeah?"

"Have you seen the Traveling Pants?" Lena went down to the kitchen to ask the question rather than just shout it.

"No. I don't think so."

"I thought they were in my room." She began to feel a touch of nervousness. "Was anybody in here cleaning or doing laundry yesterday?" She trusted her mother and the regular housekeeper, Joan, not to do anything insane, but once in a while there was a substitute.

"No. Joan was here on Friday. That's it. Are you sure you had them? That you brought them from school?"

"Yeah. I'll go back and look more," Lena said, darting back up the steps to her room. She checked everywhere, even hopeless places like her bottom drawers and a trunk she hadn't opened in months.

She knew she had brought them home for Tibby to wear to the party. Tibby had worn them and then given them back. She *had* given them back, right?

Lena thought she had, but there was enough doubt to provide modest comfort for the moment.

crazy is what crazy do

—The Black Eyed Peas

Opening night arrived, and Carmen's stomach somehow climbed into her neck. She might have thrown it up, but luckily, it stayed attached.

There were photographers, critics, hundreds of people. Andrew was trying to protect her. She could feel that. He held her hand and walked her around backstage.

Jonathan kissed her and pulled her hair.

"Lovely." Ian nodded at her decked out in her flowers. He kissed her head and she thought she might cry.

Could she do this? Did she know how? She tried to swallow her stomach back down to her stomach again.

From where she sat backstage, she listened to the first act and let the trance begin. She heard the words more clearly than she ever had before. She heard more in each word, more in each combination of words, and exponentially more in each line of words.

These were real performers. Her heart swelled to know

them. They had given so much in five weeks of rehearsals, she would have thought they'd given everything. But now she knew that they had saved something for this.

During intermission she peeked out at the theater, watching it refill. When it was almost full and the lights blinked on and off, she saw three people file in through the center door and her breath caught. Time lapsed as they walked down the center aisle: three teenage girls all in a row.

They were so big, so bright, so beautiful, so magnificent to Carmen's eyes that she thought she was imagining them. They were like goddesses, like Titans. She was so proud of them! They were benevolent and they were righteous. Now, these were friends.

Lena, Tibby, and Bee were here, in this theater, and they had come for her. Her big night was their big night. Her joy was their joy; her pain their pain. It was so simple.

They were absolutely lovely, and in their presence, so was she.

In the presence of her friends, Carmen rediscovered the simplicity she had lost. They enabled her to find the voice of Perdita as she had first understood it. It felt good to be able to go back.

But the greater miracle was her understanding of the last scenes in the play: the reunion, the end of estrangement, the end of winter. She had understood from the beginning the feeling of the girl who was lost, and now she also understood the girl who was found.

In front of six hundred and twenty souls, three of them

most precious to her, Carmen's winter ended and she felt the return of her own extravagance.

Lena was singing along to an old Van Morrison tune on the radio, driving along the New Jersey Turnpike. She'd dropped Bee off in Providence and Tibby in New York, and now she was heading back to D.C. to return her mother's car. It was four o'clock in the morning and she needed to do something to keep herself awake.

Her cell phone began buzzing in the front pocket of her skirt. That worked too.

"Hello?"

There was no connection at first, and then she heard an urgent though distant voice. "Lena?"

"Effie! Is that you?"

"Lena, are you there?"

"Yes, it's me. Are you okay? Are you in Greece?" She jabbed the radio button off. She was relieved and grateful to get to talk to Effie so much sooner than expected.

"Yes, I'm at Grandma's," Effie said, muffled, but crying openly.

"Ef? Effie?" For several seconds Lena heard sobs but no voice, and she agonized. "I am so sorry, Effie. Please talk to me. Are you okay?"

"Lena, I did something really terrible."

Even over a cell phone connection, Lena suddenly sensed that these were a different kind of tears than the ones Effie had left with. "What? What is it?" Lena tried not to drive off the road.

"I can't even tell you."

"Please tell me."

"I can't."

"Effie, what could it be? How could it be that bad?"

"It is. It's worse."

"You're making me nervous, you know. Just tell me or I'll drive into a ditch."

"Oh, Lena." More sobs.

"Effie!"

"I—I . . . your pants."

"What? I can't hear you!"

"I took your pants."

"The Traveling Pants?"

"Yes." Crying. "I took them."

"To Greece?"

"Yes."

"Effie." Now she knew where they were, at least.

"I was mad and I just—I was mad at Tibby and you and everybody and—"

"Okay, I get it," Lena said, disoriented by the rapid re-allocation of guilt between them.

"It's worse than that, though."

Lena felt the bang bang bang of her portending heart. "What?"

"I wore them on the ferry and they got wet."

"Yes."

"I hung them on the line on Grandma's terrace to dry. I never thought—"

Bang bang bang. "You never thought what?"

"It was windy. I wasn't thinking that it could"—several words were lost in tears—"or that I would lose them."

"What do you mean, Effie?"

"I went to get them and they were gone. I've looked everywhere. For the last three hours I've looked." Another crash of sobs. "Lena, I did not mean to lose them."

Effie had taken the Pants. Now Effie couldn't find them. But she had not lost them. They were not lost. "Effie, listen to me. You cannot lose them! Do you hear me? You have to find them. They have to be there somewhere." Lena's voice was as hard as she'd ever heard it.

"I've tried. I really have."

"You keep trying!" There was static on the line. "Can you hear me? Effie? Effie?"

She was gone. Lena threw the phone down on the passenger seat and clutched the wheel. She felt like she could crush it in her hands.

The Pants could not be lost. They had magic to protect them. They were not the kind of thing that could be lost. They were there, and Effie would find them. Anything else was not a thing she could think.

It had been hard for Carmen to see it end. The honors, the admirers, the catered parties, the champagne, the little egg rolls. Her singular pride in introducing her friends to the cast. But the evening had eventually come to an end.

It had been hard to say good-bye to her friends as they piled into Lena's mother's car to drive through the night and be back by morning in time for their obligations.

344

Walking back from the parking lot, Carmen had passed the theater again to savor the taste of the night.

Judy and Andrew had still been there, sleeves up and hair down, going over the points of the evening one more time. It had been hard not to cry when they hugged her.

"You did me proud, sweetie," Judy said in her ear.

"I'm not going to jinx it," Andrew said. But when Carmen let out a few tears, she saw that he had some too.

Hardest of all had been ending up back in her dorm room.

Thankfully, Julia was asleep when Carmen crept into her bed. Carmen slept a long and virtuous sleep. But as does tend to happen in the morning, Julia woke up.

"How did it go?" Julia asked pointedly.

"Weren't you there?" Carmen asked.

"No, I had other plans."

This was strange, because during one of the many curtain calls, Carmen had actually seen Julia in the audience. She knew she had, because she had been struck at that moment by the contrast between the three beacons of friendship burning like suns in her eyes and Julia, the cheapest, scrawniest, chintziest ten-watt bulb of a counterfeit friend.

"That's weird, because I saw you there."

Julia was again looking couched and furtive. "No, you didn't."

Carmen could have summoned her towering anger at this moment. She thought of it. Her power was restored enough that she could have taken on Julia as the rock-hurling Carmen of old, and Julia would have suffered for it.

Carmen could have, but she didn't. Julia had once seemed too valuable to cross. Now she didn't seem valuable enough.

She began getting dressed as Julia looked on sourly.

"I don't know what your problem is," Julia snapped before Carmen could get out of the room. "I thought we were friends."

Carmen turned. She towered a little in spite of herself. "We weren't."

"We weren't?" Julia echoed, surprise and sarcasm mixing.

"No. You know how I know?"

Julia looked heavenward, the same kind of petulant expression Carmen herself used to make. "How do you know?"

"Because you wanted me to fail. But I didn't. Too bad for you. That means we were not friends."

Before Carmen left, she thought of one more thing.

"You know what the sad thing is?"

Julia's jaw was locked now. She wasn't saying anything back.

"The way you are going, you will never have one."

As Carmen walked away, she felt sorry that she'd been taken in by a snake like Julia. But in some strange way she felt appreciative that it had happened. In friendship terms, she'd lived her life in the Garden of Eden. Her bond with her friends was so powerful, so supportive, so uncompetitive, she'd thought that was how friendship worked. She'd

346

been spoiled and she'd been innocent. She hadn't recognized how good she had it, or how bad other alleged friendships could be.

Now she knew.

If she could go back, would she do anything differently? She thought about that.

No, she probably wouldn't. It was that old idea—better to put your heart out there and have it abused once in a while than to keep it hidden away.

But jeez, a little judgment wouldn't hurt.

Poor empty pants

With nobody inside them.

—Dr. Seuss

From the moment Bee learned the state of the Pants, time had ceased flowing in its normal way and instead proceeded in nervous jolts.

"Should I call Lena again?"

"You talked to her ten minutes ago," Eric said from the back of Bee's neck, where he'd been kissing her.

"I know, but what if she heard something? What if she talked to Carmen?"

She and Tibby and Lena had done almost nothing but call each other since Lena had set off the alarms.

Bee's phone rang before she could decide. It was Carmen.

"Oh, my God."

"Lena told you." Bridget's agitation was big and her dorm room felt tiny.

"Yeah." They had deliberated waiting until after Carmen's last performance on Wednesday.

"What are we gonna do?"

"What can we do? Hope Effie isn't blinded by anger and jealousy."

Bridget paused. "I kind of wish we had someone else looking."

"Yeah. But who else have we got?"

"Grandma."

"Ugh."

Lena called Effie every hour for twenty straight. Grandma was getting annoyed, but what could she do? She let Effie take the blame.

"I'm trying. I'm trying everything." That was all Effie would say.

Lena even wished she could call Kostos to see if he was there and could help. But unfortunately, that was a bridge she had burned.

"I think I know what the problem is," Tibby said to Lena on the phone from her room in New York.

They called each other so often, they hardly bothered hanging up anymore. "What?"

"The Pants don't want Effie to find them."

"Oh, my gosh. You could be right."

"They're scared of her." Tibby suspected that she was possibly overidentifying with the Pants, but still.

"Maybe that's it."

"So what should we do?"

❈ ❈ ❈

Lena waited for twenty-two more hours and made another uncharacteristically rash decision.

"I'm going to go," she said to Carmen on the phone.

"What?"

"I'm going to Greece. I'm online as we speak. I'm buying a ticket."

"No."

"Yes." She had made up her mind. It was her fault, really. The Pants had been in her possession. It was her lunatic sister who had taken them. She was the one with the crabby grandma in Oia. Who could find them but her?

"When?"

"Thursday is the soonest I could get."

"Whoa."

"I just pressed the button, Carma. I bought it."

"You are fearsome. With what?"

"A credit card."

"Whose?"

"My mother's."

"Does she know?"

"Not yet."

"Oh, Lenny."

"You can't put a price on the Traveling Pants."

"Yeah, but maybe your mom can."

Lena started to get suspicious when Bee called on Tuesday and asked her for her flight number for the third time. "What's up?" she asked.

"Nothing," Bee said.

❁   ❁   ❁

When Lena arrived at the gate at Kennedy Airport in New York for her flight to Athens on Thursday, she was surprised to see Bee standing there with her duffel bag over her shoulder, but she was not stunned. She was stunned to see Tibby and Carmen standing beside Bee.

She laughed out loud. The first time in days. It was cathartic. "Did you come to say good-bye?" she asked, full of happy suspicions.

"No, baby, we came to say hello," Carmen said.

Bee said she'd borrowed the money for her ticket from her dad. According to Carmen, David had about a billion frequent flyer miles, so he gave her some when she pleaded. Tibby's parents had given her an open ticket voucher for her graduation present last June. They'd also loaned her a hundred bucks to get an expedited passport, which was going to be hard to repay since she'd given notice of exactly one hour at her job.

"Call us Beg, Borrow, Steal and . . . ?" Bee looked at Tibby.

"Use," Tibby said.

"I wish I was Steal," Carmen said.

"I wish I was Borrow," Lena said.

"Nobody wants to be Beg," Bee pointed out.

They had to argue at the ticket desk to get their seats together, but when the plane took off for Greece, all four of them were sitting side by side.

Lena looked right and looked left and laughed again. How

352

much it sucked to be traveling under these circumstances. But how exquisitely great it was to be doing it together.

"Are you worried they're going to kick you off the team?" Tibby asked.

As the plane soared through space, as their reckless energy dissipated and the hours stretched, they began to calculate the number of things they had blown off and people they had upset by doing this.

"Not unless they can do without a center forward." Bee explained that the coach would be furious and threaten her a lot, but then he would forgive her in time to start her in the first league game.

Tibby realized they could not talk about the length of this trip. They couldn't cast their minds forward to an outcome other than finding the Pants and bringing them home, and who could say how long that would take? But they were heading into the third week in August. It was hard not to recognize the fact that most schools started in a week and a half.

"I'm going to take an incomplete in my screenwriting class," Tibby said. In the three days she'd spent in New York since her reunion with Brian, she'd made gigantic strides on her love story, but she hadn't quite gotten to the end of it.

"I was supposed to pack up my room this week. My mom and David are moving into the new house the day after Labor Day. I'll just have to do it later."

"Eric said he'd forgive me for leaving if I wore a burka and promised not to flirt with any Greek boys," Bee said.

"Greeks do like blondes," Lena said.

"Brian offered to come and help us search," Tibby said.

"How about Leo?" Carmen asked.

"He called last night," Lena said. "I think he's going to Rome for most of next semester."

"That's sad," Carmen said.

Lena shrugged. "It's not, really. It's all right. I kind of knew it wasn't going to turn into a long-term thing."

Tibby noticed how different Lena looked from the old days of Kostos, when every time she proclaimed equanimity, she looked as if she had stolen a car.

"It's for the best," Carmen consoled her. "Lena. Leo. Your names don't sound good together anyway."

Tibby laughed and hugged Carmen's arm. "Well, thanks, Carma. That about settles it."

Lena laughed too.

"Have a thorny relationship problem? Just ask Carma," Bee said.

"You should get a column."

"Start a blog."

"I think I should," Carmen agreed. "Hey, did I tell you who came to the final performance last night?"

"Who?"

"Well, my mom and David . . ."

"Right," Lena said.

"And my dad and Lydia."

"Really?" Bee said. "All four of 'em."

"Yep. They were surprised to see each other at first, but they all had such a great time together I told them they should get a room."

Tibby laughed and listened to her friends laugh and then just sat back and listened to the flow of their familiar voices. As unhappy as she was about the Pants, she was joyful that the four of them were finally together. She felt a little guilty about it, like she was laughing at a funeral. And then she realized that the Pants wouldn't want her to feel that way.

"Do you guys realize this is the first time we've really been together since the beach at the end of last summer?" Tibby said, unable to keep her appreciation to herself.

"Yes, I thought of that too," Lena said a little sadly.

"How could we go so long?" Carmen asked.

"You're one to ask," Tibby said, but even as she said it she was filled with gratitude to have their regular Carmen restored to them.

"You know what?" Bee said.

"What?"

"I don't think it's just that the Pants are scared of Effie."

"Then what?" Lena asked.

Bridget looked at each of her friends in turn. "Look at us. I think the Pants are smarter than we even know."

At first cock-crow

the ghosts must go

Back to their quiet

graves below.

—Theodosia Garrison

It was late when they got to Valia's house, and the four of them were so tired and punchy, so confused as to their whereabouts in time and space, they felt like they'd been inhaling from a whipped cream can.

Lena was earnestly happy to see her grandmother and surprised not to see Effie. She had been girding herself for an uneasy reunion.

"Effie left for Athens today," Valia told them impassively, but a few minutes later she pulled Lena aside. "She tried her hardest, you know. She tried to find those pants all day and night."

"I know, Grandma," Lena said.

Tired as they were, they knew their purpose. Lena found two flashlights and they set out with them on the narrow cobblestone roads and paths beneath the perch of Valia's terrace.

"It's all up and down here," Tibby pointed out, waving her hand down the cliff to the dark water below. "No flat."

That made it harder to find things, Lena acknowledged to herself. Gravity always played its advantage here.

Valia shook her head at them, making no secret of her doubts, and after a while even Lena realized the futility of their method. Why struggle to light up tiny patches of the world when the sun would do the job so effectively in a few hours?

"We should get some sleep," Lena said. "That's the smartest thing to do. That way we can get up early and get to work."

They did get to work in the morning. And yet, preoccupied as they were by their loss and their mission, they couldn't help being awed by what the sun showed them.

"This is the most beautiful place I've ever seen. A thousand times more beautiful than the next most beautiful place," Carmen said.

Lena thought that too. She felt a great giddiness along with a deep satisfaction at getting to share it with them. Another unexpected gift, courtesy of the Pants, she thought.

She told them about the formation of the Caldera, really a giant crater left by what was possibly the hugest volcanic explosion in the history of the world. It sank the whole middle of the island, leaving sheared cliffs around a center of water.

"And what about those islands?" Bee asked, squinting over the water to three masses of land floating in the Caldera.

"Patches of lava left over," Lena explained.

Lena led them along the sloped paths where they thought the wind could have carried the Pants from Valia's patio. The whitewashed houses and crumbling churches, the dazzling blue of the domes and doors, the blinding pink of the climbing bougainvillea, all of it was so intoxicating to the eyes it was hard to stay focused on the job at hand. After a few hours in the sun, they took a break in the shade and tried to strategize.

"I wouldn't be surprised if someone found them," Tibby said.

"That's a good point," Lena said.

They went to town. Luckily, most of the shopkeepers spoke at least a little English. Lena went armed with a picture.

"We're looking for something," she explained to a man in a clothing shop. She pulled out the picture of the Pants as worn by Tibby last summer at the beach. She pointed to the Pants. "We lost these."

The shopkeeper looked alarmed. "You lost this girl?" He put on his glasses and held the photograph up close.

"No, she's right here," Bridget explained. "We lost those Pants."

They found a copy shop in town. Using the photograph, they blew up the image of the Pants, beheaded Tibby, and circled the Pants with a thick black marker. *LOST PANTS*, Lena wrote in English and Greek. The copy lady helped with the translation. Lena put down her grand-mother's address and number. *REWARD!*, she wrote in Greek.

While they waited for fifty copies to be made, Lena gave them a little tour.

"This is the forge that belonged to Kostos's grandfather. I think he sold it in the last year or two. That's where Kostos used to work," she explained. "That's where we kissed the first time," she added as an aside.

She took them down to the little harbor. "Did you ever see the picture I drew of this? It was one of the first ones I ever liked. Kostos and I went swimming here."

"There's a certain theme to this tour, I think," Tibby said.

"Ha ha," Lena said. As they stood on the dock she pretended to push Tibby into the water.

"How could you not fall in love here?" Bee asked.

Inspired by her thoughts of love and of beauty, of ancient places and dirt floors, Bee lifted her arms to the sky and did an arcing dive off the dock into the sea. It was thrillingly cold. She popped her head through the surface and screamed with joy.

Because they were her friends, and perfect friends in nearly all ways, the three of them screamed back and dove in after her.

They all shouted about how cold it was. They swam around screaming in their wet, billowing clothes. Bee hauled herself out first and helped the others, who were laughing and shivering so hard she was afraid they might drown from elation and harebrained stupidity.

They all lay side by side on the dock so the sun could dry them. The sky was the most perfect and cloudless blue.

Bee loved the sun. She loved her heavy, dripping clothes. She loved the water lapping against the pilings beneath her. She protested aloud at the encroachment of Tibby's cold toes against her shin, but she loved that, too.

She belonged to her friends and they to her. That much she knew, even if the Pants were temporarily mislaid.

"I think our copies are probably ready," Carmen pointed out dreamily.

They posted their signs all over the place. Throughout Oia and its environs.

"I think we should cover Fira, too," Lena suggested.

So they went to Fira that evening with fifty more. They were fanning out, posting them around the crowded tourist spots, when Bee came running.

"Lena! I think I just saw Kostos."

Lena felt the *zzzzt* of electrical current up her back.

"You never even met Kostos," Tibby said, appearing next to her.

"Well, I know, but I saw his picture," Bee insisted.

Lena looked around, trying to feel calm. She did a slow, calm survey. "My grandmother said he's not here. He hasn't been around all summer. Where do you think you saw him?"

Bee pointed to a corner with a café and a bike shop.

"What are the chances? You probably imagined it," Carmen said. She stood protectively by Lena.

"Carma, he does *live* here," Bee pointed out. "It's not

like I'm claiming to have seen him in Milwaukee or something."

"Whether he was or wasn't, he does kind of haunt this place," Lena said diplomatically. "I am the first to admit that. Anyway, let's keep going."

They posted their signs until it was dark, Lena distractedly imagining she saw Kostos everywhere.

"Now we'll go home and wait for people to call us," Lena said.

At home Lena stepped into the kitchen, where Valia had cooked up a huge feast. "Grandma, Kostos isn't on the island, is he?"

"I heard he's traveling all this summer. I don't see him vunce. I talk to Rena, but I don't know vhere he goes." Valia was pretending to be dismissive of Kostos. Like Lena, she'd spent too much time hoping.

They had a long, cozy night at home. Valia went to bed early but left them a bottle of red wine. They sat on the floor drinking and talking and talking and talking.

It was magical, but by the time they dragged themselves up to bed they realized that in spite of one hundred signs, not one person had called.

Lena was the only early riser of the group, and her body seemed to adjust most quickly to Greek time. At sunrise, she decided to take a walk.

She took a long, slow walk. First she thought about Effie and then about Bapi, and after that she let herself think about Kostos.

It was fitting, in a way, to walk and see all these ruins. Here, on this island, the place where she'd both given away her heart and seen it broken, there were ruins all around, though not all of them ancient.

Ruins stood for what was lost, and yet they were beautiful—peaceful, historic, intellectual. Not tragic or regrettable. Lena tried to keep hers that way too, and she succeeded to some extent. Why not celebrate what you had had rather than spend your time mourning its passing? There could be joy in things that ended.

Still, it surprised her how much she was thinking of him here, how often she thought she saw him. Around the corner, looking out a window, sitting at a table in a café. Not a ghost or a memory of Kostos, but Kostos as he was now.

"It's weird. Now I keep thinking I see him," she confided to Bee later that day when they were canvassing people around the Paradise and Pori beaches.

"What do you think when you do?" Bee asked.

Lena considered this question as she showered before dinner.

After the scene in the motel in Providence, Lena knew she had changed. She knew she had destroyed whatever remained of her and Kostos. God, what must he think of her now?

She wasn't who he thought she was. She wasn't who *she* thought she was. She had displayed an ugliness he hadn't imagined was there. But it was a relief, in a way. If that was part of who she was, he should know it. He shouldn't be tricked. And there was a perverse, childlike part of her that wanted to get to be ugly sometimes.

She wondered about him. Had he ever really been able to love her? Did she really love him? There was undoubtedly something beautiful in longing and wishing. Their love story stayed perfect because they couldn't have it.

But could he love her imperfection? Would he accept the fact that she wasn't always beautiful? Could he allow imperfection in himself? Would he give up being lovable for her sake?

They had their imagined love. It had been wrenching and beautiful. But she wondered now whether either of them had ever had the stomach for the real thing.

The following day they tried the port of Athinios, where the ferries came in. They posted signs and they went shop to shop and restaurant to restaurant. Valia had by now trained them how to ask "Have you seen these Pants?" in Greek. They even learned to say it in French and German.

There was one moment of excitement when an ice cream scooper said, "Oh, I saw those." But after all four of them closed in on him, they realized he meant he'd seen the signs.

"We aren't getting hopeless, are we?" Tibby asked. She couldn't hide her worry.

"No," Bee reassured her.

"We'll find them. They want us to find them," Carmen said.

Tibby sensed that none of them was willing to think about it any other way. Or at least, they weren't yet willing to say so.

When they got home from Athinios, Lena's grandmother was waiting inside her door. She practically tackled Lena as soon as she saw her.

"Kostos is here!" she said. Her fingers were pressing a little too hard into Lena's shoulders.

"What?"

"He's here. He's looking for you."

Her friends clustered around her.

"He's looking for me?" she echoed.

"Oh, boy," Tibby said.

"See, he *is* here," Bee said.

"He said he's leaving the island and he vanted to find you before he left."

Lena's heart started to rampage in its old familiar way. "Where did he go?"

"He said he vould look for you at the grove." She shrugged. "I don't know vhat, but he valked up." She pointed.

Lena knew what. "Thanks, Grandma." She paused, trying to gather her feelings around her.

"Are you going?" Valia looked like she was going to go for her if Lena didn't hurry up.

"Yes, I'm going."

With words of caution and encouragement from her

friends, Lena walked slowly up the hill. It was strange. She thought she'd found some place of calm regarding Kostos. Why was her heart racing?

Why did he want to see her? What more was there to say? She couldn't have been clearer than she had been. She was frankly surprised to think she hadn't scared him off for a lifetime.

Of the things she'd said, would she take any of it back? Did she want to? Was that why her heart was racing?

She walked up and up until the cliff leveled into a sort of plateau. She was happy to see how green it was again. The rain had been good this year.

Yes, some of the things she'd said that night had been lies. Maybe she'd correct a few of those if she could, but they represented some kind of truth, and she had needed to get it out. She was glad she had, if only so she could move on with her life.

Her heart rose at the sight of his back as he stood in their grove. Some feelings you just couldn't kill, no matter how much they deserved it. He turned and saw her as she came close.

Why did he look happy to see her? Why was she so happy to see him?

"We always come back to here, don't we?" she said.

He nodded. He looked better. Not in handsomeness, exactly. He looked straighter, fuller, stronger. He'd worn a hangdog, hopeful look last time, in Providence, but he didn't look that way now.

He rolled up his pants and they sat side by side at the edge of the pond. The water was so cold Lena yelped, and he laughed.

He doused his feet and then he reached in and washed his hands. She kept her hands in her lap. She looked at the foot of scrubby grass separating them.

"I've been unhappy," he told her. She believed him, though he didn't look very unhappy now.

"I was awful to you," she said.

He plunged his hands into the water again and shook them out. "I have a story to tell you," he said, looking at her directly.

"Okay," she said uncertainly. She had a feeling she was going to play a role in this story.

"Remember how you asked if I thought you would rush into my arms when you saw me?"

She winced. She'd said it cruelly then. She'd wanted to hurt him.

"Well, that is what I thought," he declared unflinchingly. "When I flew to see you, I packed clothes to last me for two months. I imagined I would call my grandmother and she would send the rest of my stuff in boxes. Because I did think you would rush into my arms and we would be together forever."

As painful as this was to hear, she admired his honesty.

"I called the Greek consulate. I started working on a student visa. I got transfer applications to three universities near you."

As much as she admired his honesty, she wished he would stop now.

"I brought a ring."

Lena chewed her cheek so hard she tasted blood. How could he tell her these things? They were clearly as painful for him to say as they were for her to hear. She couldn't think of any way to respond.

"I didn't think we would get married. Not in the first few years. But I wanted to give you something to show you that I would never leave you again."

She felt the boot in the head. The unexpected tears. She felt herself softening for him; she could feel her body changing.

He was tough. He was gritting his way through this confession. She could tell he wasn't going to stop until it was done.

"I worked two different jobs, almost a hundred hours a week for the last two years, and I spent almost everything I made on the ring. It was good to be distracted and also to think I could make it up to you."

Lena's friends teased her for the humming sound she made when she felt their unhappiness. She heard herself make that sound now.

"Do you know what I did with it?"

He was staring at her so fixedly she realized he expected her to answer. She shook her head.

"I threw it into the Caldera."

Her eyes were wide.

"You know what I did after that?" The recklessness with which he told his story seemed to capture the recklessness of what he had done.

She shook her head again.

"I broke into the house of my former wife and I stole the ring I had given her and I also threw that into the sea."

Lena just stared at him.

"It didn't mean anything compared to your ring, but it gave me a feeling of ending."

She nodded.

"But then Mariana called the police, and so I confessed to the crime and spent a night in jail in Fira." He told it very matter-of-factly.

"No," said Lena.

He nodded. He actually looked pleased with himself.

"I have a mug shot," he said, almost cheerfully.

She thought of it. Lovable Kostos in a mug shot. It was insane. It was funny. But she couldn't help being impressed by him. She'd credited herself with the capacity for destruction. She had underestimated his.

"My grandfather picked me up. Thankfully, I was released without fines."

"What did he say?" It was hard to picture.

"Well." Kostos's face returned to solemnity. "He pretended it hadn't happened. We never talked about it."

Lena made the humming sound again. She realized this confession was part of Kostos's penance. It was her penance too.

The sun was beginning to set. The pink light on the silvery olive leaves was as lovely as anything she could remember. She knew Valia would be putting dinner out soon.

"You are leaving for somewhere," she said.

"I take the first morning ferry. I'm flying to London tomorrow."

"To London?"

"Back to the School of Economics. They held a place."

"Oh. Of course." That was the difference about him now, she realized. He was undaunted. He was sturdier than he had been before. His anger at her had burned away the guilt. He had forced himself to get over her.

How powerful it was to give up your desires. It was like bargaining for a rug. Your only leverage was being able to walk away.

"I can start where I left off. I even got a room in my old flat."

Her throat ached. "God. It's like the clock turned back. It's just like we're back to the summer we met. It's late August and you're going off to London and I'm going back home for school."

He nodded.

"You can almost imagine away all the things that happened in between," she said.

He was thoughtful as he looked at her. "But you can't, can you?"

"No, you can't." She saw the fair orange circle of sun in the still water. She put her hands in to fur the edges. She brought cold, watery hands to her warm cheeks.

He stood up and so did she. He put out his hand to shake. Hers was still wet. "I guess we should say good-bye," he said.

It was easier to be together, to talk, now that they had both given up.

"Yes. I guess it is."

"Good luck with everything, Lena. I hope you will be happy."

"Thanks. I hope you'll be happy too."

"Well, then."

"Good-bye."

He cleared his throat a little bit as she walked away. She turned around.

"There's a full moon tonight," he said before he walked a separate way.

As soon as he was out of sight, Lena felt that old feeling of missing him. It didn't cut like a raw wound. It was the ache of a flu coming on.

Had they really gotten over each other? she wondered. It seemed more like they had gotten over themselves.

Lena was quiet through dinner, watching the tanned, beloved faces of her friends, enjoying their banter. She loved how Valia laughed when Carmen teased her.

As soon as she'd gotten home they'd wanted to know everything that had happened with Kostos, and she'd told them. But she hadn't yet figured out how to tell them how she felt about what had happened.

She crawled into bed early. She half listened to the

laughter downstairs coming from Bee and Carmen and Valia. She heard Tibby talking to a series of international operators, trying to reach Brian on her cell phone.

Lena's head was so full she expected she would toss and turn for hours, but instead, she fell asleep almost immediately. And then she woke up with a jolt. She felt there had been a dream, but it receded too quickly for her to grab even a string of it.

She heard Carmen's slow breathing beside her. The particular look of Carmen's sleeping face reminded her of a hundred other nights, a hundred sleepovers through the years. Here, in Greece, it made her feel happy. So often the world was made of jumps and starts, but tonight it was round and continuous.

She looked out the window and saw the proud full moon hanging over the Caldera, seeming to enjoy its own perfect reflection below. She knew what Kostos had meant.

She spent another minute looking at the moon, and suddenly she really knew what Kostos had meant.

She crept out of bed gingerly so as not to wake Carmen. She pulled on a pair of jeans and a faded green T-shirt. She brushed her hair and padded on soft toes out of the house.

Who knew what time it was? Who knew if he'd be there or when he'd be there? But her big feet had faith as they pulled her up the hill.

He was there. Maybe he'd been there for hours; she couldn't know. He stood up to greet her, happy, not surprised.

He needed to look at her face for only a second to know it was okay to hold her.

She cried in his arms. They weren't sad tears at all, just ones that needed to get out. She cried in his shirt. She cried for her Pants. He held her as tight as he could without crushing her.

She had willed her heart to stay small and contained, but it wouldn't be. Oh, well.

The neat leaves wrinkled under the moon. The pond made slapping, watery noises. It felt so good to be right here. These were arms that felt unlike other arms.

"Do you think you can ever forgive me?" he asked her. There was no demand in his voice. She felt like she could answer yes or no and he wouldn't hug her less.

"Maybe," she said faintly. "I think maybe so."

"Do you love someone else?" he asked. It was important to him, clearly, but he let it float.

"I tried," she said. "I don't know if I can." She talked to his chest.

She could feel him nod on her head. She could feel his relief in the way his body found more surfaces to connect to hers.

"I know I can't," he said.

She nodded at his chest. They stayed like that for a while. She realized the sun was already pushing up light at the farthest edge of the sea. It was later than she thought. Or earlier.

He unbound himself from her slowly, regretfully.

She felt cold air replace all the parts he'd been touching.

Before he broke away he put his hands on either side of her face and kissed her, strong and sturdy and full of lust. It was a new kind of kiss. It was grown up and decisive. She knew without thinking how to kiss him back the same way.

The last thing he said to her was something in Greek. He said it with emphasis, as though she would know what he meant, but of course she didn't.

And all the way down the hill as the sun rose, carelessly extending itself into the privacy of her night, she tried to remember the word.

Was it one word? Two words? A phrase? It was five syllables, she thought. It was, wasn't it? She tried to remember each of them, chanting them over and over as a mantra all the way down the hill.

First thing inside the house she wrote it down with a pencil on a piece of lined paper in her grandmother's kitchen.

She wrote it out phonetically. What else could she do? She didn't know the Greek alphabet well enough to try the right way. She was unsure of how to represent the vowel sounds.

Why did he say it like that? Like he knew exactly what he was talking about and like she would understand?

Arg. He always left her with a problem.

"Do you know what this means?" she asked her grandmother when she came down the stairs, sticking the piece of paper two inches from Valia's nose. Lena wasn't quite as private as she used to be.

Valia scrunched up her already wrinkly eyes. "Vhat is this supposed to be?" she asked.

"I don't know. I'm hoping you can tell me. It's Greek."

Grandma was nonplussed. "You call this Greek?"

Lena breathed impatiently. "Grandma, can you try?"

Valia made a martyrish fuss over finding her glasses. She squinted at the paper some more. "Lena, love, how do I know vhat this means?" she said finally.

While her friends got out of bed and dressed and took over the kitchen, making omelets out of everything edible in the room, Lena sat at the table in the middle of the action with her nose in the Greek-English dictionary.

"What are you doing?" Tibby finally asked.

"I'll tell you when I know," she said.

They put on bikinis and sundresses and packed straw bags and Lena followed them down to the beach with her face still in the dictionary. She tripped over a cobblestone and skinned her knee like a baby. Like a baby, she felt she might cry.

"What is with you?" Carmen asked.

"She'll tell us when she knows," Tibby said with a note of protection in her voice.

Lena was so preoccupied she got a sunburn on her back. She kept diligently at her dictionary when her friends went to get ice cream. She tried every spelling. Every grouping of letters until at last, with the sun at the top of the sky, she figured it out. Or at least, she believed she did.

"κάποια μέρα" was what Kostos had said. It meant "Someday."

And so she did understand.

off we go, into the wild

blue yonder.

—U.S. Air Force anthem

On the sixth day in Santorini, Lena tracked Effie down by phone at their aunt and uncle's house in Athens.

"Effie, it's me," she said. She made her voice gentle. She knew Effie was afraid to talk to her.

"Did you find them?" Effie practically exploded.

"No."

"You didn't?"

"No."

"Oh, no." She heard Effie turn instantly snuffling and teary. As mad as she'd been, Lena realized she didn't want Effie to feel this way. "Oh, no," Effie said again.

"I know."

"Since you called, I thought maybe you found them," Effie said, sniffling. She probably believed Lena would be too angry to call otherwise.

"I called because I wanted to tell you . . . it's okay." Lena wasn't sure what she was going to say until it was out.

Effie blew her nose loudly.

"It's going to be okay," Lena said again. "Okay? I know you didn't mean for it to happen. I know you tried your hardest to find them."

Effie shuddered a sob.

"It's okay, Ef. I love you."

For the longest time Effie was crying too hard to say anything back, so Lena waited patiently until she was done.

On the seventh day in Santorini, they swam for hours in the Caldera, floating with their bellies pointing to the sky. It seemed to Carmen they were putting off having to touch their feet to the earth again. The earth turned and time passed and then they would have to think about what it meant. But the hour did come, as all hours do.

"I don't think we can stay here much longer," Lena said, sitting on the sand and watching the sun go. She was the one who had to say it.

Carmen looked at her shriveled fingertips. She pressed them to her mouth.

They had been so busy with their Pants-finding attempts the first few days, but after that, bit by bit, they'd talked about the Pants less, expected less, done a little less. They'd relaxed into their long aimless stretches of talking and eating and thinking and walking and wondering about things together.

Although the overarching fact of the matter was sad, there had not been a moment since Carmen had arrived here that she'd suffered. It felt too good to be together.

There was too much joy in it, so long needed and so long overdue.

Rather, Carmen had felt an ever-growing awe at the wisdom of the Pants for knowing how to bring them together. For knowing that absence is sometimes more powerful than presence.

"I wish we could stay here forever," Carmen said.

"I do too," Bee said.

They didn't want to leave without the Pants, Carmen knew. The Pants were here, in a way. Even if they were lost, they were all around them.

"I think we might have lost the Pants a while ago," Tibby said, pressing her hands into the sand, her face abstracted. "I mean, I think we lost the idea of them. They came to us to keep us together, and I think we were using them to help us stay apart."

Carmen thought about this. "Right. It was like we had the Pants, so it was okay if we didn't see each other."

"I think that's true," Lena said. "I hadn't thought of that."

"We counted on them too much," Bee said. "Or maybe we counted on them in the wrong way."

Without thinking, they moved around to form a loose circle, like they did at Gilda's. Today there were no Pants, just them.

"They taught us how to be separate people, but we learned a little too well," Carmen said.

"We should have put them away during the school year," Tibby suggested.

"But our lives are different now," Lena said. "It used to

be we were apart for summers. Now we're apart all the time. Regular life used to be together. Now regular life is apart. It's impossible to know how to use them."

Carmen felt like she might cry. "Maybe it's too big a job to keep us together anymore."

Bee grabbed Carmen's raisiny fingers for a second before letting them go. "It can't be," she said. "But we can't expect the Pants do all the work, either."

"We're all in different places now," Carmen said, voicing her deepest fears. "Maybe our time is over."

"No," Lena said. "I don't believe that. You don't believe that, Carma, do you?"

Carmen was sitting there not wanting to believe it. And then, out of the blue, she had an idea that released her.

"I think I know what it is," she said. "We aren't in Bethesda anymore and we aren't in high school. We aren't really in our families and we aren't in our houses. Those are the places we grew up and the times we spent together, but they aren't us. If we think they are, then we're lost, because times end and places are lost. We aren't any place or any time."

She thought of their Pants. She pictured them blowing off the laundry line and into the air, floating and soaring until they silently merged into sky and sea.

"That's the thing. We are everywhere."

You are Welcome here.

—B. C. L. and T

EPILOGUE

On our last day in Greece we took a long walk and ended up on a stony precipice overlooking the water. We sat with our legs dangling into space, part of the air. The sky was cloudless and the sea was perfectly calm.

I looked at my friends, brown, barefoot, freckled, rumpled, mismatched, happy, all of us in each other's clothes. Tibby had Lena's white pants rolled up to her ankles, Carmen had Tibby's paisley T-shirt, Lena wore my straw cowboy hat, and I tied up my hair in Carmen's pink scarf.

The sky and the sea were so still and so constant that although we squinted and stared to find the line between them, the place that separated sea and sky, time and space, liquid and air, we could not see it.

I thought of what Carmen had said about us. We aren't in any one place or any one time. We are everywhere, here and there, past and future, together and apart.

And so for a long time we sat and watched in silence because the seam was invisible and the color was eternity.

And I thought about the color and I realized what blue it was. It was the soft and changeable, essential blue of a well-worn pair of pants.

Pants = Love

Girls in PANTS

the third summer of the sisterhood

AND

Forever in BLUE

the fourth summer of the sisterhood

ANN BRASHARES

RANDOM HOUSE AUSTRALIA

A Random House book
Published by Random House Australia Pty Ltd
Level 3, 100 Pacific Highway, North Sydney, NSW 2060
www.randomhouse.com.au

Published by arrangement with Random House Children's Books,
a division of Random House, Inc. New York, New York, USA. All rights reserved.

Girls in Pants first published by Random House Australia in 2005
Forever in Blue first published by Random House Australia in 2007
This bindup edition first published by Random House Australia in 2008

Produced by Alloy Entertainment
151 West 26th St
New York, NY 10001, USA

Addresses for companies within the Random House Group can be found at
www.randomhouse.com.au/offices.

National Library of Australia
Cataloguing-in-Publication Entry

Brashares, Ann.
Sisterhood 3 & 4: bindup.

ISBN 978 1 74166 288 7 (pbk.)

For secondary school age.
Female friendship – Juvenile fiction.
Teenage girls – Juvenile fiction.
Jeans (Clothing) – Juvenile fiction.
813.6

Cover photography by Zefa Images (Girls in Pants) and Micaela Vitali (Forever in Blue)
Author photo courtesy Ann Brashares
Cover design by Anna Warren, Warren Ventures
Internal design by Marci Senders
Typeset in 12-point Cochin
Printed and bound by Griffin Press, South Australia

10 9 8 7 6 5 4 3 2 1

Girls in
PANTS

the third summer of the sisterhood

Ann
Brashares

RANDOM HOUSE AUSTRALIA

For Jacob,
my own worthy boy

Acknowledgments

First and always, I would like to acknowledge and thank Jodi Anderson. I also thank, with great warmth, my editorial sisterhood, Wendy Loggia and Beverly Horowitz, and gratefully acknowledge the entire Random House Children's Books group, with special thanks to Marci Senders, Kathy Dunn, Judith Haut, Daisy Kline, and Chip Gibson. I wish to thank Leslie Morgenstein, who's been in it from the beginning. And I thank my friend and agent, the incomparable Jennifer Rudolph Walsh.

I lovingly acknowledge my parents, Jane Easton Brashares and William Brashares, and my brothers, Beau, Justin, and Ben Brashares. And last and most, my small tribe, Sam, Nathaniel, and Susannah.

We, the Sisterhood, hereby instate the following rules to govern the use of the Traveling Pants:

1. You must never wash the Pants.

2. You must never double-cuff the Pants. It's tacky. There will never be a time when this will not be tacky.

3. You must never say the word "phat" while wearing the Pants. You must also never think "I am fat" while wearing the Pants.

4. You must never let a boy take off the Pants (although you may take them off yourself in his presence).

5. You must not pick your nose while wearing the Pants. You may, however, scratch casually at your nostril while really kind of picking.

6. Upon our reunion, you must follow the proper procedures for documenting your time in the Pants.

7. You must write to your Sisters throughout the summer, no matter how much fun you are having without them.

8. You must pass the Pants along to your Sisters according to the specifications set down by the Sisterhood. Failure to comply will result in a severe spanking upon our reunion.

9. You must not wear the Pants with a tucked-in shirt and belt. See rule #2.

10. Remember: Pants = love. Love your pals. Love yourself.

In summer, the song

sings itself.

—William Carlos Williams

PROLOGUE

If you are reading this, you may know about us. Or about our Pants, anyway. If you do, you can skip ahead a few pages. If you don't, hang here with me for a minute. I'll try to make it painless.

You may say, I don't want to read a book about pants. And I can understand how you feel. (In England, when they say pants, they mean underwear. Did you know that?) But trust me, these are epic Pants. These Pants have the stunning power to transform four ordinary teenage girls into raving beauties living lives of astonishing adventure, not to mention causing delicious young men to fall constantly at their feet.

Okay, I exaggerate. They don't actually do that. But they do hold us together when we're apart. They make us feel secure and loved. They walk us to places we wouldn't otherwise dare to go. They help us know which boys are worthy and which ones are not. They make us better people and better friends. All this, I swear, is true.

And they look good along the way.

Who are we? We are we. We have always been we. Sometimes we are us. (Grammatically, it's just a fact.) It's all thanks to Gilda's gym in Bethesda, Maryland, for offering a prenatal aerobics class roughly eighteen years ago. My mom, Carmen's mom, Lena's mom, and Bee's mom bounded and sweated through a long, pregnant summer and then they each gave birth to a baby girl (plus a baby boy, in Bee's mom's case) in September. As far as I can tell, in those first few years our mothers raised us more like a litter of puppies than as actual individual children. It was later that our mothers started to grow apart.

How can I describe the four of us? Let's use the metaphor of cars.

Carmen would be a torqued-up cherry red gas-guzzler with a V-8 engine and four-wheel drive. She can make a mess of things, but she's a lot of fun, she sticks to the road, and she's got mad acceleration.

Lena would get good gas mileage. Like one of those hybrid cars. She would be easy on the environment and, of course, easy on the eyes. She would have state-of-the-art GPS, but it would be wrong sometimes. She would have air bags.

Bee would have no air bags. She might not have bumpers. She might not even have brakes. She would go a million miles an hour. She would be an ocean blue Ferrari minus the brakes.

And I, Tibby, would be a . . . bike. No, just kidding.

(I *am* old enough to drive, damn it!) Hmmm. What would I be? I would be a muscular Plymouth Duster, dark green, with a picky transmission. Okay, maybe that's just what I'd *want* to be. But I'm the one writing this, so I get to decide.

The Pants first came to us at the perfect moment. That is, when we were splitting up for the first time. It was two summers ago when they first worked their magic, and last summer when they shook up our lives once again. You see, we don't wear the Pants year-round. We let them rest during the year, so they are extra powerful when summer comes. (There was the time this winter when Carmen wore them to her mom's wedding, but that was a special case.)

We thought it was a big deal two years ago, our first summer apart. Now we're facing our last summer together. Tomorrow we graduate from high school. In September we go to college. And it's not like one of those TV shows where all of us magically turn up at the same college. We are going to four different schools in three different cities (but all within four hours of one another — that was our one rule).

Bee is the sloppiest student of us four and she got into every school she applied to. (Can you say all-American?) She chose Brown. Lena decided, against her parents' advice, to go to art school at the Rhode Island School of Design, Carmen is going to Williams just as she always dreamed, and I am starting film school at NYU.

As life changes go, it's really, really big. If you're my

dad, you say, "Hey. You'll see each other at Thanksgiving." But if you're me, you realize that life as we've known it is over. Our shared childhood is ending. Maybe we'll never live at home again. Maybe we'll never all live in the same place again. We're headed off to start our real lives. To me that is awe-inspiring, but it is also the single scariest thought in the world.

Tomorrow night at Gilda's we'll launch the Pants on their third summer voyage. Tomorrow begins the time of our lives. It's when we'll need our Pants the most.

Afterwards, the universe will explode for your pleasure.

—Douglas Adams

"Okay, Bee with Greta and Valia and Lena," Carmen ordered, shepherding a wandering grandmother with her hand. Bee and Lena intertwined their legs, trying to tip each other over, as Carmen clicked her digital camera.

"Okay, um. Effie and . . . um, Perry. And Katherine and Nicky. With Tibby and Lena and Bee."

Lena cast her a look. Lena hated pictures. "Are you getting paid or something?" she asked grumpily.

Carmen pushed her hair off her sweaty neck. The shiny black gown permitted no flow of air. She shook off the mortarboard (who ever thought of that name?) and pressed it under her arm. "Squeeze together, would you? I'm losing Perry." Tibby's three-year-old sister, Katherine, bleated angrily as her older brother, Nicky, stomped on her foot.

It wasn't Carmen's fault her friends had large families. But it was graduation, for God's sake. This was a big day.

She wasn't going to miss anybody. She didn't have any official brothers or sisters. She had to make the most of her unofficial ones.

"There is no shade," Valia, Lena's grandmother, noted bitterly.

It was a football field. Carmen briefly imagined the trouble with an elm or oak planted at the fifty yard line. The thought of this made her turn toward the raucous bunch of graduating football players, their families and admirers. It was one of the many clumps and cliques spread out over the hot field—a last stand for social order.

Carmen's grandma, Carmen senior (Seniora, as Tibby called her), cast searing looks at Albert, Carmen's father, as though blaming him for the merciless heat. Carmen could practically read her grandmother's mind: If Albert could leave Christina, Carmen's mother, what couldn't that man be capable of?

"Now's the big one, okay, everybody?" It had been a long morning. Carmen knew she was wearing everyone thin. She was irritating herself at this point. But who else looked out for posterity? Huh? "Last one, I *swear*."

She arranged the dads and full-grown boys in the back. Even Lena's dad—not because he was tall (Bee had a good three inches on him) but because Carmen was a generally thoughtful person, if she did think so herself.

Grandmothers and mothers took the next row. Valia, Carmen senior, Tibby's ancient great-grandma Felicia, who didn't know where she was, Greta nervously patting

her perm. Then there was Ari in her handsome beige suit, Christina constantly looking over her shoulder at her new husband, David, Tibby's mom with the lipstick on her teeth. And there was Albert's wife, Lydia, looking eager but also anxious that she might be taking up an extra square inch of space.

Lastly, Carmen ordered the remaining siblings into place. Effie pulled a dire face about having to kneel on a level with Nicky and Katherine. Tibby coaxed Brian from his spot on the sidelines and arranged him in the back row.

And now it was the Septembers' turn. Sitting in the front, they clutched each other in a mass of hot black polyester, leaving a space in the middle for Carmen. "Okay! Great!" Carmen shouted at them all in encouragement. "Just hold on one second."

Carmen nearly wrestled Ms. Collings from the dais. Ms. Collings was the teacher who'd sent Carmen out to the hallway the greatest number of times, but she was also the teacher who loved her best.

"We're all set," Carmen said. "Here." She demonstrated to Ms. Collings the camera placement she wanted. For a moment Carmen studied the viewfinder. She saw them all, encompassed in the little frame — her beloved friends, her mom, stepmom, stepdad, actual dad, grandma. Her friends' moms, dads, families who felt as close as if they were her own. This was her whole life, right here. Her tribe. Everything that mattered.

And this moment. This was it, somehow. All of them

celebrating a day and an accomplishment that belonged to the four of them equally. This was the culmination of a shared life.

Carmen threw herself into her pile of friends. She screamed, out of pure emotion, which got them all screaming. She felt the heave of flesh as every layer of their group seemed to sink into the whole more fully — arms wrapped around shoulders and waists, cheeks pressed together, wrinkly and smooth. Then Carmen burst into tears, knowing that in the picture her eyes would look very puffy indeed.

Granted, Tibby was in a mood. All she could see was change. All anybody talked about was change. She didn't like Bee's wearing heels for the second day in a row. She felt peevish about Lena's getting three inches trimmed off her hair. Couldn't everybody just leave everything alone for a few minutes?

Tibby was a slow adjuster. In preschool, her teachers had said she had trouble with transitions. Tibby preferred looking backward for information rather than forward. As far as she was concerned, she'd take a nursery school report card over a fortune-teller any day of the week. It was the cheapest and best self-analysis around.

Tibby saw Gilda's through these same eyes. It was changing. Its glory days of the late nineteen eighties were far behind it. It was showing its age. The once-shiny wood floor was scratched and dull. One of the mirror panels was cracked. The mats looked as old as Tibby, and they'd

been cleaned much less. Gilda's was trying to get with the times, offering kickboxing and yoga, according to the big chalkboard, but it didn't look to Tibby like that was helping much. What if it went out of business? What a horrible thought. Maybe Tibby should buy a subscription of classes here? No, that would be weird, wouldn't it?

"Tibby, you ready?" Lena was looking at her with concerned eyebrows.

"What if Gilda's closes?" Tibby opened her mouth, and that was what came out.

Carmen, holding the Traveling Pants, Lena, lighting the candles, Bee, fussing with the dimmer switches near the door, all turned to her.

"Look at this place." Tibby gestured around. "I mean, who comes here?"

Lena was puzzled. "I don't know. Somebody. Women. Yoga people."

"Yoga people?" Carmen asked.

"I don't know," Lena said again, laughing.

Tibby was the one most capable of emotional detachment, but tonight it all lay right on the surface. Her irrational thoughts about Gilda's made her feel desperate, like its demise could swallow up their whole existence—like a change in the present could wipe out the past. The past felt fragile to her. But the past was set, right? It couldn't be changed. Why did she feel such a need to protect it?

"I think it's Pants time," Carmen said. The snacks were out. The candles were lit. The egregiously bad dance music played.

Tibby wasn't sure she wanted it to be Pants time yet. She was having enough trouble maintaining control. She was scared of them noticing what all this meant.

Too late. Out of Carmen's arms came the artifacts of their ritual. The Pants, slowly unfolding from their winter compression, seeming to gain strength as they mixed with the special air of Gilda's. Carmen laid them on the ground, and on top of them the manifesto, written on that first night two years before, describing the rules of wearing them. Silently they formed their circle, studying the inscriptions and embroidery that chronicled their summer lives.

"Tonight we say good-bye to high school, and bye to Bee for a while," Carmen said in her ceremonial voice. "We say hello to summer, and hello to the Traveling Pants."

Her voice grew less ceremonial. "Tonight we are not worrying about good-bye to each other. We're saving that for the beach at the end of the summer. That's the deal, right?"

Tibby felt like kissing Carmen. Brave as she was, even Carmen was daunted by the implications of looking ahead. "That's the deal," Tibby agreed heartily.

The last weekend of the summer had already become sacred in their minds. Sacred and feared. The Morgans owned a house right on the beach in Rehoboth. They had offered it to Carmen for that final weekend, in part, Carmen suspected, because they had gotten an au pair from Denmark and felt guilty about not hiring Carmen to babysit this summer as she had done the summer before.

The four of them had promised each other in the spring that it would be their weekend. The four of them and nobody else. They all depended upon it. The future was unfurling fast, but whatever happened this summer, that weekend stood between them and the great unknown.

They all looked ahead to college in different ways, Tibby knew. They all had different amounts to lose. Bee, in her lonely house, had nothing. Carmen did; she dreaded saying good-bye to her mother. Tibby feared leaving the familiarity of her chaos. Lena flipped and flopped—one day she was afraid to cut ties, and the next she was dying to get away.

The thing they feared equally and powerfully was saying good-bye to one another.

After drawing for the Pants (Tibby won), reviewing the rules (unnecessary, but still part of tradition), and taking a brief hiatus to chew down some Gummi Worms, it was at last time for the vow. Like they had the summer before, they said it together.

"To honor the Pants and the Sisterhood
And this moment and this summer and the rest of our lives
Together and apart."

Only this time, Tibby felt the tears fall when they said "the rest of our lives." Because in the past that had always seemed like a distant road, and tonight, she knew in her heart, they were already on it.

Somebody already broke

my heart.

—Sade

That night Tibby had a dream about taxidermy. In it, her crazy great-grandma Felicia had had the Traveling Pants stuffed as her graduation gift. "It's just what you wanted!" Felicia shouted at her.

The stuffing job looked totally professional. The Pants were mounted on a polished marble pedestal and inhabited by fake legs to look as if they were jauntily midstep. As animated as they looked, you had to notice that there was no body or head or even any feet. They were connected to the marble base by a brass pipe sticking out of one pant leg.

"But they can't go anywhere," Tibby pointed out timidly.

"That's the point!" Felicia thundered. "It's just what you wanted!"

"I did?" Tibby asked, confused and guilty for having maybe wanted it. She found herself wondering if they were too heavy to be circulated among their various dorm rooms.

Now we really won't have to worry about washing them, she consoled herself in her dream-reality.

When Tibby awoke, Katherine was at her side. Katherine's head as she stood there loomed one inch from Tibby's as she lay down. "Brian's visiting." Katherine loved trying out words. She was happy with herself that she'd said *visiting* as opposed to just *here*.

Tibby groggily sat up. "What time is it?"

Katherine moved herself in front of Tibby's clock radio and studied it hopefully.

"God, it's almost eleven," Tibby answered herself.

She was about to head directly down the stairs, but then she decided to brush her teeth first. When she arrived in the kitchen, Brian was at the table setting up dominos with Nicky.

"Let's try to set up a few at once," Brian counseled patiently, arranging them in a snaking row.

Nicky only wanted to knock them over.

"Hey," Tibby said.

"Hey."

"Did you eat breakfast?" she asked.

"Uh-huh. Yeah." He seemed a bit nervous for some reason, the way his shoulders were rising toward his ears.

"What's up?" she asked him. She went to the refrigerator to inspect.

"Just, uh . . . Can I talk to you for a second?"

She closed the refrigerator and stood up straighter. She looked at him. "Sure."

"In . . . there?" He gestured toward the living room.

Tibby's eyebrows nearly joined over her nose. "In there?"

Nobody ever did anything in the living room in her house. Loretta ventured in once a week to clear out the cobwebs. And every few months her parents had a party and acted like they relaxed on those perfect sofas all the time.

Mystified, she followed him. They posed on the sofa like cocktail party guests.

"So . . . what?" she asked him, a sprout of worry in her chest. It was slightly funny how they were sitting next to each other and both facing forward.

He rubbed both palms against the denim covering his thighs.

Tibby pulled her legs up onto the sofa so she could turn to him. "Everything okay?"

"I wanted to ask you something."

"Okay. Ask."

"You know the thing tonight?"

"Uh . . . you mean the senior party?"

"Will you go with me?"

Her eyebrows compressed even further. "We're all going. Right? Lena . . . Bee . . ."

He waved a hand to acknowledge all that. "But will you go with me?"

She was utterly perplexed. "You mean like a date?" She blurted it out because it sounded so ridiculous.

"Kind of. Yeah."

Suddenly, it seemed mean to snort or laugh at the

preposterousness of this concept. She tilted her head. He was very brave to keep looking at her eyes the way he did.

She clasped her hands. It dawned on her that she was wearing a tank top and her pajama bottoms. Tibby spent an unusual amount of time in her pajamas, so it wasn't like Brian hadn't seen her in them hundreds of times. But here, in this stage-set living room, under the glare of this weird question, it only accentuated the weirdness.

"A kind of date?" she asked slowly.

"Kind of."

She wouldn't hurt his feelings. She just wouldn't. It didn't matter where this would lead them. She nodded. "Okay."

She felt raw sitting with him on the sofa. When he leaned toward her she had absolutely no idea what was going to happen. His body moved in slow motion, and she seemed to see herself and Brian from some distant spot in the room. He possessed a new kind of confidence, a deliberateness. She was both terrified and eerily calm.

So she sat still, looking into his eyes as he reached toward her face. He didn't kiss her or anything like that. But what he did felt just as shockingly intimate. The first three fingers of his right hand landed lightly on her warm face and smoothed out the rumple of consternation in the center of her forehead.

"Okay," he said.

One day in the early spring when Lena stayed home sick from school, she watched a young woman on a day-

time talk show who'd written a book about being adopted. This woman had never met or been contacted by her birth mother, and yet she spent her whole life wishing and hoping her birth mother would find her. She talked about how she didn't want to move from the home where her parents had first adopted her. She didn't like to take long trips. She always left explicit forwarding instructions when she moved. She made sure her phone was listed under her own name. She left her little trail of bread crumbs. She wanted to make sure she could be found.

Since then, Lena had thought about this woman many times, and she wasn't sure why. She didn't dwell on it. Minds worked in weird ways. Like how Lena always thought of Ritz crackers when she shaved her legs. Who knew why? And did it even matter?

But now, as she lay on her bed, filling out forms for school in September, Lena thought about the woman on the talk show again. She filled out a roommate questionnaire and she kept flashing on the woman's sad gray eyes. She filled out the dorm preference sheet and she saw the woman's twitching lower lip.

And as Lena lay back on her bed and put her hands over her face, it finally dawned on her. This woman reminded Lena of herself.

Without even realizing it, Lena had subtly resisted the idea of going away this summer. Even a week away from home made her feel slightly unglued. The thought of moving to another city in September, thrilling as it was, was also a source of agony.

Lena wanted to leave home. For one thing, she was ready. For another thing, since her dad had forced Valia, his widowed mother, to leave her beautiful Greek island and relocate to suburban Maryland, the Kaligaris house had been full of tension.

Lena looked forward to RISD. She wanted to be an artist, she was almost sure of it. Her art class this summer was the single joy in her life, apart from her friends.

And yet. And yet Lena didn't want to go. And the reason was that she didn't want to leave the place where Kostos could find her. And on a deeper level, she didn't want to put more distance—in time or in space—between now and the time when he'd loved her. She didn't want to become a different girl from the one whom he had loved.

The phone rang and Lena snatched it up before Valia could get it and yell at the innocent caller.

"Hello?"

"Hi, it's me."

"Carma. Hi. What are you doing?"

"Getting dressed. I had another waxing fiasco. What are you wearing?"

Lena cast her eye at the clock. She was supposed to meet everybody at the senior party in half an hour. She was bringing Effie as her date, because she had no other date and because Effie was spocking on some senior guy or other.

Lena then cast her glance on her open closet. She had no excitement in getting dressed. Her wardrobe had two categories: the clothing she had worn with Kostos—filled

with memories—and the clothing she hadn't—empty. She didn't want either.

"I don't know. I didn't pick yet."

"Lenny, it's a big night," Carmen cajoled. "Get dressed. Wear something great. Put on makeup. Do you need me to come over?"

"No. I'm all right." She didn't feel like setting Carmen loose in her closet.

"Don't wear that khaki skirt," Carmen warned.

"I'm not," Lena said defensively, even though it was exactly what she had planned to wear.

Unfortunately, Lena's wardrobe represented her life. It was binary, like a computer with its universe of zeros and ones. Lena had two settings: 1. Thinking about Kostos. 2. Avoiding thinking about Kostos.

Lena deeply empathized with the adopted woman on the talk show. Lena too had been abandoned by the person she thought loved her best of all. And without meaning to or wanting to, she harbored a passive, unquenchable hope that someday he would come for her.

Where there is great love,

there are always wishes.

—Willa Cather

"Brian! Brian's here!" Katherine threw open the front door and shouted the news to the top of the house.

Brian clearly longed for a real live date. He presented flowers to Tibby and a box of chocolates to Alice for the family. It was as though he'd read about dating in a manual somewhere. Nonetheless, he didn't seem to mind that his real live date was wearing jeans while he was wearing a suit jacket and tie.

"You look beautiful," he said, taking in the look of her, from the Traveling Pants, to the filmy iris blouse that showed what cleavage she had to its best possible effect, to the antique rhinestone clip in her hair, to the kohl shading along her upper eyelids. She really had tried to look pretty.

One thing about Brian was, he understood the Pants. Just like Bailey, two summers before, had understood them implicitly. The Pants, in a way, were like the ultimate

litmus test, separating the worthy from the unworthy. And no matter how he looked, Brian was the most worthy guy she'd ever known.

Few people in the course of history had ever transformed, even just physically, as much as Brian had since the afternoon two years before when Tibby and Bailey first filmed him at the 7-Eleven.

It was great and all. A supreme dork with a golden heart whom you befriend because you love him grows to six feet two, gets his dental hygiene together, accidentally breaks his hideous glasses, and morphs into a virtual heartthrob before your eyes. It was like dumbly buying a share of stock at one dollar and watching it soar to one hundred. Tibby still observed in stupefaction how girls whispered and flirted around Brian these days.

But on the other hand, it seemed to Tibby like another example of destiny's strange sense of humor. The single safest guy in Tibby's life had turned imposing. He didn't impose on purpose, she knew. He didn't desire her to be mean to her. He didn't plant these feelings in her heart to make her sad. But desire was there, his and hers, and as a consequence, it wasn't a safe relationship anymore.

"Brian, Brian, Brian!" Katherine and Nicky were literally dancing around him. Brian had earned their love the hard way, not by being their peevish older sister, but by playing every endless, tedious game they could devise and listening carefully to every harebrained thing they could think of to say. They were a lot more demonstrative than his real live date, come to think of it.

Brian's innocence gave him a funny kind of confidence. It was hard to explain. He didn't care that he had walked all the way to her house because he had no car. He wasn't self-conscious that their date car was her car. Once outside, he gallantly opened the door for her. On the driver's side. He didn't care, so it didn't matter.

Inside the car, it was private. So dark and private. He touched his hand to the inside of her elbow. She got scared, and fumbled the key into the ignition.

They were growing up. That was a fact she had to face. He had grown from a kid to nearly a man. He was eighteen years old. He wanted Tibby in a different way than he used to. He looked at her differently. He wasn't pushy or gross, but his eyes did linger on her breasts. When he put his hand on her, she could tell he was feeling the curve of her waist. And when he looked at her like that, she felt different too. It was natural, right?

In the school parking lot he reached for her hand. Hers was clammy.

What about friendship, though? What about the ease between them? Where was that going to go? And if they let it go, could they ever get it back?

That was the thing about this summer. With everything that was happening, she wondered, was there any going back?

The auditorium was dark and the DJ was loud and grating like at every school social function, but this was their last one, and for that reason, Tibby couldn't bring herself to hate it quite as much.

Brian held her hand fast. He was declaring their couplehood. Ironically, he did her more credit than himself. This spring his social star had certainly risen past hers. Not that he noticed or cared. In spite of her beautiful friends, Tibby was identified more with the disaffected artist types. Bee was a glamour jock. Carmen had turned into quite the babe, the target of a lot of underclassman fantasies, though she'd never curried favor with the ruling set. Lena flew under the social radar. And Brian, oddly, had become a darling of the social whirl—even they needed new blood occasionally—getting invitations none of the rest of them got. Tibby was one of those who sat on the sidelines in dark clothes, making cynical observations with other self-designated misfits who were too cautious to jump into the fray.

Of all the boys in school, only Brian seemed to notice how Tibby's hair had grown out, how her delicate shoulders looked in a tube top, how the Pants made her small behind look especially nice. She loved being noticed like this. And also, she didn't.

Bee and Carmen found them right away. Lena and Effie hadn't arrived yet. Effie was an infamously slow and primping date. Bee was wearing a white halter dress and her hair was brighter than the tea lights. She looked like an extremely fit Marilyn Monroe. Carmen wore a siren red slip dress, to which the boys were already flocking. As stunning as they looked in their finery, Tibby was still grateful it was she who had drawn for the Pants.

Bridget and Carmen hustled Tibby off to the bath-

room in their time-honored way. The cavernous girls'
bathroom was always the most happening spot at a
school party. "You both look unbelievable," Tibby said
along the way.

"You, Tibby, are luscious," Carmen responded. "Brian
looked like his heart was going to break when we took
you away."

An army of gussied girls were perfecting makeup,
smoking, and gossiping in front of the mirrors.

Bee took out her lip gloss. She put some on and
shared it around.

"Hey, Bee?" Carmen said.

"Yeah?"

"If you ever meet a guy and you fall in love with him,
but because of some weird genetic mutation he doesn't
seem to return the feeling?"

Bee always went patiently along with Carmen's coun-
terfactuals. "Yeah?"

"Wear that dress."

Bee laughed. "Okay."

Lena arrived a few minutes later, dressed down as
usual, in an olive green cargo skirt and a black shirt.

"Lenny, did you have to wear the ponytail?" Carmen
asked fake-irritably.

"What do you mean?" she asked.

"Come on, it's our last high school party," Bee said.

Together, they put some mascara and lip gloss on her
and coaxed the elastic out of her hair.

Looking at their faces in the mirror, Tibby felt as

though she might cry. This was the place where they'd spent the majority of school events these last four years. They had had more fun here, together, than anyplace else. This, on some level, was their real high school experience.

Carmen caught her look. "It's sad, I know."

"Let's get back out there," Tibby said. She didn't want to feel these things right now.

Back in the auditorium, they dispersed. Brian was waiting eagerly. "Do you want to dance?" he asked Tibby.

Was she allowed to say no? Was a real live date allowed to say no? As he took her hand and led her to the floor, the fast song changed into a slow one. Was that better or worse? She couldn't decide.

It would have taken her an hour to figure out how to get her arms around Brian, but he went right for it. He closed in and held her tight.

So here it was. This was a first. She had, admittedly, thought a lot about Brian's body and how it would feel. Friendship seemed to fuzz at the edges as this new thing happened.

He was so much taller than her now, her head barely reached his chest. His hands were on her waist, her hips, her back. Slowly touching the places he'd looked at for so long. She felt a lightness in her lower abdomen, a wobbliness in her legs.

This was going too fast. It was getting away from her. She couldn't do it.

Her cheeks were deeply flushed as she pulled away. "Can we go?" she asked.

"Where?" he asked.

"I'm not sure." She took his hand and led him out of the auditorium and toward the parking lot.

She suddenly had her idea. She'd get them back to basics.

He followed her into the car without complaint. In silence she drove to the seminal 7-Eleven on River Road.

He realized what she was up to. He smiled and shrugged at her under the pulsing lights of the store. He went obligingly toward Dragon Master and fished around in his pockets for change. Even as she watched him she knew he would play their old game to please her, but his life was outside of the screen now.

"Never mind," she said. She was skittish. Her legs were jumpy. A drop of sweat rolled down her spine. She couldn't figure out where to be. She was on the run.

They got back into the car. She drove to a small neighborhood park equidistant from their houses. It was another of their places.

They got out of the car and sat on a picnic table. It was quiet and dark. She was just going to have to stay still and let it catch her. She knew it.

She hopped off the table. She stood in front of him. With her standing and him sitting, their faces were at the same level. She put her clammy hands on his knees. He scooted toward her, to the very edge of table, and pulled her into his arms. He held her like that for a long time while her heart slammed out a beat.

When she looked up he kissed her first on the forehead and then on the lips. It was such a kiss. Full of pent-up desire and no uncertainties at all, he put his hands under her hair, supporting the back of her head. He paused the kiss for only a moment to say something in her ear. "I love you" was what he said.

It was beautiful to her, unlike anything she had ever felt before. It brought tears to her eyes and still more warm blood to her face.

Tibby felt the odd sensation of a wind blowing through her mind, alternately hot and sultry, then cold and bracing. And when the wind subsided, she realized that the friendship, as it had been, was gone.

Someday somebody's going

to ask you

a question that you

should say yes to.

—old 97's

Carmen was on a supremely important mission: She needed to steal her mother's fake eyelashes and she needed to do it now.

She'd gotten up early to say good-bye to Bee one last time before Bee left for camp in Pennsylvania. She'd eaten breakfast with her mom, and spent a few minutes feeling guilty about not having a job as she watched Christina trundle off to work. She'd written a long e-mail to her friend and stepbrother, Paul.

Then she'd started to feel sad about saying good-bye to Bee and it reminded her of good-byes generally. So Carmen turned to the most recent issue of *CosmoGIRL!* for solace, as she often did in moments like these. And voilà, she was swept away by the imperative need to copy the innovative use of fake eyelashes on page 23. Sometimes it paid to be shallow.

It was so different for Carmen these days, walking into her mother's room. The reason was obvious: It wasn't

her mother's room anymore. It was her mom and David's room. A woman's room was so different than a woman's room together with a man. It was utterly different when the woman was your mother and the man was her spanking-new husband, whom you'd met less than a year before.

Carmen wasn't grateful for her parents' divorce. There were so many things she'd lost. But it took David's presence now to show her what remarkable access and role-defying closeness she'd shared with her mother for all those years when it had been just the two of them.

When her father had first left, a lot of the usual boundaries had come down. She'd slept in her mother's bed almost every night for a year. Was it for Carmen's sake? Or for Christina's? Once there was no dad coming home after a hard day of work, "we girls," as her mother called them, had eaten Eggo waffles or scrambled eggs for dinner many nights. Carmen had considered it a treat, not having to saw through some hunk of flank steak and stomach the obligatory vegetables.

Carmen used to feel an easy ownership of this room. Now she treaded uncertainly. She used to flop at will on her mother's bed. It was a different bed now. Not literally a different bed, but in every other way different. She steered wide around it now.

It wasn't just that the room contained a lot of male stuff. David wasn't a slob or anything. He was always conscious that this apartment had been Christina and Carmen's long before he joined up. He commanded one

closet, three bookshelves, and a new bureau from Pottery Barn. He didn't even have pictures yet. The room now testified not so much to him but to *them*—their intimacy, the things they whispered to each other when they were falling asleep. Even when they weren't present, Carmen felt like she was invading it.

The bathroom used to bloom with female stuff— creams, lotions, makeup, tampons, and perfume. Now, in deference to *them*, Christina kept it all mostly stowed in the cabinet. Even seeing David's shaving cream can lined up next to Christina's nail polish remover made Carmen feel like she'd just crawled between them in bed.

The false eyelashes weren't in the medicine cabinet, Carmen quickly discovered. When you lived with your daughter, you left things like that in easy view. When you lived with your brand-new husband, you hid the evidence.

Carmen already knew that most of the stuff Christina didn't want David to see, she stored in the cabinet above the toilet. Yes, this was the right department, Carmen realized as soon as she'd jiggled open the sticky door. There was wart remover, there was mustache bleach, there was bikini wax and hair straightening balm and a box of Nice 'n Easy in Deep Mahogany. Carmen snaked her hand toward the back, knocking over appetite suppressants and a pack of laxatives. A plastic bottle was set rolling by the falling laxatives. Carmen watched in displeasure as it fell off the shelf and . . . splash, into the toilet. Damn.

She watched it bobbing in the toilet water. She could see it contained some kind of vitamins. She really hoped the cap was watertight.

While she delayed reaching her hand into the toilet—who hurried to do a thing like that?—she absently wondered why her mother kept vitamins in the cabinet of shame. David was all about vitamins. He ate them for breakfast. He talked about various herbal supplements like they were his best friends. What kind of vitamins would Christina keep from her dashing nutrition-man?

Carmen's curiosity was always her best motivator. She stuck her hand in the toilet and plucked out the bottle, tossing it directly into the sink and running hot water over it. She added some liquid soap. Once the bottle and her hand were sufficiently clean, she turned it over to satisfy her questioning mind.

Her head grew chill and fuzzy. The fuzz invaded her chest and expanded in her lower abdomen. The front of the label communicated precisely why this bottle lived between the laxatives and the Preparation H. But it wasn't David her mom was trying to hide them from. At least, that was what Carmen powerfully suspected.

They were prenatal vitamins. The kind you took when you were having a baby. And Christina was almost certainly hiding them from Carmen.

Tibby squinted in the morning sunlight. She was groggy and disoriented, her lips were swollen, and her

eyes felt puffy. She felt like she had a hangover, but not because she'd had any alcohol.

It was one of those mornings when you come to terms with a strange new reality. You ask yourself, Did I dream that? Did I actually do that? Did he really say that? Reality comes back in bits and pieces, and you experience the novelty of it all over again. You wonder, Will this day and this night and tomorrow and all the rest of the days be different because of what happened last night? And in Tibby's case, she knew the answer.

She put her fingers on her lips. Could you get a hangover from kissing?

Was Brian awake yet? She pictured him in his bed. She pictured him in her bed. She got the shivery feeling in the bottom of her stomach, so she stopped picturing him in her bed. Was he regretting anything? Was she regretting anything?

What would they say when they saw each other again?

Would he just drop by during pancakes the way he often did? Would he plant a wet one on her lips and wait to see if anyone noticed?

She stood up and looked at herself in the mirror. Did she look as different as she felt? Hmmm. Same black watch plaid pajama bottoms hanging down around her hips. Same undersized white tank top baring several inches of belly. Maybe not.

Her room was a big, cluttered mess. There was noth-

ing new about that, but she did notice it in a new way as she looked around. Had she ever thrown out anything in her life?

There were layers and layers of Tibby detritus both on the walls and on the floor. You could do an archaeological dig in this room and probably unearth her Fisher-Price farm if you tried hard enough. What was the matter with her?

It was dusty and stuffy and it bothered her. It was always dusty and stuffy. It didn't always bother her. In an uncharacteristic move, she walked over to the window and forced it open. It was hard going, because she had not opened this room to actual air in as long as she could remember. The paint stuck a bit as she wrenched up the sash. Oh.

The air came in and it did feel good. It was nice, open like this. The breeze blew around some of the papers on her desk, but she didn't mind.

She heard her mother downstairs in the kitchen. She thought of telling her about Brian. A part of her really wanted her mom to know. Alice would be excited. She would make a big deal about it. She loved Brian. She would love the idea of her daughter telling her about a juicy milestone like this one. It was her mother-daughter fantasy—the very thing Tibby so often denied her.

As Tibby left her room she registered the sound of the rustling leaves of the apple tree, so little heard here, and she liked it.

Tibby watched her mother in her usual morning flurry. Would she be able to slow down for Tibby's news? Tibby tried to formulate the opening sentence. "Brian and I . . . Me and Brian . . ."

Tibby opened her mouth, but Alice got there first.

"Tibby, I need you to stay with Katherine this morning." Alice already sounded mad and Tibby hadn't even refused yet.

Tibby's words dried up.

Alice wouldn't look in Tibby's eyes, indicating that she felt guilty somewhere down deep, but the guilt only made her less patient. "Loretta has to take her sister to the doctor and she can't be back till after lunch." Alice snatched the juice boxes from the shelf and shoved one at Nicky. "Or that's what she says, anyway," she added ungenerously.

"Why does her sister have to go to the doctor?" Nicky asked.

"Sweetie, she has some kind of infection, I don't know." Alice gestured the whole issue away with a sweep of her arm, as if it might or might not be true, but she couldn't spend any more time thinking about it.

Alice was flinging things into and out of her purse. "I have to take Nicky to camp and then go to the office."

"I'm not doing it," Tibby said. Not only had she lost all desire to tell her mother about Brian, she never wanted to tell her mother about anything she cared about ever.

Alice gave her a look. "Excuse me?"

"I'm not the babysitter. I'm sick of you dumping the job on me every time it's convenient."

"You're living in this house, and that means you have to help out, just like everybody else."

Tibby rolled her eyes. This fight was nasty, but it had taken place so many times they might as well have been following lines of a script.

Katherine stirred her Cheerios around in her bowl. She slopped some of the milk onto the kitchen table.

Tibby always felt distantly guilty for refusing to babysit Katherine in Katherine's presence, but she managed to get over it.

"I can't wait to go to college," Tibby muttered, as though to herself, but not really. The statement was untrue, and she said it only to make her mother unhappy.

Half an hour later, Tibby sat on the back deck with a pile of papers and brochures from NYU, while Katherine careened around the backyard. The fight with her mom had shaken all the magic right out of her. She was back on the ground, looking down at the bugs rather than up at the sky.

Eventually Katherine's appetite for independent play ran out. She appeared in Tibby's face.

"You want to climb the tree and pick apples?" This currently represented Katherine's greatest fantasy.

"Katherine, no. Anyway, why do you want those apples so bad? They're not good. They're not ripe yet. And even if they were ripe, they'd be hard and sour." Tibby had

fallen into that shameful parent-ennui where you said no before you even listened to what the kid wanted.

"Did you ever eat one?" Katherine asked.

Tibby hadn't ever eaten one, but she didn't feel like getting argued to the ropes by a three-year-old. "I'm telling you, they're gross. If they were good, wouldn't we all be eating them instead of buying apples from the bin at the A&P?"

Katherine seemed to find this kind of logic depressing. "I still want to try one."

Tibby sat there, watching Katherine sizing up the apple tree. She was too small to reach even the lowest branch, but she was undeterred. She backed up ten or so yards from the trunk of the tree, ran as fast as she could, and jumped. Her attempt was so meager and ineffective it was almost heartbreaking.

Katherine backed up for another go. She backed up farther this time for optimum speed. She ran with her arms bent tight at her elbows in a caricature of sprinting. It was so cute, objectively speaking, that one part of Tibby longed to get it on camera.

But at the same time, Tibby was annoyed. She indulged herself in pettiness. She did not want to babysit. She was annoyed with her mother. If she were to let herself be absorbed into Katherine's world, it would be almost like enjoying babysitting. Which she didn't.

So Tibby watched. Katherine was inexhaustible. Why did she want the damn apples so much? Tibby couldn't imagine the nature of her desire.

But Tibby could remember being small and wanting to jump, running and jumping just like Katherine, and imagining you were going to practically take flight—thinking you could jump so much higher than you really could.

The first thing Bridget did when she got to soccer camp was find Diana. They'd spoken on the phone and exchanged many e-mails, but Bridget hadn't seen Diana in two years—not since the day they'd left Baja. And of all the things and people she'd encountered there, Diana stood out as her single happy memory.

When she found her in their cabin, she screamed and hugged Diana so hard she lifted her off the ground.

"God." Diana examined Bee's face. She stepped back. "You look great. You grew?"

"You shrunk?" Bee asked back.

"Ha."

Bridget tossed her gigantic duffel bag onto her bunk. She wasn't big on folding or sorting. She used to pack in Hefty bags, but Carmen made her stop.

She hugged Diana again and admired her. Diana had kept her hair straightened two summers ago, but now she'd let it collect into long, pretty dreads. It looked unbelievably glamorous to Bee. "Look how you are! You are stunning and fabulous! Do you love Cornell?"

Diana hugged back. "Yeah, except I live and breathe soccer. You'll see how it is."

"You had time to find Michael, though, right? Did you bring a picture?"

Bridget exclaimed and swore appreciatively at the picture of Diana's good-looking soccer-playing boyfriend and also at the pictures of her hilariously hammy younger sisters.

"So who else is here?" Bridget asked, gesturing at the second set of bunk beds in the cramped cabin.

"Two assistant coaches." Diana got a vague look on her face.

"You met them?" Bridget asked.

"At lunch. Katie and Something," she said. She closed one eye, trying to remember. "Allison. I think. Katie and Allison."

Bridget sensed an issue. "And they are . . . ?"

"Fine. Great."

"Fine and great? Katie and Allison are fine and great?"

Diana smiled. Vaguely.

"So what's the problem?"

"What problem?"

"Why do you look like that?"

"Like what?" Diana asked, glancing downward.

Bee felt impatient. Diana was an honest person. Why wasn't she being honest now?

Diana pulled a hair elastic off her wrist and stretched it between her index finger and thumb. "You haven't . . . met the other coaches yet. Have you?"

Diana's words came slow, and Bee's came very fast. "No. Have you?"

"Uh. Not all of them. But I saw . . ." Something about

Diana's hair elastic was so fascinating her words trailed off in her deep contemplation of it.

"Who?" Bee shot out.

"You probably already . . ."

"Who?"

"I'm pretty sure you . . ."

Bridget huffed in exasperation. She grabbed the arm that wore Diana's wristwatch and held it up so she could read it. "We have a staff meeting in eight minutes. I'm going to go find out who you're talking about."

I don't have to be careful.

I've got a gun!

—Homer Simpson

Carmen was sitting at the table in the small kitchen of the apartment later that day, clutching the bottle of prenatal vitamins.

In this time of thinking, certain facts aligned themselves in Carmen's mind. Her mother had gained weight in the past couple months. Carmen had put it down to happiness, but now she felt silly for not being more observant. Christina's wardrobe had subtly but certainly shifted toward the roomier stuff in her closet. Had she stopped drinking wine? Carmen tried to think. Had she gone for a lot of doctor's appointments?

Carmen had once overheard her mom joking with her aunt about how it was easy to hide stuff from teenagers because they were so self-absorbed. She felt the sting of it now, though she'd laughed it off then.

She heard a key in the lock of the front door—her mother, arriving home from work at the usual time. Carmen stayed sitting, knowing her mother would

appear in the kitchen moments after she'd put her bags down. Carmen hadn't planned an ambush, exactly, but it came off a lot like one.

"Hi, *nena*, love." Christina's whole body looked tired as she entered the kitchen. She'd always eschewed the practice of wearing sneakers with her suit to and from work, but recently she'd caved on her dignity. Now Carmen understood why.

Wordlessly Carmen held up the bottle.

Wordlessly Christina stared at it, and slowly its significance registered. Her eyes widened, and her expression changed from confusion to surprise to dread to exhaustion and back again.

Carmen decided to skip to the crux of the matter. "How far are you?" she asked in a moderated, matter-of-fact tone, though her heart was pounding. She knew it was true, but still she wanted her mother to deny it.

Christina seemed to stiffen her spine to mount a vivid defense. She seemed to consider several possible angles. And then, before Carmen's eyes, she deflated again. Her dark red blouse appeared to crumple. "Five months."

"You're kidding." Well, there it was. "When were you planning to tell me?" Carmen's voice was flatly accusatory.

"Carmen. Darling." Christina sat down across from her. She wanted to reach for Carmen's hand, but Carmen was sitting on one, and the other was strangling the neck of the vitamin bottle. Christina withdrew her attempt.

She was quiet for a few moments, collecting her breath. "Just let me explain, okay? It's complicated."

Carmen offered something between a shrug and a nod.

"David and I have talked and thought a lot about having a baby. He hasn't had that joy in his life, as I have. We didn't know if it would be possible. But we agreed, life is too short not to try for something you want."

Carmen hated the "life is too short" rationalization. She thought it was one of the lamer excuses in the history of excuse-making. Whenever you did something because "life is too short not to," you could be sure life would be just long enough to punish you for it.

"At the very least we thought it would take me a year or two to conceive, if I did at all," Christina went on. "We never dreamed it would happen so fast. I'm almost forty-one years old."

Carmen cocked her head skeptically. With half her mind she was calculating whether they'd conceived this baby before or after their wedding. It was a close call.

"I didn't even guess I was pregnant until I was almost three months along. I just couldn't believe it. And then I needed to think about how to talk to you. The timing was not what I had wished. It's very . . . complicated."

Complicated. What a totally unsatisfying word. It was a politician's word.

"There were your exams, your senior paper. Then graduation crept up on us," Christina continued, holding

up her hands plaintively. "I didn't want any of your special things to get overshadowed by this news."

"Were you going to tell me before it was born?"

Reasonably, Christina looked hurt. "I was going to tell you this weekend."

"Do you know what kind it is?"

"You mean a boy or a girl?"

Carmen nodded.

"No. We want to wait to find out when the baby is born."

Carmen nodded again, knowing as she did that this baby would be a girl. It just had to be.

"So I guess it's due around . . ." Carmen had already calculated the baby would have to be born near her own birthday, but she left the space open for her mother to fill.

"Around the end of September," Christina supplied slowly, the look of dread intensifying.

Carmen knew, intellectually, that this was happy news on a lot of levels. Christina had a whole new life ahead of her. From about seventh grade onward, Carmen had feared the day she'd leave for college. She imagined she'd be leaving her single mother alone to defrost food and eat by herself night after night. Instead, this September, she'd be leaving a happy couple bursting with a new baby.

And besides, Carmen was finally getting the sibling she had always professed to want. If she were a big and good person, she would be able to feel and appreciate this

happiness. She would be able to congratulate and even hug her mother. But she wasn't a big or good person. She'd dashed too many such opportunities not to know the truth about herself.

"It's kind of convenient, in a way," Carmen stated, sounding robotic, like she didn't much care. "Because you can just use my room for the nursery, right? I'll be going just before the baby comes. Good planning."

The corners of Christina's mouth quivered. "It wasn't good planning. It wasn't planned like this."

"And you can even combine birthday parties. What a funny coincidence."

"Carmen, I don't think it's funny." Christina's gaze was earnest and unwavering. "I think it's serious, and I know you must have a lot of complicated feelings about it."

Carmen looked away. She knew she was being spooky. She could tell by the worry in her mother's eyes. Carmen was well known to whine and complain and lash out destructively. Christina's posture, much like that of a person girded for the arrival of a hurricane, indicated that she was ready for just such a lashing.

Carmen didn't want to give her mother anything, not even that.

Yes, Carmen did have feelings, and they were damming up behind her face, generating a mammoth pressure somewhere around the back of her eyes. Carmen was afraid her face might explode if she had too many more of those feelings just now.

Silently she handed her mother her vitamins and stood

to leave. Earlier she'd debated telling her mother that they'd fallen in the toilet, but as she strode out of the room she figured she would just let her mother go ahead and eat them.

Carmen hated herself right now, but she hated her mother a little bit more.

Oh, Carma,

I, of all people, won't dare congratulate you or anything. I swear I won't remind you how you always said you wanted a brother or sister, like all those *%&#$-all people did to me. I feel your pain. I mean, couldn't they have just gotten a dog?

I hope the Oreos provide comfort for at least an hour—just eat the box and think later. I got the kind with extra stuff in the middle, because I love you extra.

Tibby

The air in the dining hall of the Prynne Valley Soccer Academy was charged in a peculiar way. Bridget felt goose-bumpy and alert. She had an idea, but she didn't want to have that idea—to give it words or a picture. Or maybe she did want to have that idea but didn't want to *want* the idea. Maybe that was it.

The room was knotty pine from floor to ceiling. Wide planks for the walls, medium for the floor, skinny for the ceiling. It was filling up slowly with coaches, trainers, administrators, and blah blah blah. The campers wouldn't arrive until tomorrow. Every stranger looked like someone she knew. Her intensity made her invisible; she was seeing so hard she forgot about being seen.

"Bee?"

Diana's voice was behind her, but she didn't turn. Diana was a real friend, but she wasn't telling Bee what she needed to know. So Bee would find it out for herself.

There was a long table to one side. On it were sodas and an industrial-sized coffeemaker and a few plates of store-bought cookies. Oatmeal with bits of raisin.

Was it dread or hope that made her chest pound? Her toes clutched so hard inside her clogs they were falling asleep.

She sensed the presence of a significant body just off her left shoulder. She wasn't sure with which sense she sensed it. He was too far away to touch him or to feel his body heat. He was too far behind her for her to see him. Until she turned, that is.

Her eyes seemed to go in and out of focus. Was it him? Of course it was him! Was it him?

"Bridget?"

It was unquestionably him. His eyes were dark under dark, arching eyebrows. He was older and taller and different and also the same. Was he surprised? Was he happy? Was he sorry?

Her hand went protectively to her face.

He made a gesture as if to hug her, but he couldn't seem to bridge the strange air between them.

The time came for her to say something, and then it passed. She stared at him in silence. Socially, she never cared much about covering her tracks.

"How are you?" he asked her. She remembered that he was earnest. It was something she'd liked about him.

"I'm — I'm surprised," she said honestly. "I didn't realize you would be here."

"I knew you would be." He cleared his throat. "Here, I mean."

"You did?"

"They mailed out the staff list a couple weeks ago."

"Oh." Bridget cursed herself for not reading her mail more thoroughly. She hated forms (*Mother's maiden name . . . Mother's profession . . .*), and between this camp and Brown, she'd had far too many of them.

So he'd known. She hadn't. What if she had known? Would she have willingly tossed herself into a summer full of Eric Richman, breaker of hearts and minds?

It was amazing, in a way, that he occupied space like a regular human being. He was so monumental to her. For these two years he'd represented not only himself but all the complicated things she'd felt about herself.

He was looking at her carefully. He smiled when her eyes caught his. "So, from what I hear, you haven't gotten any worse."

She looked at his mouth moving, but she had no idea what he was talking about. She did not disguise this.

"At soccer," he clarified.

She'd forgotten they were at soccer camp. She'd forgotten she played soccer.

"I'm all right," she said. She wasn't even sure what she was talking about. But she said it again, because she liked the ring of it. "I'm all right."

Your chances of getting

hit by lightning go up if

you stand under a tree,

shake your fist at the sky,

and say "storms suck!"

-Johnny Carson

The only adult person in Carmen's life who hadn't smilingly congratulated her about her upcoming baby sibling was Valia Kaligaris, Lena's grandmother. Now, as Carmen sat at the counter in Lena's family's glossy kitchen and Valia sat at the breakfast table, Carmen felt grateful for that.

Granted, Valia wasn't up for chatting these days. As Carmen waited for Lena to come back from the restaurant, Valia glowered at the Cheerios box and then trudged, still in her purple bathrobe, to the darkened den, where she turned on the TV so loud Carmen could hear every word even though it was two rooms away. It was a soap opera. Apparently Dirk had abandoned Raven at the altar the very day before her identical twin sister, Robin, went missing. Hmmmm.

Carmen could privately ridicule it because it wasn't *her* soap opera. *Her* soap opera (to which she had become progressively addicted since she'd been accepted to

Williams early decision in January and stopped doing her homework) was called *Brawn and Beauty* and it would never have a plot line as dumb as this one. Carmen's addiction centered on one actor (hailing from the Brawn side of things) named Ryan Hennessey. He was absolutely, explosively gorgeous, and her one true love, no matter how much her friends made fun of her for it. He was a *good* actor. Seriously, he was. He'd done some sort of Shakespeare thing before he'd gotten the soap gig. At least, that was what Carmen had read in *Soap Opera Digest* while she was waiting with Tibby to pay for the Diet Coke at the A&P the night before.

The Kaligarises' front door opened and closed, and Lena appeared with her mother a minute later.

"Hey, Carma." Lena looked sweaty from her shift at the Elite. Ari was in her work clothes.

"Hi. How's work?"

Lena rolled her eyes.

"At least you have a job," Carmen pointed out.

"How's the search going?" Ari asked, pulling a pitcher of water from the fridge and filling a glass. "Anybody?" She held up the pitcher.

"No, thanks." If Carmen had wanted something, she would have gotten it for herself. The Septembers had broken down that barrier at each other's houses before it had even gone up. "The search is . . . uh, slow. I'm kind of, uh, not that much in the mood for babysitting this summer." Carmen realized that if she didn't rush onward, she could be questioned on this topic. "But I saw this ad

at the A&P to take care of an old lady five afternoons a week. She's kind of blind, I guess, so the job would mostly be reading to her. I called the number and left a message."

Ari put her glass down a little too forcefully on the granite counter. Lena turned to look at her mom. "You know," Ari said, her eyes animated, "that's strange. I've been thinking about that same thing for Valia. I've been thinking how much she needs some companionship to help her with her errands and correspondence and maybe take her to her doctor's appointments. I don't dare take another afternoon off work this month."

Carmen nodded.

"I was hoping Lena or Effie could pitch in, but they both got jobs early this summer."

Carmen kept her expression brightly neutral, so as not to appear to indict Lena.

Ari put her glass in the sink with a definitive motion. "How much were they offering to pay on the sign you saw?" She was getting quite enthusiastic now.

"Eight an hour."

"How about I'll pay you eight fifty if you'll look after Valia thirty or so hours a week? We could make up the schedule together."

Carmen considered, looking down at her chipped red nail polish. In this minute she could go from having no job, no purpose in life, to having one. The money was decent. It would be a little weird to have Ari paying her. But then, it was more comfortable for Ari to hire Carmen

than to hire a stranger. Carmen would frankly rather hang out in Lena's airy, spacious house than in what would likely be a stuffy, old-lady apartment.

"Well . . ." Carmen tapped her index finger on the counter. "Okay. Why not?"

"Fantastic," Ari said.

Carmen hadn't looked across the counter at Lena before this moment. So she hadn't seen how Lena had positioned herself with her back to her mother and was facing Carmen, frantically wide-eyed, mouthing the word *no* and drawing her index finger across her neck, until it was too late.

Lena waited to explode until she'd gotten Carmen up to her room and shut the door.

"Are you insane?"

"Lenny, jeez. What's the problem?"

"Why do you think Effie and I set up jobs in mid-April? Jobs we both fully hate, by the way."

"Because . . . you're well organized?"

Lena shook her head stormily.

"Because . . . you are ungrateful and uncaring grand-daughters of your recently widowed and helpless grand-mother?"

"Because Valia is a nightmare!" Lena practically shouted.

It was a good thing Valia's hearing wasn't so good, Carmen thought.

"I mean, she's an amazing and wonderful woman." Lena backtracked, looking more serious. "She really is.

And we love her. But she's awful right now! And I'm not saying I blame her for it. She's miserable about Bapi. She's miserable that she's in the States living with us. She hates my dad for making her come. She hates everything about this country. She wishes she were in her own home surrounded by her friends. She is furious at everybody, can't you tell that?"

Carmen was now feeling stupid and a bit defensive. "Maybe she is. But maybe I can handle it."

Lena shook her head. "Trust me. You and Valia are not a good combination right now."

Carmen narrowed her eyes. "And what's that supposed to mean?"

Now, and for a long time, the best way Bridget knew to settle her mind was to run. Sometimes she felt that the meditative state of the long, quiet miles helped her think. Sometimes she felt that the pure exhaustion helped her not think.

Sometimes she believed that she was running toward some sort of resolution, and other times she knew she was just plain running away. Still, it was what she did.

This late-evening run took her up and down country roads fringed by scrubby, June-green trees. The sinking sun poked an occasional sparkling ray straight into her eyes. When she got bored of the cars honking at her (was she posing a hazard in the fading light, or was it her hair?), she leaped off the road. Another girl might have been scared to run through unfamiliar woods as darkness

fell, but Bee wasn't. She knew she could outrun virtually any human being who might find her. And the bears in these parts weren't man-eaters, she was pretty sure.

It was exhilarating, if anything. The forest was young and sparse, cut through every which way by paths. She followed a deep, wide bed where she imagined a river had once lain. She pictured herself striving in this same place when the river flowed. She ran until her thoughts shortened and no longer formed lines. They flashed and blipped. She didn't follow them around the corner. She simply felt things without any hows or whys. This was how she settled herself.

Now the sun was entirely gone and Bridget knew the light would soon disappear too. The light that stayed on after the sun always felt to her like an empty promise. Ahead of her, on the dirt bed, something caught her eye. It jostled her breath out of its rhythm and sent her brain spinning. It was less than twenty yards away, and it disturbed her. She slowed her pace to keep the distance from disappearing so fast. She wanted to run wide around it, but she wanted to face it too. She was back in hows and whys.

It was a bird, she thought. A pigeon, maybe. It was clearly dead and bent into a wrong set of angles. Its head seemed to stick up from the ground in a pitiful pose. She was nearly upon it. She wouldn't stop. She would keep going. She would avert her eyes. No, she couldn't avert her eyes.

It wasn't until she was literally over the bird that she realized, in a burst, that it wasn't a bird at all. It was a mitten. It was a lost, grayish mitten with the thumb

sticking up and looking very much like the head of a bird.

She was instantly flooded by relief and reassessment. Her mind and body fell back into calm alignment.

But as she ran and ran and the sky turned a dark, bruised blue, she felt sad. And, strangely, even though the twisted body in her path had been a mitten, she found herself remembering it as a bird.

If Lena's mother's car had not overheated it wouldn't have happened. The whole summer would have gone differently.

But her mother's car did overheat, on Thursday afternoon, so Lena borrowed her father's car on Friday and dropped him at work on her way to drawing class. It was easily on the way. In fact, as she drove away from her father, who was already sweating through his white shirt, she considered absently that it was only a short walk from his office building to her class. But at the time, it didn't signify anything.

By midmorning she was deeply immersed in her drawing. At Annik's instruction, the model, Andrew, took five-minute poses. For the first few poses Lena felt so harried she could barely get a gesture out of the tip of her charcoal. But then those five minutes began to stretch out for her. The intensity of hurrying stayed, but the consciousness of time dropped away. Just as her awareness of the model's nakedness had completely bewitched her during the first few days and subsequently floated off. (In hindsight she felt ashamed of her juvenile, red-faced

self. To the seasoned artists in the class, Andrew's nudity was about as sexually charged as Lena's coffee cup.)

Lena now observed Andrew's body in extreme detail, staring without a vestige of shyness at the hollow inside his hip and the sharp ridge of his shin. When she passed deeply into this creative state, she didn't really have thoughts anymore. The muscles that controlled her arm bypassed her thinking brain, linking directly to her autonomic system. The usual Lena was just along for the ride.

She jumped when the timer rang out for the long break. A shiver radiated from her shoulders. She hated coming up to the surface like this. She didn't want to hear Phyllis's newspaper rustling and Charlie's heels slapping around in his sandals. She didn't want Andrew pulling on his robe. Not for the reasons you might think. No, really. (Though the truth was, she did regain the awkward mindfulness of Andrew's bare skin in that second when he'd pull on the green kimono and again in that second when he'd take it off.) She just wanted to draw. She just wanted to stay in that place where she understood things without thinking about them.

As Lena stared wistfully at her empty coffee cup, she recognized—almost abstractly—her happiness. Leave it to her to detect happiness rather than actually feel it. Maybe it wasn't happiness, precisely. Maybe it was more like . . . peace. At the end of the previous summer her peace had been sliced up like roast beef. The tumult had brought with it a certain strange exuberance, a feeling of living more extravagantly than ever before. But it had also sucked.

She thought back to the end of that summer, when she had first met Paul Rodman, Carmen's stepbrother. Her response to him had taken her by surprise. She had never experienced such an instant physical attraction to anybody — not even Kostos. In Paul's presence, that first time, she had spun these out-of-character fantasies about what she could mean to him, and he to her. But after he left, she retreated, as was her wont. Her romantic side went back into hiding, and after some time, her timid side took over, timidly, again.

Now when she thought about him she felt ashamed. He was one of the many things she'd been hiding from this year. He was one of the people she'd been avoiding.

In February, she had first heard from Carmen that Paul's father was sick. She felt awful about it. She had thought about Paul. She had worried for him. But she hadn't called him, or written, as she'd meant to. She had learned since, from Carmen, that Paul's father was sicker and would likely not be getting better. She didn't know what to say to Paul.

She was afraid of his sadness. She was afraid to elicit his feelings. She was also afraid not to. She was afraid she would bring it up, and there would fall that most inept failure between them: total silence.

It wasn't until this class, this feeling, that she had regained a sense of balance. The time she spent with her charcoal and her fingers and her broad pads of paper and Andrew and Annik and these deep, stabilizing stretches of meditation — it all felt like too big a gift to be received. She would have to work to receive it.

Her heart soared at the sound of the timer indicating the break was over. Back to work. It was amazing how much she could hate and love the very same sound.

And so began the fateful pose.

For starters, it was unfortunate that the door opened in the middle of the pose, when Lena was least able to process what was happening. It was unfortunate that the person who walked through the door was Lena's father. It was also unfortunate that the door was located near the model stand and that Andrew was oriented in such a way that the first thing you saw, upon bursting through the door in the middle of a pose (which you really weren't supposed to do), was a very up-close look between Andrew's legs. It was particularly unfortunate that Lena didn't recognize all of these unfortunate things in time to soften her father's experience, but instead unwittingly treated her father to a long stretch of her unabashed fixation upon the glories of Andrew.

When her father started talking, overloud, she came to. He was looming over her. It was a rude transition. It took her a moment to find any words.

"Dad, you are —

"Dad, you didn't —

"Dad, come on. Let me just — "

She started a lot of other sentences too. The next thing she knew, he had his hand clamped around her arm and was steering her back through the door, turning her forcibly away from Andrew.

Annik appeared in the hall with amazing speed.

"What's going on here?" she asked calmly.

"We are leaving," Mr. Kaligaris blustered.

"You are?" she asked Lena.

"I'm not," Lena said faintly.

Mr. Kaligaris exclaimed three or four things in Greek before he turned to English. "I will not have my daughter in this . . . in this *class* where you have . . . in this *place* where she is—"

Lena could tell her father wouldn't use the necessary descriptive words in her earshot. When it came down to it, her father was a deeply conservative and old-fashioned man. He'd grown even more so since Bapi's death. But long before that, he'd been way stricter than any of her friends' fathers. He never let boys up to the second floor of their house. Not even her lobotomized cousins.

Annik stayed cool. "Mr. Kaligaris, might it help if you and Lena and I sat down for a few minutes and discussed what we are trying to do in this class? You must know that virtually every art program offers—"

"No, it would not," Mr. Kaligaris broke in. "My daughter is not taking this class. She will not be coming back."

He pulled Lena through the hall and out onto the sidewalk. He was muttering something about an unexpected meeting and coming to find her to get the car back, and *look what he finds!*

Lena didn't manage to pull away until she was standing in the harsh sunshine, dazed and off balance once again.

It's like, how much more

black could this be?

And the answer is none.

None more black.

—This Is Spinal Tap

H ow bad could it be?

That was what Carmen asked herself as she fixed Valia a cup of tea first thing when she arrived at the Kaligaris house early Monday afternoon and brought it into the den, where Valia was watching television.

"Awful." Valia nearly spat when she tried the tea. "Vhat did you put in this?"

"Well, tea." Carmen was being patient. "And honey."

"I said sugar."

"The sugar bowl was empty."

"Sugar and honey is not the same. American honey you cannot eat."

"You can if you want," Carmen began, but realized this was not a diplomatic avenue. "Here, I'll try again." She took the teacup back into the kitchen. She located the box of Domino granulated white sugar on the high shelf in the pantry. She refilled the sugar bowl.

While she waited for the water to boil a second time,

her mind traveled to September. From a chilly distance she imagined her mom very pregnant. She imagined a baby shower. She imagined her room, filled with expectations for somebody else.

When she used to think about September, she imagined herself arriving at college, meeting her roommate for the first time, unpacking her stuff. Now she could only seem to picture what would be going on in her absence, and in those pictures, it was as though she were dead. Or as though she were the one who hadn't yet been born.

She used to be able to look forward to college. She had dreamed of Williams for so long. It was one of the best colleges in the country. The place her dad had gone. As agonizing as it was to leave her friends, college was something she'd really wanted. Why couldn't she want it anymore?

She was angry. She wasn't angry at the baby, exactly. How could she be? She wasn't angry at her mother. Well, she sort of was, but that wasn't the real root of it. She was angry that she couldn't picture her own life anymore. She was angry that her mother and this baby had somehow stolen her future and plunged her back into the past.

The pressure was building up behind her eyes again. Reflexively she snatched the phone from the wall.

"Hey, it's me," she said when Tibby answered.

"You okay?" Tibby asked. It was so nice how a person who loved you could pick up on your mood in three small words.

Carmen could hear Nicky shouting about something in the background. "I guess. How 'bout you?"

"Nicky, could you do that in the other room?" Tibby called, away from the phone. "How's Valia?" she asked into the phone.

"She's—"

Suddenly a beeping sound overwhelmed the connection. "Tibby?"

Beep beep. Beeeeeep.

"Hello?"

"Sounds like a modem." Tibby had to shout over the noise. "It must be from your end."

Carmen hung up the phone and went into the den. Sure enough, Valia had moved from the TV to the desk and was steering the computer's mouse like a race car. Carmen watched in surprise as Valia expertly negotiated her way through a series of menus into a rapid instant messaging conversation. Presumably with somebody in Greece, considering that Carmen couldn't read a single letter. She was used to the look of the Greek letters from all her years in the Kaligaris household, but she couldn't tell you what sounds any of them made.

Carmen was supposed to help Valia with her correspondence? And here she had been picturing crumply airmail paper and blue envelopes.

"*Vhat?*" Valia turned around somewhat belligerently, obviously feeling Carmen's eyes on the back of her uncoiffed head.

"Nothing. Wow. You really know what you're doing." Carmen decided to be mature and not mention how Valia

was hogging up the phone line when she really wanted to talk to Tibby.

Instead, she sat down in one of the comfortable TV chairs, mindlessly picked up the remote, and started flipping channels. *Brawn and Beauty* would be starting in seven minutes. She settled back into the chair, resting her heavy head. How bad could it be, spending the summer watching her favorite soap and getting paid while Valia burned up the lines IMing her Greek friends?

"Not that channel." Valia had turned from the computer, her hands still poised over the keyboard.

"What do you mean?"

"I like channel seven. *The Vorld Apart*."

"But you're not even watching. You're on the computer." Carmen could hear her own voice rising.

"I like to listen," Valia proclaimed.

"But I like to *watch*," Carmen said tartly.

"Who's the vun getting paid?"

Ouch. Carmen felt as though Valia had bit her. She felt the flush rising in her cheeks. "Well, could you get off the computer, then? You're hogging up the phone line," Carmen snapped in a manner that was not very mature.

Tibberon: How's it going with the ancient Greek?
Carmabelle: Ahem. Not bad. Not not bad. Not good. If you see what I mean.

"Just tell me every, every single thing. After that you can drink your smoothie."

70

Tibby felt her heart rising again. Carmen's enthusiasm was everything she could wish for. She shook her clear plastic cup of frothy pink smoothie so it wouldn't separate.

"Well, first we danced to that —"

Carmen was waving her hands around. "No, no. Back up. I want the beginning. I want to hear the whole thing, soup to nuts."

Tibby smiled in spite of herself. She liked sitting outside under the umbrella at the smoothie place on Old Georgetown Road, feeling the sun bake her calves. She crossed her legs and let her green plastic flip-flop drop onto the hot sidewalk. Truth was, she wanted to tell the whole thing, soup to nuts. It made it real again. "Okay. So back up to my house. Doorbell rings. Katherine opens the door. He's wearing the suit jacket and tie — kind of short in the arms and obviously cheap, but so, so, so, so cute. And he has —" Tibby wished her face weren't turning pink, but she couldn't help it. "A bunch of flowers. Dyed pink carnations, fairly hideous. You know, like flowers only a boy would buy, but totally perfect." Tibby needed to stop and breathe or she was going to pass out.

At that moment her cell phone rang faintly from the lower reaches of her straw bag. She pulled it out and squinted to see the number. It was her mother's cell phone.

"Hello?"

Nobody was there at first. She heard background noise. And then she heard her mother saying something to someone else. She sounded strange.

"Hello?"

"Tibby?" Her voice was ragged.

"Are you okay?"

Her mother was crying.

"Mom, are you okay? What's going on?" Tibby felt a frigid load of adrenaline hit her bloodstream.

"Honey, Dad and I—" Alice broke off. Her crying was too thick to make words. She could hear her father's voice in the background, shouting.

Tibby stood up, jamming her foot back into her shoe. "Mom, please tell me what's going on? You're scaring me."

Her mom took a few seconds to get her breath. Tibby had never heard her sound like this before. It set her mind swirling and leaping spasmodically with fearful possibilities. She paced around the table.

What? Carmen was mouthing urgently.

"We're at the hospital. Katherine is hurt." Alice paused to gain control of her breaking voice again. "She fell out the window."

Tibby couldn't move or think. Waves of cold rolled through her body. Hot hysteria began to brew under her ribs. "Is. She. Okay?"

"She's conscious, she's—" Her mother's sobs took on a more hopeful tone. "That's a good sign."

"Should I come?" Tibby asked.

"No. Please go home and look after Nicky, okay?"

"Yes. I'll go." Tibby was crying now. Carmen's eyes were tearing and she didn't even know what had happened.

Tibby needed to ask a question that summed up her

dread. But she was afraid, so she waited until the connection was dead.

"Which window?"

Lena sat on the back steps of the restaurant during her break. Inside was hot, outside was hot. She was sticky, and her apron was spattered with tomato sauce. It looked vaguely gory. Like maybe a customer had made one nasty comment too many.

She hated this job. She hated the careless food, all hurried and overcooked in vats. She hated the constant pressure to turn tables over. She hated the green vinyl booths and the way the coffee cups rattled in their saucers, filling the saucers with hot coffee, which she inevitably spilled on her apron. She felt embarrassed by the lame painting of the Parthenon frieze that stretched across an entire wall of the dining room. She hated the fake windows and the fake ivy. She was bothered by the fact that her manager, Antonis, the one with the fuzzy gray hair spilling out of his ears, still thought she spoke Greek in spite of several one-sided conversations.

She would happily sit out here in the back alley and smell the garbage if it meant not being in there. She needed time by herself. She was constantly being talked at, complained to, harassed. Even the polite customers were always waving her down, catching her eye, needing her to bring one more thing.

Some people liked being in communication with other people all day long, but Lena was not one of them.

Looking back on the relative peace of Basia's clothing store the summer before made it seem like a dream job.

Her father had pressed hard for the restaurant job. He had personally recommended her to the owner of the Elite. It was what his parents had done back in Greece. It was the life he had grown up in. Since his own father's death less than a year before, these things had become more important to him.

For most of his life her dad had rebelled against Bapi and against his upbringing. He had eschewed the restaurant business in favor of law school. He had changed his name from Georgos to George. He made a point of being American, not even teaching his daughters to speak Greek. It seemed sad to Lena that he had waited until his father was dead to start caring about the stuff his father had always wanted him to care about.

"The restaurant business is very practical," her dad had told her on several occasions, implying that being an artist was not very practical. "It's a good business," he'd say, and she was sure it was a good business. For somebody else. She sort of wondered whether he'd ever stopped and considered who she was. Did he really imagine she was going to start a restaurant in the proud Kaligaris tradition? Could he not see how wrong it was for her?

It had been four days since the disaster in her drawing class. She hadn't been back and she was missing it terribly. She could stand this job if she had her drawing to look forward to. She could tolerate Valia's loud misery and her parents' tension at home if she could draw. But without it, she felt like she was sinking.

74

"Okay," Lena said. She didn't really want to leave anyway. She would stay and water the plants if that were her only excuse.

Annik left supplies out on a free easel. It was like leaving drugs out for an addict. It had been Lena's easel; that's why it was free. At first Lena just stood in the back of class and watched people draw. Then her fingers started itching for a piece of charcoal. She ambled over to the easel, just drawing with her eyes at first. She hesitated. Then she picked up the charcoal and she was lost until the bell rang.

Annik came over. "That's lovely," she said, studying the three poses of Andrew laid out on the sheet. "Do you want to go outside and talk for a minute?"

"Okay." Lena expected they'd talk in the hallway, but Annik led her down the hall, up a ramp, and out into the courtyard. Annik rolled up to a bench, and Lena sat down on it. The dogwood trees rustled and a small fountain gushed appealingly in the middle. Various sculptures and found-object works, one involving a stack of car tires, decorated the perimeter.

"Are you comfortable drawing Andrew?" she asked. Annik's hair was a beautiful red, made only more so by the sunlight. There was orange and gold and chestnut and even pink in it. Annik was fairly young, Lena realized, probably in her late twenties, and her face was delicate and pretty. Lena wondered, absently, if there was a man who loved her.

"Yes," Lena said. "I felt a little awkward the first day, but then it went away. I don't think about it anymore."

"That's what I thought," Annik said. "How old are you?"

"Seventeen. I'll be eighteen at the end of the summer."

Annik nodded. "Can I tell you what I think?"

Lena nodded.

"I think you should take the class."

"I think I should too. I wish my dad felt that way."

Annik put her hands on her wheels like she was getting ready to roll away.

Lena wondered, as she had many times before, what had happened to Annik that made her need a wheelchair. Had she always been in a chair or had she grown up on her legs like a regular kid? Had she had an accident or a disease? Lena wondered what of Annik's worked and what didn't. Could she have a baby if she wanted to?

Though Lena wanted to know, she didn't dare ask. She shied away from the intensity that might come from asking such a question. Intimacy came faster when a person wore their pain and poor luck for all to see. And yet, not asking felt like an act of neglect or cowardice. It kept a distance between them that Lena regretted.

Annik rolled back and forth a little, but she didn't go anywhere just yet. "You do what you need to do," she said.

Lena wasn't sure whether this meant take the class or listen to your father, but she had a pretty strong suspicion it was the former.

"I'm not sure how I'd pay for it, for one thing," Lena mused.

"I'm allowed a second monitor," Annik said. "You'd

need to help set up and clean up every day, including mopping. But you'd get free tuition."

"I'll do it," Lena said instantly, not aware of making the decision.

Annik smiled openly. "I'm so glad."

"I'm not sure what I'm going to tell my dad," Lena murmured, half to herself.

"Tell him the truth," Annik said.

Lena shrugged, knowing that this was the piece of Annik's advice she was not going to take.

There are many things

that we would throw away

if we were not afraid that

others might pick them up.

—Oscar Wilde

Tibby sat frozen on a chair in the den watching Nicky watch cartoons. Her thoughts came together and broke apart, occasionally punctured by the sadism of *Tom and Jerry*. Her whole body hurt; every bone ached when her mind flashed on Katherine. She let herself think of Katherine for only a second at a time and then she pulled away, because it hurt too much.

Nicky didn't know anything yet. They didn't want to scare him. Whereas Tibby was good and scared, wanting desperately for the phone to ring, but only if it was good news.

Tibby was not raised religious. For the early part of her childhood, her parents were devout atheists, spewing Marx's "opiate of the masses" rhetoric. Nowadays Tibby wasn't sure what they believed. They didn't talk about it anymore.

But Tibby was not them. As far as Tibby was concerned, you couldn't have someone you loved, really

loved, die and not believe in some kind of god. It was the only way to look at it. And besides, Bailey herself—as she had lived, not as she had died—had been proof that somebody or something existed beyond the realm of rational things.

And when Tibby thought of Bailey, it made sense, because a god who was smart enough to want Bailey back as soon as possible was also smart enough to see the beauty of Katherine. Katherine was too good for the world Tibby lived in. Tibby belonged there just fine, but not Katherine. Katherine was brave and generous and passionate. If she weren't on God's dance card, then who would be? Tibby would stand in the corner of heaven, if she ever made it there, but Katherine, like Bailey, would be doing the polka or the bunny hop or maybe the bus stop with God.

Please don't take her yet, Tibby implored. *She's only three and we love her too much to survive without her.*

Tibby was asking selfishly. Because she knew it was her fault. She had opened a window that was always shut. Why had she done that? She knew Katherine wanted to climb the apple tree. She knew that was how Katherine fell out the window. *It wasn't on purpose. Please, God, believe that.*

It was an accident. It was horrible, but not nearly as horrible as the ways in which Tibby had failed her little sister on purpose. Tibby was jealous and resentful. She hurt Katherine's feelings on the pretense that small kids didn't have actual feelings. And yet Tibby knew in her

heart they did — possibly the deepest feelings of all.

If Tibby had loved Katherine as she deserved, maybe she wouldn't have fallen out the window. If Tibby had paid attention to her and given her a boost to the branch of the apple tree, then Katherine wouldn't have been climbing out anybody's window. If Tibby hadn't been so preoccupied with Brian, maybe this wouldn't have happened.

Love was the best padding anybody could have. And though irrepressible Katherine deserved it a million times over, Tibby hadn't given it.

I do love her, God. I love her so much. Tibby just wanted a chance to do better.

The phone rang and Tibby threw herself on top of it.

"Tibby?"

It was her dad. She ran the phone into the kitchen so Nicky wouldn't hear. "Dad?" Her body was shaking.

"Honey, she's doing better. The doctors say she's going to be okay."

Tibby gave herself full permission to cry now. She wept and sobbed and heaved and shook. Her dad was doing similar things on his end.

"Can I come?" she asked.

"She's still getting X-rays. Her skull is fractured, which is the most serious thing. She also broke her wrist and her collarbone. We're hoping that's the extent of it. She's talking and alert now, but I'd rather you stay home with Nicky for a couple more hours. Bring him over around six when things settle down here, okay?"

"Okay. But I want—I want to see her so bad, Daddy. . . ." Tibby's voice got swallowed up in tears.

"I know, honey. You will."

"Tib, it's me, Carma. We've been terrified all day. Lenny made me stop calling your house, and then she called five more times. I'm so glad K's gonna be okay. I'm thinking about you. Please call when you get a second. I love you." *Beeep.*

"Tibby! It's Bee! God, Lena called me here to tell me about Katherine. I'm still shaking. She's going to get better so fast, though. I know it. Call me? Love you." *Beeeep.*

"Tib, sorry I kept calling before. It's Lenny. I just couldn't stand waiting. I'm so glad the news is good. I'll come visit tomorrow, okay? Hang in there. We love you." *Beeeep.*

"And I saw it really close, so I wanted to get it." Katherine was propped up on pillows in her hospital bed, slightly woozy from medication but still eager to recount her adventure to Tibby and Nicky, who were both sitting cross-legged on the foot of her bed.

Tibby nodded eagerly, trying not to show her agony at each word of the retelling. Her heart ached at the sight of Katherine's bruised, bandaged head, her cast, her sling and multiple cuts and scrapes. It was made almost more

84

heartrending by the fact that Katherine didn't seem to notice.

"I couldn't reach it, so I climbed." Here she looked remorseful. "I'm not supposed to climb. But I almost got it, so I climbed more. And then"—she looked to Nicky for this bit—"I falled."

Nicky was entranced. Rarely had his sister done anything so interesting. "On the ground?" he asked breathlessly.

"First I grabbed on the bottom of the window," she explained. "I tried to climb back in because my fingers hurt because I was hanging."

Nicky nodded, eyes wide and unblinking.

"I couldn't climb back in, so I saw the soft bushes and I falled."

"Oh," Nicky murmured.

"They aren't very soft because I crushed my skull," Katherine added conversationally.

"Katherine!" Tibby could not take this. The images were too awful to bear. She turned her head to get hold of herself. When she turned back, she lay across the bed on her stomach and grabbed Katherine's two bare feet. She tried to smile. "You are so strong and brave, you know?" She turned to Nicky. "Isn't she?" She knew his was the compliment Katherine would treasure.

"Yes," Nicky said solemnly.

"But you have to promise you will never do something like that again, right?"

"I promised. I already promised Mommy and Daddy that."

Tibby held the pair of small feet up to her face, pressing one to each cheek, and closed her eyes. She was overcome by tenderness and relief mixed with guilt and regret. She breathed deeply and willed back the tears. She didn't want Katherine to see any more crying.

"Brian!" Katherine shouted, with remarkable glee for a girl who had in fact crushed her skull less than eight hours earlier.

Tibby looked up. She had already felt so many things today, she couldn't imagine feeling any more.

Brian's face was wrenched, but he kept his expression bright as he came over to hug the noninjured parts of Katherine. "You are all in one piece, Kitty Cat," he said. "Good job."

Katherine beamed. "I falled out Tibby's window."

Brian cast the briefest of glances at Tibby, but she could read in it his protectiveness of her. "That's what I heard."

Tibby wondered how he'd heard. It was so like him just to come over to the hospital.

Tibby let Katherine's feet go as Brian looked at her in his particular way—projecting all the things he was thinking from his eyes to hers. He was worried about Katherine, but he was worried about Tibby, too. He wanted her to feel better, not to feel bad or responsible. He also wanted—or did she imagine this?—to convey to her that what had happened between them had really happened, that he meant what he had said to her.

She wanted something too. Just one little thing: for them to go back to how they were before.

Carmen lay on her bed thinking about Katherine, worrying about Tibby, and generally wondering things. Her mother was sleeping even though they'd finished dinner only an hour before. Once again, David had not made it home in time for dinner.

David was working on a big case. Seeing his schedule up close convinced Carmen that she did not ever want to become a lawyer. At least, not the kind David was. For a few weeks he'd come home by seven most nights for dinner, but in the last month he never came home before eleven, and even at that hour he was fielding calls on his cell phone. A few times he'd left home for the office one morning and hadn't come home until the next morning. Then he'd taken a shower and gone back again. Carmen had always suspected that people who worked that hard secretly didn't *want* to come home, but she knew that wasn't true of David. He was desperate to be home with Christina. He adored her. Carmen could see that he felt genuinely guilty and sad for every dinner he missed. And that was pretty much all of them.

According to Christina, he was working on a "big deal." One gigantic company gobbling up a different gigantic company, as Carmen understood it. And all David wanted to do was finish this "big deal" before the baby came. Which was why he worked twenty hours a day.

Carmen studied her ceiling, dotted with the glowing constellation stickers she'd excitedly arranged there when she was eight. There should be a law disallowing eight-year-olds from decorating their rooms, especially where stickers were involved. Why had her eight-year-old self saddled her seventeen-year-old self with so many dumb decals and see-through unicorn window appliqués? They were impossible to get off.

The truth was, she continued to have a soft spot for the glowing stars, but tonight they made the ceiling seem closer rather than farther away.

Thinking about her eight-year-old self reminded her of her four-year-old self, who was responsible for packing her closet with so many beautified (er, mangled) dolls. And that reminded her of her baby self, who had also inhabited this very room. And that, of course, reminded her of babies again.

She wanted to leave a hole when she left for college. That was selfish, maybe, but she did. She wanted to step out of the picture of her old life and leave a big, generous cutout waiting for her return. Giving her the *chance*, at least, to come back.

But now it felt like the minute she stepped out of her life, it was going to close up around her as if she'd never been there at all. The picture would re-form almost instantly with a new family in the place of her old one, and she could never come back again. That was how it felt to her. She was scared to disappear. She was scared to lose her place.

The ceiling was pushing down on her. The pressure beneath her eyes was pushing up. She felt like her eyeballs were in a vise. She got out of bed and turned on the light. She wiggled her mouse to wake her sleeping computer. She went online, and without really planning to, she brought up the Web site for the University of Maryland. Slowly she clicked around inside the site. It was the usual higher-education propaganda. She found herself clicking on the admissions link, and from there to the online application. The university offered rolling admissions. She wondered if they were still rolling. Her hand caused her to click on the Print icon.

Her eyes lighted ever so briefly on the stack of booklets and papers from Williams College. Health forms, dorm info, a course guide, a map showing the leafy spot in western Massachusetts where the campus lay, more than seven hours north of home.

She listened to the buzz and spit of her printer and wondered. What if she didn't go away after all? What if she didn't disappear?

Aerodynamically, the bumblebee shouldn't be able to fly, but the bumblebee doesn't know it so it goes on flying anyway.

—Mary Kay Ash

"I took on an extra shift at work," Lena told her father at dinner when he asked about her day. "I'm going to do the first dinner shift, from four to seven." She looked down at her pasta as she said it.

"Excellent," her father said.

"How is little Katherine doing?" her mother wanted to know. "Did you get to stop by there today?"

"Yeah." Lena smiled at the thought of Katherine's excited retelling. The tragedy had become the single most thrilling incident in Katherine's short life. "She's great. Only she has to wear a hockey helmet till the end of the summer."

"I wore a hockey helmet," Effie recalled, scraping her salad fork annoyingly across her plate. "Didn't I, Mom?"

"For a week," Ari answered. "You had a concussion, not a fracture, thank God."

Lena chewed a piece of bread. What was it about little sisters smashing their heads? Lena had never had so much as one stitch.

"Vhat kind of sauce do you call this?" Valia asked in an overloud voice.

"Pesto," Lena's mother said with finality.

"It does not taste good." Valia inspected it with her fork.

They were all quiet and waited for the moment to pass. Even Effie had been ground down into acquiescence.

A while later, Lena stood at the sink doing the dishes. She stiffened when she heard her grandmother pad into the kitchen behind her.

"I did IMs with Rena today."

"Oh?" Lena did not turn around. She did not like these conversations.

"She tells me Kostos and that voman are not living together now."

Lena closed her eyes and stood with her hands in the warm suds. She was glad Valia could not see her face.

Valia had many things to be bitter about, and Kostos was one of them. Her greatest dream was to have her handsome, beloved surrogate grandson, Kostos, marry her beautiful granddaughter Lena. She didn't seem to realize that her own hurt and disappointment were magnified a thousand times in Lena herself. If she had, maybe she wouldn't have brought up the news from Oia as often as she did.

The baby expected by Kostos and Mariana, the reason for their hasty marriage and Lena's heartbreak at the end of the previous summer, did not materialize. That was the first thunderclap to arrive, sometime in December. Valia

kept Lena roiling on this news for weeks. No one knew exactly why or what happened, but there was endless speculation. Valia was so biased, Lena doubted that any of her information was reliable. For all she knew, there was a bouncing baby Kostos, beloved by all.

Then, as now, Lena both wanted these rumors to be true and she didn't. The better part of her didn't. It was all she could do to get over Kostos and keep moving on with her life. She couldn't open her mind to any what ifs or she would be hobbled by them. She didn't want to know about Kostos. Whatever had happened, it was over. But still, *she did want to know*.

Valia's very presence and her connection to Oia was a thorn in Lena's heart, aggravating the wound whenever it seemed to be healing.

"Kostos stays in an apartment in Vothonas, near the airport. He has a job for a house-building company."

Lena couldn't control her thoughts. She would have if she could.

Had the baby miscarried, so that Mariana owned his sympathy? Or had it been a hoax, so that Kostos despised her? Had Kostos grown to love his wife? Or hate her? Would there be a different baby, if not the first one? These were the regular thoughts she'd had thousands of times. Now she had new ones to add: Were Kostos and his wife really separating? Or was he temporarily relocating for a new job, and she would soon join him?

Lena would have considered electroshock therapy if it meant getting rid of these thoughts.

"That's interesting," she said faintly to the wall. She couldn't let Valia see how these news bulletins affected her.

Valia launched into her opinions, and Lena stopped listening. She finished up the pots and pans as quickly as possible, made a polite excuse, and rocketed up to her bedroom. She called Tibby and talked about nothing in particular. She cleaned her clean room.

She got into bed with a book and tried, as she had so many other nights, not to think about Kostos.

"He's a little taller, don't you think?" Bridget's question floated up to the rafters a few feet above her head. Some of it made its way down to Diana in the bottom bunk.

"Uh. Yeah, I guess."

Bridget tapped her toes against the metal rail at the bottom of her bunk. "God, he is cute. In my memory, I didn't exaggerate that part of it."

"Bridget?"

It was the deep, slow, irritated voice of Katie across the cabin.

"Yeah?"

"Will you shut up?"

Bridget laughed. She appreciated bluntness. "Okay."

She was happy. She couldn't help it. She was happy that Katherine was okay. She was happy that she felt happy instead of miserable at the thought of Eric Richman sleeping in a bed less than one hundred yards away. Bridget tapped her toes some more. She made a

rhythm approximating "Walk on the Wild Side." She tried turning onto her stomach. She cleared her throat. "Can I say one other thing?"

"No," Katie barked, but her bark belied a certain amusement.

"Please?"

"What is it, Bee?" Diana asked wearily.

She'd had over twenty-four hours to digest the fact that she would be spending the summer with the mythical Eric. She'd seen him twice that day. They'd smiled at each other, though they hadn't spoken. She was getting the same fizzing feeling she'd had when she'd met him the first time. And that was dangerous, maybe. But she was different now. She felt different.

"I'm not sorry he's here," she informed Diana. "I think I might be okay about it."

LennyK162: Talked to Bee finally. Cannot believe about Eric.

Carmabelle: Cannot either. She said she's okay, though.

LennyK162: Do we believe her? Do we go to Pennsylvania and drag her home?

Carmabelle: Let's give it a week.

Today was the day Valia had her doctor's appointment. Her kidneys had apparently been doing something funky, so she was supposed to get something or other checked once every two weeks at the hospital.

It was their first outing, and Carmen welcomed it. Just leaving the house had to be good. Even if they both

got squashed by a bulldozer on their first step down the front walk, it would be preferable to another long afternoon spent in the darkened Kaligaris den.

Besides, today was also the day Carmen got to wear the Traveling Pants, and nothing magical was going to happen sitting inside with Valia close enough to squash it.

They'd only been together for one week, and already Carmen and Valia were in a rut. After madly IMing and yelling at the computer—and at Carmen—for a couple of hours (while also listening to the TV), Valia's energy would start to fade. Sometime around three o'clock she would change to a soft chair and her head would start to nod and swerve as sleep tried to claim her. This was around the time that *Brawn and Beauty* came on. Carmen would perch at the edge of her chair, and gingerly, slowly reach for the remote control. Then, waiting long minutes if necessary, she would watch for Valia's wrinkly lids to shut. Then she would wait even longer. Then . . . slowly she would shift down the volume and slowly scroll through the channels. Her heart would be in her throat at this point. Once she got to channel four, she would imagine victory at hand, she would yearn for that first look at Ryan Hennessey's turquoise eyes . . . and then . . .

Valia would shoot straight up in her chair and bellow, "Zat is not my show!" and Carmen, in pitiful defeat, would turn back to Valia's show. And then the cycle would start again.

So Carmen was shamefully grateful to Valia's misfiring kidneys as she and Valia shut themselves into

Carmen's car. She was deaf to Valia's ten-minute harangue about how Carmen didn't hold the steering wheel right.

They were absurdly early for the appointment, thanks to Carmen's eagerness, so Carmen was the picture of flexibility when Valia insisted they stop at the ice cream shop around the corner from the hospital. Who was Carmen to turn down ice cream?

Valia wanted pistachio. No, she didn't, she wanted butter pecan. No, that would not be good.

"Vhy do they have the cookies in the ice cream?" she demanded to know.

"Vhat do they mean by this . . . *jimmies*?"

"Who vould eat that purple thing?"

Carmen saw the look on the face of the girl behind the counter, and it was familiar. It was a look that she imagined she herself had worn for roughly thirty hours the week before.

Finally, after an excruciating number of questions and unsolicited criticisms, Valia settled on peppermint ice cream, of all things. It was a garish red, and slimy-looking.

Valia took one bite and shoved it toward Carmen. "I hate it. You eat it."

"I don't want it."

"I hate it." Valia kept pushing it at her.

Carmen was fuming. She hated Valia's nasty peppermint ice cream too. And furthermore, she hated Valia. Valia was a big, fat baby. Carmen hated babies. She hated old people. She hated everyone in between. She hated everyone.

Except him.

He was a guy—maybe her age or a little older—who walked into the store just as Carmen was dodging the slimy red ice cream.

She didn't hate him, though at her rate, perhaps she could learn to. He wasn't Ryan Hennessy or anything, but some quality about him struck her nonetheless. His straight hair was yellowish brown and a little bit unkempt. His eyebrows were almost blond and his freckles made him look kind of jaunty, like he didn't care about anything too much. His eyes, on the other hand, made him look like he did.

She looked at his face for a moment too long. When she turned her head back, she saw the scoop of ice cream bobbling on Valia's cone, and it was too late to fix it. Sure enough, the scoop plunged to the ground and skidded a foot or so. Valia, incensed, shouted something at Carmen in Greek and then made a show of striding away. But the peppermint ice cream didn't just look slimy. Valia's heel hit the trail of ice cream, and Carmen watched in horror as the old lady went down hard. Carmen's shout and Valia's scream mingled and merged in the air.

Almost instantly Carmen had Valia in her arms. Valia was lighter and drier than she would have imagined. Her eyes were squeezed shut and her face was twisted in pain. Carmen could tell that her right leg had crumpled in the wrong direction. When Valia opened her eyes, Carmen saw the blurry tears in them, and she felt awful. Her own eyes filled with tears.

"Oh, Valia," Carmen murmured, trying to get a strong hold of her under her arms. "I am so sorry." She heard a little sob escape her own mouth.

At once Carmen saw another pair of arms in the mix. It was the guy she did not yet hate. He was helping her lift Valia from the sticky linoleum.

Now the few other patrons gathered around and the counter girl appeared, bouncing nervously from foot to foot.

Valia moaned. "My leg is hurt," she said. "Don't move it. Please."

"Okay," Carmen said soothingly. "It's okay."

"If you'll just rest your arm over my shoulder I can support your leg," the guy coaxed her. He got himself in position and nodded to Carmen as if to tell her it was time to lift. She complied.

Valia moaned again, but they had her off the floor.

"Valia, the emergency room is right around the corner. We'll take you right there, okay?" Her voice couldn't have been gentler.

Valia nodded. The ferocity had abandoned her features for once, and they settled sort of sweetly into her face, even in spite of her obvious pain.

Ready? the nonhateful guy mouthed to Carmen. Suddenly they were partners.

They began to walk, Carmen murmuring reassuring things into Valia's ear. On the way out of the shop, Carmen's arms were so occupied she couldn't catch the door as it swung behind her. The sharp edge of the metal

doorframe caught her hard on the back of her arm. Carmen did all she could not to stagger or groan. She pressed her lips together and tried not to release the tears loading up her eyes. She noticed that the guy was looking at her. He glanced at her arm. She didn't see the blood until he did.

She shrugged a little. *It's okay,* she mouthed over Valia's head. She vowed not to let her tears go.

In the emergency room, they eased white-faced Valia carefully into a chair. Then Carmen shifted into a mode of pure efficiency. She talked her way to the front of the line, collecting forms she promised to fill out as soon as Valia was in the hands of a doctor. By some miracle, Carmen discovered that one of the emergency room doctors spoke Greek, and before long Valia was safely, gratefully in an examining room, the Greek words a palliative in her ear.

Then Carmen remembered about the nonhateful guy. When she returned to the waiting room, he was still there, elbows resting on knees in a plastic emergency-room chair.

"Thank you," she said immediately and earnestly. "That was really, really nice of you."

"Is she okay?" he asked.

"I hope so. There's a doctor who speaks Greek, which made her happy. He seemed to think she might have torn a ligament in a knee, but he didn't think she broke any bones, which is the good news. They're gonna do an X-ray just in case."

It was funny to have all this to say, to have this whole project in common with a guy whose name she did not know.

She sat down next to him. He produced a damp paper napkin he'd been holding. "For you." He pointed to her arm.

"Oh, God. Right." The blood had stopped flowing and started to dry, but it looked a bit gory nonetheless. She wiped it off with the napkin. "Thanks."

"Are you okay?" he asked.

"Totally fine. It's a scratch." It was more than a scratch, but she liked the feeling of being brave.

She looked at the streaky red napkin. He looked at her.

"So . . . thank you so much. Again," she said quietly. Carmen wanted to signal to him that he was free to leave, but he didn't appear to want to leave just yet.

He was still looking at her, like he was trying to figure something out.

"I work here," he offered to the silence.

"Really?"

"Well, volunteer is more accurate. I'm premed, so I, you know, want to spend time in the real world of medicine. To see if I'm up to it."

"I bet you are." Carmen blushed, surprised that she had let that out of her mouth.

"Thanks," he said, looking down for the first time.

They were silent for a minute or two. He was wearing brown Pumas. He had the goldish sparkle of whiskers on

his face like a real grown-up man. His hair had the extra shiny quality of someone who spent a lot of time in a pool. His shoulders were wide and his torso was strong and lanky—most definitely the build of a swimmer.

"Is she your grandmother?" he asked.

"Oh. Valia? No. She's . . . well, she's my . . . actually, she's my friend Lena's grandmother. I was bringing her here for some tests—I mean, not the emergency room. That wasn't part of the plan."

"Right." He smiled. He was looking at her upper arm again.

Shallowly, she felt pleased that she'd injured a part of her body she felt was particularly good to look at.

"Maybe you'll have to come back again. For the tests," he said.

"I'm sure I'll be back," she said. "Valia can't drive here—especially now—and I have a car all to myself right now and . . ."

He nodded. He got up to go. "Maybe I'll get to see you again. I hope so."

"Me too," she said faintly, watching him go. She felt her heart streaming into different parts of her body, places she hadn't felt it beat before.

And yet, as she went back over the conversation, she felt a trace of apprehension. Valia was her friend Lena's grandmother. Carmen was bringing her for tests. Carmen had a car to herself.

Carmen was also getting paid eight fifty an hour. She realized she could have mentioned that, too.

Hit the point once.

Then come back and

hit it again.

Then hit it a third time—

a tremendous whack.

—Winston Churchill

Today was a day during which Bridget would almost certainly look upon the face of Eric Richman, and he would look upon hers. It made getting dressed a different project than usual. Usually she didn't care that much. Or if she did, it was to satisfy her exuberance (like the shiny, shiny pink pants) or her idiosyncracy (like the pilly green turtleneck everyone hated).

This morning, it was more her vanity calling out to be satisfied. Did she want the ponytail high? Nah. Too severe. Braids? Carmen looked saucy when she arranged her hair into two braids on the sides, but Bee's pale hair made her look like Heidi. Anyway, how much did she want to use that particular weapon?

The Hair, as Tibby called it. It had launched a thousand comments. Cars honked and delivery guys whistled; even respectable men looked too long. Hairdressers exclaimed over it as though it were a living miracle. The Hair. Marly's hair, Greta's hair. In fact, it was nothing

more than a bunch of dead cells sprouting out of her scalp, but it was her birthright.

Do I want you to notice me? she wondered, leaning so close to the mirror that her eyes formed one large Cyclops eye.

The mirror in the cramped cabin was speckled with gray and only showed the story from midhip to midforehead. If she backed up, she'd be sitting in Katie's messy bunk.

She shouldn't care about this so much. She felt an annoying buzzing around her head: expectations, clustering like so many mosquitoes. She did not like those. She refused to have them.

She would just . . . throw on the first pair of shorts she found. And okay, so they were the really nice short blue Adidas ones. And the first top. Well, the second, because that was the white tank with the racing back, and it looked better than the first one. And the hair. She'd just leave it down. She was not setting a trap. She was not! She was just . . . in a hurry. A coach could not be late. She pulled a hair elastic around her wrist just in case.

She loped out of the cabin barefoot, swinging her cleats by the laces. She'd grown so much, she would probably be taller than Eric in her cleats.

Five coaches were already milling around on the center field. One of them happened to be Eric. Not that her eyes went there first.

Having finally read the camp's handbook in the hour after sunrise when she couldn't sleep, she now knew the

deal. The camp was split into girls' and boys' sides. Each side was broken into six teams. They played soccer for four hours every morning. They put the boys and girls together for speed and agility training for an hour after lunch, and then for the other activities—swimming, waterskiing, hiking, rafting, and all kinds of other campish things. After dinner they had a couple of free hours. Usually there was a movie or something.

Now that she'd bothered to look at the roster of coaches, on which Eric Richman's name did indeed appear in twelve-point type and which had sat folded inside an envelope in her room at home for several weeks, unread, Bridget knew she was assigned to coach a boys' team. That was all right. Diana was coaching one on the girls' side, that was the only negative. They would have had fun together.

Bridget sat down in the middle of the field and plucked out the socks she'd balled up in her shoes. She pulled them on and laced up her cleats. She felt the warm sunshine on the top of her head.

It's different now. It's all different, she was telling herself. But she was not sure her self was listening. Eric circled close to her, with the slightly bemused expression he had often worn around her two summers before. She followed him with her eyes.

The campers were gathering. They were supposed to all be between the ages of ten and fourteen, but the boys particularly were so varied it was almost comical. Some looked like little kids. Some looked nearly like grown men.

She saw Manny, assigned to be her trainer, whom she'd met during coaches' meetings the day before. She waved to him and he waved back.

The boys' director blew his whistle. Joe Warshaw. He'd played for the San José Earthquakes, a major claim to fame. Bridget jumped to her feet, shaking out her legs. This was exciting. She'd coached unofficially in Burgess, Alabama, the previous summer. She'd coached at clinics. She'd assisted the JV coach at school a bunch of times. But she'd never coached her own team before.

She knew her reputation preceded her. She'd already heard whispering behind her back at breakfast that morning. She was not only the youngest coach but also the only high school all-American this year.

She spent most of her life in places where her soccer accomplishments didn't matter that much. Her friends weren't athletes. They were as supportive as they could possibly be. All three of them had cried at her awards ceremony. But they didn't understand what it meant— nor did she really want them to. She loved how much they loved her for everything else. Her dad, always pre-occupied, thought being an all-American was basically comparable to making varsity. And her brother had come to a grand total of one of her games. But here it was like being a celebrity. These kids worshipped the things she'd accomplished. And Eric. He, of all people, knew what it meant.

She ended up at Eric's side as the director called out the teams. Not entirely on purpose. He was the only one

she knew. (How strangely she knew him.) And it was a perfectly natural place to stand.

It's not like I'm going to do that again, she promised herself.

Sometimes when she thought of Eric, and now more powerfully when she saw him, she felt some achy nostalgia for her old self. For the dauntless, daring soul she used to be. There was something vaguely enchanted about that time. There were certain qualities you possessed carelessly. And you couldn't retrieve them when they were gone. The very act of caring made them impossible to regain.

Not all of that spirit was gone. She still had it, but she had a more tempered version. That time with Eric in Baja had been both the height of that magic and its calamitous end. He had managed to inspire both.

She was a bit more fragile now. Or no. Maybe she was less fragile. Maybe she had come to terms with her injuries and knew how to protect them. She was more self-protective, that was true. But she was a girl without a mother. She had to protect herself.

Bridget had the sense that she was already popular among her constituency. The boys assigned to her made a big thing about it among themselves. As they gathered around her now, some looked boldly admiring and others just looked terrified. She had several capable, well-muscled kids. One of them, a blond, spoke English with an accent. For some reason, the face that drew her belonged to a broad-faced, freckled, sharp-featured kid

with long, gangly legs and extremely large feet. He had a great face—all eagerness—but even just standing still made him look uncoordinated. He was going to be a project, she could tell.

While their teams put on their jerseys (Bridget's team was sky blue), she found herself standing near Eric again. "You're popular, aren't you? I've never felt like such a letdown," Eric said, laughing, and she was pleased if he meant what she thought he meant.

"So how's it going?" she asked him coolly. She wanted him to know she was different now. "You look tan."

"I just got back from two weeks in Mexico."

Bridget felt her face strain. What was he trying to say to her? She'd never been the kind of person who'd overthought people's motives, and she didn't feel like starting now.

From his face, he seemed to recognize that he had already shoved them into slightly awkward territory.

She cleared her throat. "How was it?"

He was uncomfortable. "We stayed with my grandmother in Mulege. And then we traveled down to Los Cabos and ended up in Mexico City for a few days."

Bridget heard one word louder than the others. He was doing that *we* thing. What was we? Who was we? She wasn't going to stand here wondering.

"Who is we?"

He paused. He wasn't looking at her anymore. "We? Oh, uh, me and Kaya. My girlfriend."

Bridget nodded. His girlfriend. Kaya. "Wow. Good for you."

Had he wanted to tell her this? Had he not wanted to tell her?

"See you," Bridget said numbly, walking away to stake a place for her team to gather. She wished she could have blasted those buzzing, swarming expectations with a can of bug spray.

You had hopes, admit it. She hated dishonesty, especially in herself. *You know you did.*

Lena stared out the window of the bus. It was empty, so she pulled her legs up onto the seat and hugged them, loving the feeling of the Traveling Pants against her skin. It had been a wonderful afternoon of drawing, almost magical. Partly because of wearing the Pants, partly because she felt she was really making progress.

She pictured the last pose of the day—twenty minutes. She loved the long pose best. They had a new model now, Michelle. She had round hips and long, hyperextending arms. Lena had no thought of assessing the model in terms of beauty. Michelle represented a series of drawing challenges. Lena looked out the window of the bus, but she saw Michelle's elbows.

Lena liked her time on the bus, and the slow walk from the bus stop to her house in the sweet end-of-day light. It gave her a transition between the meditation of her class and the sharpness of home.

This night she was greeted sharply. Her father was yelling before she could put her bag down.

"Where have you been?" He hadn't changed out of his suit yet. He did not look relaxed.

She kept her mouth shut. She had a feeling he knew where she hadn't been.

"I dropped by the restaurant on my way home from work to say hello and you were not there," he rumbled.

She shook her head. She felt the dull thud starting in her chest. She would wait to find the extent of his knowledge before trying any damage control.

"You don't work the dinner shift, do you?"

She shook her head again.

"You were at that art class, weren't you?"

Was there any point in denying it? There were many stated rules of the Pants, but she realized there was an unstated one too: You couldn't lie in the Pants. At least, she couldn't.

She needed to start breathing again. "Yeah."

His faced moved and twitched in anger. His eyes bulged. That was the thing she always dreaded. She and Effie knew that when his eyes went like that they were in serious trouble. It had happened very rarely throughout their childhood. But in these long months since he'd brought his unwilling mother to live with them, it happened a lot more often.

Lena's mother appeared in the front hall behind him. She was distressed. "Let's talk about this in a calm way. George, why don't you change before dinner. Lena, get yourself settled." She had to pull George away like a coach walking a prizefighter back to his corner.

Lena ran upstairs and closed her door. She waited to see if she needed to cry. She endured a couple heaves. A tear soaked into the knee of the Pants. Her cheeks were blazing and her pulse was throbbing all around her body.

Dinner was a quiet, tense affair. Effie was at a friend's house. Valia's complaints—freshened by her knee injury—actually broke the tension rather than added to it, so thick was the air. At least someone was talking.

Afterward, Lena and her mother and father closed themselves up in the den.

Her father's anger wasn't as hot, but it seemed to have gotten deeper. "I've done some thinking, Lena."

She was sitting on her hands.

"I am deeply troubled that you've lied to us."

Breathe in. Breathe out.

"You know I've never been happy with the idea of art school for you," he went on. "It's impractical, it's expensive, and at the end of four years, you'll have no job prospects. You can't seriously think you'll make a living as an artist."

Lena looked at her mother. She knew Ari was stuck. She didn't disagree with her husband, but she didn't agree with him either.

"After seeing that class, I felt it was wrong for you in other ways too. It's not a good atmosphere for a young girl. Some parents may accept that kind of environment for their daughters, but I can't." At least he wasn't yelling. "I've told your mother this already. I can't support your decision. We will not pay for you to go to

RISD. We will pay for a regular university, but we won't pay for that."

Lena was stunned. "Isn't it a little late for this decision?" Her voice sounded raw.

"You can find a program, I think. Your grades are good. Some universities are still taking applications. If not, you can apply for next fall and stay home and work to make money."

I'd rather die, she felt like shouting at him. But she didn't. She said nothing. What could she say? What would matter to him? Certainly not her feelings.

He was punishing her for disobeying him. He was dressing up his punishment in clothing of practicality, pretending he was being a good father, but she knew what it was.

She pulled her hands out from under her. They felt as cold as marble. Her blood had stopped circulating through her body.

She got up slowly and walked out of the room. He wouldn't hear her words. She doubted he'd hear her silence, either.

Patrick: I'm mad.

SpongeBob: What's the

matter, Patrick?

Patrick: I can't see my

forehead.

There was a funny thing about Carmen, and she knew it all too well: She could understand and analyze and predict the exact outcome of her crazy, self-destructive behavior and then go ahead and do it anyway. It was called premeditation, and it caused people to have to go to jail for their whole lives as opposed to just a few years.

What made a person like that?

As Carmen once again lay in wait for her tired mother, pretending to flip casually through a magazine in the living room, she was full of guilty premeditation.

She kindly waited to pounce, though, until her mom had taken off her shoes and lain down on the living room couch. Now that the truth was out about the baby, Christina's stomach was expanding remarkably.

"I got a call from the admissions director of University of Maryland today," Carmen said conversationally, flipping the pages of the magazine a little too fast.

The truth was, Carmen wasn't excited about the prospect of spending her freshman year at the University of Maryland. It was a decent school, but it wasn't a fantastic one, like Williams. It was huge and anonymous where Williams was small and personal.

What Carmen was excited about, in some perverse way, was telling her mother.

Christina was too tired even to express the extent of her confusion. "*Why?*"

"Because I applied there, and the admissions lady wanted to tell me they were making a special allowance and letting me in."

Christina tried to sit up a bit. "*Nena*, I have no idea what you are talking about."

"I'm thinking about going to UM instead of Williams."

Now Christina sat the whole way up. "Why in the world would you do that?"

"Because maybe I'm not ready to leave home just now. Maybe I want to stay and help out and be part of the baby's life." Carmen tossed this off as though she were describing her plans to get a manicure.

"Carmen?" Her mother's look was satisfying. She was definitely and certainly paying attention to Carmen's future and nobody else's at this particular moment.

"What?" Carmen blinked innocently.

Christina inhaled and exhaled yoga style a few times. She settled back onto the cushions and thought awhile before she opened her mouth to talk. "Darling. In my

selfish heart, I want nothing more than for you to stay home. I hate the thought of you leaving. I'll miss you terribly. You know that. I want you to stay with me and David and the baby. In my selfish heart, that is my fantasy."

Carmen felt tears bulging out of her lids. She'd swung from pure insouciance to tears in under twenty seconds.

Christina's voice was soft as she continued. "But a good mother doesn't just obey the wishes of her selfish heart. A good mother does what she believes is the best thing for her child. Sometimes they are the same. This time they are different."

Carmen pawed at her cheeks with the back of her hand. What kind of tears were these, exactly? Tears of joy? Agony? Fear? Confusion? Maybe a few of each?

"How do you know that?" Carmen's voice was full and high with emotion. "How do you know they aren't the same?"

"Because Williams is the right place for a girl as smart and capable as you, *nena*. You belong there."

"I belong at home."

"You'll always belong at home. Going to Williams doesn't mean you won't belong at home."

"Maybe it will," Carmen said.

"It won't."

Carmen shrugged and wiped her eyes again with the back of her hand. "I feel like it will."

Lenny,

You sounded so sad on the phone earlier, we thought these might cheer you up. The lady at the candy store said she never knew a person who only liked root beer—flavored jelly beans, and to be honest, the all—brown bag doesn't look quite as attractive as the tropical fruit mix, for example. But you are you, Lenny, and we love you like that.

XXXXXXXXXX OOOOOOOOO,
Tib + Carma

Tibby was outside her window. She was looking up at it, clutching the sill with her hands, feeling the emptiness under her feet. Inside was warm yellow light, and outside, where she was, it was dark. She could feel the apple tree somewhere behind her, but she couldn't see it. Her hands hurt, her arms were lifeless. She wanted to get back into her room so badly. How had she gotten here? Why had she done it? She couldn't drop down into dark emptiness, but she couldn't get back inside, either.

"Tibby? Tibby?"

Tibby opened her eyes and took a moment to orient herself. She was slumped in a movie theater chair. The lights were on. The screen in front of her was blank. Margaret was ever so gently waking her.

"Hi, Margaret. Hi. I fell asleep, didn't I?"

"You did. Don't worry. Your shift is over. I jis took care of the garbage for you, so that's all sit."

Tibby looked at her gratefully. "Thanks so much. I'll get yours next time, okay?" Groggily she sat up and let the dream ebb away. She didn't used to fall asleep in movies. But working in a theater could do that to you. Once she'd taken the tickets for the four o'clock show and made sure everyone was in their seats and vacuumed the lobby, she was allowed to watch. That was the whole reason she'd asked for Margaret's help to get her this job.

But now she'd seen *The Actress* fourteen times. The first three or four were pretty good. But slowly after that, the suspense drained out of the suspense. The spontaneity of the love affair shriveled to nothing. By the tenth or twelfth time, Tibby could practically see the gears working in the actors' heads. She could practically see the cheap manipulations of the camera work. By the fourteenth time . . . well, she fell asleep.

As a lifelong movie lover, it was sad, in a way, for her to watch the magic of the illusion dry up like a piece of macaroni left overnight in Katherine's booster seat. It made Tibby feel dull and flat. And watching the excitement on the faces of the audience just made her feel worse. She knew that every audience member was taken in by the big swelling climax, with the cellos and violins and gigantic close-ups of earnest, rapturous faces. They felt it was all happening magically and powerfully for them alone. Of course they didn't consider that they were

clutched in the fist of this elaborate fraud. It didn't matter.

Tibby had gotten accepted to the film program at NYU on the strength of the movie she'd made about Bailey the summer before. She was about to spend four years learning how to make films. She'd thought it was what she wanted more than anything. But now Tibby was beginning to wonder.

She imagined, depressingly, what it must feel like to be a wedding officiator or a doctor who delivered babies. You'd watch these people in the middle of their personal wonders, imagining for themselves a pure, unique once-in-a-lifetime experience. And then an hour or two later you'd watch somebody else do the same thing. What they thought were miracles were your breakfast, lunch, and dinner.

It was sad that what you once thought were marvels on the screen were really manipulations. What you thought was art was just some gimmicky formula.

Bridget discussed it with Diana at night after the campers were in bed. They sat on the edge of the lake, tossing rocks into the still water. Bridget outlined her strategy, which was pretty simple. She'd just avoid Eric. She would stay away from him and throw herself into other things—her team, her training, hanging with Diana, and making new friends. And besides, she got three weekends off, and so would Eric. Chances were, they'd be off on different weekends. It didn't need to matter so much that she and Eric were working at the same camp. It was a big camp.

At a prebreakfast meeting the next morning, the directors gave out assignments to the staff. Besides coaching, they each were assigned partners with whom they would preside over afternoon activities and chaperone certain meals, evening events, and special weekend trips.

It was long and somewhat boring and Bridget tuned it out, surreptitiously glancing at more of the pictures Diana had brought—more Michael, her roommates, her soccer team at Cornell—until she heard her name called.

"Vreeland, Bridget. Rafting and kayaking. Two-thirty to five weekdays. And you've got Wednesday breakfast, Monday lunch, Thursday dinner, and Sunday night moonlight swim. Weekend trips TBA," Joe Warshaw read out.

She shrugged happily. It sounded fun. She didn't know the first thing about rafting or kayaking, but she was a quick learner. And she, more than anyone, loved swimming at night under the stars. Joe was flipping pages on his clipboard. "Vreeland, Bridget, you'll partner with . . ." He was scanning for a name. "Richman, Eric." Joe didn't even look up when he read it. He went on to the next assignment.

Bridget hoped she was hallucinating. Diana cast her a panicked look. If Bridget was hallucinating, then so was Diana.

It was so outrageous Bridget almost wanted to laugh. Was this somebody's idea of a joke? Had somebody from Baja phoned ahead to say that Bridget and Eric shared by far the most wrenching history, so be sure to put them together?

She looked up and Eric caught her eye. She was frowning.

"You can change it," Diana said under her breath. "Talk to Joe after. He likes you. He'll change it."

Bridget marched over to Joe after. "Hey. Can I ask you something?"

"Sure."

The kitchen staff was beginning to set up for breakfast.

"Can I, uh, change partners? Would that be all right?"

"If you give me a good reason." He seemed to anticipate what she was going to say, because he started back in before she could open her mouth. "And I mean a medical or professional reason. I don't mean a personal reason. I don't accept personal reasons."

"Oh." She racked her brain for something that sounded medical or professional. Oozing sores? Would those help? Contagious foot fungus? Multiple personalities? She could make a case for that last one.

"Good. Stick with your partner. Everybody always wants to change at first." He piled up his papers and stood to leave. "You'll do fine."

God is subtle. But not

malicious.

—Albert Einstein

The ferocity was back on Valia's face, and it was more ferocious than ever. They were due in the hospital again, this time for the double whammy of blood testing for Valia's kidneys *and* physical therapy for her knee. She'd refused to get into the car with Carmen, on account of Carmen's allegedly holding the steering wheel wrong. So Carmen was steering Valia down the sidewalk in her wheelchair, much like a mother pushing the stroller of a very grumpy baby.

Ashes to ashes, diapers to diapers, strollers to strollers, gums to gums, Carmen mused as she pushed Valia along. Who said she hadn't gotten a babysitting job this summer?

There was a reason she was breezing along the two-plus miles to the hospital in the very teeth of the mid-July heat, but she did not yet know his name. And anyway, how much better it was to be outside, sharing Valia with the universe rather than having her in a small dark room, all to herself.

With one hand on the wheelchair, Carmen opened her phone with the other hand and pushed the Lena button.

"Hi," Carmen said when Lena answered. "Are you done work?"

"I have lunch and dinner shifts," Lena said. "I'm on break."

"Oh. Listen—"

Carmen broke off, because Valia had snapped her head around and was scowling, the lines around her mouth deepening. "I don't vant to hear you talk on the phone," Valia declared. "And how you can push with vun hand?"

"You have to go," Lena said knowingly, sympathetically.

"Oh, yes." Carmen snapped the phone shut. Ferocity was etching lines on her face too. One of the advantages of a baby over Valia, say, was that not only were babies considerably cuter but also they couldn't talk.

Carmen pushed the last mile with a clenched jaw. At the hospital she went first to the kidney floor, number eight. As Valia barked at other, non-Carmen people who were trying miserably to help her, Carmen got to roam around in the hallway. In forty minutes she saw many faces pass, but not the one she wanted to see.

It wasn't until they reached the knee floor, number three, and Carmen had been prowling that hallway for twenty minutes that she saw the guy whom she did not yet hate poke his head around the corner. When he saw her, the rest of his body came too.

"Hey!" he said, striding toward her and smiling. God, he could wear a pair of jeans. Had he grown even better-looking in the days since she had seen him?

"Hey!" she said back. Her stomach reacted forcefully to the sight of him.

"I realized I forgot to ask you your name last time," he said. "I've been wondering for a week."

"Did you come up with any ideas?" Carmen asked.

He thought. "Um . . . Florence?"

She shook her head.

"Rapunzel?"

"Nope."

"Angela?"

She squinched up her nose in displeasure. She had a very fat second cousin named Angela.

"Okay, what?" he asked.

"Carmen."

"Oh. Hmmm. Carmen. Okay." He tilted his head, fitting her to her name.

"What about you?"

"My name is Win." He said it sort of loud, as though he were expecting an argument.

Carmen narrowed her eyes. "Win? . . . As opposed to lose?"

"Win as opposed to . . ." He had a slightly pained look on his face. "Winthrop."

"Winthrop?" She smiled. Had she known him long enough to tease him?

"I know." He winced. "It's a family name. I hated it

from the beginning, but I didn't learn to talk till I was two, and by that time it had stuck."

She laughed. "Why *do* we let other people name us?"

"Yeah," he said indignantly. "Why? Somebody should change that."

"I remember that skier in the Olympics," Carmen recalled. "Her parents let her name herself and I'm pretty sure she chose Peekaboo."

He nodded sagely. "Well, yeah, there is that."

She smiled. *Win.* Huh. Win, Win, Win, Win. She didn't mind at all.

"How's your . . ." He pointed to her arm.

Not coincidentally, she was wearing her most flattering sleeveless shirt, which offered a long view of her tanned, curvy upper arm. Both of her arms, actually.

"It's fine. Practically all better."

"Good."

"How's Valia doing? Ligament, right? Anterior cruciate?"

She nodded happily. Carmen's main problem with guys was that she had nothing to say to them. She loved the fact that she and Win (Win, Win, Win) had all these things to talk about even though they didn't know each other.

"Carmen? Caaaaarmen?"

It was the sound that chilled her blood, that dried her bones and made her lunch crawl back up her throat. Carmen tried to keep her face bright. "That would be Valia. She needs me. I better go."

"She doesn't sound happy," Win observed.

"Well . . ." Carmen bit her lip. She didn't want to vent

her suffering to Win. It just seemed wrong here. "Valia's had a rough time." She dropped her voice to a low volume. "She lost her husband less than a year ago, and she had to move here from the beautiful island in Greece where she was born and spent her entire life and . . ." Carmen felt genuinely sad for Valia as she described it. "She's just really . . . sad."

Win looked solemn. "That does sound rough."

"Yeah. I better go," Carmen said. She wasn't sure she could endure the Valia wail another time.

"She's lucky about one thing, though," Win called after her.

Carmen turned her head as she walked away, feeling her long hair swing over her shoulder like a girl in a movie.

"What's that?"

"She has you."

Lena felt too fragile to go back to drawing class for a few days. She knew her father would be watching her closely now. She waited until she felt strong enough for a confrontation before she dared to go back.

She asked Annik if they could talk during the long break, and Annik agreed. This time Lena led the way to the courtyard. Annik had been so pleased when Lena had first told her about RISD. Annik rattled on about all the teachers she knew there. Now, with the change in plans, Lena felt like she had to tell her that, too.

"So he says I can't go. They won't pay for it," Lena explained numbly.

Annik's mouth narrowed. Her dark eyes widened within their frames of reddish eyelashes. She seemed to hold back. She probably knew it didn't help to trash a person's parent, no matter what he'd done. "He says you can't go or he won't pay for it?" she asked finally, flatly.

"I guess both. I can't go if they don't pay."

"Are you sure about that?"

Lena shrugged. "I hadn't really thought about it."

"You should. People go to art school who don't have any money. There are two ways. I'm guessing that you wouldn't qualify for financial aid?"

Lena shook her head. They lived in a big, nice house with a pool. Her father was a successful lawyer. Her mother had a good income.

"Then you'll have to win a merit scholarship," Annik said.

"How do you do that?" Lena was afraid to be hopeful.

"I could call my friend—" Annik stopped herself. She put her hands together.

Lena counted Annik's rings, nine altogether.

"If I were you," Annik went on, changing course, "I'd go on the Web site or call them up and find out. And if they tell you no, then ask some more questions until you get somebody to tell you yes."

Lena looked doubtful. "I'm not really good at that kind of thing."

Annik looked impatient. Not mad or dismissive, but definitely impatient. "Do you want to go to art school or stay home?"

"I want to go to art school. I can't stay home."

"Then figure out how to do it." Annik put her hand, briefly, on Lena's elbow. "Lena, I think you could do something good. I think you have talent, possibly a lot of it, and I don't say that lightly. I want you try. I can see it's what you love. But I can't fight for you. You have to fight for yourself."

"I do?"

Annik gave Lena an encouraging half smile. "You do. You've got to take up some space, girl."

So the first strategy wasn't going to work. Not only was Bridget not going to avoid Eric, she was going to see him constantly. Somebody up there was having a sick laugh at her expense.

Bridget took a long run on her break after lunch and tried to formulate plan B.

She and Eric weren't going to be strangers, so they were going to have to be friends. She could do that. She could treat him like a regular guy. Couldn't she?

She could try to forget that he was her first and her only. She could put aside the disastrous effect their brief fling had on her life. She could ignore—she could try really hard to ignore—the mighty attraction she felt to him. She could make herself accept that he did not feel that same attraction for her.

Bridget was breathing hard now, running up a steep hill, curving round and round. The forest cosseted her on either side.

The truth was, she had never felt so overwhelmingly drawn to anyone. In the two years since they'd seen each other, she had questioned this particular magnetism Eric had for her. Was it real? Or was she so caught up in a mania of her own making that summer in Baja that she had imagined it?

Seeing him again this summer answered her question. It was real. She responded to him the same way, even though she was different.

What was it about Eric? He was handsome and talented, yeah. But lots of guys were. She had adored Billy Klein back in Alabama the summer before, and she had even felt attracted to him, but it wasn't like this. What made you feel that stomach-churning agony for one person and not another? If Bridget were God, she would have made it against the law for you to feel that way about someone without them having to feel it for you right back.

Bridget reached the top of the little mountain. Suddenly the trees fell away, and she could see furrowed hills and steamy valleys on and on. The camp, in which all of this agitation was contained, was small and circular. From this height, it was small enough to put her arms around.

Bridget knew what to do. She couldn't control her basic response to Eric. But she could control her behavior. She had been tough and single-minded then, and she was now, too. Just as she'd found a way to seduce him back then, she could find a way not to do it now.

She had a weekend at home coming up. She would pull herself together. And when she got back to camp,

she would contain herself: She wouldn't flirt, she wouldn't tempt, she wouldn't pine, she wouldn't grieve. She wouldn't even yearn. Well, maybe she'd yearn a little, but she'd keep it to herself.

She began the run downhill, fast and just a little bit out of control.

Yes, they would be friends. They would be pals. He would never know what she really felt.

It was going to be a very long summer.

can I buy you a drink,

or should I just give you

the money?

—Failed pickup artist

"Come on, Tibby! We're going!"

Tibby was standing in the front door of her house, watching Bee jump up and down on the lawn and shout at her. Her yellow head radiated light in the darkness.

"Where are we going?" Tibby asked flatly.

"It's a surprise. It'll be fun. Come on!"

Tibby walked out onto the summer lawn, feeling the bits of mown grass sticking to her bare feet. "I don't want a surprise. I don't want to have fun."

"That's exactly why you need some."

Carmen was at the wheel of her car, honking the horn and waving out the window. Tibby could see Lena in the front passenger seat.

Bee came close and bent her head toward Tibby's. "Come on, Tib. Katherine is bouncing back like a little Super Ball. You're allowed to feel okay, you know? I have one night before I go back to Pennsylvania. I'm not spending it without you."

Tibby ran back to the house to tell her parents she was going. Usually her parents went out on Saturday nights, but since Katherine's accident they stayed close to home. And besides, since they'd fired Loretta, who was going to cover for them?

Tibby trudged to Carmen's car without bothering to get shoes. "I don't want to go," she announced to the group, once inside the car.

"You don't even know where we're going," Lena pointed out.

"I still don't want to go."

Carmen released the break and drove off anyway. "The lucky thing for you, Tibadee, is that your friends don't listen to you."

Tibby shook her head humorlessly. "I don't really see how that's lucky."

"Because we love you too much to let you fester in your room for the rest of the summer," Carmen clarified. *Fester* was her word of the week.

"Maybe I like to fester," Tibby said.

"But festering . . . does not like you." Carmen nodded decisively, as though this were the last word on the subject.

Tibby sat back and let the comfortable nattering swirl around her. Listening to her friends' voices felt like hearing a familiar symphony, with one instrument coming in and layering atop another. The way the cadences linked and harmonized made her feel safe.

Until Carmen pulled into the parking lot of the Rockwood pool.

"Why are we here?"

"We're going swimming," Bee offered.

"Why don't we just go to Lenny's?" Tibby asked.

"Her parents are home. And Valia is asleep," Carmen explained.

Enough said. No sane person wanted to wake up Valia, and her bedroom window faced the back of the house.

"Well, this pool is closed." Tibby felt sour as she said it.

"Just come on, okay?" Bee said.

Tibby followed them over the bridge of the piddling creek that used to seem to her like a roaring waterway connecting parts unknown. It was probably just for sewage. She followed them up the endless steep stairs that used to seem to her like the stairway to heaven. They approached the locked gates, then fanned out to the sides.

Tibby was starting to get an even worse feeling about this.

"This is the place!" Bee called out, pointing up at the one part of the fence not spangled by razor wire. Bee was already climbing by the time they'd gathered at the foot of it. "Up and over," she called gaily, making it look as simple as mounting a bike.

"I'm not coming," Tibby said.

"Why not?" Carmen and Lena both turned to look at her.

This was the kind of stunt she would normally have gone along with. But the thought of climbing the fence made Tibby feel almost physically sick. She couldn't explain all the reasons, but she knew she wasn't doing it.

"I just don't feel like it," she said.

Bee paused on the other side of the fence. They were all obviously disappointed that they couldn't get Tibby excited about their plan. Bee reversed her climb. Now Tibby felt bad.

"But you guys go ahead," she said, trying to lighten her voice. "Seriously, go. I don't mind. Besides, you need someone to stand guard here . . . you know, like, just in case." It sounded pitiful to Tibby's own ears.

"I wish you'd come. It won't be as fun without you," Lena said.

"Next time," Tibby answered, feeling like a big loser.

So there she sat, slumped against the side of the fence—the outside, the wrong side—pretending she was standing guard, while she listened to her friends strip down to their underwear and splash into the water. They were more subdued than they would have been if Tibby had gone along. But still, they were willing to play.

"Carma, I will pay you back, I swear."

Carmen rolled her eyes. "Shut up. Why are you saying that? We don't pay each other back. We're not keeping score."

Tibby actually paused from her insane flurry of activity to look appreciatively at Carmen. "So I won't pay you back."

"Thank God." Carmen took a tube of cherry-flavored Blistex from the mess of stuff on Tibby's dresser and put some on. "Eleventh floor, right?"

"Yeah, check in at reception. Ask for Dr. Barnes. There's a little kids' lounge in case you have to wait."

"No problemo. It's my home away from home." Carmen held up Tibby's soft charcoal T-shirt and considered stealing it.

"Katherine's going to be very happy about this."

Carmen returned the shirt to the mess. "And it's good practice for me, right?" Her voice had turned sober.

Tibby sensed her mood and touched her wrist. "I think you already got it down, Carma."

Carmen led the way to the foot of the stairs, where Katherine was waiting eagerly, her yellow backpack strapped over both shoulders, her hockey helmet tipped at a slightly rakish angle.

"Ya ready, baby?"

Katherine stood up on her kitchen chair, and with no regard for her cast put her arms up in a point like a diver. She jumped to Carmen.

Tibby helped her load Katherine into the baby seat they'd fastened into Carmen's car, and hopped into the copilot seat. First Carmen dropped Tibby off at work, and then she drove to the hospital. As they parked, Carmen enjoyed the good spirits of Katherine, chirping away from the backseat, never complaining once about her driving, in contrast to, say, Valia.

As they whooshed through the automatic doors into the giant lobby, Carmen lifted Katherine into her arms. Sweetly, Katherine clung to her like a koala, her hockey helmet wobbling just under Carmen's chin.

"Can I push the button?" she asked in the elevator.

"Yes, eleven. One one," Carmen steered Katherine's index finger in the right direction.

Her excitement over this made Carmen feel as though she'd just awarded Katherine a lifetime of good fortune. "Nicky always gets to push," Katherine explained, pushing several extra times.

Carmen couldn't keep her eyes from scanning the halls. Her heart was beating a lot harder and faster than normal. Of course she was thinking about him. Of course she wanted to see him. But on the other hand, she didn't.

She rested Katherine on the reception counter in pediatrics. "Katherine Rollins to see Dr. Barnes," she said to the woman behind the desk.

The woman wrote Katherine's name down and located her file. "Do you want to play in the playroom for a few minutes, sweetie?" she asked Katherine.

"Can she come?" Katherine touched her pointing finger right to Carmen's cheekbone.

"Of course," the woman said, and gestured them in the right direction.

Carmen couldn't help looking over her shoulder as she walked. A part of her really wanted to see him. A big part.

Well, another time, she thought, entering the confines of the playroom. It was bright and sunny, involving a few other children and lots of toys and miniature furniture. Carmen would have to content herself with standing or sitting on the floor, because there was no way she was fitting

into an Elmo chair. And if by some miracle she did fit in, she wouldn't be getting out. She pictured herself walking out of the hospital with a red plastic Elmo chair attached to her butt.

"Hey, you." She put Katherine down in front of a bead maze and straightened her helmet. "What do you want to play?"

Katherine danced around, utterly pleased. She brought over a Noah's ark, a xylophone, two puppets, and a book. Carmen knew that Katherine was always miffed at how Tibby's friends came over and spent time with Tibby. Now she had Carmen all to herself.

Carmen heard a girl's giggle from behind the big doll-house set up in the corner. She also saw a few parts of a man popping out—the girl's father, no doubt. Carmen figured she and Katherine could take over the dollhouse once those two vacated. Twin boys were throwing Nerf basketballs at each other. Carmen observed that somebody had taken a few bites out of one of the balls.

"How about this?" Katherine was shaking the animals out of the ark.

They played. There were a lot of singletons in this version of Noah's story, probably due to loss and theft, but Katherine didn't seem to care. Carmen was the hippo, the elephant, the lion, and the penguin. It was good, because Carmen had always had a knack for animal sounds and voices. With the penguins, she really got into a character. In this case, her penguin was a mafioso, kind of like Marlon Brando in *The Godfather*, only in a penguiny way.

Katherine was laughing so hard she stopped making any noise. The people behind the dollhouse were laughing too. The twin boys were circling them eagerly.

Suddenly Carmen realized that the leg extending from one side of the dollhouse had a brown shoe on the end of it. A brown Puma, specifically. She cut off the penguin's soliloquy. Moments later, a face appeared over a miniature gable.

She put both hands over her eyes in complete humiliation. "Hi, Win." Could she have been any louder?

He came entirely out from behind the dollhouse. He was fighting the impulse to smile. No, probably the impulse to laugh. At her.

"Hi, Carmen," he said. He crawled over to where she was sitting cross-legged on the floor. He pushed the inner part of her elbow and made the arm she was leaning on collapse. "Can I tell you I've never heard a more entertaining penguin in my life? I didn't even know penguins could talk."

"Ha ha," Carmen said, straightening her arm again. She tried to pull herself up and recapture some tiny amount of dignity.

She cleared her throat. "Win, this is Katherine. Katherine and I are friends. Katherine, this is Win."

Katherine stood up somewhat importantly. "Hi," she said.

Win pointed to her helmet. "I like your stickers."

She nodded. "I crushed my skull."

Carmen looked aghast. "You didn't crush your skull, sweetie. You fractured it."

Katherine waved this off as an uninteresting detail.

"And it's getting better really fast," Carmen added, possibly for her own sake.

Carmen could tell that Win was fighting to look serious. "Hey, Maddie."

A lovely girl with brown skin poked her head over the dollhouse. "This is Katherine," he said.

Katherine headed straight for the dollhouse. "Hey. Can I see that thing?"

"If you don't mess up the living room," Maddie allowed. Maddie looked to be about four, enough older than Katherine to be totally seductive.

Win was sitting close to Carmen on the floor. She could feel the heat from his body. She could smell him. He smelled a little salty, like cashews, and a little sweet, like mango shampoo. She felt woozy.

"I'm surprised to see you here," she said, feeling shy after all her bellowing and swaggering with the plastic animals.

"This is what I do."

"I mean, I know you work here—" she started.

"No, this is specifically what I do. Nine to two I work in pediatrics, mostly here in the playroom. I play with kids when their parents need to talk to the doctors."

She raised her eyebrows. "Really."

"Yeah. And if you need work, I'd hire you in a split second. You got the place rocking with that penguin."

She squeezed her eyes shut. "Stop."

"Only it doesn't pay very well," he said.

"How much?" she asked.

"Nothing."

"That's not so good."

"It pays better than my job after two. Then I go up to geriatrics to amuse and entertain the old folks. They're always goading me to buy them stuff out of the vending machine. I'm going into debt with that job."

A nurse appeared at the door of the playroom. "Katherine Rollins?"

Carmen got up. "Hey, Katherine. It's our turn."

Win got up as well. "Your . . . sister?" he asked.

"No. I'm an only child," Carmen said. She had no idea why she said that. It was true, yes, but true in such a narrow and ungenerous way it felt more like a lie.

"She's . . . ?"

"My friend Tibby's little sister. She fell out a window a few weeks ago. She's going to be fine, but she has to get checked out a lot to see how she's healing. Tibby was supposed to bring her, but her job added on a shift today, and she's trying to save money for—" Carmen looked up. "Why am I telling you all this?"

He shrugged, smiling. "I don't know."

"Come on, Katherine," she called. Katherine was having trouble parting with Maddie and the dollhouse.

"You can tell me more, though," he added. "I'll listen to anything you want to tell me."

She heard in his voice, in its particular hopeful tone, that he meant it. She knew he meant it in a real way and not just a charming or flirtatious way. He was sincerely

curious about her; he was utterly observant. She could tell that he did want to know her. And on one level this made her as happy as anything she could possibly imagine.

And on another level it made her sad. Because the girl he wanted to know wasn't her. He wasn't seeing her for how she was. He was seeing her as a kind and selfless person who cared about the people around her. He was coming to all the wrong kinds of conclusions.

And worse than that, she was letting him.

Show me a girl with her

feet planted firmly on the

ground and I'll show

you a girl who can't put

her pants on.

—Annik Marchand

"Vreeland! For God's sake, quit sunbathing and help me get some of these things in the water!"

Bridget opened one eye and sat up on the dock. She started laughing. Eric was trying to pull four kayaks into the lake at once, and he wasn't looking so graceful.

"Dude," she bellowed in a perfect imitation of her cabinmate Katie's low, sloppy drawl. "You're late. I can't keep covering for you like this." Bridget lay back down, resting on her elbows, letting the Traveling Pants soak up some sunshine. She'd already set up all the rafts, oars, life preservers, water shoes, and both double kayaks. She was always early, he was always late. He was always pretending to be put out by the small amount of work she left for him to do.

"I see it's the usual horde of campers," he said.

It was another joke between them. Three weeks into camp and almost no one came for their activities. Rafting just wasn't as sexy as extreme mountain biking, it would

appear. Well, there was a small group of boys who appeared now and then, but according to Eric, they weren't there for the boats.

If it hadn't been a no-flirt zone, Bridget would have batted her eyes and said, "Well, why *are* they here, do you think?" But she didn't.

"Why are you scaring the campers away?" Bridget asked. The sun made her yawn.

"Because I don't want to work. I want to sit on my ass."

Bridget smiled at that. She knew how he killed himself on the soccer field. But sitting around was mostly what they did from two-thirty to five. It was shaping up to be a beautiful rhythm—drive yourself and your team relentlessly in the morning and laze about in the sunshine with the guy you loved all afternoon.

She got to her feet. She'd scrupulously worn her least sexy Speedo one-piece for the last few days, but it was dirty. Besides, today was not just any day. It was a Traveling Pants day. She had brought them back with her from her weekend at home, and their presence now lent a particular sweetness to the air even stronger than the wafting smell of honeysuckle. Today she wore them over her best green bikini. Anyway, Eric probably didn't even notice or care. (Did he?) Why did she bother to think about it?

When she got too hot, she carefully peeled off the Pants, folded them, and put them on the dock. She shook her hair out of its braid. For her pleasure alone she did a high, arcing dive off the dock and into the lake. She

plunged down deep, not stopping herself until she touched the pebbly bottom. She took her time getting back up. She had always had good lung capacity. When she surfaced, Eric was watching for her.

"What? Are you, like, a whale?"

She pretended to be offended as she bobbed there. "Thanks a lot. Eric, girls don't mostly like to be called whales. Ask your girlfriend if you are unsure."

"Humans aren't supposed to stay under that long."

"Speak for yourself." She swam over to the row of plastic kayaks. "Hey, you want to try one of these things?"

This was a novel idea. "Sure. We might as well look like we know what we're doing."

She pulled a double one loose from the rocky shoreline and into the shallow water. She sat herself down in the front and put her oars into place. He followed her into the water.

As he climbed aboard he made a point of jostling the boat as much as possible, which got her laughing again. He settled in.

"I think you forgot something," she said.

He looked around. He shrugged.

"A paddle?"

"Oh, that." He sat back, tipping his face to the sun. "Are those really so important?" He was trying not to smile.

"I'm not sure it counts as kayaking if you just float around," she said. But she put her paddle inside the boat and lay back herself. They floated for a while.

Even in just a week, there had been so much down-

time spent together that Bridget was relaxed with him. They talked about things. It was weird to be killing time with someone about whom you felt passionate.

She'd plucked up the courage to mention Kaya, casually, at least once or twice every day. She wanted him to know she understood. She wanted him to know she respected that he had a girlfriend and she wouldn't try to get in the way.

He lifted his head. "Bee," he said.

"Yeah?"

"Bee!"

She looked up. He sounded sort of urgent.

"What?"

"No, *bee*!"

He pointed, and she suddenly felt a buzzing around her ear. She yelped and swatted it away and it went to her other ear. She hopped up to her feet. The kayak teetered violently.

The bee went from her to him. It flew into his hair. He jumped up to his feet and caused an even greater disturbance.

She screeched, laughing. She rocked the boat, trying to stay on her feet. He shouted and rocked back. She crashed into the water first. She heard his splash soon after. When they came up they were both laughing even harder.

She sputtered and coughed the water out of her nose. "I think we really look like we know what we're doing."

Lena approached Annik before class. She was sweaty and sticky from the restaurant, and her feet hurt and her

shirt was filthy, but she was pretty pleased with herself nonetheless. "The woman at the financial aid office at RISD said if I get my portfolio to the committee by the fifteenth of August I could still qualify for scholarship money."

Annik smiled big. "Nicely done."

"I warned them my dad is going to ask for his deposit money back, and I asked her to keep me enrolled anyway. She said I have to come up with a deposit by the end of this month."

"Can you do it?"

"I just took on three more shifts at my waitressing job. I really hate it, but it pays."

Annik clapped her on the back. Wheelchairs built up a person's muscles, Lena decided.

"That's what I call fighting," Annik said appreciatively.

"Qualifying and getting are different, though," Lena told her. "There is one full scholarship left to give out, and they have over seventy portfolios already under consideration."

Annik looked at the ceiling. "Well. You better do something good, then."

After class, Annik waited for Lena while she did her mopping. "Do you have an hour to spare?" she asked.

Lena figured she could call home and make an excuse. "Sure." Effie would cover for her if necessary.

"I want to see what you can do with a longer pose. I'll sit for you. I certainly can't stand for you." Annik seemed to enjoy her own joke.

Lena was timid to laugh. "Are you sure you want to?" she asked.

"I'd be happy to do it. I'll set up over here." She rolled over to the windows. "We've got about an hour left of decent light."

Lena felt a little self-conscious setting up her easel. It was weird staring straight at your teacher, but once Lena got drawing, she became immersed. She drew without pause for thirty straight minutes. Then Annik stretched her neck a little and Lena worked for thirty more. She'd never done more than a twenty-minute pose, and it was exciting.

Her self-consciousness returned when it was time for Annik to look at her work. Annik looked at the drawing carefully, wheeling a little back and forth. Lena bit her pinky nail and waited.

"Lena?"

"Yeah?" It came out a little squeaky.

"This is not a bad drawing."

"Thanks." Lena knew something else was coming.

"But you didn't draw my chair."

"What do you mean?" Lena felt instantly embarrassed.

"I mean, you took the drawing down to my shoulders. You would certainly see a good bit of the chair at that angle, but you left it out. How come?"

Lena felt her cheeks warm. "I'm not sure," she said almost inaudibly.

"I'm not trying to give you a hard time," Annik said.

"It's just that the chair is a big part of who I am, you know what I mean? I have all kinds of deep and complicated feelings about it, resentments, of course, too, but it is part of me. I don't picture myself without it. I'm surprised you left it out."

Lena felt bad. She'd thought maybe it would seem critical of Annik if she drew the chair. She hadn't been sure what to do about it, so without really thinking, she'd avoided it.

"You could make a really fine drawing, Lena. I can tell this is the right approach for you — portraits, long poses. I can see how deeply you respond to gestures and facial expressions. You'll excel at it if you work hard." Annik said it like she meant it. "But Lena?"

"Yeah?"

"You've got to draw the chair."

Tibby had never liked Loretta until Loretta got fired.

The main reason Tibby didn't like her was because Tibby was too old to be in Loretta's jurisdiction, and yet Loretta acted like she was Tibby's babysitter anyway.

And then there was the time Loretta put Tibby's best cashmere sweater in the dryer and shrank it so small even Katherine couldn't wear it. Tibby knew it was petty, but she nursed a long grudge.

In spite of all that, Tibby was appalled when her parents let Loretta go. Appalled and guilty.

"It wasn't her fault." Tibby defended Loretta to her parents when she heard the news. "If it was anybody's

fault, it was mine for leaving the upstairs window open."

But her parents stuck by their decision, and Tibby was left feeling horrible for Loretta. In the too many hours she spent in her cluttered room (windows safely shut), Tibby thought a lot about Loretta and missed her.

Tibby had never realized before what an easy spirit Loretta had. She hardly ever took offense at anything. She managed to defuse even the tensest Rollins family episode with her lightness and good humor. She was the master of deflecting and distracting both Nicky and Katherine from whiny behavior. This was something Tibby now sorely missed, as she listened to her mother square off and feud with Nicky day after day, sending him into paroxysms of loud brattiness. Tibby wondered how her mother had learned so little during these years of Loretta's wise example.

One night Tibby stayed up too late and got overly weepy. She wept bitter tears of sorrow for knowing Loretta didn't have a job anymore, for knowing it was her fault that Loretta didn't have a job anymore, and also for never having told Loretta how great she was.

The next morning Tibby found Loretta's address in her mother's book. She clipped her hair in the barrettes Loretta had given her two Christmases ago, pulled on her most cheerful yellow shirt, got into her car, and set off to the far reaches of Prince George's County. She had nothing but a map of the greater Washington, D.C., metropolitan area and a lot of guilt to guide her.

It took her two and a half hours (one and a half spent

getting lost), but the look on Loretta's face when she saw Tibby made it worth it. Even if Tibby spent twenty-four hours getting lost on the way home.

"*¡Tibby! ¡M'ija! ¿Cómo estás? ¡Dios te bendiga! ¡Ay, mira que hermosa estás! Cuéntame, ¿cómo te va?*" Loretta exploded in Spanish.

Not only did Loretta not appear to harbor any resentment; she hugged Tibby like a long-lost daughter. Loretta's eyes filled with tears as she planted several kisses on Tibby's face.

Tibby was still blinking in surprise when Loretta pulled her into the small house and introduced her to various family members as though they knew all about her. Loretta gestured to the pale woman on the couch in her bathrobe. "She no get up. She have"—Loretta pounded her chest in demonstration—"infection."

That was Loretta's sister, Tibby realized. It made Tibby feel even worse.

Tibby sat at the dining room table with Loretta, who kept patting her hand and asking exactly how Katherine was doing.

"She's getting better so fast. She's great. She misses you, though," Tibby added quickly. Tibby then presented Loretta a picture of beaming Katherine in her hockey helmet, which Loretta promptly kissed. Loretta wanted to know all about Nicky, and she even wanted to be sure that certain leftovers were not spoiling in the fridge. Loretta cried a lot, both out of sadness and joy, and said many things in Spanish, which Tibby could not understand.

The thing Tibby could understand was that Loretta truly loved Katherine. She loved Nicky. She even loved Tibby, for God knew what reason. How could Tibby's parents fire someone who loved their kids this much? It was wrong.

Loretta insisted that Tibby stay for dinner, so Tibby accepted. Then Loretta and her niece and another sister buzzed around in the kitchen for the next hour preparing a feast, while Tibby sat on the sofa with the sick sister, watching a TV show. Tibby was handed a big glass of orange soda and banned from helping in the kitchen.

Tibby watched the actors motoring away in Spanish and let her mind go. She was moved by Loretta's capacity to love, even when her employment had ended in such a bitter way. Loretta didn't seem concerned that the whole thing was so unfair, that Tibby's parents had lashed out vindictively.

Some people spent their lives wallowing in resentments, and other people, like Loretta, let ill fortune wash right over them.

When the table was revealed to Tibby with a great flourish, she saw how proud Loretta was. In honor of Tibby, Loretta and her niece and sister had made steak.

Tibby tried to keep the look of alarm off her face. She was moved by this gesture. Clearly this wasn't the kind of household where they ate steak every night. And so Tibby chewed the meat with as much vigor as was possible for a girl who had been a vegetarian since she was nine.

Heard melodies are sweet,

but those unheard

Are sweeter; therefore, ye

soft pipes, play on.

—John Keats

"Let's call her . . . Good Carmen," Carmen said.

It was Saturday and they had spent most of the morning at the farmers' market. Now Lena and Tibby were both lying on the deck in back of Tibby's house, chins on hands, nodding.

"This guy who works at the hospital, you see, keeps running into this girl, this Good Carmen." Carmen sat up in her lounge chair and crossed her legs Indian style. She breathed in the pineapple smell of Lena's sunscreen. "Good Carmen is taking care of Valia. She's being stoic and selfless. She's taking care of Katherine. She's doing it all out of the goodness of her heart. The problem is that this guy thinks Good Carmen is me."

"Is he cute?" Tibby asked.

Carmen narrowed her eyes. "Tibby, have you been listening to anything I'm saying?"

"All of it. I just need a little context. What's his name? What's he like? How much do you care what he thinks?"

Carmen considered. "Well. Hmmm." Truthfully, even thinking about him was fun. Talking about him was jubilation. "Is he cute, you ask? I mean, he's no Ryan Hennessey, of course —"

"No, he's not," Tibby shot back. "He's real, for one."

"Yes. He is real. He does have that going for him. And yes, he is cute." She couldn't keep the smile off her face.

"He's really cute," Lena said. "I can tell. Look at you."

"What's his name?" Tibby asked.

"Win." She realized she said it in the same slightly argumentative tone he did. She was already taking his side.

"Win?" they both asked.

"Yeah. Short for Winthrop. What can he do? He didn't name himself."

"I like it," Lena stated.

Tibby studied Carmen for a long minute. "Oh, my God. Carma Carmeena Carmabelle. You like this guy, don't you?"

Carmen was blushing.

"This is amazing. This is new," Tibby continued. "You do like him."

"But he doesn't like me. That's the problem. He is a good person. He's premed. He volunteers at the hospital all day long. He likes Good Carmen."

"So why not set him straight?" Lena asked.

"Because he won't like me anymore."

"Why don't you try it?"

"Because I'm scared to. I don't want to ruin it for him.

158

I'd rather he have his idealized version of me than introduce him to the real thing. I like the way he thinks of
me—I mean Good Carmen."

Lena lifted her sunglasses. She was resolute. "Carmen,
that's just sad. Be yourself. If he doesn't like you for
yourself, then he ain't worth it."

"Hallelujah," said Tibby.

Carmen studied them suspiciously. "What's with you two?"

Bridget sat with her clipboard on her lap at the side of
the soccer field, chewing on a piece of grass. She didn't
even bother to lace up her cleats these days. She went
around barefoot. She even played barefoot. It was
unorthodox, she knew, but who really cared?

Eric was pacing a few yards away. He was watching
his team doing dribbling exercises. She didn't get that
screaming feeling in her cells quite so much now when
she saw him. She was getting used to him.

"Blye at forward," she said to no one in particular.
She'd put Lundgren, the Swede, on defense. He was ver-
satile. The European kids always had the best fundamen-
tals. Naughton, her special favorite, she put in the goal.
He was completely uncoordinated, but he had a weird,
seemingly dumb magnetism for the ball. At the moment
she had her team carrying out an elaborate pattern of
sprints. She wanted to get her roster in order before they
got back.

Suddenly her clipboard was in shadow. "Away. No
spying," she ordered without looking up.

Eric stepped back about one foot. "You're crazy to put Naughton in the goal."

"I'm crazy to put him anywhere. No spying. No peeking. No Peking. No Beijing."

"It's friendly advice."

"All friendly till we beat you soundly."

"Ooooh. I'm scared."

She looked up at him finally. He pretended he was going to step on her feet. She put her hand over her eyes, squinting in the sun. She smiled at him, and a nice thought passed through her mind. *I think we're really friends.*

Eric had joined her and Diana for dinner the past two nights. At first Diana seemed alarmed, but she got used to him. You could get used to almost anything. They spent three hours sitting at a table in the cafeteria discussing the relative merits of each of their teams like the three big soccer dorks they were.

Bridget and Eric hung out now even when they didn't have to. He joined her for her evening runs sometimes. They ate their lunch on the field together (except Mondays, when they pretended to chaperone in the dining hall) and talked strategy. They didn't make a big deal of it or anything.

She could do this. She could. It wasn't that hard. She loved him, maybe so, but she also loved being with him. She could be happy with just that. She didn't need any more.

Finally, finally, at last the strange air of their

encounter was dissipating. Her new relationship with him had almost entirely eclipsed the old one. She felt like she could trust herself with him now.

Bridget watched her breathless team streaming back toward her across the field. She stood waiting for them like a proud mama. Naughton was the first one in her face. She frankly suspected he'd cheated a corner or two, because he wasn't all that fast. "Hey, Naughty, how'd you do?"

"Good." He was trying to catch his breath.

"You all get water," she ordered the group. "Then we'll get to work."

Naughton continued to hang around her, not quite balanced on his bumpy knees, while the others got water. He was always asking her stuff. He was her project, and he knew it. "You running tonight?" he asked her.

"Probably. Maybe a short one."

"Can I come?"

This was new. "Uh . . . I guess. If you have anything left after I finish with you all today."

He looked eager. "I'll keep up. Don't worry."

This made her remember things that had happened two years ago. How she would foist herself upon Eric when he tried to lead runs in Mexico. She would bother him and show off and flirt outrageously. God, had she really done that?

She was still thinking about this as she and Eric walked to the dining hall for lunch a couple of hours later.

He noticed she was quiet, but he didn't bug her.

Joe Warshaw intercepted them at the front of the room. "Just the two I need," he said, pulling them off to the side. He sort of winked at Bridget as if to say, "See, your partner's not so bad, is he?"

Bridget looked down at her toes.

"We've planned a rafting trip this weekend," Joe explained. "It's an overnight down the Schuylkill. It's an easy stretch, one portage. We've got eight kids signed up. Esmer was supposed to do it, but he has to take off this weekend, and you two are both on. Do you mind?"

"Does it matter if we mind?" Eric asked. He knew the way of Joe.

Joe smiled brightly. "No, actually."

"Well, then," Eric said.

"I'll tell the kitchen guys to get all the tents and stuff packed into the van. I'll make it easy for you, how's that?"

Eric and Joe talked logistics while Bridget's mind raced around the place. She was going on an overnight camping trip with Eric. Oh, God. She trusted herself to stick to the friendly banter during meals and even lake duty. She had mastered that subtle art. But sleeping close to him in a sleeping bag under the stars? She wasn't sure she trusted herself to be able to do that.

Hey, girlies,
    41 days!!!! Do you know where your bikinis are?
                                                        Bee

It came to her in a dream. It really did.

Lena was dreaming about Valia and her mother and Effie and all kinds of incongruent bits and pieces. And in her dream she went into the dining room—or a place that she knew was the dining room even though it looked kind of different. And instead of her family members sitting in the chairs, there were drawings of them—big wide sheets of paper with charcoal drawings propped on the chairs. Lena not only liked these drawings, in her dream, but she knew that she had made them.

And when she woke up, she knew what her portfolio project was going to be. It wasn't so much that she wanted to draw a series of portraits of her family. It was that she knew it was the right thing to do.

She decided to start with her mother, the source of all things. Besides, she knew she could make her mother agree to it. After dinner, she scouted the house for the right place to pose her.

"Sit there." Lena pointed to the living room couch, green velvet, with pillows carefully arranged. She studied her mother. No. She didn't really repose in the living room very often.

"Let's try the kitchen," Lena said, and her mother followed her there. She sat Ari down at the kitchen table. Better. But her mother was never really sitting down.

"Stand, okay?" Lena said. She let her mother gravitate to her own spot at the counter. That made sense. Without thinking, her mother put her chin in her hands, her elbows resting on the granite counter, waiting for Lena to pick.

"Don't move," Lena said. "That's good." She brought a stool opposite her mother and propped her drawing board on her lap. Lena made herself look for a long time before she started. She wanted to see all that was real and also what was there. She didn't want to let herself shy away.

She started. She liked the softness of her mother's skin contrasting with the gleaming granite countertop, the way the skin of her elbows puddled a bit upon it. Her mother eschewed softness, longed for hardness, but softness was what she had.

Lena wanted to capture her mother's worn, slightly bagging knuckles with the hard permanence of her wedding ring pressing as it now did into her mother's cheek. She considered her mother's severely glinting diamond studs, a twentieth anniversary gift from Lena's father, sitting in her soft, tired earlobes.

Drawing wasn't a passive exercise, Annik liked to say. You had to find the information; you had to go in after it.

Lena pushed herself to look deeper into the tentative set of her mother's eyes, the lines burrowing toward her lips, made more pronounced by the careful, deliberate way she held them.

Ari wanted to support Lena in some way. She would sit for this drawing until every one of her limbs went to sleep. But she needed to stay allied with her husband, too. She'd made too many compromises already this year to pull out. She was an appeaser, maybe, but by now she was accountable herself.

Lena saw these conflicts fighting in each quadrant of her mother's face. She saw the tiny fault lines betraying the feelings that pulled her mother apart. Ari was so placid in some ways, her smooth hair, her plucked brows, her elegant clothes in every soft shade of beige. And in other ways, Lena could see she was waging an internal war.

Lena imagined herself a field marshal, overseeing the hostilities between her mother's eyebrows. Then she imagined herself a cartographer, mapping out each curve and concavity between Ari's cheekbone and her jaw. She imagined herself a blind person, feeling her way around her mother's neck and collarbone with her charcoal. She pictured herself the size of a mite, crawling over the canyonlike hollows of her mother's shoulders.

When Lena brought the drawing in to Annik the next day, Annik was plainly excited. She was near speechless.

"Do you think I got the chair?" Lena asked timidly.

Annik hugged her, knocking Lena's legs into her wheels. "I really do."

Should we have stayed

home and thought of

here?

—Elizabeth Bishop

"Hey, Naughty."

Bridget hadn't told Naughton exactly the time of her run that evening, but he was there nonetheless. She wondered how long he'd been waiting by the road at the foot of the hill. Eric, this evening, had not come.

They ran in silence for quite some time. The air was so heavy you could practically feel the water squishing around in it. Bridget had to hand it to Naughty. The uphill stretch was fairly brutal—she liked to start a run tough—and he kept right with her even when he looked like he was going to die.

He was fourteen. He seemed infinitely younger than she, but she realized with some mortification that he was no more distant from her age than she was from Eric's.

He kept turning his head to look at her. He was nervous.

She paused briefly at the top of the mountain to enjoy the view. It was part of her ritual. The silence was

punctuated by Naughton, who was breathing so hard she was afraid he might blow out a lung.

She waited until they were headed downhill to get conversational. "How's it going?" she asked him.

"G-g-ood." He worked hard for the word.

He waited until they had finished the four-mile loop and begun walking to unburden his heart. "Um, Bridget?"

"Yeah?"

"Do you like Bridget or Bee?"

"Either. Both."

"Okay, uh, Bee?"

"Yeah?"

"I wanted to tell you something."

"Okay."

Silence.

"Uh . . . never mind." Sweat made his whole face shine.

"Okay."

He couldn't bear to leave it at that. "I, uh, think you're . . . pretty amazing."

"I like you, too, Naughty."

He cleared his throat. "I think I'm talking about a different kind of like."

"Like a girlfriend?" She cut to the chase. This could take all night.

He was surprised. "Yes."

"I'm your coach, Naughty. You know I can't be your girlfriend." That hadn't been good enough for her, back

in Baja, had it? Why did she think it was good enough for him?

"Do you have a boyfriend?" he asked.

This would have been an easy out, but she didn't feel like lying. "No. Not really."

"Maybe after camp?" he proposed. "I could wait."

He was so much sweeter and more rational than she had been. Why seal off all hope? "Maybe someday. Who knows what will happen?"

A few hours later, she was sitting next to Eric on the dock. The sun was setting behind the trees and she was feeling thoughtful.

"Can I apologize to you for something?" she asked him, kicking her bare feet back and forth in the warm air.

"What do you have to apologize for?" he asked lazily. His hair was messed up from drying with the lake water in it. His face was stubbly and relaxed in a way it had never been with her that first summer.

"Two summers ago."

He winced a little, but he let her go on.

"That kid Jack Naughton wants to be my boyfriend. He's sweet, but it made me think of myself. It made me remember how I behaved to you, and I felt so ashamed." She cracked a piece of wood off the dock and threw it into the water. She let out a breath. "I'm sorry I did that. You must have thought I was so ridiculous."

Eric's face was pained. He was silent for a long time.

She brought her feet up onto the dock and hugged her knees to her chest. She pressed her chin against one

brown knee, afraid to look at him. She could feel the weight of her loose hair drying against her back.

They hadn't talked about this before. In all their many hours spent together, they hadn't mentioned the fact that they'd known each other—much less *known* each other. They never talked about "us." There wasn't any "us."

But now, she was raising the specter of "us," wasn't she? Not to reawaken it, she promised herself. That was not it. Her mind supplied a funny version of the famous *Julius Caesar* line: *I come not to praise us, but to bury us.*

Eric rubbed a hand through his hair. "I didn't think you were ridiculous," he said at last, a little defensively. "It was more complicated than that."

"But it was all my fault. I know it was."

He looked terribly tired. One side of his mouth was flat and the other pointed down. She could tell he didn't want to talk about this anymore.

"I won't bring it up again," she said softly. Her eyes pricked with tears that she did not want him to see. "I promise. We can forget it ever happened."

When he finally talked his voice was so quiet she could barely hear him. "Do you think I could forget it?" He brushed his hand over his eye. "Do you really think it was all you? That I didn't want it too?"

Brian was over, so Tibby stayed in her room. Brian came to see Katherine almost every day. He was transforming her arm cast into a masterpiece, drawing a fierce

and sprawling dragon with her Magic Markers, adding a little more each time he came.

Brian also came to see Tibby, Tibby suspected, but she did not want to see him. He would catch her every so often skulking to the kitchen to forage for supplies and ask her, by his hollow-eyed looks, why she was avoiding him. And she just kept avoiding him because she didn't have an answer.

Tibby was perched on her bed, having left the door open a few inches so she could hear Brian's voice but not be seen. That was when Carmen arrived. Brian was careful enough to leave her alone, but with Carmen there was no such luck. Carmen walked in and closed the door behind her.

"What are you doing?"

"What do you mean?"

"Why won't you see Brian? The poor guy is dying."

"He's here to see Katherine," Tibby said defensively.

Carmen was not a particularly patient person. "Shut up. He loves Katherine, I know, but he wants to see you."

"Why can't I just be by myself if I want?" Tibby asked churlishly.

Carmen sighed. She was in one of her tough-love moods. "Because Brian loves you. And I am pretty sure you feel the same way. So what are you doing? Like it or not, you're going to NYU in a month and a half. You can't just leave it like this."

Tibby was tired of hearing it. Her mom had been in her room singing the very same tune not twenty-four

hours before. "Why is everybody in such a hurry to shove me and Brian together? Why does he have to be my boyfriend? Are you not a real person if you don't have a boyfriend? Why does everybody have to be in love with somebody?"

"You don't have to be in love with somebody," Carmen replied. "But it so happens that you are. And besides, Brian means more to you than just being your boyfriend." Carmen looked around distastefully at the mess. "Is this about Katherine?" she asked. "Because Katherine's getting better fast and you're the one acting broken."

"It's not about Katherine," Tibby said, just to get Carmen off her back. "It's not about anything. And anyway, maybe you're wrong. Maybe I just don't like Brian in that way."

Carmen sized her up. "Are you honestly telling me that you don't like Brian in that way?"

Tibby couldn't say no without lying, so she decided to say nothing instead.

"Hi, Dad. It's me."

"Hey, bun! How good to hear your voice. What's up?"

Carmen and Al talked pretty regularly on Sunday evenings, so a call on a Thursday night did tend to prompt the old "What's up?"

Carmen had been, in her slightly sick way, excited to tell her mother she would not fulfill her lifelong dream of going to Williams College. It turned out she was not at all

172

excited to tell her father. She'd put this call off a hundred times.

"I . . . um . . . How's Lydia?"

"She's great." Her dad obviously knew she was stalling.

"How's Krista?"

"I think she's fine." Al was always more circumspect on this subject. He didn't want to make it seem like Krista was the girl who lived with him while Carmen was the girl he talked to on Sundays. In spite of the fact that this was true.

"Tell her I say hey, okay?"

"Of course. She'll be happy. Now, tell me. Is everything good with you? How's your job?"

"It's . . . fine. Listen, I'm calling because . . . well, because . . ." She had to make herself say it. "Because I'm thinking a lot about this fall."

"Okay . . ."

"I might not be ready to leave home just now." She said it so fast it came out like one long word.

"Bun, explain what you mean."

"With Mom and David, and Mom expecting the baby and everything. It's hard to picture leaving right now."

"Okay . . ."

"I might just stay here this fall. I might even go to U of Maryland. I got accepted there, you know, like, just in case."

"Oh, I didn't realize that."

"It happened recently."

"So. You say you *might* stay home this fall?"

"I think I probably will." She let out a breath she'd been holding for at least a minute.

"No Williams, then."

"Maybe not."

"Maybe not?"

"Probably not."

"Probably not."

"Yeah. The thing is, I have to call them at Williams and tell them. I can't just hold the spot if I'm not going to use it, you know?"

"Yes, I'm sure you're right about that." Her dad didn't sound mad, really. He sounded calm.

"So I'll go ahead and call 'em, I guess."

She could hear her father switching the phone to his other ear. "Bun, why don't you let me take care of it, okay? I put down a big deposit already, and I might need to work with them a bit to get it back."

"Oh, no. Do you think . . . ?" Carmen couldn't stand the thought of her dad getting stiffed for thousands of dollars along with everything else.

"I think it will be fine," he said. "You let me handle it, okay?" He was so calm.

Was it possible her mother had gotten to him first? Carmen detected the faint smell of a parental plot. Even divorced parents were capable of such things when they got concerned.

"Thanks, Dad." Once again, tears jumped into the breach. "Are you sure you're not disappointed?" Her

voice disobeyed her and cracked on the last syllable.

He sighed. "If you want to go to Williams, I want you to go to Williams. If you want to go to Maryland, I want you to go to Maryland. I want you to be happy, bun."

How did she get such nice parents? How did such nice parents turn out such a disaster of a daughter?

He wasn't done being nice. "I love you, Carmen. I trust you to make the right decisions."

Carmen felt that an anvil had mysteriously replaced her lower intestines. Sometimes trust felt like the worst gift in the world.

It's the same old story.
Boy finds girl, boy loses
girl, girl finds boy, boy
forgets girl, boy
remembers girl, girls
dies in a tragic blimp
accident over the Orange
Bowl on New Year's Day.
—The Naked Gun

The rafting went smoothly. This time there were no dive-bombing bees. No splashing or tipping or crashing overboard. Bridget and Eric made a convincing show of knowing what they were doing.

Meanwhile, the campers, eight boys, did plenty of splashing and colliding and smacking each other with their oars. They had a blast while Bridget and Eric were all business.

During the long hours of floating along the hot, quiet river, Bridget had lots of time to regret her last conversation with Eric. It had changed the mood between them. Of course it had. The ease had vanished. They were suddenly considerate and polite. She really hated that.

Tension of all sorts had risen. She felt self-conscious pulling her T-shirt up over her bikini when she got hot, even though everyone else was in bathing suits already. She averted her eyes from Eric's bare chest, even though she'd seen him like that plenty of times before. While she

braided her hair, she looked over to see him looking, and they both instantly cast their eyes down.

When the rain began soon after their dinner of bland, camping-style beans and rice, they both looked slightly stricken. There were three tents: two four-person tents for the campers. One two-person tent for the leaders. The two-person tent looked comically small to Bridget as she began to set it up.

She could guess that Eric had bargained on getting to sleep under the sky. So had she. That way, he could be on one side of the campsite and she on the other, and they could avoid this whole conundrum. The wind blew harder and pushed fat drops of rain down on them as if to make its point. They would all be sleeping in tents tonight.

Bridget was usually good at stomping out tension. It was a special talent of hers. She would march around boldly, crushing it underfoot, not paying it any mind. But this time, it was tricky. It wound its stalks around her ankles and held her fast.

She didn't know where to go to change out of her bathing suit. She didn't want him to see her brushing her teeth or her hair. Obviously she didn't want him to spot her peeing in the woods. She didn't want to walk into him wearing just his boxers, or worse. She felt nervous about the thought of him watching her climb into her sleeping bag in her nightshirt.

When she thought of her recklessness with him two summers before, she recoiled. How could she have done that? She didn't even know him then.

Maybe that was exactly how she had done that.

Eric gave her a good long time by herself in the tent before he politely asked if he could come in. He was so polite, he was soaked.

Lying in her sleeping bag, her hair bundled under her neck, she turned her back to him, like she wasn't noticing him getting into his own sleeping bag not two feet away. She wished they could laugh about this, but she couldn't find a way.

There they were lying in a tiny orange tent, side by side. The rain beat down. She could smell his shampoo and his wet skin. It was awkward in a magical way.

She was too embarrassed to consider the tantalizing possibilities that lay before them if she were to let her mind go free. Really, what she most wanted to do was to reassure him. She didn't pose a threat. She didn't. She wanted to prove it to him.

She turned so she was lying on her back looking up. He did the same.

She cleared her throat. "Tell me about Kaya," Bridget said. "What's she like?"

Eric didn't answer right away.

"I bet she's beautiful."

He let out a long breath. "Yeah. She is." He sounded a little guarded. He was private about these kinds of things.

"Light hair or dark?"

"Dark. She's actually half Mexican, too."

"That's cool." Bridget, absurdly, wished she could find some way of being half Mexican. "Does she go to Columbia?"

"She just graduated."

To Bridget, it sounded so old and sophisticated and totally winning to be half Mexican and have just graduated from Columbia. She felt herself developing an inferiority complex as she lay there stupidly in her sleeping bag, shrinking into her underage, non-Mexican skin. She didn't even want to say anything else, for fear of measuring up even stupider and more juvenile next to his dazzling girlfriend.

Why had Bridget invited Eric's girlfriend into their little orange tent?

He turned on his side, facing her, and propped his head on his hand. Talking a little, even about this, had made things easier between them. "Hey. I want to hear about *your* friends."

This was bait she could not resist. And so she spent her nervousness on chirping and blabbing and yammering away, just as stupid and juvenile as could be.

Lena's next hurdle was a big one. It was Valia. Lena had been avoiding her grandmother so scrupulously for so many months, it was almost terrifying to look right at her.

Lena half hoped Valia would refuse to pose, but she didn't. She sat behind the desk in the den and looked at Lena straight on.

"You can work at the computer, if you want. I could draw you that way," Lena offered.

Valia shrugged. "I am done vith the computer today."

Lena calculated it was already late in Greece; that was probably the reason.

"You could watch TV, if that would be more comfortable."

"No. I vill just sit here," Valia said.

Lena had to stiffen her spine. She was looking for a way out, and Valia was looking right at her. Lena made herself be brave.

It was rough at first. Lena had been avoiding Valia's obvious pain, and her own associated troubles. Seeing Valia's face, she couldn't ignore that pain. Drawing Valia meant not only seeing it but going in after it. Lena felt that her only hope was to try in stages.

How much her grandma had aged in the past year. Valia's skin was so wrinkled it looked like it might fall off her bones. Her once-dark eyes were watery and faded, with a bluish tinge around the irises. They looked out from the folds of skin as if from inside two grottos.

Bapi had loved Valia. Lena imagined that even when they were old, Bapi had seen Valia as the young, beautiful woman she had been. Now there was no one to see her that way, and as a consequence, she had shriveled up.

Lena suddenly grasped her challenge. She was going to try to see that Valia—Bapi's Valia—in this face, if she could. She wouldn't just find the sorrow, plentiful though it was. She would be like an archaeologist. She would unearth the former Valia; she would rediscover her in the midst of all the ravages.

Now Lena was really looking, and Valia stood up to it.

She looked right back. Lena had never done a drawing with her subject gazing directly into her eyes. It was like a staring contest fought to a stalemate.

Lena the archaeologist saw clues in the shape of Valia's eyebrows. She borrowed a little from Effie, who some people thought resembled Valia. She saw her father in Valia's mouth and chin. Lena was drawing what she saw, but she was allowing the past to inform the way she interpreted it, if that was possible. She could see the beauty if she really tried.

Valia's usual aggressive frown was slowly sifting out of her features. The parts and places that made up her face took on new, more natural shapes. Lena realized that Valia liked being looked at. And that made Lena consider, sadly, how little anybody had looked at her. They were all afraid of her. They kept their eyes averted from her. Who needed another tragedy in their day? They politely ignored or submitted to her complaints just to make them go away. They all basically wished *she* would go away. Or at least, they wished her anger, her suffering, her loneliness, her discontent, and all of her complaining would go away. The rest they would be okay with.

It was no wonder Valia was angry. Her son had brought her here by near force and now spent the entire time wishing she weren't here. And Valia really *wanted* to go away, that was the thing. They wanted her gone; she wanted herself gone. What a mess.

Lena drew and drew. Valia was an exceptional model.

Far better than the professionals at school, who got paid fifteen bucks an hour. For seventy minutes, Valia stood stock-still without a single sigh or moan or wriggle.

After a while, Lena felt tears in her eyes, but she didn't stop for them. How lonely Valia was! How much she loved being seen, finally. What a tragedy for all of them that they had starved her so.

When Lena finished, she got up and kissed Valia on the head. They hadn't touched each other in months. Valia seemed shaken by it.

Shyly Lena offered Valia the picture. *I've seen you. I think I finally have*, Lena said silently.

Valia looked at it for a long time. She didn't say anything. She nodded brusquely, but Lena believed that on this strange Saturday afternoon, they had seen each other.

The next morning at breakfast, Valia was back to her usual tricks.

"Who made this coffee?" she demanded, acting as though she might very well spit it on the table.

"I did," Lena shot back. "Don't you like it?"

"It's the vorst," Valia said heartily.

Lena clapped her eyes on Valia's and wouldn't let them go. "So don't drink it, then."

Her entire family stared at her in astonishment, and Lena felt quite pleased with herself.

"Hi, Carmen? I hope this is the right Carmen. If this is the right Carmen, then this is Win. If not, it's . . . it's still Win and sorry to bother you. Even if this is the right

Carmen, I might be bothering you and I'm sorry if I am. I found your number on the . . . well, never mind. I'm not like a stalker or anything. I swear to God. I've never called somebody up out of the blue like this. But I have to admit I've been thinking about you, and . . ." *Beeeeeeep.*

Somewhere in the middle of the night, Bridget felt a tiny tickle of hair against her arm. She opened her eyes without moving a single other muscle. In sleep, Eric had rolled toward her. His head had come so close as to graze her shoulder. She felt breathless. Their bodies were curled in the same direction, hers distantly cupping his. The bottoms of their sleeping bags almost touched.

What little sleep she had had that night was light and full of surface dreams. She couldn't go under any deeper, being this close to him. She wondered if he noticed at all how close their bodies were, how their breath mixed. Or was his sleep innocent and sound?

Gingerly, glacially she moved her foot. She held her breath until, through her sleeping bag, she could feel, ever so lightly with her big toe, the shape of his heel. She prayed he wouldn't notice or stir. He didn't. He slept.

She withdrew her foot, feeling sorry.

She would have given anything for him to want her again. But she would have given even more for him to trust her.

Don't ask me any

questions right now.

I'm grumpy and I'll

probably make fun

of you.

—Effie Kaligaris

Tibby was standing at the front of the theater, waiting for the one o'clock show to end. She'd stopped watching the movies altogether. These days she preferred to stand by the front windows and look out. One afternoon the box office lady was sick, and Tibby got to take over in the tiny room. That was fun—safe, contained, predictable.

Tibby wondered, once again, about the wisdom of her career choice. She wondered if maybe NYU had any openings in accounting. Or maybe they offered a program for future tollbooth attendants. Or cashiers. She pictured herself enjoying a career in one of those liquor stores in bad neighborhoods where you sat behind a thick sheet of bulletproof Plexiglas and people paid for their stuff through a slot in the window. That sounded about right.

She spotted a little group across the street, and she experienced that split second of objectivity when you see

someone you know before you realize you know them. The tall one, of course, was Brian. Tibby constantly had to relearn what he looked like now. When he had been the lowliest of dorks, his unkempt hair—longish, unbrushed, needing a cut—had played a role in the vicious circle that had been Brian's appearance. Now it looked conspicuously cool, neglected in exactly the right manner. She bought his clothes for him at Old Navy a couple times a year, so there were no pitfalls there. He had learned to like taking showers of his own accord. That helped too.

The little figure with the giant, lolling, hockey-player head was Katherine, of course. Every time Tibby saw that hockey helmet, she felt her guts constrict. Her facial muscles pulled into a grimace, even when she fought against it. The sight of it made her feel angry and it made her want to cry.

Nicky was holding Katherine's other hand. Even he had become more protective of her.

They crossed the street and approached the doors of the theater. Katherine caught sight of Tibby in the plate-glass windows. She waved so fervently her helmet slid to the side, the chinstrap bending her ear in half. Tibby opened the doors for them.

"We're going to see a movie at *your* theater!" Katherine shouted.

Tibby straightened the helmet. She was always doing that.

"Hey, look." Katherine pointed to her head.

"What?" Tibby said.

"Stickers!" Katherine was exultant. "Nicky helped me do it."

The hockey helmet was indeed plastered with stickers, every superhero and cartoon character in the history of cheap merchandising.

"Wow. Nice," Tibby said.

"Now I might never want to take it off," Katherine declared triumphantly.

Tibby felt her breath catch. There was some torture in this she couldn't even identify. God bless, Katherine. How could she be how she was? How could Tibby be so different? Why was she so pained when Katherine really was okay? Tibby wasn't the one who fell out the window. Her concern for Katherine had become a waste; Katherine didn't need it. Who was it really for?

Forgetting about what had happened for a moment, Tibby looked instinctively at Brian. And Brian touched her tenderly on the hand, enveloping her in a look of support that didn't have anything to do with whether he wanted to kiss her or not.

Carmen had saved Win's telephone message and replayed it fourteen times in one hour. So why was she in the hospital—the very place where he worked—hunkered over a book in a corner, wearing sunglasses and a hat? It was Wednesday afternoon and Valia had her usual physical therapy session. Carmen knew where to find Win. Win might even be looking for her.

Instead, she picked the most remote spot she could find, which happened to be a deserted hallway in labor and delivery. It was nice and quiet for a while, but suddenly there was a virtual gaggle of pregnant women waddling toward her. She bent her head and tried to read a few more pages, but she was distracted. So much for her solitude. There was nowhere to run in this place.

All the women and their spouses were piling into a room. Carmen was imagining what it could mean—a big, wild rave for the pregnant folks?—when something began to dawn on her. She looked at her watch.

For the most part, she meanly ignored anything her mother said that contained the words *labor, birth, pregnancy,* or *baby.* But vaguely in the back of her mind she knew her mom and David were coming to a childbirth class at this very hospital.

Could it be? Could it?

Oh, man.

She tried to get back into her book, but she couldn't. For pages and pages, Jane Austen's elegant banter went into her eyes and stopped short of her brain. Carmen was curious now. Once she framed a question, it was so hard for her not to answer it. She put her book in her bag and walked down the hall. She stopped at the room where the pregnant women had gone. It had a frosted glass window, fairly convenient for snooping. She saw the couples sitting on the floor. The men had their legs spread out with their rotund wives between them. It looked pretty peculiar, frankly. The teacher stood behind a table at the front.

Carmen had come to the conclusion that her mother wasn't, in fact, part of this strange class when she peered farther in to the back and saw the familiar angle of dark hair. Christina was easy to miss because even with her big round belly, she seemed to be shrinking against the wall.

Everybody was a couple and Christina was alone. Why was that? The current exercise involved the men massaging their wives' shoulders, and Christina just sat there.

Where was David? Carmen watched in puzzlement until Christina reached up her arms to massage her own shoulders. That was all Carmen needed. The ache in her chest caught her by surprise and propelled her straight through the door and into the room.

"Can I help you?" the instructor asked her.

"Hold on just a sec," Carmen said. She went to her mother. "What's going on? Where's David?"

Christina's eyes were pinkish. "There was a big emergency on his case. He had to fly to St. Louis," she whispered. To her immense credit, there was lots of sadness in the way she said it, but no blame. "What are you doing here, *nena*?"

"Valia has physical therapy," Carmen explained.

Christina nodded.

The instructor appeared in front of them. "Are you registered for this class . . . ?" she asked Carmen. She didn't say it in a snotty way, but she obviously preferred complete order.

Carmen looked from the instructor to her mother and

190

back again. She pointed to her mother. "I'm her partner."

The instructor looked surprised. Politically, it was her responsibility to be open to all kinds of couples. "Fine. That's fine. We're starting with some labor massage techniques. Just follow the rest of the class to get started."

Carmen situated her mother between her knees and began massaging her tense shoulders. Carmen had strong hands. She felt like she was good at this. She heard a little hitch in her mother's breathing, and she knew Christina was crying.

But she knew Christina was crying because she was happy, and that gave Carmen her own feeling of happiness unlike anything she'd felt in a long time.

Hey, you beautiful girls!

My dad just sent me a pile of stuff from Brown.

My roommate's name is Aisha Lennox. Doesn't that sound cool?

I'm gonna live with her. We're gonna know her. How weird is that?

Bee

Lena thought the drawing of Effie would be the easy one. She didn't dread it. She didn't overprepare. She sauntered in. Lena was not a saunterer, and for good reason, she decided. She always ended up regretting it.

"Where do you want to be?" Lena asked. "Your room? Your bed? Someplace else?"

"Um." Effie was painting her toenails. "Can you just do it here?" She was sitting on the floor in front of the TV in the den. Some reality show was blaring. Effie had her chin resting on her knee and was giving full attention to her toenail, as though it were one of the more demanding things she'd ever grappled with.

"I guess," Lena said. "Do you mind if I turn the TV off?"

"Leave it on," Effie said. "I won't watch."

Lena didn't question this. She had an instinct that bossing your model around was no way to get her to loosen up. No matter how stupid she was being.

Lena settled on a profile. Effie's knees bent, her chin down, her toes flexed. She started sketching.

Effie was no Valia. She moved around as though modeling for Lena's picture wasn't even on her to-do list.

"Sheesh, Ef. Can you hold still?"

Effie flashed her a look. She went back to her toenails.

Lena tried. She really did. It was hard to draw a moving hand. Lena let it blur. It was hard to draw someone's character when they kept their face turned away. She tried to suggest the resistance in Effie's pose. It was the only thing that felt true.

And then Lena had to ask herself, why was Effie resisting so hard? It was true they'd been missing each other this summer. They'd both gotten jobs early. They'd both spent as much time away from the house as possible.

Was her relationship with Effie another casualty of the Valia debacle?

Had it gone more wrong than Lena knew?

"Effie?"

"What?" Effie snapped, still not turning her head.

Lena's mouth seemed to work a little better with a charcoal in her hand. She opened it. "Ef, I feel like you don't want this to work. Like you're mad at me."

Effie rolled her eyes. She made a show of blowing dry the shiny pink polish on her big toe. "Why do you think that?"

"Because you won't look at me. You won't sit still."

If Effie had been Lena and Lena had been Effie, this could have taken all day. But luckily, Effie was Effie. When she finally turned, her face was full of expression.

"Maybe I don't want you to go to art school."

Lena put down her pad. "Why not?" She couldn't help showing her astonishment. She always just assumed that Effie sided with her in any struggle against her parents, just as she always sided with Effie, even when Effie was wrong. Did Effie actually agree with her parents this time? Did she resent that Lena was causing more turbulence in their already turbulent home?

Effie's eyes were full of tears. At long last she capped her polish and tossed it aside. "Why do you think?" she demanded.

Lena felt her own eyes pulling wide open. "Ef. I don't know. Please tell me."

Effie put her face in her hands. "I don't want you to go. I don't want you to leave me here . . . with all of them."

On her knees, Lena made her way the few feet to her sister. She put her arms around Effie. "I'm so sorry," Lena said honestly. "I don't want to leave you." She felt Effie's tears against her shoulder and she held her tighter. "I hate to even think about leaving you."

The beautiful thing about getting someone to tell you what was wrong was that you could tell them something to make it a little better. Lena made a mental note that she should try it more often.

In the lobby a while later, Carmen was hugging her mom good-bye when she saw Win. He smiled eagerly, doubling his pace to get to her, like he was afraid she might slip away.

"Carmen!"

"Hey, Win," she said. She couldn't help smiling at him. He was too sweet not to. Win and Christina were looking at each other. Win was probably wondering which distant relative of which distant acquaintance Carmen would be accompanying to the hospital now.

"This is my mom, Christina," Carmen said. "Mom, this is Win."

"Nice to meet you, Win," Christina said.

Carmen saw him through her mother's eyes and was again struck by his exceeding gorgeousness. Carmen found most guys who looked that good intimidating, but Win was different. He was not arrogant or scary. He had a self-deprecating smile and a shuffling posture totally at odds with the usual "I'm gorgeous" swagger.

"Nice to meet you, too," he said earnestly. "I thought you must be related. You're beautiful like Carmen."

If Carmen had just heard about this statement rather than actually listening to it in person, she would have groaned and rolled her eyes and told Mr. Slick to get out of town. But hearing him say it and seeing the look on his face as he did, she believed it was the most innocent and sincere compliment she'd ever gotten. And so did her mother, apparently.

Christina flushed with pleasure. "Thank you. I like to think I look like her."

Carmen felt unbalanced, buffeted as she was by all the goodness. She had no idea what to say.

"Carmen saved me today," Christina volunteered to Win, emotion all through her voice. "My husband couldn't make it to childbirth class, and Carmen came to my rescue. She's my partner and coach. Can you imagine?" Christina was laughing, but her eyes were full of tears. Carmen had heard about pregnant women being extra emotional, but jeez, this was a bit much.

Win stared at Christina with rapt attention. And then he turned to look at Carmen. She'd wished many times for a boy like Win to look at her this way. But now it was wrong. The stuff her mom was saying made it all worse.

She opened her mouth to say something. And then she realized. "Oh, my God! I have to get Valia! I'm gonna be late for her." Oh, God. She could practically hear the bone-splintering howl from the eighth floor.

"I'll come," Christina said, running after her to the bank of elevators.

"Bye, Win," Carmen shouted over her shoulder.

He looked a little sad as she waved to him through the narrowing gap of the elevator door. As soon as it closed, Christina burst. *"Nena*, who is he?" She was obviously excited. "He is . . . he is just *adorable*! And the way he looked at you."

Carmen's face was hot. "He does seem . . . nice." She didn't want her mother to see her flustered smile. She wished she could get her mouth into a normal shape.

"Nice! He's more than nice! How do you know him?"

Carmen shrugged. "I don't really know him. Or I guess I do kind of know him." She chewed the inside of her lip. "But he doesn't know me."

To the man who only has a hammer in the toolkit, every problem looks like a nail.

—Abraham Maslow

It took four evenings for Tibby to pounce on the garbage bags and take them out to the alley before Margaret could get there first. Margaret was so experienced at her job, having worked at this very Pavillion Theater for well over twenty years, and so dedicated to it, that it was nearly impossible for Tibby to manage to do her coworker even this one small favor.

"Tibby, thanks!" Margaret said brightly when she saw the empty cans. "You're jis sweet."

"I'm returning a favor," Tibby said.

Tibby watched as Margaret put her sweater in her employee locker (no pictures pinned up inside, Tibby noticed) and collected her purse, in exactly the same manner she did every evening. Tibby knew Margaret would take the bus on Wisconsin Avenue to her home, which was somewhere north of here. She couldn't exactly guess what Margaret did with her free time, but she felt almost sure Margaret did it alone.

Suddenly Tibby felt inspired. "Hey, Margaret?"

Margaret turned, her purse dangling neatly from the crook of her elbow.

"Do you want to get some dinner with me?"

Margaret looked utterly bewildered.

"We could just get something quick, if you want. We could go right around the corner to that Italian place."

Why not spend some time with a gravely lonely person? Tibby thought, silently applauding herself. Wasn't that a worthy thing to do? Tibby felt sure it was something a good person would do.

Margaret looked around, as though to see if perhaps Tibby was talking to someone else. The muscles around her mouth twitched a little. She cleared her throat. "Excuse me?"

"Do you want to have dinner?"

Margaret looked a bit frightened. "You and me?"

"Yes." Tibby was beginning to wonder if she had overstepped.

"Will, uh, okay. I giss I could."

"Great."

Tibby led the way around the corner. She had never seen Margaret outside the movie theater. It was kind of strange. She wondered how many times Margaret had *been* out of the movie theater—other than when she was home. In her pale pink cardigan, with her white vinyl purse with gold buckles and her bewildered expression, Margaret looked like an innocent victim of some time-travel mishap.

"Is this place okay?" Tibby asked, holding open the door to the restaurant.

"Yes," Margaret agreed in a slightly quavering voice.

Tibby had been to this restaurant before and it had seemed perfectly normal. But now, with Margaret at her side, the place struck her as raucous, dark, nightmarishly noisy, and totally wrong.

The hostess showed them to a table. Margaret perched on the very front of her chair, her backbone stiff, as though ready to flee at a second's notice.

"They have good pizza," Tibby said feebly.

Did Margaret eat pizza? Did she eat anything? Margaret was terribly thin, nearly as small as a child. There were certain clues to her age: the loose skin of her neck, the texture of her blond ponytail. Tibby knew she had to be in her mid-forties. But in almost all other respects, Margaret looked just shy of puberty.

What had happened to her to make her like this? Tibby wondered. Had there been a tragedy? A loss? Was there some terrible thing that had caused her to step off the conveyor belt of life around the age of fourteen?

Or, more insidiously, had she just taken the cautious route time and time again? Had she cut off more and more potential branches of life until it had narrowed to just one?

Was Margaret scared of love? Could that be it? Had she left the building just around the time everybody else started hooking up?

Tibby looked at Margaret beseechingly. She wanted

to say or do something to make Margaret feel comfortable, but she could not figure out for the life of her what that might be.

"Do you like pasta?" Tibby asked. "I've heard it's pretty good here."

Margaret looked at her menu as though it were a devilishly tricky test. "I'm not sure," she said faintly.

"You could just get a salad," Tibby suggested. "Or if you don't like this kind of food, I totally understand."

Margaret nodded. "Maybe a salad . . ."

Tibby felt a stab of sadness, because she knew Margaret wanted to please her, too. Margaret was desperately uncomfortable, but she didn't want to let Tibby down.

Who was doing whom the favor in this exercise?

Slowly the hot air of righteousness leaked out of Tibby, and she realized what an idiot she was. She had dragged poor Margaret far out of her comfort zone, congratulating herself on doing Margaret this great charity. But Tibby wasn't giving solace to a lonely woman; she was basically torturing her. What had she been thinking?

"Maybe I don't feel like Italian food," Tibby said brightly, wanting only to offer Margaret some salvation. "Why don't we walk back by the theater and grab some ice cream and then I'll walk you to the bus stop?"

Margaret look colossally relieved, and that gave Tibby a small piece of happiness. "Sure thing."

As they walked, Tibby remembered how her uncle Fred had this line he brought out on the occasion of nearly

all family birthdays. Her parents would moan about their children growing older, and he'd say, "Growing up is for crap, but it's better than the alternative."

Well, for the first time Tibby realized there was an alternative. It was walking right next to Tibby, licking her orange Creamsicle and breaking Tibby's heart.

"He caught me again," Carmen told Lena, sipping her iced cappuccino and enjoying the air conditioning at the Starbucks on Connecticut Avenue.

"What do you mean?" Lena asked. She wasn't eating her cookie, and Carmen really wanted it.

"Win caught me in another random act of kindness at the hospital."

Lena laughed. "Busted."

"I feel like I was shoplifting or something. I didn't know what to say to explain myself."

"Did you tell him it was an accident? You didn't mean it? You'll never do it again as long as you live, so help you God?"

Carmen laughed too. "Good Carmen strikes again. What are we going to do with that girl?"

"Tie her up in the bathroom."

"Good idea."

Lena was squinting at her in thought. "Maybe you actually *are* Good Carmen. Have you ever thought of that?"

Carmen considered the way she'd knowingly polished off her mother's last coveted pint of Ben & Jerry's the night before. "Nah."

Lena still wasn't eating her cookie, so Carmen broke off a piece of it and ate it. "So guess who's sleeping on my couch tomorrow night?" Carmen asked.

"Who?"

"Paul Rodman. He's driving up from South Carolina and I convinced him to crash here. I haven't seen him in months."

Lena shifted uncomfortably in her chair.

"He asked about you."

Lena nodded timidly.

"He always does. It's the part of the conversation he actually initiates."

Lena looked down at her large feet in their large cork-bottomed flip-flops. "How's his dad?" she asked.

Carmen stopped chewing. She had been corresponding with Paul by e-mail. She got more words out of him that way. "He's not good. Paul drives hours to see him every week. It's so sad."

Lena was nodding as Carmen's cell phone rang. Carmen scratched around in the bottom reaches of her bag until she found it.

"Hey?"

"Carmen, hi. It's David."

"What's up?" Most of the warmth in her voice evaporated.

"I just wanted to thank you. The way you took care of your mother yesterday. You don't know how much it meant to her. And to me, too. I wanted to be there so bad myself and I really just can't tell you how—"

"It's fine," Carmen interrupted. "No problem."

"Really, Carmen. I really—"

"Okay." She didn't want him to keep going on about this. "Are you still in St. Louis?"

"No, I'm home," he said heavily.

Why was she annoyed at him? It wasn't his fault he worked like a dog. He had a family to provide for now. He took his responsibilities seriously. Blah blah blah.

"So I'll see you later," she said.

"Oh, Carmen—one other thing?"

"Yeah?"

"I left my phone recharger in the hotel in St. Louis. Could I borrow yours?" It was well known that they had the exact same cell phone. Sometimes it seemed like the only conversation piece between them. He had the ring that sounded like a polka. He thought it was hugely entertaining.

"Sure. It's in the outlet by my night table," she said.

"The hotel said they'd send mine back. I told them I'm going to need it."

Why were there conversations always so stilted? "Yep. You are," Carmen said. "Well, bye."

"Bye."

She hung up. When she put her phone back in her bag, she realized the recharger was coiled in the bottom of it. Oh. Oops.

Lena was squinting, trying to figure out whom Carmen was talking to. "David?" she finally guessed.

"Yeah."

"I knew it wasn't anybody you liked very much."

"I like him all right," Carmen said, the slightest petulance creeping into her voice. She sighed. "I should be nicer, shouldn't I?"

"I'm not answering that."

Carmen got a mischievous smile on her face. "I know what to do. I'll invite Win to have dinner with my mom and me and David." She laughed. "That'll set him straight."

Tibby:
Beach equipment + tunes.
No techno crap, as per discussion.

Bee and Me:
Food. A lot. Mostly high-calorie snacks with extra trans fats. (I think I like those. What are they, anyway?)

Lena:
Other household goods.
(Kleenex in addition to toilet paper, missy.)

Please make your donations ($60, and I mean cash money) to the Rehoboth Beach First Annual Precollege Dream Weekend Fund, aka Carmen's wallet.

And I mean soon, dang it.

Since Lena had heard about Paul's being in town overnight, she'd been thinking of him. Finally she got up the nerve to call him at Carmen's, and she asked him to come over. He wasn't in her family, obviously, but she felt a pressing urge to draw his picture.

She didn't want to avoid him anymore.

That afternoon, charcoal in hand, she met him at the door. She hugged him stiffly. She felt her heart jump a little at the way he looked. Older, sadder, even more handsome.

Somewhat mutely, he followed her to the kitchen.

You two are way too much alike, Carmen said about Lena and Paul and their combined inability to carry on a conversation. Carmen had had high hopes for them once.

"Do you want anything to drink?" she asked him.

He looked nervous. "No, thank you."

She gestured for him to sit down across from her at the kitchen table. She ran a hand through her hair. She'd brushed it for this occasion. "I have kind of a weird favor to ask of you," she said.

Now he really looked scared. But not unwilling. "Okay."

"Would it be all right if I drew a picture of you? It would take around an hour or an hour and a half. Just a sketch of you from here up." She indicated at her collarbone, lest he run from her house in panic. "You see, I'm making a portfolio of drawings of people, because I'm trying to win this scholarship to RISD. Otherwise, I can't go to art school, and I really want to. Do you think that would be okay?" She had never said so much to him all at one time.

He nodded. "I'd like that," he said.

She had an idea. "Maybe we'll go outside."

He followed her out to the backyard. She didn't picture him on a lounge chair by the pool or anything. She surveyed the possibilities. There was a tree stump in the far corner, by the fence. It had been a giant, beautiful oak that had grown old and gotten a disease, so her parents had had it cut down before it got the chance to fall on their house. It was strong and sturdy, suitable for Paul. She steered him to it, then ran to fetch herself a chair and her drawing board.

"You ready?" she asked.

He sat squarely. The stump was the perfect height for him. Lena's feet would have been dangling, but his rested solidly on the soil. He put his hands on his knees. This could have looked stiff for another person, but for Paul it looked right. She noticed he wore a large gold class ring on the pinky of his left hand. It was the one thing that didn't fit.

She backed up a bit. She wanted to draw more of him. "Do you mind if I do a three-quarters?"

"That's fine," he said.

She clipped her paper to her board. He watched her carefully. This caused her to clip her knuckle. It hurt, so she sucked on it for a second. She put her hair back in a ponytail. She poised the charcoal over her paper.

"Should I look at you?" he asked.

"Um. Yes," she said. Paul was always remarkably direct in his gaze, so this felt right for him. On the other

hand, she felt the pressure building as their eyes met for long moments. She didn't feel about Paul the way she did about other people.

The lines of Paul's face gave the impression of being straight and square. Strong, square jaw; square forehead; squared-off cheekbones. But when she looked harder and longer, she saw many unexpectedly round things. His eyes, for instance. They were large and circular, innocent and almost childlike. But at the outside corners she saw he had faint, fanning creases, proto–laugh lines that she suspected didn't come from laughing. And at the inside corners, the thin skin where his eyes met his nose was blue and slightly bruised-looking.

His mouth was surprisingly full and curvaceous. It was a lovely mouth. She lost herself in the very tiny up-and-down lines at each corner that separated his lips from his cheeks. You wouldn't expect such a sensitive mouth on so large and strong a person. She felt a little manic, looking at it boldly and for a long time. And then she felt guilty for taking advantage of this drawing opportunity in such a way.

She drew his shoulders and arms in big, loose gestures. When she got to his hands, she tightened up a little.

Her hand hesitated over the ring. She made herself open her mouth. "Can I ask you about the ring?" she said.

The fingers on his other hand instantly enclosed it. He looked down. It was the first time he'd broken the pose, even minutely, in almost forty minutes. "Sorry," he said, realizing this.

"That's okay. Don't worry," she said in a rush. She suddenly felt protective of him. "You can take a break. You deserve one."

"No. That's okay." He was looking down now. His neck arched gracefully and sadly. The tilt of his neck spoke so eloquently that her fingers itched to start another drawing.

It was a miracle how when you looked hard enough, when you really sought out information, there was so much to see, even in a person's tiniest gesture. There was so much feeling, such a dazzling array of things that your words, at least Lena's words, could never say. There were thousands of images and memories and ideas, if you just let them come. There was the whole history of human experience somewhere contained in each of the bits, the most universal in the most specific, if you could only see it. It was like poetry. Well, she had never really found poetry in poetry, to be truthful. But she imagined this was what poetry might be like for someone who understood it and loved it.

Either it was like poetry or it was like getting really, really stoned.

The ring was off and Paul had it cradled in his palm now. He looked at her again. "This is my father's. He went to Penn, too, so he wants me to have it."

Lena stared at him solemnly. She wondered if the swelling compassion she felt for him was finding its way out of her eyes. "He's sick. Carmen told me."

Paul nodded.

"I'm so sorry."

He was still nodding, slowing it down. "It's rough. You know?"

"I do," she said with feeling. "I mean, I don't. I do and I don't. I don't exactly, but I feel like I do. My bapi—my grandfather died last summer." Suddenly she felt a horror at her words. "Not that it's like that!" she practically shouted. "Not that that is what is going to happen!" Lena really hated herself sometimes.

Paul's expression was undeservedly kind. It was all sweet forgiveness. And even gratitude to top it off. "I know you do, Lena. I can tell you understand."

They just stared at each other, but for the first time the silence didn't feel shamefully insufficient. It felt okay.

"Do you want to take a break?" she asked him again.

"Okay," he agreed this time.

The stump was big enough for two. She sat next to him cross-legged. She leaned into him a little, and he let her. The sun shone down on them benevolently.

The corners of her drawing, where she left it in the grass, flapped gently in the breeze.

She wanted to finish it, but she didn't feel rushed. She realized she'd begun the drawing so she could tell Paul she was sorry.

Jiggle it a little

it'll open.

—Pinky and the Brain

I t was another day in the rut.

Valia had used up most of her energy IMing her friends back home. It was the one time of the day she looked alive. Now they sat in the darkened den, Carmen preparing to wage another war of attrition, with the TV as the prize.

She hadn't gotten her Ryan Hennessey fix in days. She tried to picture him. For some reason she couldn't picture him. She stood up. "Valia, we're festering. We have to get out of here."

"Ve do?"

"We do. It's a beautiful day. We need a walk."

Valia looked sleepy and cranky. "I'm vatching a show. I don't vant to valk."

"Please?" Carmen suddenly felt so desperate she didn't care about their standoff of sullenness. Let Valia win this round. "I'll do all the work. You just sit in your chair."

Valia considered. She liked being pled with. She liked her obvious power over Carmen. She shrugged. "It's too hot."

"It's not so hot today. Please?"

Valia wouldn't give Carmen the satisfaction of saying yes outright, but she looked at her wheelchair with resignation.

Carmen took the opening. Gently she heaved Valia's skinny body into her wheelchair. "Okay." Carmen checked for her keys and her money and wheeled Valia right out the door.

The sky was perfectly blue. Though it was August, the swampy deep-summer haze had momentarily lifted. It was so good to be out. Carmen walked aimlessly, letting her mind wander. She tried to look at the world through Valia's eyes, to imagine how each suburban vista looked through the eyes of an old woman who had spent her life on an Aegean island. Not so good, obviously. But when Carmen looked up and saw the sky, she knew it was the same sky. She wondered if Valia saw this lovely, azure sky and knew it was her same sky.

For some reason, a picture pushed into Carmen's mind of a restaurant she'd been to with her mom a few times. She didn't remember the name of it, but she knew exactly where it was. She pointed them in the direction of it and walked. She felt hungry all of a sudden.

At the restaurant, Carmen was pleased to see they still had tables with large white umbrellas set up outside. Red geraniums flowed from wooden boxes along the

whitewashed walls of the little terrace. Carmen had never been to Greece, but she imagined that if you just looked at a small patch of the wall or looked up at the white umbrella against the sky, maybe it would look a little like this.

She set Valia up at a table. There were no other diners.

"Vhy are ve here?" Valia demanded.

"I need a rest and I'm also kind of hungry. Do you mind?"

Valia looked annoyed but martyred. "Does it matter if I mind?"

"I'll be right back," Carmen promised.

They didn't have waiter service at the café tables, so she went to order from the counter inside. It was after lunch and before dinner, so the place was pretty deserted. She felt a bit illicit as she studied the menu. It wasn't Greek food precisely, but it was Mediterranean. She recognized a lot of the dishes from things she'd had at Lena's house. She knew the Kaligarises weren't cooking that stuff at the moment. Lena explained that her dad thought it made Valia homesick. He tried to steer her away from everything that might make her homesick. He didn't want Valia cooking, even though it was what she had done her whole life.

Carmen ordered stuffed grape leaves and something hot that strongly resembled spanakopita. She ordered an eggplant dish, a Greek salad, a few squares of baklava, and two large lemonades. She paid up and carried it all to the table, setting all the dishes between her and Valia. "I bought us a snack. I hope that's okay."

Valia gazed at it all disdainfully.

Carmen put a steaming spinach pastry on a little paper plate and handed it to Valia with a fork. "Here, try some."

Valia just sat there with it, smelling it, completely still.

Immediately, Carmen regretted her impulse, just as she ended up regretting almost all of her impulses.

Valia didn't want to be here. She was going to hate the inauthentic food. She could already hear Valia's litany of complaints.

You call this food?

What is the green mess? This is not spinach.

As the moments passed, Carmen felt worse and worse. Why did she have such stupid ideas? More than that, why did she actually carry them out?

Valia held the plate up close to her face. She looked like she was going to take a bite, and then she stopped. Carmen watched in wonderment as Valia put it down on the table and bent her head.

Valia just sat like that with her head bent for many long moments, and then Carmen saw the tears. Lines of tears bumped down Valia's wrinkly face. Carmen felt her own throat constricting. She watched as Valia's face slowly collapsed into pure sorrow.

Carmen was up and out of her chair. Without thinking, she went to Valia and put her arms around the old lady.

Valia was stiff in Carmen's arms. Carmen waited to be pushed away, or for some other signal of Valia not wanting to be hugged anymore, especially not by Carmen.

But instead, Valia's head got heavier as it sank into Carmen's neck. Carmen felt the soft, saggy skin against her collarbone. She hugged a little harder. She felt Valia's tears, damp on her neck. She realized, sort of distantly, that Valia's hand had made its way to her wrist.

How sad it was, Carmen thought, that you acted awful when you were desperately sad and hurt and wanted to be loved. How tragic then, the way everyone avoided you and tiptoed around you when you really needed them. Carmen knew this vicious predicament as well as anyone in the world. How bitter it felt when you acted badly to everyone and ended up hating yourself the most.

Carmen tenderly patted Valia's hair, surprised that for once that it wasn't she who was acting awful. It wasn't Carmen who was being needy, but rather feeling needed.

She thought about Mr. Kaligaris and all of his theories about protecting his mother. Yes, smelling Greek food made Valia sad. He was right about that. And being held by another human seemed to make her sad too. But sometimes, Carmen knew, being sad was what you had to do.

"I vant to go home," Valia croaked into Carmen's ear.

"I know," Carmen whispered back, and she understood that Valia wasn't talking about 1303 Highland Street, Bethesda, Maryland.

"Have fun with Michael." Bridget lifted her eyebrows suggestively. "But not too much fun."

As she helped Diana put her duffel bag into her car, Bridget felt a strange rolling sensation under her eye-

balls. Her head was aching and she was tired. She was happy for Diana that she was going back to Philadelphia to spend the weekend with her boyfriend, and she was sorry for herself that she was staying here.

She decided against stopping in the dining hall. Friday night dinner was one of the better meals, involving an ice cream sundae buffet where she was always happy to return for seconds and thirds. But tonight she wasn't hungry. "I gotta go to bed," she muttered to herself, trudging through the parking lot and past the equipment sheds.

The camp felt strangely empty. It was middle weekend, so the vast majority of campers went home. Only about a quarter of the staff remained to keep an eye on things.

As she pulled off her clothes and crawled under her covers, Bridget was grateful that her cabin was quiet for once. She bundled herself up as tight as she could. It was at least eighty degrees outside; why was she so cold? The tighter she bundled, the colder she felt. She was shaking. Her teeth were chattering. The more she focused on it and tried to stop, the more they chattered and clacked. Her cheeks burned.

She was getting a fever, she concluded. She meant to do something about this. Maybe she could steal a couple of Advil from Katie. She kept imagining herself doing this, without actually doing it. She passed, gradually, into a state between awake and asleep. She imagined getting another blanket. She imagined drinking a glass of water. She could not figure out whether she was doing it or not. She puzzled and tortured her brain trying to figure out

what was and wasn't real. She must have drifted like that for a long time, because it was dark when she was startled by the presence of somebody next to her.

"Bee?"

She tried to orient herself. It was Eric's face, floating near hers.

"Hi," she said softly. She didn't want to pull the blankets from around her chin, because she hated the idea of a draft reaching her hot skin.

"Are you okay?

"I'm okay," she said. Her teeth were chattering again.

He looked worried. He pressed his hand to her forehead. "God, you're hot."

She meant to laugh and make a joke about this, but she couldn't summon it. She was too tired. "I think I got the flu."

"You got something." Tenderly, almost automatically, he pushed her hair back from her forehead. It was so nice, how he did it. She felt strangely cozy and happy inside her fever.

He moved his hand to touch her flushed cheek. His hand felt remarkably cold. "Do you want to take something? Should I see if the nurse is around?" His eyes were fixed on her, full of concern.

"Don't worry, it's not a big deal." Her fatigue made her talk extra slow. "I always run high fevers. My mom used to say"—she had to take a break to work her energy back up—"I'd get to a hundred and six degrees with just a little cold." She didn't mean to sound tragic when she

said this, but she must've, because Eric looked distraught. He knew about her mother. She had told him almost the first time they'd met.

"I'm not sure if the nurse is here, but I'm going to get you something. Do you take Tylenol or Motrin or something like that?"

"Anything," she said.

"I'll be right back. Don't go anywhere, okay? Promise?"

She coughed up a tiny laugh. "That I can promise."

"You have to let Valia go home," Carmen said to Ari, following her into the Kaligarises' kitchen.

First she'd had to get Lena's blessing. Then it had taken Carmen two days to get Ari alone in a room, but Carmen was nothing if she wasn't dogged.

Ari put the mail down on the kitchen counter and turned to Carmen in surprise. "I'm sorry?" Ari's eyes were large and lovely like Lena's, but dark and indefinable, where Lena's were fair, green, and fragile.

"I know it's none of my business," Carmen backtracked, "and I know you and Mr. Kaligaris probably don't want to hear my opinion." Carmen always called Ari Ari and she always called Mr. Kaligaris Mr. Kaligaris. She couldn't remember a time when it was different.

Ari nodded slightly, inviting her to pursue that unwanted opinion.

"I really think that you and Mr. Kaligaris should let Valia go back to Greece." Tears welled in Carmen's eyes,

219

and she felt so annoyed by her ready-to-wear emotions. "She's dying here."

Ari sighed heavily and rubbed her eyes with the backs of her hands. At least this wasn't entirely news to her. "How can Valia take care of herself? Especially now, with her knee? Who is going to look out for her if not us?" She didn't sound like she was voicing her own conviction, but more like she was reciting somebody else's.

"Her friends? She has her friends, and they are like her family. I can understand that. The only time I've ever seen her look happy is when she's IMing Rena." Carmen kneaded her hands, sort of amazed to hear herself take on Ari like another adult. "Valia is too depressed to get herself a glass of water, but I swear she could have programmed the computer herself if it meant making a connection to home."

Ari looked at her, pained and tired, but with tenderness, too.

Couldn't Ari see that Valia wasn't the only one suffering? Carmen had never seen Ari so tense, and Mr. Kaligaris hadn't always been as angry and rigid as he was now. Couldn't Ari see the toll it took not only on her, but also on her daughters?

Carmen knew she wouldn't have been able to have this conversation if Mr. Kaligaris were here. But she trusted Ari to love her. Ultimately she trusted Ari to read her good intentions and, hopefully, the truth.

"Carmen, sweetheart, I'm not saying you aren't right. I appreciate what you're trying to do. But it's compli-

cated. Really, how can Valia go back to that house she shared with Bapi for fifty-seven years? How could she tolerate the pain of living there without him? Sometimes change is the right thing."

Carmen couldn't help looking sour. She was no friend of change. "I know that. I know being back in her house on the island will make her sad. Of course she'll be sad. But that's her home. That's her life. She can handle being sad. I'm sure of that. What she can't handle is being here."

There was that law of life, so cruel and so just, that one must grow or else pay more for remaining the same.

—Norman Mailer

Tibby couldn't fall asleep. She sat in her bed and looked out the window at the hazardous apple tree. The apples were growing plump and red now. How had she never even tried one?

She associated them with having fallen, that was part of it. She could viscerally recall the smell of the over-sweet, rotting, fermenting apples from seasons past that fell without ever being picked. That smell and the sight of the marauding worms and beetles nauseated her. She loathed the apples wounded on the ground, but she had never thought to pick one from a branch.

The tree seemed to be considering her just as she considered it. She felt its judgment. It wasn't judging her for leaving the window open. That wasn't her crime. Her crimes were deeper and more numerous: She wasn't big enough to love Katherine as Katherine deserved. She wasn't brave enough to love Brian as he deserved. She wasn't strong enough to keep the things she loved alive

(Bailey, Mimi), nor was she wise enough to grasp the meaning of their deaths.

Tibby was good at hiding. It was the one thing she knew how to do. She was good at sealing herself in a little box and waiting it out. But waiting for what? What was she waiting for?

She thought she'd learned a lesson from Katherine's fall out the window. The lesson was: Don't open, don't climb, don't reach, and you will not fall. But it was the wrong lesson! She had learned the wrong lesson!

The real lesson embodied in Katherine's three-year-old frame was the opposite: Try, reach, want, and you may fall. But even if you do, you might be okay anyway.

Flexing her feet under the covers, Tibby thought of a corollary to this lesson: If you don't try, you save nothing, because you might as well be dead.

Time passed for Bridget in the strangest way, a little forward, a little back. She was vaguely aware of Katie and Allison returning to the cabin. They probably assumed she was asleep, but that didn't stop them from flipping on the light and gabbing noisily and turning on music. She suspected they'd been partying with the other remaining staff. They smelled like it, anyway.

Sometime after that, Eric returned. He sized up the situation with Katie and Allison. He was furious. "Can't you see that Bee is sick? Why are you making all this noise? What the hell's wrong with you?"

Even through her haze, Bridget could tell this was not a side of Eric she'd seen before.

"Dude. Back off," Katie snapped. "Why are you barging into our cabin and telling us what to do?" She was too drunk to yield her ground, even if Bee was sick.

Eric knelt next to Bridget. He put his hand on her forehead again. He bent down close to her ear. "I don't really want to leave you in here with the two of them. You want to come back with me? My cabin is empty this weekend. You can sleep."

She nodded gratefully. She was only wondering how she was going to get from here to there without freezing to death. She wasn't wearing anything but her underwear under the blankets.

He had an idea for that, too. He put his arms under her and scooped her up, still tucked inside her blankets. He carried her out of the cabin and into the night, with Katie and Allison watching his back in surprise and indignation.

She felt light in his arms. She rested her burning face against his neck. She was shivering again. He pulled the blankets closer around her and rested his chin lightly on the top of her head.

She was trying her hardest to remember each of these things he did, to mark them in her brain permanently, because they were immeasurably sweet. Maybe they were the sweetest things that had ever happened to her or ever would. She kept hoping that this, unlike all those blankets she imagined getting and glasses of water she

imagined drinking, that this was real. *Please let it be real*, she thought wistfully. *And if it's not, let me just stay here anyway.*

He pushed open the door of his cabin with his back and put her very gently into a bed—his bed, she hoped. She wanted to smell his smell. He was careful to tuck her blankets around her snugly. She tried to stop shivering.

"I'd put another blanket on you, but I don't want you to get overheated, you know?"

She nodded. She noticed he'd been carrying a bag, also, looped around his wrist. "Here." He unloaded a bottle of Advil, a bottle of aspirin, a bottle of water, a bottle of orange juice, a thermometer, and a paper cup. "The nurse isn't back till Sunday, but I got into the infirmary in case we need anything else."

She fluttered her eyes, trying to focus on his solemn face. "It was unlocked?"

He shrugged. "Now it is."

He filled the cup with water and poured two pills into his palm. "Ready?" He helped her to sit up in bed.

She tried to figure out how to get her hand out without letting any cold air in. She stuck her hand out up by her neck, keeping the rest of the blanket tight around her. She thirstily drank the water and another cup and another with her little T. rex arm.

"Poor thing. You were thirsty," he said.

She took the pills, wincing as they went down. Her throat felt swollen.

"Thank you," she said, lying back down. She felt tears fill her eyes at the extravagance of his kindness to her.

He put his cool hand on her cheek again. "I am worried about you," he said quietly. And looking at his face, she could never again question whether they had really become friends.

He took the thermometer out of its case. "Open up."

"Are you sure you want to know?" she asked. She knew she was hot.

He nodded, so she opened her mouth. He waited for the mercury to settle. It didn't take very long. He studied it with his eyebrows furrowed. "God, it's 104.7. Is that safe?"

"I've been there before," she said faintly. Why did she have to do everything in such dramatic fashion?

"Should I call a doctor?" he asked.

"I think I'm going to be okay," she answered truthfully. "I'm not scared or anything."

He lay on the bed opposite her, propped on his side, watching her carefully.

"I'm going to call your dad," he announced, sitting up. He got his cell phone from the top drawer of his bureau.

"Don't call my dad," she said softly. "He's not . . . there."

"It's midnight. Where would he be?"

"No. I mean." She took a break. "He's just not there. In that way." She was too tired to explain any better.

He looked at her, the corners of his mouth turned down. He looked deeply troubled about that.

He lay down across from her again.

The more she wanted to stop shivering, the more she shivered. She didn't want him to worry about her.

He couldn't stand to watch her shake. He got up and came over to her. He picked her up inside her ball of covers and moved her over on the bed. To her great astonishment and joy, he lay down alongside her. He put his arms around her and tucked her face into his neck, and she felt as though her fevered heart might burst.

He held her as though he thought he could absorb her fever and her sickness and her sadness at not having a mother or even a father she could count on. He stroked her hair and lay with her like that for hours.

And maybe he did absorb her ache, because in his arms she finally fell asleep.

By four A.M., daylight was beginning to haunt the sky. Tibby did not want the sun to rise without some real measure of awakening.

After these hours she felt as though she knew the tree in a new way and the tree knew her. It wasn't an unfriendly tree, but it did pose a challenge to her.

Somewhere around two o'clock, Tibby had remembered she had the Traveling Pants. They had been sitting for a shameful number of days under her bed. She'd been hiding from them. Somewhere around three, she put them on.

She hoisted up the window sash and sat with her elbows on the sill, resting her chin in her hands. The tree waved. Katherine had thought she could reach it from

the window but, in fact, she couldn't. Tibby could reach it but thought she couldn't. Tibby's mother's ovaries seemed to produce a heartier strain of egg as they got older.

Tibby put one foot out the window and then the other. She sat on the sill. She looked down. It was far. She would feel incredibly stupid if she fell. She and Katherine could wear matching hockey helmets. Tibby smiled in spite of herself, knowing what a huge kick that would give Katherine. She wondered if Nicky would be similarly willing to help with the stickers.

Tibby caught a sturdy branch with two hands and held it tight. She knew just where she needed to put her feet. She tried to figure out how to do it so that her weight would not at any time be up for grabs. Then she remembered that this was kind of the point.

When she hoisted herself off the window, she would have to transfer her weight completely to her hands for a second or two until she could place her feet. She would just have to do that.

Okay.

Yes.

Like, now.

Tibby looked at the ground. She could already see a couple of wormy apples languishing in the dark grass. The ground was psyching her out, so she looked at the sky.

She lifted; she swung. She actually screamed in that moment. But before her scream had gotten all the way

out of her mouth, her feet were on the lower branch. She was balanced. She was safe.

She passed herself down slowly, branch by branch. She had a bit of the monkey in her after all. She hung from a low branch by both hands, skimming above the ground with her feet. Then she let go.

The fall was small, but it was grand. Her hands hurt like crazy. Her whole body was shaking with nervousness and pleasure. Her chest was so full she could barely fit a breath into it. She felt like she was living someone else's life.

She crept around the house to let herself in the front door. Before she even turned the knob, she realized it would be locked. And so would the back door. And so would the side door. She was locked out of her house.

This struck her as so unbearably funny that she rolled around on the grass and laughed until she cried.

Sometime toward morning, Bridget's fever broke. As dramatically as it had gone up, it came down. She was hardly aware of what was happening when the air around her suddenly turned from bone-cold to sweltering hot. The sweat seemed to pour from every inch of her skin. When she awoke with a start, she realized she had thrown off all her covers in her sleep. More alarmingly, she was lying in her underwear, still circled in the arms of Eric's sleeping body. Now she was afraid to move. Whether Bee was sick or not, this would not look good to Kaya, for example. She didn't want Eric to wake up and see how it was.

She thought she could very carefully untangle the sheet from the bottom of the bed and cover herself with it before he woke up. She was feeling remarkably lucid as she grasped the edge of the sheet between the first and second toes of her left foot. Moving as slowly and smoothly as she could, she pulled her foot toward her.

How funny and strange that she and Eric had slept in the same space twice in less than two weeks. And not for having chosen it. Not for having wanted to sleep together at all. (Well, maybe she did . . . but no longer at his expense.)

In a way it was a tragic waste, and in a more profound way it was the most romantic thing she had ever experienced. Two years before, they had slept together in the figurative sense; this summer, in the literal one. The former had split her in two. And the latter made her feel whole. The first summer had made her feel abandoned. This made her feel loved.

Sex could be a blissful communion. But it could also be a weapon, and its absence, sometimes, was required for the establishment of peace.

Eric shifted and she halted her foot abruptly. Still asleep, he pulled her closer, so her whole self was pressed against him, his arms and chest against her bare skin. He sighed. He probably dreamed she was Kaya. She also dreamed she was Kaya, the one he truly loved.

Bridget wanted to enjoy this, but she couldn't. She couldn't bear to think of him waking up and feeling embarrassed and compromised after he had cared for her with

such perfect kindness. She wanted to protect him from that.

She waited until his breathing sank into a rhythm again, and she started back up with the sheet. Morning was almost fully upon them, and the sun was streaming through the window, illuminating their twined bodies. *Don't wake up yet*, she begged him.

She had gotten the sheet almost up to her thighs when he awoke. *Oh.*

For a moment, in that transition, he clung to her hard. And then, in stages, he seemed to recognize the yellow hair spread over his arms and to realize who it was he held like that. Confused, he looked at her full on, at the two of them together, and then he looked away.

"I'm sorry," he muttered, pulling his arms from her.

How she missed them. She pulled the sheet up over herself. The bedding under her was soaked with sweat. "Please don't say that," she said.

Bridget had always believed that the night was more dangerous than the day. But in the preceding twelve hours, her conviction had reversed itself. The night protected her and the morning laid her bare.

"I didn't mean . . . ," he began, flustered.

"I know," she said quickly.

He couldn't look at her anymore. "Are you feeling . . . ?"

"So much better," she supplied.

He was up on his feet, turned away from her. "I . . . uh, I'll let you get dressed. Grab anything you want of mine. T-shirt or whatever." He pulled a pair of shorts over his boxers.

There were so many things she wanted to say to him. So many shades of the words *thank you*. So many routes to get to an apprehension of love. Not *that* kind of love. This kind of love. Any kind of love, really.

She wanted to say these things to him, to make him understand her feelings and also to make him know that though this thing between them was fragile and strange (she knew, she really knew it was!), he was safe.

But it was too late. He was already gone.

This "telephone" has too many shortcomings to be seriously considered as a means of communication. The device is inherently of no value to us.

—Western union internal memo. 1876

"Mom?" Carmen strode into her mother's room and toward the closed door of her bathroom. "Hey, are you okay in there?"

Carmen was nervous to begin with because her mom had stayed home from work, explaining she was a little under the weather. Carmen had made her scrambled eggs for breakfast and Christina had only picked at them.

Christina had been in there a long time. Carmen heard a moan and then nothing.

"Mama?" She knocked on the bathroom door. "Is everything all right?" She felt her heart pounding. When her mother opened the door a moment later, her face was white.

"Mama! What's going on?"

Even Christina's lips were white. "I think . . . I'm not sure . . ." She put her hand on the doorframe to steady herself. "I think my water broke."

"You . . . you . . . you do?" Carmen felt like she'd been transported to one of those old-fashioned movies where

the wife goes into labor, only in this version, Carmen was the bumbling husband.

"I think so."

"Does that mean . . . ?"

Christina transferred both hands to her spherical stomach. "I don't know. I don't feel like I'm in labor."

"It's too early!" Carmen shouted at her mother's stomach, as though the baby should know better. "The baby isn't due for four more weeks!"

"*Nena*, sweetie, I know."

"Should I call the hospital?"

"I'll call my midwife," Christina said. She walked slowly toward the phone.

"Do you . . . feel okay?" Carmen asked, watching her mother call.

"I feel like I'm . . . leaking." Christina pushed a button and waited. She waited longer while the receptionist paged her midwife.

Carmen paced while Christina alternately talked and listened. When she hung up she looked scared, and that pushed Carmen's heart from a trot to a canter. "What?"

Christina's eyes were teary. "I have to go to the hospital to get checked. If my water really broke, I have twelve hours to go into labor naturally and after that they induce. The fear of me getting an infection is bigger than worrying about the baby being early."

"So the baby is coming . . ."

"Yes. Soon," Christina said faintly.

"Where is David?" Carmen asked. It was obviously the thing Christina was thinking about.

"He's, uh . . . he's . . ." Christina put her hands over her face. She was trying not to cry, and that made Carmen feel worse. "I'm trying to think. . . . He's been away so much. I think he's in Trenton, New Jersey. Maybe he's in Philadelphia now. I'm not sure."

"We'll find him!" Carmen shouted, further alarming them both. "We'll call him!"

"First we'll go to the hospital, okay? The midwife said go right over."

Carmen's hands were clammy and she raced around ineffectively. "Have you got your bag? I'll drive."

Once in the car, Carmen watched her mother intently.

"*Nena*, honey, keep your eyes on the road. I'm okay."

"Are you having . . ." Carmen wasn't sure what the right terminology was, having diligently tuned it out most of the summer. ". . . labor?"

Christina kept her hands on her stomach, her eyes vague, as though she were feeling for some message tapped in Morse code from within. "No. I don't think so."

"Does anything hurt?" Carmen asked.

"Not really. My back is cramping, but it's just uncomfortable. Not really painful."

Once they were at the hospital and Carmen had landed her mother with a resident to get checked out in an examining room on the labor and delivery floor, she called David's cell phone. It went right to his voice mail without even ringing. That wasn't a great sign. She left a

message for him. She meant to sound calm, mature, and informative, but as soon as she hung up she knew she sounded more like semihysterical.

She shot up at the sight of her mother's face, at the door of the waiting room.

"What?" Carmen said softy, inwardly screaming at herself to be calm.

"My water did break," Christina said. She looked overwhelmed. Her voice was quiet and she was clearly scared.

"Okay."

"I'm not in labor, though."

"That's good, right?"

"Yes."

"So now what? We go home?"

"I have to stay here," Christina said. "They want to keep an eye on me until eight tonight. Then they'll induce."

"Induce means like . . ."

"They give you chemicals to make you go into labor."

Carmen nodded solemnly.

"But I told them we can't do it until . . . I can't have the baby until . . ." Carmen watched in agony as the tears brewed in Christina's eyes. "I can't do it until David gets here." The tears spilled over, and Carmen pulled her mother into her arms. Christina let herself cry for real, and Carmen wondered if this had ever happened before in her whole life.

Christina always took her mothering so seriously, she

hardly ever let herself cry or act scared in front of Carmen. Carmen felt scared too, but at the same time she felt grown-up. She felt proud that her mother was letting Carmen take care of her this time.

Holding her mother, Carmen wanted, really wanted, to be brave this time.

"I'm going to go get David," Carmen promised her. "I'm going to get him and bring him home so you can have the baby together, okay?"

Carmen sat in the hospital lobby trying to calculate. The timing was bad on almost every front. Grandma Carmen, Christina's mother, was still in Puerto Rico with her aunt. Everybody, David included, was getting travel engagements out of the way in time for when the baby arrived. But the baby apparently had little consideration for anyone else's plans. Carmen was beginning to wonder if this baby was going to have a few things in common with its big sister.

Carmen couldn't leave her mother alone while she got David. It could take a while. Her mother was not yet in labor, true, but who wanted to sit in the hospital without someone who loved you?

The thing to do was call one of the people Carmen trusted most in the world. Of those three, Bee was out of town, and Carmen had misgivings about Tibby and hospitals. She called Lena. Lena didn't answer her regular phone or her cell. Not surprising, since she often didn't carry the cell. Carmen didn't feel like leaving another

crazy-girl message. She called Tibby. By some act of fate, Tibby picked up after the first ring.

"Can you come to the hospital?" Carmen begged, her voice runny with tears. "My mom's water broke, and David is out of town, and I have to find him before my mom's doctor gives her medicine to get the labor going. Can you keep her company until I get back?"

"Yes," Tibby said instantly. "I'll be there in a minute."

"Keep your cell with you, okay? I'll call."

"Okay."

They both hung up.

Carmen's call came not long after Tibby woke up. It had been a long night. It was tiring, after all, staying up till dawn watching a tree, climbing down that tree, and then getting locked out of your house for a few hours and not getting into bed until after seven in the morning. It was. Ask anybody.

And it was surreal sitting in a chair next to Carmen's mother on a bed in a labor room at the hospital listening to the fetal monitor bleep. It was made even more so on three and a half hours of sleep.

Tibby wondered at the mountain that was Christina's belly. She remembered pretty well her own mother's pregnancies with Nicky and then Katherine. She was thirteen for the first and almost fifteen for the second. She hadn't found the whole thing at all amusing at the time.

But fear not, she reminded herself and, silently, Christina. *We at the Tibby Corporation have a new policy*

toward younger siblings and even babies generally. We like them and like for them to be safe. We even admit that we love them, though not more often than is necessary.

"How are you feeling?" Tibby asked. She somehow felt that, much as she cared about Christina, she wasn't the best person for this job.

"Just fine," Christina said, through a mouth that was tense. Her eyes were distracted.

"Are you sure?" Suddenly Christina was doubled over.

"I think so," Christina said grittily, clenching her jaw.

Tibby was on her feet and fluttering nervously. "Should I . . . get the midwife, do you think?"

"I — I don't . . ."

Christina couldn't talk, which said to Tibby she should get the midwife.

The midwife, Lauren was her name, was filling out papers at the nurses' station. "Uh, Lauren? I think Christina is maybe having some trouble."

Lauren looked up. "What kind of trouble?"

Tibby raised her palms skyward. She was not a doctor. She was not a nurse. She wasn't a mother or anybody's husband. She couldn't even vote yet. "I don't know," she said.

Lauren followed her into Christina's room. "Are you having contractions?" she asked Christina.

Christina sat up holding her stomach. "I'm not sure."

Lauren looked at the paper spooling out of the monitor. "You, my dear, are having contractions."

"But I'm not in labor." Christina said it half as a statement and half as a question.

"I would say you are in labor."

"But it's too early," Christina said. Her eyes weren't focusing quite right. "I thought tonight—"

"Tonight we'd induce if you didn't go into labor naturally. You are going into labor naturally from what I can see."

"But David and . . ." Christina closed her eyes and put her chin to her chest.

"Another one, right?" Lauren said. "You're getting into a pattern—every seven minutes or so. Let me check your cervix, okay? Lie back and open your legs."

Tibby did not like the sound of this. She floated toward the door.

Lauren was one of those plain-faced, plainspoken people who liked to say and do embarrassing things as flatly and as often as possible. Like Tibby's eighth grade health science teacher, who said the words *breast* and *anus* so often you'd think she'd never heard of pronouns.

Tibby loitered in the hallway until Lauren appeared at the door. "She's at three centimeters," Lauren announced.

"I don't know what that means," Tibby said.

"It means her cervix is opening. That's what happens when you're in labor. When her cervix is all the way open—that's ten centimeters—she'll be ready to push the baby out."

Tibby had one more question and Lauren couldn't very well answer it for her: *How did I get here?*

"How long will that take?" Tibby asked.

"Hard to say for sure, but it's still early labor. It'll probably be a few hours at least."

242

Tibby hoped, really and truly hoped, that Carmen and David would be back by then.

Lauren was looking at Tibby seriously. She actually had very pretty brown eyes. Her no-nonsense look was countered by a streak of dark purple liner under her eyelashes.

"Tibby, you need to get in there with her. She's a little freaked out. She could use some support." Lauren turned to go.

"Um, excuse me," Tibby said politely, "but I am, uh, Christina's daughter's friend, if you see what I mean?"

Lauren shrugged. "Yeah. But you're who she's got right now."

Frantically Carmen called David's cell phone again and got his voice mail again. She paced up and down the sidewalk at the entrance to the hospital. She called Irene, David's secretary, and got *her* voice mail. Why did important things have to happen at lunchtime? She called the family number at Lena's house and barked out a message that she couldn't come for Valia today. Somewhat hopelessly, she called David's cell phone again and hung up on his voice mail. She threw her bag on the sidewalk.

"Carmen?"

She turned around and saw Win. Of course it was him. He took in her general dishevelment and her teary eyes. "Are you okay?"

"My mom's about to have a baby and I can't find her husband," Carmen burst forth. "Her water broke and the

baby isn't supposed to be born for a month. But now they want her to have the baby tonight so she doesn't get some kind of an infection."

Carmen couldn't quite believe she was talking particulars about her mother's amniotic fluid with a boy on whom she had a crush. But she was scared and she wanted to do the right thing and she didn't even know how to do it. Win's concern was so apparent it was heart-rending. "I promised her I'd find David."

"Her husband?"

"Yeah."

"Do you have any idea where he is?" Win asked.

"He's been traveling a lot for work," Carmen explained balefully. She was walking in a tighter and tighter circle until she was basically spinning on the sidewalk. "We weren't on high alert yet, because the baby wasn't due yet. I have to find him right now!" Her voice was climbing, tinged with hysteria.

"Okay. Okay. Does he have a cell phone?"

"It's not even ringing! He might be on a plane or something." Or it might have run out of batteries, and someone who offered to lend him her recharger might not have done so, she added miserably to herself.

"You tried his office?" Carmen appreciated how much he wanted to help her. He was a good person.

"His secretary was at lunch. I'm going to drive over there," Carmen muttered. "What else can I do?"

"Can I come?" Win looked intent.

"You want to?"

"Yeah."

She was now running toward her car and he was following her, stride for stride. "Can you get out of work?"

"I'm on lunch break. I'm done with pediatrics for today and the old folks can do without my antics and my pocket change for one afternoon."

"You're sure?"

He looked at her as seriously as if she'd asked him to plunge to the bottom of the Atlantic Ocean with her. "I'm sure. I'm sure I'm sure."

Carmen drove. She felt like Starsky and Hutch as they pulled up to the curb and leaped out of the car. He followed her to the elevator and then to the reception desk.

Mrs. Barrie greeted Carmen warmly, and Carmen explained where she was going without breaking her gait. Christina had worked at this same law firm since Carmen was a toddler. Carmen knew her way around the place.

Carmen and Win staked out Irene's desk, and thankfully, she returned from lunch ten minutes later. "What can I do for you, Carmen?" Irene asked, looking confused. Carmen wore a bandana on her head, do-rag style, and her feet were in flip-flops.

"We need to find David." Carmen's intensity was such that Irene seemed to shrink back from her own cubicle. "I think my mom's gonna have the baby soon," Carmen explained, "but don't tell anybody anything yet."

Irene, good soul that she was, got right with the program.

"Oh, my." Briskly she pulled up the calendar on her computer. Her long fingernails clickety-clicked on the keys until she got to the right day. "Your poor mother. We'll find him."

Carmen sometimes got the feeling that everybody rooted for her mother. She was probably like a poster girl for legal secretaries. She'd won the respect and ardor of a handsome young lawyer without even meaning to.

"He has a meeting in Trenton this afternoon. He's renting a car there and driving to Philadelphia. He's supposed to stay in a hotel in Philly tonight. He has a meeting scheduled there tomorrow morning and then he comes home. And wait." She studied her notes a little more closely. "He told me he was hoping to stop off and visit his mother in Downingtown on his way to Philly."

Carmen was thinking. "Do you know the number of the meeting place in Trenton?"

"Yes." Irene looked it up and called it. She went through several people and several bits and pieces of conversation before she hung up. "He left already."

"Oh." Carmen chewed her thumbnail. "How about the car rental place?"

"Yes." Irene called them, too. She listened for a bit and put her hand over the receiver. "He rented the car and left about twenty-five minutes ago."

"Shit," Carmen mumbled. She walked in a small circle. She realized Win was watching her carefully. But she was too preoccupied to be self-conscious or even to consider all the ways in which she was diverging from Good Carmen.

"Do you have David's mother's number?"

Irene winced. "I don't think I do." She riffled through her Rolodex and then scrolled through her computerized version. "No, I'm sorry."

"The address?" Carmen asked without much hope.

Irene shook her head. "I don't know David's step-father's name, do you?"

Carmen should have known it. She had certainly heard it before. But in her efforts to tune out most of the things David said, she'd tuned out this potentially helpful bit of information.

"We should leave a message at the hotel in Philadelphia just in case," Win suggested.

Irene nodded and did it. "He hasn't checked in yet, but they'll have him call as soon as he does."

Carmen's brain was working fast. "Can you call the rental car company again?" she asked.

Irene did it without asking questions. Carmen held out her hand for the phone. "Can I talk?"

"Sure." Irene handed it over.

Carmen talked to a representative for a few minutes. As soon as she hung up she looked at Win and Irene brightly. "I have something. They can't get hold of David in his car, but they can tell us where the car is."

"Really?" Win looked impressed.

"Yeah. And like I always say, thank the Lord for satel-lite systems." She laughed at herself. "I don't really go around saying that."

Win smiled at her, also clearly relieved that they had a lead. "How far is Downingtown?" he asked.

Irene shrugged. "I think about an hour and a half."

Win and Carmen looked at each other. "So let's go," Win said.

"You think so?" Carmen asked, suddenly nervous about the extent to which she'd embroiled an innocent guy in her drama. "You sure you want to come with me?"

His eyes told her she should take this for granted. "I'm sure I want to come with you."

Of course she found it in

the last place she looked.

If she hadn't found it,

she'd still be looking.

—Susannah Brown

Lena walked into her father's study with expectations so low, she would have been happily surprised if he'd taken a paperweight from his desk and thrown it at her.

He was thumbing through a stack of papers on his desk. He was listening to Paul Simon. It was one of about three CDs he ever listened to, and he always struck Lena as slightly tin-eared and immigrant in his appreciation. The song was perky and polished, something about a camera that took bright color pictures. To Lena the song was like an A-plus paper, a math problem where you showed your work, a form fully filled out. But it didn't sound to her like music. She liked her colors dingier.

Her father looked up at her over his half-glasses. He turned the music off.

"Do you mind if I make a drawing of you?" Lena had practiced saying this in her head so many times, the words had long ago lost their ordinary feel and had begun to taste funny in her mouth.

He waved her to the empty seat across from his desk. He was prepared for this. Lena's mother had no doubt warned and mollified him.

Lena's paper was already clipped to her drawing board and her charcoal was squeezed into her clammy hand. She hadn't come in willing to take no for an answer. She sat down. "You don't need to do anything special." She'd practiced saying that, too.

He nodded absently. He didn't need to be asked twice. He was already back to his papers. But she noticed he kept his face angled straighter now, only his eyes cast down. The lenses of his glasses glinted, but his eyes within them appeared shut from where she sat.

She watched him for a long time before she began to draw. She made herself do this. She didn't care if it made him uncomfortable.

For a while she saw what she expected. She could have drawn his angry face with not only his eyes closed but with hers closed too. This was how she pictured him, and this is how he looked. She saw what she felt, and what she felt was his anger. She had certainly suffered for it. Why else was she here?

She knew what she felt. But what did she see?

She began to wonder. With drawing, you were always pitting your feelings and expectations against what the cold light offered your optic nerves. Like the first time you tried to mix colors to paint water. You thought you'd be using a lot of blue and maybe green. But if you made yourself see, you ended up with a lot more gray and

brown and white, and even weird unexpected colors like yellow and red. And if you tried to paint it again, it would all be different. You couldn't paint the same water twice.

She remembered once standing with her mother on a street corner in Georgetown and watching a painter at work. Her mother let her watch for a long time, and as they were walking away, Lena remembered asking how come he used so much brown.

As a child, you were taught to see the world in geometric shapes and primary colors. It was as if the adults needed to equip you with more accomplishments. ("Lena already knows her colors!") Then you had to spend the rest of your life unlearning them. That was life, as near as Lena could tell. Making everything simple for the first ten years, which in turn made everything way more complicated for the subsequent seventy.

And now her feelings about her father made a mask over his actual features. She had thought that her challenge would be to paint his anger, to confront it. But now she knew that wasn't the challenging thing. The challenging thing was to see past it.

She stared at him without blinking until her eyeballs dried and her vision blurred. She wished she could turn her father upside down. Sometimes you could see things more truly when you forfeited your normal visual relationship with them. Sometimes your preexisting ideas were so powerful they clubbed the truth dead before you could realize it was there. Sometimes you had to let the truth catch you by surprise.

Lena looked away and closed her eyes. She opened them and looked back at her father's face, but only for a second. It could catch you by surprise, or maybe, if you were bold, you could catch it.

She turned away, and then turned back for a little longer. She was seeing more now. She was holding on to something. She took a deep breath, carefully keeping herself in this other visual dimension. This place where she saw but didn't feel.

Her hand was finally connecting charcoal to paper. She let it fly. She didn't want to bog it down with thinking.

Her father's face was no more to her than a topographical map. The mouth was a series of shapes, nothing more. The downturned eyes were shadings of darkness and light. She stayed there a good, long time. She was careful not to blink too hard or too long for fear that this new way of seeing would abandon her.

She wasn't afraid of him anymore. The scared part of her was waiting out by the mouth of the cave; the rest of her had gone in.

She saw something in her father's mouth. A little tick. Another tick, and then a sag.

She wasn't scared anymore, but was he?

The trick of drawing was leaving your feelings out, giving them the brutal boot. The deeper trick of drawing was inviting them back in, making nice with them at exactly the right moment, after you were sure your eyes really were working. Fighting and making up.

And so her feelings were coming back in, but they were a

different kind this time. They were guided by her eyes, rather than the other way around. Tentatively, she let them come. A good drawing was a record of your visual experience, but a beautiful drawing was a record of your feelings about that visual experience. You had to let them come back.

She saw her father's fear, and it so surprised her, she could barely contemplate it. What was he afraid of?

She could imagine if she tried. He was afraid of her disobedience. He was afraid of her independence. He was afraid of her growing up and not being the kind of girl he could feel proud of—or the kind of girl Bapi would be proud of. He was afraid of being old and powerless. He was afraid she would see his vulnerability. But also, she suspected, he wanted her to see it.

She felt her fingers softening around the charcoal. Her lines got looser. She felt sad and moved by these things she saw in his face. She didn't want to make it hard for him to love her. But at the same time, she couldn't deny who she was to make it easy.

Her fingers were flying. The muscles in her father's neck quivered slightly with the great effort of holding still for her. He was trying. He really was.

That moved her too.

After almost two hours she set him free. "Thank you," she said earnestly.

He pretended he didn't notice so much.

She held the drawing board facing out as she left, so he could peek at the results if he wanted to. He didn't peek.

But later that night, when she was going to bed, she

251

tiptoed past the kitchen, where she'd left her drawing of him propped on a chair. He stood alone in the quiet room. And even though she just saw his back, she knew he was looking.

Win offered to take the wheel so Carmen could work the phone. Half an hour into the drive they had to stop for gas. He bought two Cokes and a bag of Corn Nuts. Carmen had never had Corn Nuts before, and she loved them. They could barely hear each other over the crunching, so they found themselves shouting, which they both thought was incredibly funny once they realized it. The laughter made Carmen's eyes start running again, and the salt made her lips burn.

She was tired and punchy and worried and also happy that they were driving toward David and doing everything they could.

By her calculation they had four hours to find David and get back to her mom. He was only an hour away now. It would work. It had to work. She felt confident that Tibby could keep her mom company for the waiting part, and David and Carmen would be there in time for the inducing part, when the real drama started.

Win was a good driver. He was confident and sharp about it, and yet effortless too. For some reason, the look of his hands on the wheel (at ten and two—Valia would have approved) struck her as masculine and even sexy.

Furthermore, he had an excellent profile. Not a Ryan Hennessey profile exactly—Win's nose was a tiny bit

crooked, and his upper lip went out a little farther than his bottom one. But on him, it worked. It was fun how you could get away with watching someone when they drove. He concentrated on the road, and she braved a full look at him.

They barely knew each other, and yet they always had a project together. It was the opposite of most of her romantic relationships, which were all form and no content. Carmen was infamous for writing out talking points to use with the boys she dated. She never searched for things to say to Win.

"You're close to your mother, huh?" he asked her thoughtfully.

"Yes." It was the Good Carmen answer instead of the Whole Carmen answer. "What about you?"

"I'm close to both my parents," he said. "I'm the only one, so it gets intense sometimes."

"Me too," Carmen chimed in. Then she remembered. "Until today, I guess."

"Pretty strange, becoming a sister at the age of . . . how old are you?"

"Seventeen," Carmen said.

"Seventeen," he echoed.

"Almost eighteen. And you?" she asked. These were questions they could have gotten out of the way on an awkward date two months ago, but somehow they hadn't.

"Nineteen."

"And yeah, it is strange. Stranger than I can say."

"I had a sibling for a short while." He tried to say it lightly and conversationally, but it didn't come out that way.

"What do you mean?" Carmen wanted to know, but she didn't want to demand anything. "I mean, if you want to tell me."

"I had a little brother. He was born when I was five and he died just before I turned six."

"Oh." Carmen's tears were so near the surface these days, even a fourteen-year-old tragedy concerning a person she didn't really know called them up. "I'm so sorry."

"It was a long time ago. But he is part of my identity, you know?"

She didn't know, but she could try to guess. She nodded.

"I still think about him sometimes. I dream about him too. I try to remember what he looked like. It's hard to remember, though, either because of time or because of strong feelings. I sometimes think the stronger you feel about someone, the harder it is to picture their face when you are away from them."

Carmen's tears were falling now, and she tried to hide them from Win. He would interpret her tears as belonging to Good Carmen. He would think she was crying selflessly, for him and his family's pain. Whereas Bad Carmen was crying because Win had spent a lifetime missing a baby who'd been lost, and she'd spent a summer resenting a baby who hadn't yet come.

Tibby was learning something about her future. She was learning that it would not include having children. Not unless she adopted some.

Christina was in hell, and Tibby could barely watch it. With each contraction—and they seemed like they were coming all the time now—Christina seemed to lose some of herself. When she came down she was less focused, less coherent, less recognizable. Tibby glanced at the printout. One line followed the baby's heartbeat and the other followed the quaking of Christina's uterus. It reminded Tibby of a seismogram. Christina had gone from a five on the Richter scale to about a twenty. If Christina's stomach were California, then California would be under the ocean by now.

Tibby tried calling her mother again, but there was no answer. Alice would know all about this stuff. She would know how to help. She was punching in Carmen's cell number when a nurse appeared in her face.

"You have to put that away," she snapped, pointing at Tibby's cell phone. "It interferes with the equipment. You could get thrown out of here."

Tibby considered that possibility with a certain amount of longing.

"Can you give her some medicine or something?" Tibby asked Lauren when she popped her head in. Tibby was afraid of this much pain. She didn't know how to get close to it.

Lauren came over and put her hands on Christina's shoulders. "You doing okay, honey?"

Christina tried to focus. It didn't look like the question made any sense to her. The answer was so profoundly *no* that the question hardly applied.

"In her birth plan she specified natural childbirth. That means, basically, no drugs," Lauren explained to Tibby. "That's partly why she's working with me instead of an OB. Midwives don't prescribe the heavy stuff."

It didn't seem a good sign that they were talking about Christina rather than to her. "An OB is . . . a doctor?" Tibby asked, wondering for a moment if a doctor wouldn't be a good idea right now. If she were Christina she would want the heavy stuff. She would want the heaviest stuff, and every bit of it they had. She would want them to knock her out so completely that she wouldn't wake up for a week.

"It seems like you should make that plan when you're actually giving birth. Then at least you know what it feels like," Tibby opined, but Lauren wasn't listening.

Lauren was now studying the printout with some degree of interest. "Christina, let me check you again, hon. These contractions are coming fast and furious."

Christina was shaking her head. "No. I don't want to." Her legs were clamped shut.

"We'll wait until this contraction is over." Lauren stroked Christina's shoulders in a way that was meant to be soothing, but Christina was not soothed. She was writhing. She pushed Lauren away. "I can't. I'm not ready." Christina's voice was breaking up into sobs.

Lauren cast a look at Tibby that seemed to say she was certainly the most horrendous labor partner any pregnant woman had ever been saddled with. Tibby did feel bad. Not because of Lauren—she didn't really

care what Lauren thought—but because of Christina. Christina was alone here. She didn't have her husband or her sister or her daughter or her mother. She had Tibby.

Tibby's instinct was to get on the bed with Christina, but her muscles were fighting with her. They were remembering Bailey, and more recently, Katherine. Tibby did not have happy associations with beds in hospitals. Who did?

Christina was in a ball. She was crying quietly. Tibby suffered a deep ache in her chest, climbing up to her throat.

"I need to check you, Christina. I need to see where you are," Lauren said.

She's right there! Tibby felt like screaming. *Leave her alone!*

"I'm not ready," Christina said, weeping.

Lauren tried to uncurl Christina, but Christina fought her off.

Tibby couldn't stand it anymore. She got on the bed with Christina. She grabbed her hands and squeezed them hard. That seemed to get her attention.

Lauren still pulled at Christina's legs.

"She said she's not ready!" Tibby roared.

Lauren looked taken aback, like Tibby had smacked her. Then, to Tibby's utter astonishment, Lauren put her face to the side of Tibby's head. She kissed her temple.

As if this day could get any stranger.

"That a girl," Lauren whispered. "Fight for her. She needs you."

Tibby pulled Christina up by her hands. She looked into her eyes. "Christina, I'm here. Look at me, okay?

Hold my hands. Squeeze them as hard as it hurts." That was something Alice used to say to Tibby when she had to get a shot.

Christina was coming down from a contraction. She looked lost, but slowly she zeroed in on Tibby.

Tibby knelt by her. "I'm here. You're okay. Show me how much it hurts."

The pain mounted again in Christina's face. She squeezed Tibby's hands so hard, Tibby saw them turning white. She tried her hardest not to flinch. The pressure mounted until Tibby half expected to see her ten severed fingers lying on the mattress.

"That's good!" Tibby shouted. "I feel it! That's so great!"

Christina's eyes were tracking hers now. Tibby felt, on some level, that that was the right thing.

"I need to check her. I think this is happening," Lauren said to Tibby under her breath. "Help me, okay?"

Tibby did not know what *happening* meant. She did not want to know what *happening* meant. She straddled Christina's legs, so she was practically sitting on her, though carrying her own weight. "Tina, Lauren's gonna do her thing. Stick with me, okay. With my eyes. Are you watching?"

Christina nodded.

"Squeeze my hands. Can you do it?"

Christina allowed Lauren to examine her cervix, though she was desperately uncomfortable. Tibby's hands were mottled white and purple.

"My goodness," Lauren said breathlessly. "This is

fast. Christina, you are ten centimeters and ready to go."

Tibby stared at Lauren, dumbfounded. Wasn't Lauren supposed to do this kind of thing every day? Why did she allow herself to get surprised? She said this was going to take hours. As in several. Not as in one. Did Lauren have any idea what she was doing?

Tibby hadn't even gotten hold of Carmen. She hadn't wanted to scare her. She'd thought they had *hours*. She'd thought Carmen would still have enough time to get back. Now what? What were they supposed to do now?

Christina started crying again. There was a whole lot of blood on the bed, under Christina's legs.

Tibby didn't want to show her fast-rising fear. If she panicked, where would that leave Christina? She needed to get them focused again.

Christina was in a new kind of pain, making a new kind of noise. Tibby tried not to be alarmed. It wouldn't help.

"You need to push, hon," Lauren said. "You're feeling the pressure and that means you need to push. You're almost there!"

"No!" Christina was suddenly livid. "I'm not ready! I can't do this! David isn't here! Where is he? Where is Carmen? We took the classes! This baby is not due for *four weeks*!" In her anger, Christina had tuned herself right back in. She let go of Tibby's hands, rolled back onto her side, and curled into her ball.

Tibby could see from her body that Christina was fighting a ferocious urge.

"She needs to push. I can see it," Lauren said. "Don't fight it, Christina. It's time to have this baby. You gotta let go!" She was trying unsuccessfully to get Christina's attention.

Tibby tried pulling her up again, but Christina wouldn't budge. "Tina, will you look at me? Do you see me? You can do this! I know it!"

Christina wouldn't look. "I can't."

We are born believing. A

man bears beliefs, as a

tree bears apples.

—Ralph Waldo Emerson

Roughly twenty minutes south of Downingtown, Carmen realized there was another sizable topic she and Win hadn't considered.

"Are you going away to school next year?" he asked her without looking at her. He was bearing down on a slow Nissan in the fast lane.

"Um." She licked her lips. "Yes."

This was the obvious moment to say where she was going. It suddenly struck her how badly she wanted to say she was going to Williams. She wanted Win to think she was smart.

She tapped her bare toes against the dashboard. But she wasn't going to Williams. She was going to Maryland, and she didn't want to lie to him anymore. She liked him too much to keep doing that.

"I'm going to Maryland," she said. She quelled the urge to spout her near-perfect grades and her academic honors. She left it at the truth. If he didn't like the truth, well . . . then that was a good thing to know.

"Oh."

Did he find her disappointing?

"What about you?" she asked. It was strange that she didn't know. Carmen was a great student. She cared about that kind of thing. Most boys she assessed almost like a brand, and where they went to college added or subtracted from their cachet. Win was different. She'd gotten to know him from the inside, it seemed.

"I go to Tufts. In Boston." He smiled a little and tipped his head toward her. "I was kind of hoping you were going somewhere up around there."

I was! she felt like shouting at him. *I could have! I almost did!*

But she stayed quiet, which was good in a way, because when her cell phone started ringing she heard it right away and snapped it open.

It was Tibby, trying to be calm.

"Oh, my God! Oh, no! Tell me you are kidding," Carmen roared into the phone.

Tibby wasn't kidding.

"We'll be there as fast as we can," Carmen said helplessly.

"What happened?" Win asked.

"She's in heavy labor," Carmen said, a little sob getting past her. "It's going fast. She's asking for David and for me."

"Man," Win muttered. He took his foot off the gas pedal. "What do you want to do? Keep going or turn around now?"

"Turn around," she answered. As soon as he flicked

the blinker she thought better of it. "No, keep going. It's David's baby, too. We have to tell him. He'll be heart-broken if he doesn't even know."

Win seemed to think that was a good answer. He got back into the left lane of the highway and pushed the speed. He was going eighty-five and Carmen wasn't complaining.

The news shook her and sent her mind back to Bethesda to be with her mother. Carmen knew Christina was scared. She was probably in a lot of pain. "I was her labor coach," Carmen murmured.

She *was* close to her mother. Underneath everything was that. It wasn't just the good answer, it was true. How else could you explain how powerfully she felt her mother's distress?

Her mother told her once that when you feel someone else's pain and joy as powerfully as if it were your own, then you knew you really loved them. Right now Carmen knew she had the pain part right. The joy . . . well, she still had work to do on that.

Win expertly took the exit for Downingtown. Carmen focused her energies on the map. She was a good map reader. They had the cross streets and the car make and the license plate number. That would be enough informa-tion, they both hoped. God forbid David had parked in an underground garage or something.

The coordinates led them to a housing development. Carmen screamed when she saw the green Mercury. She screamed out the letters and numbers of the license plate. Win was laughing and yelling too. The two of them

267

stormed the front door of the recently built clapboard house. Carmen fidgeted, trying to restrain herself from ringing the doorbell more than twice.

A woman appeared at the door. Carmen saw David behind her and immediately started waving and yelling. It was all a flurry after that. Carmen couldn't remember who said what, but five minutes later, Carmen, Win, and David were speeding south toward Bethesda, Maryland.

"I forgot my rental car," David muttered from the backseat, still whitish gray in the face.

"It's okay. Somebody can take it back for you," Carmen reassured him. She looked from Win, in the driver's seat, to David. "By the way, David Breckman, this is Win —"

Was it possible that she didn't know his last name? Here they'd run the gauntlet of emotions, he'd experienced everything with her from Valia's friable ligaments to Katherine's hockey helmet to her mother's unexpected labor, and she really didn't know even that? "Uh, what's your last name?"

"Sawyer."

"Win Sawyer," she murmured.

"Thanks for your help, Win," David said robotically. He was trying to call the hospital on Carmen's cell phone. Her battery was almost gone.

"What's yours?" Win asked her. They were in their own world.

"Lowell."

"How do you do, Carmen Lowell?"

She smiled at him gratefully. "Ask me later."

By Baltimore, they were flying down 95 at just as

many miles per hour. Carmen was incensed when a siren started blaring behind them. Win groaned.

"Oh, you're joking," Carmen said.

Win pulled onto the shoulder. Carmen opened her door.

"Carmen, no!" Both Win and David were yelling at her. "You're not supposed to get out of the car!"

Suddenly a policeman was yelling at her over his bullhorn. It made her angrier. She slammed the door and crossed her arms over her chest.

"My mother is in the hospital about to have a baby without her husband, and you are holding us up!" She practically exploded.

After an impassioned chat with the policeman, Carmen got back in the car.

Win looked a bit shell-shocked. He and David both looked defeated, as though expecting tickets and fines of hundreds of dollars and also to go to jail.

"He said he was sorry," Carmen reported instead. "Go ahead."

"*What?*" both Win and David yelled at her.

"Win, go!" she said. And Win obliged. "He offered us an escort but I said no," Carmen continued once they'd gotten back up to speed. "I told him no, but please radio ahead to his fellow cops and tell them to leave us alone."

Win was trying to hold back his smile. Carmen couldn't think about whether she was being Good Carmen or not. She couldn't keep track anymore.

David was shaking his head. "Win, this girl is a force of nature."

Win cast a sideways look at Carmen. "I'm getting that impression."

"We need some help here." Lauren and Minerva, the labor and delivery nurse, had pulled Tibby aside. "I'm not getting through to her," Lauren added. Like Tibby didn't know that.

Aren't you the professionals? Tibby felt like screaming at them. *Aren't you supposed to know how this goes? I'm seventeen! I'm not even supposed to be here!*

Minerva cleared her throat. She was a stocky Filipina. "This isn't a medical issue. It's an emotional issue. Do you know what I'm saying?"

"You mean Christina is freaking because her husband isn't here?" Tibby asked impatiently. She was tired. She was scared.

"Yes," Lauren said. "And she doesn't want to let the baby go. She's gotta release it, she's gotta make the leap. We need to help her so she feels safe."

Tibby knew a thing or two about leaps. She turned and strode back to Christina. She felt like a soldier going back into battle. She'd already done the sensible thing of putting a pair of hospital scrubs over the Traveling Pants, which she still wore from the night before. She prayed they would bring Christina some of their magic by association, but she wasn't crazy enough to leave unwashable Pants uncovered in such a circumstance.

Christina was fighting. And all in a rush, she reminded Tibby powerfully of her daughter. Like Carmen, Christina was a fighter, all right, and also like her daughter, she was fighting to total destruction.

Tibby got on the bed. She held Christina by her shoulders. Inside herself, Tibby made Christina a promise. *If you leap, I will. We'll do it together.*

Tibby could be a fighter too. At least, she could try. She propped Christina up on her pillows. She held Christina's face between her hands.

"Tina. I know it's hard. You don't want to let go. I know how it feels. I mean, not having a baby. Obviously I haven't had a baby, but—" Okay, she was getting off track.

To her amazement, she saw a look of mirth flit through Christina's eyes. Here and then gone. If Christina could even consider laughing at Tibby, then maybe they were in business.

"David and Carmen are coming. And they want to see this baby so bad. And the baby wants to come out, so you gotta do it." Tibby figured she would just talk. Christina was listening to her now. Her body was shaking from head to toe, but she was listening.

Lauren and Minerva had their latex gloves on. They were positioning themselves at the foot of the bed for the main attraction. Christina allowed them to pull her onto her back. Her knees were bent. She was in position.

Christina let out a whimper. She was bearing down, crumpling up her face.

"Let go! You can do it! I know you can. You're

Carmen's mom, right? You can do anything! Right?"

"Tell her to push," Lauren muttered. "She needs to push or we're all in trouble here."

"Tina, push!" Tibby said it so loud she felt her eyeballs rattling. "You can do it! Get that baby out of there, would you?" Tibby didn't even care what she was saying, because Christina was listening.

Christina was clinging to Tibby now, holding her tight around her neck, looking for strength. It made Tibby feel strong. "You know how much we love you! You know how happy David is going to be to see this baby! Just picture Carmen's face!"

Tibby was just as hysterical as Christina, but Christina was pushing now, and both Lauren and Minerva looked nearly delirious with relief.

"Tibby, I'm pushing!" Christina whimpered.

"You are! You are unbelievable! You are a star! You are the hero! You are the bomb!" Tibby was shouting; she was beyond herself. Somewhere back there was self-consciousness, and here, right up here, was she.

"Tibby!" Christina cried. She was getting some control now.

Tibby kept right on yelling and screaming, the dumbest, silliest things. She wasn't even listening to herself anymore.

Contractions came, and with each came a push. Minerva and Lauren were shouting their encouragement too, but the world had shrunken to just the two of them — Tibby and Christina, a funny pairing most every other day of the year.

Christina kept her eyes fixed on Tibby's, on Tibby's very pupils, and Tibby did not blink. As long as she could keep Christina right there with her, she could make a difference.

"I see the baby's head! I feel it!" Lauren shouted.

"Oh, my God. Did you hear that!" Tibby thundered. "She can feel the baby's head!"

Christina smiled a real honest-to-God smile.

"The baby is right there. *Right there!*" Tibby was beside herself. She had Christina's shoulders in her hands, then her face. "You got it! You know that?"

"I got it!" Christina cried. She was coming to life.

"I feel it," Lauren said. "I feel the hair."

"Tina, your baby has hair!" Tibby screamed. "Can you believe it?"

Christina looked like she liked the idea of a baby with hair. "Carmen had hair," she said faintly, "when she was born."

"Well, lucky thing, that is. I love hair. Hair is great!" Tibby was giddy now. She pushed long, sweaty strands of Christina's hair off of her neck.

"One more push, and this head is out," Lauren said. She left Tibby to her own insane translation.

"Tina, one more big one! Biggie. Big big big push. Don't you want to meet your baby?"

Christina went all out. She screamed bloody murder. Her face turned dark purple.

"And . . . it's . . . a . . . baby!" Lauren shouted.

One more gigantic push and the rest of the baby followed the head. Tibby was afraid to look down, because

it was all pretty damn gory. But Lauren raised this wriggling, slimy, purple little body up.

Tibby could barely breathe. The baby waved its hands and let out a cry. It was a very tiny person, a real person, who had hands to wave and a cry to cry.

Lauren landed the purple body on Christina's chest and Christina sobbed. She held her baby and cried. Tibby watched in wonder and cried too.

The professionals did their professional stuff between Christina's legs. Then they cut the cord, weighed the baby, and did a few other medical things. Then the baby, now more pink than purple, arrived back in Christina's arms.

Christina held the baby to her breast, and Tibby knew it was done. Christina's little world remained at two, but the second one wasn't Tibby anymore. That was as it should be, sad and happy at once.

Slowly Tibby unfolded her limbs and climbed off the bed. She wanted to leave quietly, to let Christina have her unadulterated joy.

But before she did, she planted a kiss on Christina's head. "You kicked ass," she whispered. It wasn't quite the wording of a Hallmark card, but it did express her true feelings.

Near the door, she bumped into Lauren, bustling about. Lauren paused. "Tibby, you have an unorthodox coaching style, but it is very effective. Would you be available for future labors?" Lauren was half laughing, but Tibby could see she'd been crying too. She was wiped out.

"No way." Tibby stopped. She needed to know something. It felt important, like her future suddenly hung on the answer. "Hey, Lauren?"

"Yeah?"

"Don't you get used to this? I mean, haven't you done it hundreds of times?"

Lauren pushed her hair behind her ears. Her purple liner was smudged. Her face was shiny with sweat. "Yes." She looked at her hands. "But no. It's a miracle. It's different every single time."

To love another person is

to see the face of God.

—Victor Hugo

The three of them, Carmen, David, and Win, crashed into labor and delivery with such speed and force you would have thought they were each having a baby of their own.

Tibby's was the first familiar face they saw. She was wearing hospital scrubs with a lot of scary-looking stains, standing in the hall with a bewildered expression. As soon as she saw Carmen she burst into tears. "You have a baby!" she screamed.

"We do?"

"Oh, my God."

David was darting around, trying to find Christina.

"Over here!" Tibby grabbed him by the shirt and pulled him into a room.

It was a hospital room and, of course, it featured a bed. The bed featured a flushed woman in a pale pink gown, and she in turn featured a tiny, blanket-wadded bundle topped by a knit hat the size of a tennis sock.

Carmen was surrounded by shouts and yells and exclamations of surprise and joy, so many and so voluble that she couldn't tell which one came from whom—not even if it came from her own throat. She let David beat her to the bed, but she was a fast second. With expansive arms she pressed herself on her mother and this baby and even David. Christina was laughing and sobbing, and Carmen felt her own breaths coming out in those same general types of contortions.

"We have a baby!" David pulled away a few inches to try to get a grasp on the situation. "Right?"

Christina was the madonna now, calm and wise. She laughed at his tortured face. "Yes, this one is ours."

Tears were coursing down David's face. He needed to make sure of Christina before he grappled with the idea of this baby of his. "Christina, I am so sorry—I don't know how—"

Christina pressed her hand to his face. "Don't say anything else about that. I had Tibby. We have a beautiful, healthy baby." She looked at Carmen. "You too, *nena*. Right now I have everything on the earth that I want."

With trepidation Carmen and David both peered at the tiny thing.

"Do you want to know what it is?" Christina asked.

Carmen was so overwhelmed, she'd forgotten about that whole issue. That had mattered to her once, hadn't it?

"It's a boy," Christina said joyfully.

"Oh!" Carmen let out another scream, but she thoughtfully directed it away from her mother's ear. "We have a boy!"

David cried some more.

Carmen looked over her shoulder at the door of the room. She wanted to share this deep pleasure with Tibby and Win, but both of them had gone.

Carmen realized she needed to find them. She also needed to give her mother and David and their baby a moment together.

She backed up a little, seeing the three of them framed in a triangle. Her mother's face radiated such relief and joy that Carmen felt her own face pressing itself into that same shape, without even thinking. Her connection was so overpowering, she felt like her mother's face was her own, her mother's heart was beating with hers, her feelings were the same.

And she remembered the thing about being able to feel someone else's joy and knowing that you loved them.

Good and Great Carmen,

This is a day for miracles. Put on the Pants, and take one for your very own.

All my love,

Tibby

When Carmen found the Traveling Pants neatly folded with the note right outside the door to her mother's hospital room, she raced into the bathroom and pulled them on.

Then she took the elevator up to geriatrics. Win stood by the vending machines. He was searching his pockets for change. It so happened that neither of them had eaten anything but Corn Nuts in many hours.

Her impulse was to hug him, and she didn't give herself the time to chicken out. She just threw her arms around him. "Thank you so much, Win!" she exclaimed with a full throat. "Thank you for everything."

"I'm sorry we didn't get to her in time," Win said into her hair. His arms had made their way around her, too.

"I think it's okay. I think everything is okay now."

"Hey, I didn't mean to disappear before. I just didn't want to get in the way of your family and everything," he explained.

"I know, but I needed to see you." She pulled away a little, to give him some room.

He didn't seem to want to take it. He put his face back into her hair, pressing his cheek against her ear. "I need to see you, too," he murmured.

He held her closer. She let her body relax into his, feeling his breathing. She felt his backbone under her palms. Her heart was beating only a few inches from his.

"I need to say something to you," she said over his shoulder.

He lifted his head. He let her back up from him a little. He had a look on his face that said it was girding for disappointment.

"There's this thing I've been worrying about, and I have to set it straight."

His look of apprehension grew.

She breathed out. "I think you might think I'm a good person, and I wanted to let you know that I'm not. I am mean and selfish most of the time."

He tipped his head, confused.

"You are too good for me," she explained.

"That's impossible."

"No, seriously, Win. You are a good person, and I'm only pretending to be one. I've given you this false impression that I'm selfless and kind. And I'm not."

Win raised his eyebrows. "God, that's a relief. You may think I'm good, but I was starting to feel pretty intimidated."

"Really?"

"Oh, yeah."

"I got eight fifty an hour to babysit Valia." She figured she might as well go for full disclosure.

"Man, you deserved a hundred."

She laughed. "Funny thing was, I ended up really caring about her. That part was free," she added.

He studied her for a long moment, a quizzical look in his eyes, before he opened his mouth. "I used to be fat."

Carmen felt her eyebrows floating upward. "Excuse me?"

"I used to be fat." Win shrugged. "I was the fat kid. Since we're uncovering our inner selves, I might as well throw that in."

She couldn't help glancing over his body in case there was a hundred pounds she had forgotten to notice. There wasn't.

"The summer I was thirteen my parents sent me to fat camp. The next summer I grew six inches and got serious about swimming. But still, a fat kid lives inside me."

Carmen tried to fit this piece into the puzzle of Win. It did fit, in a funny way.

He cleared his throat. "So as I see it, I'm the pretender. You're too good for me."

"That's impossible," she said.

He moved closer again. He looked in her eyes for a long time. Then he tugged, most intimately, on a belt loop of the Pants. "If you're too good for me and I'm too good for you, what does that mean?"

"We're just right?"

He smiled. "Can I?" He wanted to put his arms around her again.

"Please."

In front of the candy machine, under the glare of fluorescent hallway lights, surrounded by the smell of old people, he put his lips on hers. He kissed her soft and slow at first, and then deeper.

He buried his head in her neck. He pushed her hair aside and kissed her there. She let out a small sigh.

"I've wanted to do this for so long," he murmured into her ear.

"Mmmm," she said. She found his lips again with hers. With abandon, she kissed him. Perhaps for the first time ever, she kissed without a single thought about how it was or what it was or what it meant. She kissed from the inside.

An old lady wheeled out of her room and caught them in the act. "Can you two lovebirds take that somewhere else?" she clucked.

Carmen and Win both started laughing, running for the elevators. They held hands as they descended and as they strode through the lobby.

Carmen walked, and squeezed his hand, and suddenly she had the strangest impression that Good Carmen walked before her, a few feet in front of her, like a ghost, a glistening spirit.

This was a day for miracles. Carmen overtook that spirit. She walked right into Good Carmen and absorbed her into her soul. Let her fight it out with Bad Carmen if she needed to.

And, thus, the hospital doors opened and Whole Carmen emerged, newly born, into the world.

My shoe is off

My foot is cold

I have a bird

I like to hold.

—Dr. Seuss

Tibby wasn't done leaping yet.

Dazed in the fading light, she stumbled down Connecticut Avenue. Cars rushed by; people went around. Tibby felt like she'd been sucked into a wormhole of heightened experience and then spat back out into the regular world. The world was regular, but she wasn't regular anymore.

The wormhole happened to be pretty messy. Back at the hospital she'd washed her hands and face and shed her stained gown. She'd taken off the Pants and made away with just the pair of scrub pants on her legs. She hoped she wouldn't get arrested for it. Still, she felt sticky. She didn't want to think about that too much.

She needed to find Brian. She didn't want to get comfortable with the ground yet.

She knew he'd be at home. At her home. She pointed herself in the right direction.

A block from her house she saw him walking toward

her. She didn't question that. It was one of those days.

They didn't run into each other's arms or anything. He walked toward her and when he reached her, she turned 180 degrees so they were walking in the same direction. They walked like that for a while. She reached for his hand. He held on.

"I have an idea," she said.

"Okay," he said. He didn't ask what it was. He was willing to go along.

They walked blocks and blocks and then up a long hill up to Rockwood pool. Then they step-jumped over moving water. And then ascended that long staircase. By the time they got to the fence, it was dark. And they were good and high. A high place was what you needed for a leap.

"Here's where it's good to climb up." She pointed to the break in the barbed wire.

Brian seemed to think that made sense. She led the way; he followed. For such a chicken she really was a pretty good climber. She jumped the last five or so feet to get herself in the right spirit. He appeared gracefully by her side.

"You ready?" she asked.

"I think so," he said faithfully, even though he didn't know what she was talking about.

She began unbuttoning her shirt and his eyes widened slightly. She cast it off. She was wearing a pretty bra. That was nice. She saw her skin glowing in the warm evening air. She pulled off the aqua green scrubs. This

was new. She slipped them off and folded them carefully. Her underpants were pink and not embarrassing.

Brian's eyes glanced off her and then back on. They were careful, surprised, hopeful. And longing. There was that, too. He was looking for permission to let his eyes stay on her. And with her eyes, she gave it.

"Now you," she said.

He took off his own shirt and jeans in a matter of seconds. He left them in a pile. His skin glowed just as brightly above and below the boxers that she herself had picked out for him, three pairs for nine dollars at Old Navy. She hadn't realized she'd be seeing them again in this context. She drew in a sharp little breath. She had pictured him in her mind many times before. This was better.

She held his hand again. They let their eyes run over each other unchecked. What was there to hide anymore? She didn't want to hide anything.

She led him to the edge. She picked the deep end on purpose.

They stood side by side, their toes curled over the edge. She looked at him, right in his eyes and he looked in hers. This was going to be fun.

One. Two. Three.

And so they jumped together.

Bridget's body felt better. Dramatically ill, dramatically better, that was her all over.

Learning about the birth of Carmen's baby brother

gave her great joy. The news came like a dash of cold, fresh water on her soul. She spent almost a week's pay sending flowers and balloons to Christina.

But, still, her heart hurt. She wanted to see Eric. She needed to see him. She craved his presence. But he was gone. Saturday he disappeared without a trace.

He wasn't in his cabin. He wasn't in the dining hall for three meals in a row. Finally she sucked it up and went to Joe. "I seem to have lost my partner," she said, trying to sound casual.

"You like him now, do you?" Joe said smugly.

She felt like smacking him. "Do you know where he went?" She couldn't bring herself to say Eric's name.

"No idea," said Joe.

She tapped her bare foot against the floor planks of the main office. "Do you know when he'll be back?"

"He better be back by Monday," he said. "We've got a tournament starting."

She hated Joe at this moment, San José Earthquakes or no. He was a guy who rode his own agenda hard, and he didn't care about yours. "Did he say anything to you?"

"He said he had to take off for a couple days. That was it."

Bridget stalked away angrily. She practically screamed when a chunk of the pine floor dug itself deep into her big toe. Why didn't she wear goddamn shoes? What was the matter with her?

Where had Eric gone? Why? Did he need to get away from her? What had happened between them?

That evening she tried running, but she felt weak. She couldn't eat. She called Lena, Carmen, and Tibby on the common phone in the staff lounge and left messages for all of them. That made her feel panicky. Why couldn't she find them? She felt terribly alone.

She thought to call Greta, but she didn't know how to get her feelings up and over the transom. How could she explain? Eric wasn't her boyfriend. He wasn't her anything. Why did she feel like she needed him so desperately?

She sat on the dock at the lake and watched the clouds thicken. She wished it would rain hard and long and clear everything away. Rain never came when you asked for it.

She couldn't sit. She paced. She kicked a soccer ball around an empty field. The lightning in the distance wasn't the real thing. It was empty, dissipated and fake: heat lightning. It brought no rain.

As much as she prided herself on making this summer with Eric different from the one before, it was beginning to seem eerily similar.

Like before, she was laid open by a glimpse of intimacy, and when she tried to find it again, there was no one and nothing there. Eric offered, whether he meant to or not, some giant idea of love. But she only grasped it long enough to know her poverty. He pushed her to destroy herself. He made her want and then gave her no satisfaction.

Why did he do this to her? Why did she let him? How could she give herself away like this, even after she'd already learned such a bitter lesson?

She wished he hadn't found her in that feverish, vulnerable state. She wished he hadn't worried over her and taken care of her and held her all night. Having it was ecstasy, but its sudden, inexplicable loss was too painful to bear. She'd rather go through her life doubting such a thing was possible than knowing it was real and she couldn't have it.

What a pitiful waste she was. She was willing to give away, to throw away, the very best she had. For what? It was one thing to sacrifice yourself for a great cause. It was another to destroy yourself for a person who didn't even want you. It was an act of self-immolation, a sacrifice nobody wanted, that did nobody any good. What could be more tragic than that?

She thought she was independent and strong, but she got one small taste of love and she was hungrier than anyone. She was ravenous.

All the drawings had been difficult, but Lena saved the hardest for last.

She'd procrastinated. She'd gotten a manicure and pedicure with Effie. She'd spent mornings shopping and cooking for Carmen's household, wanting to help out with the new baby. She and Carmen had spent happy evenings together on the floor talking about drawing and Win and the beach, simply watching the baby breathe.

But now the time had come. Her portfolio had to be postmarked by the following day; she couldn't put it off any longer. When the house was quiet and the light was

good, she pulled on the Traveling Pants and sat herself in front of the mirror in her bedroom, and got to work.

It was one thing looking at other people's troubles. It was another looking at your own. If feelings and expectations made it difficult to see a loved one's face, how blind were you to your own face?

But one surprising thing, Lena found as she looked at her face in the mirror, was that it wasn't as familiar to her as some. Yes, she had looked at herself plenty over the years. But her face wasn't as rutted in her brain as her mother's or her father's.

Lena had a funny relationship with her face. She wanted it to be beautiful, and she also didn't. She looked at it with the desire to find some overriding flaw that would kick her from one category (beautiful) into another (not). And she also looked at it with the fear that she'd succeed. Either way, she usually didn't find it.

It was like what Tolstoy said in *Anna Karenina* about all happy families being alike. Lena felt that all pretty faces were all alike—straight, even, regular. It was the ugliness, the sadness that set them apart. Lena couldn't find that much objective ugliness in hers. But the sadness was apparent.

As she began to draw the outer edge of her cheek, she realized she had the look of a person who was waiting. Not impatient, not tortured, not frustrated. Just waiting. What was she waiting for?

The eight-thousand-pound elephant in the middle of her room snorted in irritation. Kostos, of course. The one

who was always there while she studiously avoided him.

She was still waiting for him to come back to her, even though he wasn't going to. She was still holding out for something that wasn't going to happen. She was good at waiting. That seemed like a sad thing to be good at.

Release me, she begged, silently, of her elephant.

She needed to be free of him. She needed to get on with her life. Maybe even to fall in love again. She had a candidate in mind.

It was easy to wish to let go of the torture and the heartbreak and the missing Kostos. It seemed easy, at least. But there was a catch. To let go of the pain, she had to give up the other parts too: the feeling of being loved. The feeling of being wanted and even needed. The way Kostos looked at her and touched her. The way her name sounded when he said it. The number of times he'd written *I love you* at the end of his third to last letter. (Seventeen—once for each year of her life.) And yes, she did still read those letters. Time for a full confession: She did.

It wasn't the suffering she willfully clung to. It was the precious stuff. But the precious stuff attached her, irrevocably, to the pain.

She waited for Kostos to come for her. She waited for him to release her. She lived quietly, passively, at the margins of other people's bigger lives: her father's, Kostos's. She took up the space they left for her.

She couldn't wait for Kostos anymore. That was the thing she learned from the face she saw in the mirror and

on her paper. There was one person who could release Lena, and Lena was looking right at her.

Beezy,

Call me, would you? These are for you, and they are full strength, so wear them well. (And carefully! I had to say that, Bee. I'm worried about you.) I am here. I can be there in a flash. Call me.

Love,
Len

I just need your star for

a day.

—Nick Drake

Bridget didn't see Eric until late Monday morning. She felt like the universe could have exploded and cooled and spat out a few new galaxies in the time that had passed.

He didn't look at her and she didn't look at him. Or she didn't let him see her looking at him, anyway. He was an avoider, wasn't he? She hated avoiders. She hated being one. How could a person transform from her hero to her destroyer in so short a time?

The intercamp tournament began Monday. Because it was tournament week, she and Eric got off lake duty. This was the time of the summer when everybody lived and breathed only soccer. Eric and Bridget stopped needing to see each other.

By Tuesday afternoon, Bridget's team had already taken their first two games. Usually she drove her players hard, but she was fun. Now she drove them harder and she wasn't fun. She was vicious.

Eric's team had also won two of two games. As angry as she was, Bridget had to grant that Eric was probably the best of the coaches. He was patient and he was intuitive, and he already had three years of Division I soccer under his belt. Bridget was considered by the other staff to be talented but unpredictable and inexperienced. And she had a few real cases on her hands. Everybody agreed Eric's was the team to beat. So Bridget determined to beat them.

Maybe it wasn't the most mature way to deal with her anger. But she had a lot of dangerous energy, and it was better used in soccer than in, say, operating heavy machinery.

So she knew her team and Eric's would meet in the final on Friday. She spent every moment until then working on her lineup and her strategy. She had a few really fine players: Karl Lundgren, Aiden Cross, Russell Chen. She knew exactly what to do with them. It was a player like Naughton who required some thought. She scouted Eric's team. She scheduled surreptitious meetings of her own team by flashlight in the woods after dinner. She took them on early-morning runs. She had to hold herself back from setting a crushing pace.

Three or four times in those days that passed, Eric looked up at her and waved or tried to catch her eye. She kept her head down. She wasn't going to hope anymore.

Thursday night, she found the Traveling Pants bundled up inside a Jiffy bag in her mail cubby with a note from Lena. She was in business.

Friday morning she got up at five. She was too preoccupied to sleep. She put on her team's blue jersey. She brushed her hair and wore it down. As an afterthought she applied mascara and a little blue eye shadow. The color matched her eyes, her Pants, her mood, and her jersey. Team spirit and all.

She went outside to consult her notebook in the streams of first sunlight that crept across the ground. She was still stuck on Naughton. Everybody deserved a chance. Everybody had something to give.

In a fit of inspiration, she went to his cabin and woke him up. "Get dressed and meet me at the south field," she told him. He had a hopeful look about him, which she suspected related to something other than soccer. "*Naughty*. Nothing like that. I need to figure out what to do with you." He knew he was an unconventional player. If he didn't, he should have.

When he got out on the field she ordered him into the goal. In one way, Eric had been right. Naughty's deficits made him a terrible choice for goalie. But on the other hand, there was something about him . . . .

"Ready?" she called lining up with the ball fifteen or so yards out from the goal. She kicked one straight at him, hard but not very hard. He moved away from it and fumbled the ball with his hands, allowing it into the box. His big feet weren't good and his hands were worse. She wondered why he'd stuck with soccer since first grade, as he'd proudly told her that he had.

"Let's try another one." He threw her the ball and she

stopped it neatly with her foot. She tried several more straight shots on goal. He couldn't just stand there and catch a ball coming right at him. He felt the need to move. He screwed it up almost every time.

She decided to try out her theory. She stood farther back and gave herself a little room to run. She kicked the ball hard, sent it sailing right into the top left corner of the goal. She watched in amazement and also satisfaction as his body took off in the direction of the ball. He leaped high, and with arms outstretched, he caught it. "Wow. Nice," she called out.

Inside she was screaming, but she didn't want to make a big deal.

She sent him several more hard, angled shots and he pulled each of them down. He couldn't tend goal when it meant just standing there. He couldn't be given any time to think, or his mind sabotaged him completely. But he could move. He had a remarkable, almost spooky sense for where the ball was going to be, and the faster it came, the farther away it was, the more impressive his ability.

On her final shots, she actually challenged herself to get one past him. Only her last and finest shot made it into the goal.

She went over to him and shook his hand. She smacked him hard on the back. "Naughty, you have something. I don't know what it is, but it is something."

"You look amazing," Tibby said, sitting across from Christina at the small table in their kitchen. Christina

bowed her head modestly. She peeked proudly at her baby. It would appear that she felt amazing too.

"I am lucky, is what it is," Christina said, hiking the baby up a little in her arms. "But Tibby, listen." Christina cast her eyes at the closed door. "I wanted it to be just the two of us"—she paused and glanced at the baby—"well, the three of us—for a few minutes, because I wanted to ask you something. It's kind of serious, and you don't need to say yes and you don't even need to answer right away."

"Okay." Tibby couldn't help feeling a little nervous. "You aren't going to ask me to be your labor coach again, are you?"

Christina snorted so loud in her laughter that the baby startled. "No. I promise."

Tibby laughed too.

"Not that you weren't everything I needed," Christina said more seriously. "You were." Her eyes looked perilously shiny, and Tibby felt her own eyes getting like that too.

"I wanted to ask if you would be the baby's god-mother."

Tibby's eyes widened.

"I know it sounds heavy, but it doesn't need to be. You played a special role in his life already. I want to acknowledge that. I'd love to think you would continue to share your life with him a little."

Tibby didn't need to think. "I'd love to."

"Seriously?"

"Absolutely," she said.

"Great."

"Do I need to offer religious guidance?" Tibby asked with some trepidation.

Christina shook her head. "No, no. Teach him film-making. Or teach him about cars. Take him to movies I won't let him see."

Tibby nodded. She liked this idea. "God, wait till I tell my parents," she said joyfully. "I'm a teenage single mother."

Christina's laughter came out in a snort again, but the baby didn't notice this time.

Carmen appeared at the door. She was wearing a tangerine sundress and her skin was tanned and glossy.

"So what did she say?" Carmen demanded.

Christina beamed. "She said yes."

"Congratulations to all three of you," Carmen said.

"Thanks. And where are you going, Miss Gorgeous?" Tibby asked.

"She's going out with Win." Christina looked as happy as if it had been her own date. "Have you met him yet?"

Tibby shook her head. "I can't wait to. So what's he like?" she asked.

Carmen pointed to her pink, wrinkly little spud of a brother. "Well, he's no Ryan Breckman. . . ."

The championship game was a long, fierce defensive grind. By late in the second half, both teams were exhausted. It was soccer's version of the rope-a-dope.

Bridget put her best and brightest on defense. She did virtually nothing on offense. Even Naughty got some playing time at center forward. She kept Mikey Rosen in the goal. He was balanced and competent. On regular and even on good shots, he didn't mess up. And anyway, her defense was so strong and so psyched up, she didn't think his job would be all-important.

The thing was, she wasn't coaching her team for the win. Not yet. That made her strategy simpler. She was going for a tie of the 0–0 variety. Her team did not grasp exactly why this was so, but they trusted her.

"Defense," she said to her subs. "Defense," she said to every player every time she opened her mouth. "Defense!" she screamed at the top of her lungs when any ball passed centerfield. She was single-minded. *"Non passerat,"* she muttered to them. Sometimes it was easier to concentrate fully and completely on one clear objective.

She paced her sideline and Eric paced his. He saw what she was doing, but he couldn't figure out why. She liked him confused. He needed to change his strategy to fit hers, and it put his team a little off their game, just as she had hoped it would.

The final whistle passed the verdict she'd hoped for: tied at zero. Now they just had to gut it out through the overtime, to prevent the Golden Goal.

The entire camp had gathered on the sidelines by this point. They were screaming for blood. It was frustrating to watch this long without a single goal. Without even a particularly thrilling attempt on goal.

She pulled her team close around her. All eyes stayed locked on hers. As a coach, this was just what she wanted: to feel totally attached and in sync with each of her players. Her intensity was catching. She didn't need to make a big speech. She just held their eyes. "Zero," she said in a whisper. "Can you do it?"

They shouted and yelled and spilled back onto the field.

Amid all the yelling and bullying from the fans, her team stayed the course throughout the extra time. No heroics. They played hard, gritty defense. They made their coach proud.

Another whistle signaled the end of the game and the beginning of the shootout to determine the winner.

The ref tossed the coin and Bridget's team won the first kick. This was just how she wanted it to go. She nodded to Russell Chen. He wasn't as great an all-around player as Lundgren, but he was a sublime kicker, and having held back all game, he was ready to explode.

Her heart pounded as Eric's goalie took his position and the other team members clustered in the center circle. The refs took their positions and Russell set up at the penalty mark. She watched the ballet of guesswork between kicker and goalie, and then Chen made his shot. Bridget's heart soared as the ball fired straight into the top of the goal. Eric's goalie guessed wrong. He didn't get a finger on it.

Her entire team and roughly half the fans erupted in cheers. Telepathically she warned them not to lose

focus yet, and being in sync as they were, they seemed to receive the message.

Now Eric's team got their turn.

There was no question whom he'd choose to kick. Jerome Lewis was probably the best player in the camp. He walked out to the penalty mark.

Bridget's team watched her breathlessly. They knew she had something up her sleeve. She poked Naughton in the shoulder. "Go get 'em," she said.

He looked surprised, like he didn't think she actually meant it.

"Go!" she yelled.

He went. Slowly. Everybody was whispering and chattering as they watched his slow march to the goal. Even the refs looked back at her as if to say, "Are you sure this is what you mean?" She waited until Naughton was in position before she nodded to the ref.

For once Eric was staring directly at her. He was competitive, sure, but now he looked more concerned for her sanity. His players were smiling at each other smugly in the center circle.

Bridget put her eyes on Naughton and kept them there. He needed to know she believed in him.

According to camp rules, this was sudden death overtime. If Lewis made the shot, the shootout would continue to the next round. If he missed it, the game was over.

The ref blew his whistle. Usually, as the opposing coach, you hoped for the kicker to blunder it. In the

strange case of Naughton, it was the opposite. *Please let this guy get a good shot off*, Bridget thought.

Lewis launched a magnificent shot. The entire camp was perfectly silent as they watched the ball stab through the air toward the goal. Naughton seemed to jump the very instant the ball left Lewis's foot. That was one thing, Bridget decided. Naughton had incredible eyes.

The ball flew, Naughton leaped, and the two came together at the very uppermost corner of the goal. Naughton pulled the ball out of the air and landed with it in his hands. He looked so surprised at his accomplishment that he stumbled and let the ball dribble from his grasp. Luckily it dribbled out of the goal rather than into it.

Stunned, the crowd burst into cheers. Bridget watched with pleasure and pride as her team rushed the goal and carried Naughton out on their shoulders. They carried him to his coach, placing him at her feet. Amid the cheering, she hugged him and planted a fat kiss on his cheek. He seemed to like that.

She graciously allowed them to dump the icy contents of the water cooler on her head. Then it was time to shake hands with their opponents. They lined up, Bridget at the back, and slapped or shook hands. The last two to come face to face were the coaches.

"You win. Of course," Eric said gallantly, bowing to her like she was a Japanese businessman and not a girl who loved him to oblivion.

She couldn't help locking on his eyes for a moment. *I didn't, though, did I?*

"Lenny. Hey. It's Bee. I'm fine. I really am. Stop worrying right now! But I do want to talk to you. I'm ready to come home. I miss you so bad. Hey! I heard the baby's name! I love it! Was it Carmen's idea? She must have laughed for an hour. Call me . . . no, never mind. It's impossible to call me here. I'll call you. And don't worry! Okay? I miss you." *Beeeeep.*

I have

Immortal longings in me.

—William Shakespeare

Lena thrust her portfolio at Annik. She was girding herself for a long wait, and suddenly feeling strangely impatient. But it wasn't like that. Annik put down her pencil, put on her glasses, and began flipping through right away.

Not three minutes later she closed it and looked up.

"It doesn't matter if you get the scholarship," she said.

Lena cocked her head in confusion. "It matters to me," she said.

"You will get it," Annik said, almost dismissively. "Unless the committee guys are blind or completely idiotic." She smiled at Lena. "The reason it doesn't matter is because you've done it. Whatever happens after is a little of this or a little of that. A little car wreck. A little dread disease. A little heartbreak. Now you are an artist."

Annik said the word *artist* like it was the best possible thing you could say of someone. Better than being a superhero or an immortal.

"Thank you. I think."

"It's not like it's a gift I'm giving you. You did it yourself."

"You helped."

"I hope so. You've done more and better than I imagined."

"I'm getting there. I'm really beginning to think so."

"You are. I can see it. I can feel it."

Lena smiled at the thought of all the seeing and feeling that went on in this room. "Hey, can I ask you something?"

"Sure," Annik said.

"I've been wondering for a long time. I feel like I should probably just ask."

Annik nodded encouragingly, almost like she knew what Lena was going to say.

"Why are you in a wheelchair?"

Annik clapped her on the back in her Incredible Hulk way. "God, I thought you'd never ask me."

Win was waiting outside her apartment building with the car running. Carmen had never imagined there would be a boy with whom she would want go to Target to shop for school stuff. It was yet another project they had together, more light-hearted than some.

Carmen burst through the front door to collect her shopping list and her debit card. She'd forgotten to bring them when a bunch of them had met for breakfast—Tibby, Brian, Lena, Effie, and Win—at the Tastee Diner a couple of hours before.

Carmen slowed to a pause in the living room. She was struck by how different the apartment felt to her in these days since Win, since the baby. The walls felt closer in

and yet the floor seemed slightly farther away. It was quiet. For once the air conditioners were mute. The tiniest hint of autumn blew in the open window. Maybe that was why the air felt new to her.

She was in a hurry; she had things to do. This apartment waited for her nonetheless. It always waited.

She knew that when she turned the corner of the hallway she would find her mother in her room with the baby. And there she was. She and baby Ryan were curled up in the bed.

They spent their mornings nursing and sleeping. Carmen often visited them in her free moments, kissing the baby's fists and swaddling him like a burrito before he kicked his way out again. Now Christina was sleeping, and Ryan was starting to wriggle. Carmen put her hand on his miniature back, admiring the efforts of her small brother.

She felt so different about him than she had expected. He was hers, and she ached at his fragility and his temper and the shape of his ears, already just like hers. But she also respected that he was Christina and David's.

She had expected, before he was born, that he would be part of her old world, vying for her space and all that she claimed. But he wasn't. He belonged to the new world. They both did, together.

Bridget's victory wasn't so sweet. Well, except for her players. It was sweet for them. They strode around the camp like superheroes for the rest of the week, clucking and retelling the major points of the game (there weren't many).

309

She was happy for them. She had grown to love them.

She'd had a blessed, one-day return home to Bethesda, and seeing her friends made her feel like life made sense again. When she came back to camp, she hung out with Diana and slept and ate, building up her strength again. She knew she could withstand her injured heart, but it took work, and in some moments, a lot of faith.

She realized she wasn't completely finished with Eric. She could keep her sadness to herself and wonder forever what had really happened. Two summers before, she had been mute. She had taken it all upon herself and let it churn and spoil inside of her. But she didn't feel like doing that anymore.

She waited until the camp was mostly quiet and went searching for him in his cabin. It brought back memories of a certain other experience long ago, fetching him from his bed. That time she went in after him. This time she was prim as a pilgrim. She knocked politely and waited.

He came to the door and opened it. Did he look slightly afraid of her, or did she imagine that?

"Would you mind taking a walk with me?" she asked. She was going to say something to reassure him that she wouldn't jump him or anything, but was that really necessary? Hadn't she proven her good intentions? Hadn't they earned her anything? Or could you never live something like that down? Could a girl ever really repair her reputation in the ways that counted?

He nodded. He disappeared for a few seconds and returned wearing a T-shirt and shoes along with his shorts.

They just walked for a while. She had her hair bunched up in an elastic. She wore a beat-up football jersey over the Pants. She'd tried wearing shoes for a week, but now she was back to bare feet. She'd decided she could accept a splinter every now and then as the cost of foot freedom.

Without thinking they wandered down toward the lake and ambled onto the dock. She sat down and he sat next to her. If they had a place, this was it.

The moon was full, and bright enough to make shadows of them on the quiet water. She liked their watery selves.

"I'm just going to talk for a while and you listen. Okay?" Why had she added the *okay*? She didn't mean to ask him for permission.

He nodded.

"I may talk about stuff you don't like," she warned him.

He nodded again. He looked tired, she realized. Even in this frail light she could see the bluish half-circles under his eyes. He looked as though he hadn't shaved in a while.

"I thought we became friends this summer," she said. "I didn't know if it would be possible after what we did — I did — two summers ago, but then it happened. I was happy. I loved being your friend. I admit I may have had some other thoughts too, but they didn't matter to me nearly as much as being your friend. I was happy to be close to you on any terms." Bridget needed to be honest tonight. That was the reason she was here.

He looked down, fiddling with the worn leather watchband around his wrist.

"I wasn't trying to be your girlfriend. I know you have

one. I accept that. I didn't want to get in the way of it. I am happy for you if you are happy with her. I'm not saying it wasn't hard for me, but I meant it . . . I mean, I mean it. I wanted you to trust me."

Still looking down, he appeared to nod.

"And we spent time together and we did stuff and we had fun. At least, I had fun. And I thought you had fun." Her voice was getting a little wobbly, but she pushed ahead. "And then when I got sick you took care of me. You took care of me as nicely as anyone ever did in my life. Even if our whole lives pass and we don't see each other or talk to each other again, I will never forget it." She paused so that the tears wouldn't drown her words. She wanted to keep them in her eyes if she possibly could.

"I trusted you. I thought you cared about me. Not like a girlfriend. I'm not talking about that. I trusted you to be my friend. And then you just disappeared. I couldn't figure out what happened. I felt so close to you and then you were gone. You made me believe in you and then you let me down. Is that how it is with you? Do you let people get close just so you can disappoint them?" She brushed the tears out of her eyes before they could fall.

Eric was looking up now, his eyes serious and shiny like hers. "Bee. *No.* That's not how it is with me."

Her chin quivered, though she wished it would not. "Then how is it?"

He sat up a bit straighter. He studied his knuckles. He opened his hands and shut them again. "I'm just going to talk for a while, and you listen, okay?"

"Okay."

"The reason I don't like to talk about what happened two summers ago is because I hate myself for it. I'm not saying you didn't do your part; you did. But I could have resisted. That would have been the right thing to do. But I didn't because I wanted the same thing you wanted, and that was wrong. You think it was just you, but I wanted it just as much. You should know that."

She could hardly move. She watched his face and listened.

"The reason I disappeared after you got sick is because I needed to go to New York and it couldn't wait. I drove up there and saw Kaya because I needed to tell her that I couldn't be with her anymore."

Bridget sucked in a little breath.

He looked sad. "I thought I loved her. Two months ago, I told her I loved her. I couldn't let that stand. It seemed wrong."

Bridget wanted terribly to ask him questions, but she also wanted to do her fair share of being quiet. She pressed her lips shut.

He opened his hands and put them together like he was going to pray. "And the reason it was wrong is because I knew I couldn't really love her if I felt something so much bigger for somebody else."

Bridget was frozen. She was scared to think through what he meant in case he didn't mean what she thought he meant.

"And the reason I've been mostly staying out of sight is because when I'm near you my thoughts don't go

straight. I need to get them straightened out before I do anything else stupid."

Bridget grabbed a look at him. Hope was filling her chest even as she tried to push it back out.

"When I was in New York, all I wanted was to rush back to you. But what would that mean? That I dumped Kaya so I could be with you? That I was a guy who'd forget a girl he thought he loved in five hours or less?" He was shaking his head. "And anyway, I didn't want you to feel responsible for breaking us up. I know you weren't pulling for that. All summer you were selfless enough to respect the thing with Kaya, and I wasn't. That sucks. I didn't feel like I deserved to come running back to you. I felt ashamed."

Bridget couldn't follow all these thoughts at once. She couldn't figure out which way they led.

"There is one thing I feel sure of, and I know it is right. All these days I keep coming back to this one thing. We spent that night together, me holding you, and I felt something stronger than I ever felt for anybody else, and stronger than I even thought it was possible to feel. It blew me away. On theory alone, that made me know I couldn't be with Kaya anymore."

He shook his head again. He looked sort of disgusted with himself, but tempted to laugh too. "I've been wanting to be rational, to believe my decision about Kaya is theoretical and not just driven by my insane, out-of-my-head attraction for you."

"Is it . . . ," she asked breathlessly, ". . . theoretical?"

He looked at her face very closely. "Not at all."

You guys!
 6 1/2 days! Ahhhhhhh! Yahhhhhhh! Wahhhhhhh!
                                        Carma

The letter came to Lena postmarked from Providence, Rhode Island, at almost the last moment it could have before the end-of-the-summer beach trip. Lena's heart throbbed as she opened it, but she knew it wouldn't determine her fate, even if the answer was no.

Because Annik was right. She was an artist. She would find her way no matter who said what. Her fate didn't belong to anyone else anymore.

The letter didn't say no; it said yes. Lena closed her eyes and allowed the pleasure to seep through her. She was strict with herself about feeling joy, but this moment she had earned.

She went into the kitchen and literally sat on the letter, thinking about it for a long time. She would go and she could go. She didn't need her parents' money and she didn't need their permission. She thought about that, too. She didn't need it, but she wanted it. That's what she realized.

She put on a neat navy skirt and a pretty linen blouse. She brushed her hair smooth and put pearl earrings in her ears. She borrowed her mother's car to drive to her father's office.

Mrs. Jeffords, her father's secretary, sent Lena in without announcing her.

Her father looked surprised to see her in the doorway. Indeed, he was so surprised, he appeared genuinely

happy at the sight of her, like he'd forgotten everything that had happened in the preceding two months and returned instinctively to his old tenderness.

"Come in," he urged, standing up.

She was still holding the letter when she sat down across from him. "I heard from art school about the scholarship," she said.

"You got it," he said evenly.

"How did you know?" she asked.

He looked placid, almost philosophical. "Because I saw your drawings. When I saw them I knew you would get it."

This was one of the less direct compliments she had ever received. If it even was one.

"Daddy, I don't want to upset or disappoint you. But I really do want to go. I want you and Mom to want it with me."

He sighed. He put his elbow on his desk and rested his cheek in his palm in a boyish way. "Lena, I'm afraid I'm the one who's upset and disappointed you."

She didn't hurry up and nod, but she wasn't going to argue, either.

"You should go to art school. You proved it to me with those drawings just as you proved it to the scholarship people."

She kept her expression in check. She didn't trust him yet. "So it's okay with you, then?"

He thought about this for a while. "I'm honored that you're asking me when you earned the right not to have to."

Her chest ached. "I want to ask you," she said. "It matters to me what you say."

"The answer is yes."

"Thanks."

She got up to go.

"Lena?"

"Yes?"

"When I began to realize, with your mother's help, the depth of my recent mistakes"—he cleared his throat—"I felt proud of you for not going along with them."

"You didn't make it easy," she told him honestly.

Valia123: Ο Θεος με Βοηθά ερχομαι σπιτι. Ο George τελικά ηρθε στις αισθυσεις του. Η Effie θα ερθη μαζι μου στο σπιτι σε μια εβδομάδα ραρθακαλώ κάνετε τις ρυθμίσεις με τη Pina, εαυ μπορειτε να την διαθεσετε, για να αερισετε το σπίτι μου.

God help me, Rena dear, I am coming home. George has finally seen the sense in it. Effie will fly home with me in one week. Please make arrangements with Pina, if you can spare her, to air out my house?

RenaDounas: Πολυαγαπημευη Valia, Κλαίω διαβάζουτας αυτό. Ποσο ευτυχισμευοι θα ειμαστε να σε εχουμε στο σπίτι που αυηκεις.

Dearest Valia, I cry as I read this. How happy we will be to have you home where you belong!

317

I have tried in my way

to be free.

—Leonard Cohen

"Hi, Dad."

"Carmen? Hi, bun! How are you?"

She felt slightly sheepish, but she couldn't let this wait any longer. "I'm fine."

"How's the baby?"

"He's great. He kicks like a black belt."

Albert laughed appreciatively, even though it was the baby of his ex-wife and her new husband they were talking about.

"How's your mom?" He asked it in a genuine way.

"She's great, too. She says it's all coming back to her, even eighteen years later."

"I'm sure it is," her dad said a little wistfully.

"So, Dad?"

"Yeah?"

"I've been thinking."

He waited patiently, though she sort of wished he would interrupt.

"Do you think . . . um . . ." She pulled her heavy hair

off of her sweaty neck. "Do you think Williams might consider taking me back again?"

"Do you think you want to go there?"

Carmen didn't want to seem like she was making her decisions rashly, so she didn't belt out her answer, but rather, paused. "I do."

"What about Maryland?"

Carmen chewed her lip. "I was thinking I might board there, you know, get the college experience and still be close to home. But then I realized I really, *really* want to go to Williams. Do you think they'll take me back? God, I mean, what are the chances they would keep a spot?" Her voice ended squeaky and she didn't sound calm anymore.

"I'll tell you what," her dad said. "Let me call."

Carmen made attempts to clean her room while she waited. In truth, she did that spasmodic, surface re-arranging, like putting the random AA battery into her sock drawer to get it out of sight, that would only make the job bigger when she got down to real cleaning.

Less than ten minutes later, the phone rang. She pounced at half a ring. So much for calm.

"Hi?"

"Hi." It was her dad again.

"Did you talk to them?" she blurted out.

"I did. And Williams College says you're good to go."

"They'll take me?"

"Yep."

"Just like that?"

"Yep."

"You're kidding."

"Nope."

"Seriously?" Carmen was afraid to let herself be happy quite so soon.

"I'm happy for you, bun," her dad said. "I can hear in your voice that it's really what you want."

"It's really what I want," she echoed.

She shook her head, feeling the nerves sizzle and zing all over her body. "I can't believe it's that easy."

He didn't respond. "You better start packing," he said instead. "And you have fun at the beach with your friends this weekend."

"I will. Thanks."

After she told him she loved him and hung up the phone, she got another sneaking suspicion. Could this have been a case of parental collusion again? Maybe even deceitful parental intervention?

Had her dad ever called Williams and told them she wasn't coming? Had he ever gotten his deposit back? Was this another case of her parents knowing her better than she knew herself?

It was really annoying, in a way. But then, it was good to be loved.

Carmabelle: Will you pack the green tube top, so I can be extremely tricky and steal it the first minute you turn away?

Tibberon: Sure. But how am I going to figure out who took it?

Carmabelle: I'm excited.

Tibberon: I'm excited too.

For three long days, Bridget left Eric alone so his thoughts would go straight. And at the end of the third day, just when she thought she couldn't stand it anymore, his head, thoughts and all, appeared by her bed, where she lay.

"Would you mind taking a walk with me?" he whispered.

She jumped out of bed. She followed him out of her cabin in her T-shirt and boxers. Suddenly she remembered something Carmen had said in the beginning of the summer. "Can you wait for me for one second?"

She left him outside and went back into the cabin. She found her white halter dress from the senior party still balled up in the bottom of her duffel bag. She hadn't thought she would be wearing it. She shed her clothes and pulled the dress over her head. Luckily, the silky material didn't hold its wrinkles.

The Pants would have been her first choice, of course, but she'd had to send them back to Lena. And besides, she didn't want to be greedy. She'd already gotten what she needed from them.

"Okay," she said, reappearing beside him in the darkness. Her feet were still bare and her hair was loose.

He blinked and took a step back to get a better look at her. "God, Bee," he murmured. She wasn't sure what that meant, but she wasn't going to press him on it.

They walked side by side down toward the lake. She tried not to bounce on her feet, but she couldn't really help it. She was happy. Her hand collided with his briefly

and it set her nerves singing. After all they had been through together, all the things they'd felt and now spoken, they didn't even know how to touch each other.

They took their usual spots at the dock. Bridget could practically see the warmth they'd left on the weathered planks from last time. She swung her legs over the water, loving the empty air under her bare toes. Their bodies made no shadows tonight; they were fully contained.

Eric pulled a little closer. His expression was wistful. "You know what?"

"What?"

"When I saw your name on that list of coaches before the summer started, I had a premonition. I knew you were going to turn my life inside out again." He didn't sound so sorry about it.

"If I had seen that list, I wonder if I would have come," Bridget mused.

He let out a breath. "Did you dislike me so much?"

"Uhhhh. Dislike?" She smiled a little. "No. That's not the word. I was afraid of you. I didn't want to feel like that again."

"It was hard, wasn't it?" He was sorry, she knew.

"I was a little out of control."

"You've grown up since then."

"Some. I like to think so."

"You have. You are different. And also not."

She shrugged. That sounded about right.

"I'm sorry I disappeared," he said sorrowfully. "I didn't

mean to hurt you. I didn't know if you felt what I felt. I was worried it was just me."

"It wasn't."

"Now I know."

They considered these things.

"I'm glad I didn't read the coach list. I'm glad I did come," she said after a while.

"Me too. We had to find each other eventually."

"Really?"

"Yeah. We were meant to be."

She loved that idea. "You think?"

"I do."

"Is that what your thoughts told you? When they went straight?" she asked. Her heart was swelling inside her ribs.

He smiled, but he looked serious too. "Yeah. It is. Maybe that doesn't sound so straight. Maybe that's not what I was expecting them to tell me. But they did. So there you go."

"How did they know?"

"Because when I lay with you in my bed, there was a moment when I could feel everything you had been through, and I had this idea that if I could make you happy, then I would be happy, too."

Bridget was too full to talk. She leaned her head against him. He put his arms around her, and she put hers around him. He'd said them simply, but these were words enough for a lifetime. He could make her happy. He had.

Last time they had started at the end. This time they started at the beginning. You couldn't erase the past. You couldn't even change it. But sometimes life offered you the opportunity to put it right.

Maybe tomorrow they would kiss. Maybe in the next weeks and months they would figure out how to touch each other, to translate their feelings into gestures of every kind. Someday, she hoped, they would make love.

But for now, all she wanted was this.

Following the light of

the sun, we left the old

World.

-christopher columbus

The Morgans' beach house had sandy carpets. The fridge was empty but for one half-loaf of moldy Wonder bread. The pots and pans looked as though they had been washed most recently by Joe, their almost-two-year-old.

It was also staggeringly beautiful, pitched on the sea grass in a low field of dunes set just eighty yards or so back from the Atlantic Ocean.

The first thing they did when they got there was to tear off their clothes (by previous agreement they'd all worn bathing suits under them) and run yelling and screaming straight into the ocean.

The surf was big and rough. It clubbed, tackled, and upended them. It might have seemed scary, Tibby thought, except that they were all holding hands in a chain so the undertow couldn't drag them down the beach. And that, in addition to all the hollering and taunting and shrieking, made it fun.

The second thing they did was collapse on the warm sand. The afternoon sun dried their backs as they lay there, shoulder to shoulder. Tibby's heart still pounded from the thrill of the water. She had pebbles in her bathing suit. She loved the feeling of the sand under her cheek. She felt happy.

She wanted to let this happiness be her guide. She wouldn't look forward with trepidation. She wouldn't rev her brain like that.

There would be the inescapable good-byes. The nitty-gritty ones. Like when she would watch Lena and Bee drive away to Providence in the U-Haul on Thursday. She could picture Bee laying on the horn for the first five miles away from home. Then there would be the moment on Friday when she'd kiss Carmen and watch her roll off to Massachusetts with her dad and all fifty million of her suit-cases. There would be the good-byes at the train station on Saturday morning when she and her mom would board the Metroliner for New York City. Her father would clap her on the back and Katherine's chin would tremble and Nicky would shuffle and not kiss her back. Tibby could picture it if she tried. And the good-bye to Brian. She knew that one wouldn't stick for long. Brian was supposed to go to Maryland, because it was almost free, and yet she suspected he hadn't gotten an 800 on his math SAT for nothing. He would find his way to her. She knew he would. It was a good thing she had scored a single room.

But this moment was for the Septembers and for them alone. This was their weekend out of time. She would live

in the happiness of each one of these moments, no matter how finite. Together, the Septembers could just be.

They all showered (the hot water ran out after Carmen's and before Lena's) and made a late lunch of grilled cheese sandwiches and brownies, feeling sun-tired and extra hungry, the way the ocean makes you feel.

The first cell phone rang just after lunch.

"Really? How great!" Carmen was laughing into the phone. She moved it a few inches from her mouth. "Win saw Katherine in the kids' lounge at the hospital today," she explained to Tibby. "The hockey helmet is off!"

"I know. She misses it." Tibby smiled appreciatively. She liked Win. She gave Win the big thumbs-up. But she found herself wishing that he weren't joining them just now.

The second call came from Valia. Valia apparently couldn't find the photocopy of the drawing Lena had made of her, and wanted urgently to bring it back to Greece. Valia had new life in her—and she was putting it all into packing. Valia then insisted on getting Carmen on the phone so she could tell her something about the new soap opera she had adopted, the same dumb show Carmen was always watching.

The third call was for Bee. Tibby watched Bee melt into the phone and she knew it was Eric. She could never begrudge Bee—or anyone she loved, for that matter—a voice that could give her so pure a look of happiness.

Tibby sat on the kitchen counter and considered the sheer number of voices that had joined their lives.

Then Brian called on Tibby's cell phone. He wanted to

talk to her, and she wanted to talk to him—just for a few minutes, at least.

As soon as Tibby hung up, two other phones started ringing simultaneously. Lena caught Tibby's glance. "What's going on here?" she said. "It's like a joke."

Tibby nodded. "Only I can't figure out if it's funny or not."

Dinner was a chaotic affair, what with the phones ringing and Carmen almost burning down the house when she forgot about the rice. There wasn't much peace. It was sort of wonderful in the sense that it reassured Tibby how rich and funny and interconnected her world was. It was sort of sad in the sense that she'd imagined that world would stop for this one weekend, so that they could just exist together in solitude. But the world hadn't stopped for them. If anything, it had sped up.

Hours later, midnight had come and gone and Tibby couldn't sleep. She sat on the floor of the small, sandy bedroom and couldn't help feeling a little bleak. It wasn't that their night hadn't been fun; it had been. After the kitchen fire was brought under control, they decided to abandon the stove altogether and had milkshakes and peanut butter fudge for dinner instead. They ate so much of it they had all lain groaning and exhausted on the living room floor.

There were so many things to talk about, so many new people to process, so much future bearing down on them, they had barely gotten started. They had listened to

music and fallen into sugar-induced slumber and crawled off to their various bedrooms.

Tonight, for the first time, the world had felt too big to contain and digest within their small circle of friendship. Was this the way the future was going to go?

They were growing up. It was inevitable, and Tibby had learned enough this summer not to stand in its way. There were boyfriends and families and big plans burning just ahead of them.

But please, God, she couldn't do it if it was a trade-in. She couldn't strike the bargain if growing up meant drowning out the friendship that stood at the very center of her life, the thing that gave her strength and balance.

Darkness closed her in the house and the black waves beat against the shore for all to hear. All of a sudden Tibby felt claustrophobic. Perhaps for the first time in memory, she felt more afraid of a small, confining space than the big, infinite one. Without thinking, she tiptoed out of the bedroom, down the stairs, and out into the air.

Tibby felt like she was walking into a dream, a happy dream, when she saw the three distant silhouettes sitting on the sand. She laughed at the sight of those three familiar heads. It was like a dream too, in that she knew more than she really could know. She knew what they were feeling; she knew it was the same thing she was feeling, and in that knowledge she felt the strength of their connection.

It seemed as though they were waiting for her, even though they had no practical reason to know she would come. When Tibby got close enough, Bee reached up for

her hand and pulled her down into their little cluster.

"Hi." Tibby's voice was quiet, but almost giddy.

"This is where the cool kids go," Bee said, laughing.

Lena shrugged. "I guess nobody could sleep."

"We have too much stuff to talk about," Carmen mused.

A wave washed close to their feet. This didn't give anybody the idea to move.

They tightened their circle, and Carmen set the Pants in the middle, making a circle of their summer as well.

Tibby breathed out, finding inexpressible comfort in her friends' faces. Before her eyes, this night had transformed into a gift of reassurance. This was the future. Life would get busier and more varied, populated both by beautiful things and unfortunate circumstances. If their friendship demanded exclusivity or solitude, it couldn't work. If it required that everything go as planned, it would turn brittle, and ultimately it would break. On the other hand, she knew that if they could be flexible and big, if they could encompass change, then they would make it.

Tibby remembered her dream about taxidermy and understood in a new way the beauty of the Pants. The Pants could move along with them.

"Whatever happens," Bridget said, "we will find each other. We always will."

I'm going back to the

start.

—Coldplay

EPILOGUE

For our last hour at the beach, we exchanged gifts instead of saying good-bye. We didn't plan it that way, exactly. It just kind of fell into place, like us all finding each other on the beach in the middle of the night. We each wanted a few things we could hold on to.

The sun streamed pink and orange behind our heads, and the ocean churned dark. The sand felt softer in the sweet light. The air was warm and comforting.

I can't tell you all that was said and what was felt. I just can't. But I'll tell you what happened and you can imagine it. You'll do better with your imagination than I could with my words.

Carmen got to go first, because she is the least patient. Not about getting, about giving. "For the walls of our dorm rooms," she announced, handing them out.

Carmen had found four long, vertical frames and pasted three photographs into each of them. The first photo, on the top, was the one of our mothers, as young,

happening, late-eighties moms sitting on a wall, arms around each other's shoulders, wearing jeans. The photo was familiar to us now. A little speckled. A little old. A little heartbreaking to remember Marly, as it always was. The next photo, in the middle, was also old, one I barely remembered ever seeing. It was the four of us as toddlers, our faces peeking over a couch. We looked like a miniature girl band. Carmen looked like the singer. I, small and confused, looked like the one who plugged the instruments into the amplifiers. It made me laugh. The bottom photo was from graduation, the four of us in the same order, the same faces, the same expressions.

The crying started for each of us around then. It was inevitable. It was like that feeling of being outside in a rainfall without a raincoat or umbrella. You fight getting wet for a while and then you just surrender to it and you realize it feels pretty nice. You wonder, why do we fight the things we fight when giving in to them isn't so bad at all?

Bee went next. She passed out tiny jewelry boxes. We pulled the tops off all at once.

On four delicate silver chains dangled four tiny, identical charms. Of pants. They were tiny silver charms in the shape of pants, just like our Pants. Now they *were* our Pants, in a new and different way.

Bee explained how Greta first spotted one in a jewelry kiosk in the middle of the mall in Huntsville, Alabama. And how she and Greta made a joint project of hounding the jeweler, Mr. Bosely, until he came up with three more.

We all put them on each other, fiddling with clasps, holding up hair. I pressed the tiny charm flat against my sternum, knowing it would live there now. We couldn't look at each other except in little bits. It was hard to feel so much.

Lena handed hers out next. She had even wrapped them. We tore the paper off with different degrees of care: I folded the wrapping paper for future use, Bee tore at hers savagely and sat on the crumpled paper so it wouldn't blow down the beach.

Lena had made four nearly identical drawings and framed them, one for each. She'd drawn the Traveling Pants twice, front and back. But she'd drawn them upside down and side by side so that together they formed a big W. Next to it Lena added the letter *e*. The picture said *We*.

I went last. I handed out videocassettes with specially decorated labels. "We have to go inside for this," I said.

I had already made sure the Morgans' VCR was in working order. So once we'd scrambled up the beach and into the house, it didn't take me long to get the movie fired up.

It was short. Just ten minutes. Most of it was stuff from my own parents' collection, but I'd managed to get stuff from Tina and Ari too. I'd even given the two of them and my mom a little preview a few nights before in our den, though I made them keep it a secret. The three of them wept while I crowded up all close to the TV and pretended not to. The three moms hugged afterward. That made me feel happy.

The first part was on old-fashioned Super 8 film, atmospheric and a little jerky, showing us crawling around in Lena's backyard. Well, Lena was timid about crawling, so we mostly nudged and rolled her. I was a stringy baby, bald and purposeless. Bee's hair looked like white feathers adorning her head. She was a fast crawler. Her mother had to pull her away from the side of the pool. Bee's brother, Perry, made a brief appearance. He didn't move much, but he did find a bug in the grass. Carmen had perfect brown ringlets, giant eyes, and a very loud voice with which to coax inert baby Lena.

By the time we were two, some parent or other had sprung for a real video camera. The next part showed the four of us girls lined up on four plastic potties. Lena sat patiently, her elbow on her knee, her chin in her palm. I was tiny and seemed to be falling into mine. Carmen was trying to yank a Mary Jane off her foot. Bee finished first. "I'm done!" She stood up and shouted at someone off camera.

The next bits were fast takes, a catalog of joint birthday parties, bad haircuts, and complex orthodontia. Siblings, parents, grandparents, and other relatives filtered through in various fashion mishaps.

The last one was a long shot, taken when we were about seven. I didn't even understand the significance of it when I'd picked it out and smoothed it into the end of the movie.

It was taken at Rehoboth Beach, probably within a mile of this very place. The camera showed the four of us

holding hands in the rough surf, jumping waves, shouting and screaming.

It was just like now. Exactly as we had done the afternoon before and early that morning. As I looked at the screen I could feel the cold, salty water covering my hands, linked with Bee's on one side and Lena's on the other. I could hear Carmen's shrieks of joy in my ear. Different times we lined up in a different order. It didn't matter the order.

The image stayed on the screen and we all watched it, even when it went still.

Back then was exactly the same as now. To brave the undertow, we had learned to hold hands.